SURPRISE ATTACK

Without warning, a brilliant flash of light came from across the landing field to the northeast.

"Cover!" Thrr-mezaz snapped as the sharp *crack* of the explosion slapped across them. He leaped into the partial cover of the Human-Conqueror aircraft. Crouching down, he peered out past the aircraft's beak, just in time to get his midlight pupils dazzled by the flash of a second explosion. He twisted his head away with a curse; but he'd gotten enough of a look to locate the focal point of the attack.

The Mrachanis' storehouse.

"Communicators: full attack alert," he shouted as a third explosion flashed reflected light from the nearby buildings, the sound hammering into his ear slits. "Tell the warriors guarding the Mrachanis to get them out of there and to cover."

He got a faint shout of acknowledgment and threw a quick look around him. Two of the Zhirrzh warriors had the Human-Conqueror facedown on the ground; the others had unslung their laser rifles and were kneeling around the base of the aircraft, weapons swinging around uncertainly as they searched for something to use them on. From another edge of the landing field one of the ground defenses opened fire, sizzling rapid-fire laser pulses into the air in half a dozen directions. Somewhere in the distance he could hear the faint sound of laser rifles joining in. . . .

ALSO BY TIMOTHY ZAHN

The Blackcollar
Cobra
Blackcollar: The Backlash Mission
Dark Force Rising
Dead Man's Switch
Cascade Point
Cobra Bargain
Cobra Strike
A Coming of Age
Heir to the Empire
The Last Command
Spinneret
Time Bomb & Zahndry Others
Triplet
Warhorse
Distant Friends
Conquerors' Pride

Conquerors' Heritage

TIMOTHY ZAHN

BANTAM BOOKS

TORONTO • NEW YORK • LONDON • SYDNEY • AUCKLAND

CONQUERORS' HERITAGE
A BANTAM BOOK : 0 553 40854 2

First publication in Great Britain

PRINTING HISTORY
Bantam edition published 1995

Bantam Books are published by Transworld Publishers Ltd,
61–63 Uxbridge Road, Ealing, London W5 5SA,
in Australia by Transworld Publishers (Australia) Pty Ltd,
15–25 Helles Avenue, Moorebank, NSW 2170,
and in New Zealand by Transworld Publishers (NZ) Ltd,
3 William Pickering Drive, Albany, Auckland.

Printed and bound in Great Britain by
Cox & Wyman Ltd, Reading, Berkshire

Conquerors' Heritage

1
"Searcher Thrr-gilag?"

Slowly, Thrr-gilag lifted his gaze from his contemplation of the stained restraint suit resting across his legs. "Yes, Ship Commander Zbb-rundgi?"

"The *Diligent* is ready to lift," Ship Commander Zbb-rundgi said. "We're waiting on your arrival."

"Thank you," Thrr-gilag said. "I'll be just a few hunbeats longer."

Zbb-rundgi's eyes flicked around the alien study group's private conversation room. "The disassembly crew can deal with the rest of the equipment, Searcher," he said. "There's nothing here you have to supervise."

"I understand," Thrr-gilag said. "As I said, I'll be a few hunbeats longer."

Zbb-rundgi's midlight pupils might have contracted slightly. At his distance Thrr-gilag couldn't tell for sure.

"The Overclan Prime's instructions were quite clear, Searcher," the ship commander said. "We were to leave as soon as we were ready."

"And we're not yet ready," Thrr-gilag told him. "You may return to the ship and make any final prelaunch preparations. I'll be there in a few hunbeats."

This time there was no doubt about the pupils. "As you wish, Searcher," Zbb-rundgi said stiffly. Turning, he stalked out of the room.

"That was foolish," a distant voice said in the silence. "Ship Commander Zbb-rundgi holds great favor among the leaders of the Cakk'rr clan, as do the Elders of his family. It is not wise for one in your position to antagonize him."

"My position is that of duly appointed speaker of this mission, Chrr't-ogdano," Thrr-gilag reminded him, fingering one of the darklight sensors in the restaint suit, still partially caked with red dirt from the Human Pheylan Cavanagh's escape attempt. "Until the Overclan Seating revokes that appointment, I'll do whatever I deem necessary. Whether it irritates Ship Commander Zbb-rundgi or not."

"Thrr-gilag, you will look at me."

With a sigh Thrr-gilag raised his eyes to the faint shape floating in the air before him. Chrr't-ogdano, Elder of the Kee'rr clan and chief observer here on Base World 12. And if the look on his mostly transparent face was any indication, he had even less respect for Thrr-gilag's official standing right now than Ship Commander Zbb-rundgi did. "Don't play word games with me," the Elder bit out. "By title you may still be speaker of the mission. The position I refer to is that of the Zhirrzh whose actions allowed the Human prisoner Pheylan Cavanagh to be rescued by his people."

"The blame for that will fall wherever it may," Thrr-gilag said. "Until that time I don't think a certain degree of respect is too much to ask."

Chrr't-ogdano's tongue flicked out in scorn. "Authority is something that can be assigned; respect is something one must earn. If you're too young or too drunk with the taste of power to understand that, then perhaps you shouldn't have been given the speakership in the first place."

Thrr-gilag pressed his tongue against the top of his mouth, choking off the words that wanted to come out. "I'm sorry if I've disappointed you," he said instead. "I did the best I could."

Some of the hardness faded from Chrr't-ogdano's face. "What has happened has happened," he said, his voice heavy with resignation. "Only history now can judge your actions."

Which was not to say, of course, that Chrr't-ogdano hadn't already made up his mind about history's likely evaluation. Or that Ship Commander Zbb-rundgi and the rest of the mission hadn't, either.

And to be honest, Thrr-gilag couldn't really blame them. True, the scheme he'd improvised to recapture Pheylan Cavanagh had worked out exactly as he'd anticipated, a point he planned to emphasize when he presented his case before the Overclan Seating. They'd let the Human into the alien spacecraft and allowed him to activate it, giving the watching Elders valuable information about its operation. Then, again as anticipated, a sudden, clear look at one of the Elders had distracted the Human long enough for Thrr-gilag to slash away his restraints and inject a minuscule amount of tongue poison into his shoulder. New information, a prisoner recaptured with minimal trouble, it should have been little more than a sidelight to the day's report.

But none of them had known about the Human fighter warcraft poised overhead to strike. And the fact remained that if the prisoner had been safely under guard in his cell when the enemy swooped down a few hunbeats later, the rescue might have been thwarted.

Or maybe the Humans would simply have demolished the encampment, raised every Zhirrzh in the mission to Eldership, and taken Pheylan Cavanagh back anyway.

Thrr-gilag shivered, the edge of his tongue scratching lightly against the inside of his mouth at the memory. Those fighter warcraft had been unbelievable. Incredibly fast, incredibly maneuverable, incredibly destructive. In coloration and performance they'd matched perfectly the warcraft that had slashed to a sudden halt the beachhead advance on the Human world of Dorcas, warcraft his brother Thrr-mezaz had suggested might be the mysterious Copperhead warriors mentioned in the Human recorder.

Or could they possibly have even been the exact same warcraft?

Thrr-gilag frowned as that ominous thought struck him. If the Copperhead warriors had been able to slip out past the Dorcas encirclement force . . . "I want to speak with my brother," he told Chrr't-ogdano. "Thrr-mezaz; Kee'rr, commander of the Zhirrzh ground warriors on Dorcas."

"Now?" Chrr't-ogdano asked, taken aback. "Wouldn't it be better to speak with him from the *Diligent*?"

"To appease Ship Commander Zbb-rundgi, you mean?" Thrr-gilag asked pointedly.

"To appease the dictates of common sense," Chrr't-ogdano shot back. "Or do you wish to still be here when the Human warcraft return in greater numbers?"

Thrr-gilag sighed. "They won't be returning anytime soon," he said. "As I've already explained to Ship Commander Zbb-rundgi. It's been nearly six tentharcs since the rescue—if the Humans had had more warcraft nearby, they would certainly have attacked by now. Any future attack must therefore be coming from one of their worlds. At least another fullarc away, probably more."

"That's an assumption."

"It's the consideration of a specialist in aliens and alien cultures," Thrr-gilag snapped, suddenly tired of all these arguments. No one had questioned Svv-selic like this when *he'd* been in charge. "A pathway to Thrr-mezaz, if you please."

"I obey," Chrr't-ogdano said, glowering, and vanished.

Across the room the door opened, and one of the technics came in pushing a carrier. "Anything new on our prisoners?" Thrr-gilag asked her.

"They're still asleep," the technic said as she pushed her carrier over to one of the three remaining tissue-analysis units. "But their metabolic levels seem to be recovering from the trauma of the transfer aboard ship. The healers think a few more hunbeats should do it."

"Good," Thrr-gilag said, finding a minor flicker of gratification in the fact that this, at least, seemed to be working out. It wasn't the taste of power on his tongue that was delaying their departure, as Chrr't-ogdano and Zbb-rundgi both seemed to think. It was, rather, an overriding concern that their two new alien prisoners might die from their mysterious injuries before they even made it off the planet. Transferring them aboard the *Diligent* had been risky enough, in the healers' opinion, and Thrr-gilag wanted the aliens to have as much time as possible to settle in before they were subjected to the stresses of liftoff.

Ship Commander Zbb-rundgi hadn't been able to grasp that concept. Or was simply too nervous about anticipated Human attacks to care about healers' warnings. But as long as Thrr-gilag stayed outside the *Diligent*, he retained the final word on when the ship lifted. "Have the Elders been able to learn anything about their injuries?"

"They're still doing studies," the technic said, the last word almost lost in the brief screech of ceramic against ceramic as the tissue analyzer came up off the floor and onto the carrier. "So far they're as puzzled as the healers are."

There was a flicker beside Thrr-gilag, and Chrr't-ogdano was back. "I have a pathway to Commander Thrr-mezaz," he growled. "Begin."

"This is Thrr-gilag," Thrr-gilag said, wondering what had taken Chrr't-ogdano so long. There was supposed to be a permanent straight-line pathway between here and all three of the Zhirrzh beachheads. Had something gone wrong? "Base World Twelve was attacked about six tentharcs ago by Human fighter warcraft of the type described in your last report. Question: are you certain both of those warcraft are still on Dorcas?"

Chrr't-ogdano nodded and vanished again. Thrr-gilag waited, watching the technic maneuver the tissue analyzer to the door and counting the time to himself. It would take around fifteen beats, he estimated, for each repetition of the message, beginning with whichever communicator Chrr't-ogdano had made contact with on the Zhirrzh homeworld of Oaccanv. From that Elder, then to another, and possibly another, until the message reached the shrine of someone who was also serving as communicator with the Dorcas ground force. Then a similar delay as Thrr-mezaz's return message wended its way back along the same route. The last time he'd talked with someone at the Dorcas beachhead, the round trip had taken roughly 120 beats. It ought to be something similar this time.

He was up to 190 beats when Chrr't-ogdano reappeared. " 'Both warcraft are still here,' " he delivered the message. " 'Are you injured, my brother?' "

Thrr-gilag flicked his tongue in a wry smile. That was Thrr-mezaz, all right. He would be the overprotective worried big brother until both of them were raised to Eldership. Probably even after that. "I'm fine," he said to Chrr't-ogdano. "You?"

" 'Last I checked, I was still here,' " the reply came back a hunbeat later. At least Thrr-mezaz hadn't lost his dry sense of humor. " 'How badly was your base damaged?' "

"Hardly at all," Thrr-gilag said. "It was an extremely precise attack."

" 'They were somewhat less so here. How many spacecraft did they use?' "

"We saw only five fighter warcraft," Thrr-gilag said. "Though there might have been others outside our detection range. Why? Is the number important?"

" 'It could be,' " the answer came back. " 'If we had some idea of how many warcraft the Humans had committed to their search, it might give us an idea of the size of their overall force. Unless they were just checking systems at random and had immensely good luck.' "

"I doubt that was it," Thrr-gilag said. "We know they also looked at Survey World Eighteen. The *Diligent* and *Operant* nearly caught that group, but they got away."

" 'Then they must have covered all the likely systems in the area around the battle site,' " Thrr-mezaz concluded. " 'That's a huge number of systems.' "

"Much too huge," Thrr-gilag agreed, frowning. "They must have had some way to narrow the possibilities down."

" 'I concur,' " the answer came back. " 'Unfortunately, that leads to two troubling conclusions. First, that they were able to get extremely detailed readings of our environmental requirements from the survey ships; and second, that they have a detailed catalog of all the systems in this region. I can't see how else they could have limited their search enough to have succeeded so quickly.' "

Thrr-gilag grimaced. "I'm afraid I have to agree with you," he said. "Unless they've found a way to track ships through the tunnel-line. That would have done it, too."

" 'Don't even joke about such things,' " his brother warned. " 'That's how rumors get started; and the more impossible the story, the faster it spreads. I presume you're evacuating your base?' "

"Yes," Thrr-gilag said. "We've been ordered back to Oaccanv. Where I'll no doubt be called before the Overclan Seating."

" 'No doubt. Be careful how you speak to them. The Too'rr clan was not at all happy with you for taking Svvselic's place as speaker of the study group.' "

At least that was one thing they couldn't blame on him. "Not my doing," he told his brother. "Our Elders demanded Svv-selic be demoted after he let the Human get too close to the pyramid."

" 'Be careful anyway.' "

"Of course." Thrr-gilag frowned. "Is anything wrong there? The pathway seems longer than it was five fullarcs ago."

The delay this time seemed even longer; and Thrr-gilag was just wondering if he should send one of the other Elders to try to get Chrr't-ogdano back when he reappeared. " 'We've lost the pathway you and I spoke through back then,' " the Elder repeated Thrr-mezaz's words, his faint voice gone suddenly grim. " 'One of our communicators disappeared two fullarcs ago. Prr't-zevisti; Dhaa'rr.' "

Thrr-gilag felt his midlight pupils narrow with shock. "How in the eighteen worlds did that happen?"

" 'Human warriors raided one of the pyramids and took his *fsss* cutting,' " the reply came. " 'We tracked him back to their encampment, at which point his reports via his family shrine abruptly ended.' "

"They killed him?"

" 'Or else somehow managed to capture him. All we know is that in the fullarcs since then he hasn't been heard from. Not here, nor at his family shrine on Dharanv.' "

"I see," Thrr-gilag murmured. "How did the Humans breach your defense perimeter?"

" 'They didn't have to. As it happens, all four pyramids are outside the encampment.' "

"Outside?" Thrr-gilag echoed. "Whose flat-headed idea was *that*?"

" 'Mine. It was an experiment to see if the Elders could help supplement the sentry line.' "

Thrr-gilag flicked his tongue. "The Dhaa'rr leaders aren't going to be at all happy about this."

" 'Their unhappiness has already been expressed to me,' " the dry response came. " 'I expect they'll be expressing it to you, as well, once you're up before the Overclan Seating.' "

"I appreciate the advance warning," Thrr-gilag said, checking the time. The alien prisoners should have had enough time to recover now. At least as far as they were going to. "I have to go now, my brother. Keep yourself safe, and I'll speak with you again soon."

" 'I'll be careful,' " Chrr't-ogdano repeated the words. " 'You, too. Farewell.' "

"Farewell." Thrr-gilag nodded to the Elder. "Thank you, Chrr't-ogdano. You may release the rest of the pathway now. It's time to go."

"Good," Chrr't-ogdano grumbled. He gestured toward the door with his tongue. "What about the pyramid? Are you still planning to leave it here?"

"We're hardly going to be able to watch the Humans when they return without it," Thrr-gilag pointed out, frowning at the worried expression on the Elder's face. "Why? Are you afraid?"

"After what happened to Prr't-zevisti?" Chrr't-ogdano countered. "Of course I'm afraid. You would be too."

Thrr-gilag grimaced, reaching behind his head to touch the small scar at the base of his skull, arguments and soothing words swirling through his mind and dissolving into silence on his tongue. Theoretically, of course, nothing the Humans did to an Elder's *fsss* cutting there should have any effect on the rest of the finger-sized organ, safely nestled in its shrine niche 250 light-cyclics away. At the first sign of danger, all Chrr't-ogdano and the other Elders should have to do would be to flick back to their shrines, and they'd be perfectly safe.

But theory was one thing. A group of nervous Elders worried for their survival was something else entirely. And to be fair, as far as Thrr-gilag knew, the theory had never been tested.

"The observers on Study World Eighteen," Chrr't-ogdano said. "Remember the report? They felt the pain of the Human Elderdeath weapons."

"But they were still anchored at their cuttings watching the Humans," Thrr-gilag reminded him. "But you have a point. Very well. Inform Ship Commander Zbb-rundgi that I've reversed my decision and that the pyramid is to be taken back home. And tell him we'll leave as soon as it's aboard."

"I obey," Chrr't-ogdano said, looking more than a little relieved.

He vanished. Alone again, Thrr-gilag stood up, pressing the edge of his tongue hard against the inside of his mouth as he draped the restraint suit across his shoulders. So here they were again: the Zhirrzh at war with yet another new alien race. Aliens who, like all the others who had gone before them, had attacked them on sight. Aliens with powerful explosive missiles and small but vicious fighter warcraft, who used Elderdeath weapons with a free hand. Aliens who owned twenty-four worlds, against eighteen worlds of their own, who held at least eight other alien races under their domination.

Aliens who wielded the terrifying weapon Pheylan Cavanagh had described for him. The awful killing device called CIRCE.

Taking one last look around the silent conversation room, Thrr-gilag headed for the door and the ship that lay beyond. And hoped fervently that Warrior Command and the Overclan Seating hadn't sliced off more than they could eat.

2 It was just over 250 light-cyclics to Oaccanv: nearly thirty-five tentharcs at stardrive speed. Three and a half long fullarcs for Thrr-gilag to lie in his cabin, studying the records of Pheylan Cavanagh's imprisonment and sharpening his knowledge of the Human language. And wondering what might be happening elsewhere as they flew through the darkness between the stars.

Fortunately, he didn't have to wonder in similar darkness. Ship Commander Zbb-rundgi had quietly instructed everyone aboard—unofficially, of course—to ostracize the young upstart searcher who had allowed the Human prisoner to escape and, probably more important, had treated the ship commander's advice with perceived contempt. But neither Nzz-oonaz nor Svv-selic seemed interested in taking the order seriously, and they kept

Thrr-gilag up-to-date on the progress of the Zhirrzh expeditionary forces currently in Human space.

The Elders' reports were sparse but generally favorable. On all three Human target worlds the defending warriors appeared to have been taken by surprise, though that hadn't stopped them from counterattacking with their explosive missiles and Elderdeath weapons. But they'd been routed, usually after only a tentharc or two of fighting, fleeing out into wilderness areas. Beachheads had been established and encirclement forces deployed in orbit, and now it was largely a matter of securing the territory and waiting to see how the Humans would respond to this returning of the war to their gatestep.

If this *was*, in fact, merely a turning of the war back on its creators.

It was a disturbing thought, and one which occupied the corners of Thrr-gilag's mind throughout the voyage. He trusted the Elders, certainly, and the Elders' report had stated unequivocally that at that first contact the Humans had been the aggressors. But at the same time, Thrr-gilag found it hard simply to ignore the words of Pheylan Cavanagh, who seemed to have been equally convinced that it was the *Far Searcher* and the other Zhirrzh survey ships which had fired first.

Probably the Human was lying. Almost certainly the Human was lying. But still, a thin edge of doubt remained. Thrr-gilag could only hope that when he got to Oaccanv, he would be able to erase that edge.

"All rise and prepare for service," the intoning voice of the chamber hailer boomed out. The words echoed faintly from the loudspeakers throughout the huge room, an echo quickly drowned out by the scuffling of a thousand Zhirrzh rising from their couches. "The Overclan Seating of the Zhirrzh people is now in session," the hailer called over the noise. "All honor the Overclan Prime."

Behind the podium the doors swung open, and the Overclan Prime stepped into view. For a few beats he stood in the doorway, silently surveying the crowded chamber. Then, holding aloft a *kavra* fruit for all to see, he sliced through it twice in the ancient ritual of openness and trust. Placing the lacerated fruit on the low table beside the door, he wiped his fingers on a cleaning cloth and continued forward. He walked between the two shrines—the larger, in standard white ceramic, for the general Overclan family; the smaller, of carved black stone, for the Overclan Primes themselves—nodding with respect to each as he passed. "I greet the Speakers of the Thousand Clans," he said, seating himself on his couch and gesturing for the Speakers to do the same. "We are met to consider the disturbing events of four fullarcs ago that necessitated the evacuation of Base World Twelve. Searcher Thrr-gilag, Kee'rr; Searcher Svv-selic, Too'rr; Searcher Nzz-oonaz, Flii'rr: step forward."

His two colleagues beside him, Thrr-gilag walked up to the witness box beside the podium, the sweet-sour after-taste of the poison-neutralizing *kavra* juice mixing with the acid nervousness on his tongue as he tried to read something—anything—from the Prime's expression. Hoping to get some idea where the titular leader of the Zhirrzh race stood on all this.

But the Prime's face was a mask. And small wonder. For five hundred cyclics, ever since the founding of the Overclan Seating, this family-without-a-clan had given its sons and daughters to live and work in the sprawling complex that served the Overclan, its members allied to no one, beholden to no one, favoring no one, opposing no one. No Zhirrzh could have risen through those select ranks to become Overclan Prime without long ago learning how to bury all personal thoughts and prejudices deeply within him.

"Searcher Thrr-gilag," the Prime said, those deep eyes boring into him. "As designated speaker of the alien specialist group on Base World Twelve, you bear the ultimate responsibility for the events of four fullarcs ago. Events that resulted in the escape of the Human prisoner of war, the evacuation of an importantly placed Zhirrzh base, and the raising of eight Zhirrzh to Eldership. We have read your reports, along with the comments and opinions of your communicators and those Elders who were assisting in your studies. Now we wish to hear your thoughts."

And my excuses? Thrr-gilag wondered. But again the Prime's face gave him no clue as to what the other might be thinking. "You have heard the facts of the incident," he said, forcing himself to look out at the rows and rows of clan Speakers gazing back at him. The Speakers, and the hazy cloud of silent Elders that filled the domed ceiling above the couches. "The Human prisoner was able to block the sensors of his obedience suit with mud," he continued, "and was able to seize both myself and one of my technics before we could move away. He held us as shields against the warriors and demanded entry to the newly arrived alien spacecraft."

"And did you so fear Eldership that you called off the warriors?" a voice growled from the first row of couches.

Thrr-gilag focused on him. It was a very well-known face: Cvv-panav, Speaker of the powerful Dhaa'rr clan. "I did not fear Eldership, Speaker," he said. "Indeed, I'd already risked that result by ordering the warriors to use flashblind weapons against the Human. They proved ineffective."

"Then you should have ordered them to use lasers," Cvv-panav insisted.

"Perhaps," Thrr-gilag said. "I agree, the situation was potentially dangerous. But I also saw in it a way to gain valuable information."

Cvv-panav sniffed. "We were already gaining valuable information—"

"The Speaker for Dhaa'rr will be silent," the Prime interrupted mildly. "What information do you refer to, Searcher Thrr-gilag?"

"The alien spacecraft had been damaged during its capture," Thrr-gilag said. "Zhirrzh observers had watched as its crew brought it to a landing, but that crew had been severely injured, and it was not known how long they would survive. It occurred to me that if we allowed the Human aboard the craft, our Elders would be able to see how the flight sequence was initiated. I therefore gave the order to allow him access to the craft."

"A dangerous risk," one of the other Speakers said. "And for so slight a gain. Our warrior searchers would surely have been able to learn the craft's secrets."

"Besides, the aliens *have* survived," Cvv-panav added. "Which means that the risk was for nothing at all."

"Perhaps," Thrr-gilag said. "But I didn't know that then. As for the aliens, their survival is still greatly in doubt."

"What is not in doubt is the fact that your gamble failed," Cvv-panav shot back. "The Human has returned to his people with knowledge about the Zhirrzh. You should have killed him."

"That may not have done any good," Thrr-gilag said, bracing himself. Here it came; and it was not going to be well received. "In my opinion it is not impossible that the Humans have Elders of their own."

He'd expected a roar of outrage from the assembly, or at least a hissing gasp of astonishment. The deathly silence was more unnerving than either of the other two reactions would have been. "Have you proof?" the Prime asked.

"Not as yet," Thrr-gilag said, trying to keep his voice and tail steady. "But there are indications. The Human was quick to notice our *fsss* scars, asking many questions about them. Furthermore, he also had a similar scar just so"—he traced the place on his abdomen—"indicating a spot from which a *fsss*-sized organ had clearly been removed."

"An interesting location for a *fsss* organ," the Prime commented. "Was this removal determined by medical instruments or direct Elder observation?"

"Both," Thrr-gilag said. "I ordered the Elder observation after our discussion about the *fsss* with the Human."

"A discussion which I stated at the time should not have occurred," Svv-selic put in. "It provided information—"

"The searcher will be silent," the Prime said. "Allow me to point out, Searcher Thrr-gilag, that five other Human bodies were briefly examined after the space battle. None showed any sign of such scars."

"Yes, I know," Thrr-gilag said. "And if the Humans do indeed have Elders, that might indicate that they're socially still in an extremely primitive state."

"Impossible," Cvv-panav snorted. "They have a highly advanced technology."

"Technology level and social structure are not necessarily related," Thrr-gilag said. "The Human Pheylan Cavanagh was apparently equivalent in rank to a Zhirrzh ship commander. If he, and he alone of all his warriors, had had his *fsss* removed, it might indicate that the Humans are at a stage comparable to Zhirrzh society before the First Eldership War."

For a few beats the chamber was silent. "Considering the barbarism of that era, that would be unpleasant news indeed," the Prime said at last. "Yet it would be consistent with the savagery of their attack on our survey ships. Can we assume we're dealing with a clan-structured feudal system, then?"

"Possibly," Thrr-gilag said. "But we mustn't forget that they're aliens. We can't simply project our own history onto them."

"And we similarly mustn't forget that wisps of imagination don't condense into hard ceramic," Cvv-panav said contemptuously. "To spin such a theory from a single Human scar walks the line between fever dream and stupidity."

"Perhaps," Thrr-gilag said, feeling his midlight pupils narrow with annoyance. "I would remind the Speaker that one of the Human's first actions was to try to reach the pyramid of our observers and communicators. That would imply some knowledge of its purpose."

"Coincidence," the Speaker said. "Or simple curiosity."

"Was it also coincidence that the Human warcraft who found Study World Eighteen immediately sought out and attacked the observers' pyramid with Elderdeath weapons?" Thrr-gilag countered. "Or coincidence that the Human forces on Dorcas deliberately stole a *fsss* cutting?"

He paused for breath . . . and as he did so, he suddenly noticed that all eyes in the vast chamber seemed to be frozen on him. He glanced at the Prime, back at the first row of speakers, settled on the thunderous expression of Speaker Cvv-panav . . .

He looked back at the Prime, feeling his tail begin to

speed up. Was Prr't-zevisti's disappearance supposed to have been a secret?

"Your initial testimony is hereby at an end, Searcher Thrr-gilag," the Prime said, his voice and face still unreadable. "You will stand down and await further examination. The Overclan Seating thank you for your time."

"The honor is mine, Overclan Prime," Thrr-gilag said, a sinking feeling at the base of his tongue as he stood up from the couch. His words were long gone into the air, with no way to retrieve them. If the expression on Speaker Cvv-panav's face was anything to go by, Thrr-gilag might soon wish he could vanish along with them.

The other testimony was finished, and the Speakers were filtering out for the midarc meal, when the summons Thrr-gilag had been dreading finally came.

"You are called to the private office of the Overclan Prime," the Elder told him, his voice and manner short. "Follow me."

Thrr-gilag sighed silently. "I obey," he said.

It was a long, lonely railcar ride—nearly half a thoustride long, in fact—down the deserted underground tunnel that led from the rear of the Overclan Seating chamber back to the two main office buildings of the complex. Eventually, they reached the end and returned to ground level. Leaving the railcar, Thrr-gilag followed the Elder to an elaborately carved door with large wooden rings in place of the usual doorknobs, and the look and smell of great age. "Enter," the Elder said, gesturing to the door. Taking a deep breath, Thrr-gilag gripped the ancient wooden ring and pulled the door open.

The room turned out to be a small, intimate conversation room, furnished with no tables and only a handful of couches. Three Zhirrzh were waiting for him: Cvv-panav, the Speaker for Dhaa'rr; Hgg-spontib, the Speaker for Kee'rr; and the Overclan Prime himself. None of their expressions were especially encouraging. "Come in, Searcher," the Prime said gravely, gesturing to a row of *kavra* fruit on a ledge beside the door. "I presume you know the Speakers for Dhaa'rr and Kee'rr."

"Yes, Overclan Prime," Thrr-gilag said, nodding politely to each of them in turn. Picking up one of the *kavra* fruit, he sliced through it twice with the cutting edges of his tongue and dropped it into the disposal container beneath it. "How may I serve you?" he asked, wiping his hands on the cleaning cloth hanging beneath the ledge.

"The alien prisoners have been brought to the complex," the Prime told him. "They're being prepared for interrogation in the medical center."

"I see," Thrr-gilag said. He'd instructed the healers to let the aliens recover from the stresses of landing before moving them: strictly speaking, he should have been informed of any transfers. Under the circumstances he wasn't really surprised that he hadn't. "How well did they withstand the journey across from the landing field?"

"I'm told they're quite weak, but that their metabolic readings are stable," the Prime said. "I expect to be able to speak with them in a few hunbeats." He eyed Thrr-gilag. "Before we do, though, Speaker Cvv-panav has some questions concerning your testimony of this premidarc."

"More specifically, concerning your glaring breach of security," Cvv-panav bit out. "I want to hear what you know about the Prr't-zevisti incident on Dorcas. And how you learned of it."

"I spoke with my brother, Commander Thrr-mezaz, just before we were evacuated from Base World Twelve," Thrr-gilag said. "He told me that Prr't-zevisti's *fss* cutting had been captured and that Prr't-zevisti himself had not been seen since then. That's all I know."

"And did Commander Thrr-mezaz happen to mention that this incident was to be kept a secret?"

Thrr-gilag felt his tail speed up. "No, Speaker, he didn't."

"Do you generally consider discussions with warrior commanders to be the stuff of casual conversation?" Cvv-panav persisted.

"Not at all, Speaker," Thrr-gilag said. "I've always treated such information as private and privileged."

"And yet you simply blurt out this private and privileged information without any thought whatsoever?"

Thrr-gilag looked him straight in the eye. "I would not have thought, Speaker, that testimony before the Overclan Seating would be considered casual conversation."

"I would agree," Speaker Hgg-spontib spoke up from his couch on the Prime's other side. "In fact, I'd venture to say there are many other Speakers wondering why it required a slip of a young searcher's tongue for us to learn of this incident. One might think the Dhaa'rr were attempting to keep vital information to themselves, for their own private purposes."

"The death of a Dhaa'rr Elder is a private matter for the Dhaa'rr clan," Cvv-panav growled back. "Not a gossip item for idle conversation."

Hgg-spontib's midlight pupils visibly contracted. "Are you suggesting that members of the Overclan Seating have nothing better to do than indulge in idle gossip?"

"What the Seating does or does not do hardly matters at this point," Cvv-panav snapped. "There were probably two thousand Elders observing the meeting, not counting those of the Overclan itself. Thanks to this loose-tongued young fool, the news is probably all over the Elder community by now."

"You overstate your case somewhat, Speaker Cvv-panav," the Prime spoke up mildly. "For one thing, you know perfectly well that nothing connected with a war can be considered the exclusive property of a single family or clan. For another, the first leaks most likely occurred four fullarcs ago, when Searcher Thrr-gilag first learned of Prr't-zevisti's disappearance. The pathway for that conversation included an Elder with only marginal warrior security classification."

"Really," Cvv-panav said, throwing a cold look at Thrr-gilag. "About as I would have expected."

"Perhaps," the Prime said. "But before you become too indignant, let me point out that the reason Searcher Thrr-gilag was using a nonsecure pathway was that the Dhaa'rr had not yet provided another properly secure Elder to fill the pathway gap left by Prr't-zevisti's disappearance. Two entire fullarcs after that disappearance, I might add."

It was Cvv-panav's turn to narrow his midlight pupils. "And how would you know that, Overclan Prime?"

The Prime met his glare without flinching. "Because the Overclan has been monitoring all nonwarrior pathways between Zhirrzh outposts and expeditionary forces ever since that first contact with the Human warcraft."

Cvv-panav threw Hgg-spontib a look. "I don't recall the Seating being consulted on this matter, Overclan Prime."

"That's because it wasn't," the Prime said. "I considered it a matter of Zhirrzh security, and therefore acted without consulting the Seating. As was both my right and my duty."

"I'm not sure all the Speakers would accept such an interpretation of the Agreements," Cvv-panav said. "One might think the Overclan was attempting to keep vital information to itself, to paraphrase my colleague Hggspontib. For its own private purposes."

"Walk carefully, Speaker," the Prime warned him quietly. "Inflammatory accusations can be as damaging as any security breach."

"So can the appearance of impropriety, Overclan Prime," Cvv-panav countered. He glanced at Thrr-gilag, as if suddenly remembering that there was a low-level witness sitting in on this high-level argument. "But this isn't the time for such discussions," he added. "We should instead be seeing if our prisoners are ready to answer some questions."

"Yes," the Prime said. "Communicator?"

An Elder appeared. "Yes, Overclan Prime?"

"Go speak with the healers in the medical center. See if all is prepared."

"I obey."

Thrr-gilag cleared his throat. "I would remind the Overclan Prime that the prisoners are still very weak," he said. "If pushed too hard, they may die."

"All the more reason to question them while we can," the Prime said. "In any event, that decision is now in the hands of Searcher Nzz-oonaz."

Thrr-gilag felt his tail twirling faster. "May I assume, then, that I've been removed as speaker of the mission?" he asked, just to make it official.

"Be thankful you haven't been removed from the mission entirely," Cvv-panav put in acidly, his tone making it clear that he'd argued for precisely that outcome. "By all rights, the escape of your Human prisoner should have earned you far more than simply a demotion. A public censure at the least; perhaps even criminal charges."

The Elder reappeared. "All is prepared, Overclan

Prime," he said. "The healers and alien-specialist group are waiting."

"Very good," the Prime said, rising from his couch. "Speakers, Searcher: come."

The medical center turned out to be a somewhat more compact version of the room on Base World 12 that the technics had hurriedly converted into a prison for Pheylan Cavanagh. In the middle of the room, lying on rolling beds and covered by a portable glass security dome, were the two prisoners. Nearly forty Zhirrzh were present, busy at the various monitoring consoles along the walls or gathered four-deep around the dome gazing at the aliens. Thrr-gilag spotted Svv-selic and Nzz-oonaz standing beside the glass, along with a number of the technics and healers who'd been with them on Base World 12. Only a handful of the observers appeared to be Speakers from the Overclan Seating.

And standing off to one side, Thrr-gilag spotted someone else, someone he hadn't seen for several cyclics. Gll-borgiv, an alien specialist from the Dhaa'rr clan.

"Searcher Nzz-oonaz will perform the interrogation," the Prime said as a technic by the door handed each of the newcomers a translator-link earphone. They crossed to the dome, a respectful path opening up for them through the crowd as they did so. For a few beats the Prime gazed at the aliens, then nodded to Nzz-oonaz. "You may begin."

"I obey, Overclan Prime," Nzz-oonaz said, sounding more than a little nervous. "During their brief conscious period back on Base World Twelve we established that they spoke at least some of the language of our Human prisoner. I'll try that first."

He pressed a little more closely against the dome and cleared his throat self-consciously. "Aliens of the

Mrachani," he said in the Human language. "I am Nzz-oonaz; Flii'rr. Can you hear me?"

For a dozen beats nothing happened. Then, slowly, one of the aliens opened his eyes. "I hear," he said, his voice almost too soft to hear. A beat later the words were echoed by the translator-link in Thrr-gilag's ear slits. "I am Uhraus. Ambassador to your people from the Mrachanis."

"Did he say *ambassador?*" Hgg-spontib muttered from beside Thrr-gilag, pressing his translator-link tighter against the side of his head.

"Yes," Thrr-gilag confirmed, frowning at the aliens. Yet according to the warriors who'd captured it, the alien spacecraft had opened fire on them with the same Elderdeath weapons the Humans had used.

Nzz-oonaz was obviously thinking along the same lines. "Do Mrachani ambassadors usually attack unknown spacecraft on sight?" he demanded.

For another few beats the Mrachani's gaze seemed to drift around the crowd gathered before him. Almost, Thrr-gilag thought oddly, like a dramatist measuring an audience before beginning his performance. "We came to bring warning," the alien sighed at last, closing his eyes tiredly. "And to offer the assistance of the Mrachanis in your struggle against the *Mirnacheem-hyeea.*"

Nzz-oonaz threw Thrr-gilag a questioning look. Thrr-gilag flicked his tongue in a negative: the word didn't mean anything to him. "What is this *Mirnacheem-hyeea* you speak of?" Nzz-oonaz asked.

"The *Mirnacheem-hyeea* are those who attempt to dominate all within their reach," the Mrachani said. "In their language the name means Conquerors Without Reason." He opened his eyes, closed them again. "The Humans."

Conquerors Without Reason. Thrr-gilag let the words

roll around in his mind, tasting the implications. Ominous implications, indeed.

"We appreciate your warning," Nzz-oonaz said. "What assistance do the Mrachanis offer?"

"The Mrachanis need your help," the alien murmured, his voice fading even further. "We need your—" He took a deep, shuddering breath. "Help."

"What assistance do the Mrachanis offer?" Nzz-oonaz repeated.

There was no answer. "Healer?" Nzz-oonaz asked, looking over his shoulder at one of the consoles.

"He's gone back to sleep," the healer reported. "And their metabolic efficiency appears to be dropping again. Shall I attempt to awaken them?"

Nzz-oonaz looked at the Prime. "Overclan Prime?"

The Prime was gazing at the aliens, his face hard. "How much risk would there be to their lives, Healer?"

"I don't know," the healer admitted. "We still know very little about their biochemistry."

"We won't risk it, then," the Prime said. "Let them sleep, and we'll continue the interrogation later. I want a full watch to be kept, healers and Elders both."

"I obey," the healer said. Gesturing to a technic, he began issuing orders.

Cvv-panav took a step closer to the Prime. "I should like to continue our discussion of last fullarc, Overclan Prime," he said. Quietly, but with a note of insistence in his voice.

"No need," the Prime said, turning to Hgg-spontib. "I'm sure Speaker Hgg-spontib will not argue that this contact has grown far beyond the proprietary rights of the clans who first contacted the Humans." He looked over at the sleeping aliens. "Or perhaps we should call them the Human-Conquerors," he amended grimly. "It appears that would be a more appropriate name. At any rate, I'm assigning Gll-borgiv; Dhaa'rr, to this study group."

"I protest, of course," Hgg-spontib said. "The Dhaa'rr have yet to suffer any damage at the hands of either of these alien species. If any new searchers are added, they should be from the Cakk'rr, who at least have the claim of having captured these Mrachanis for us."

"I've already discussed the matter with the Speaker for Cakk'rr," Cvv-panav put in. "There is no searcher of the Cakk'rr of adequate expertise. She has therefore agreed to defer to the Dhaa'rr in this matter." His tongue twitched. "As the Overclan Prime said earlier, nothing connected with a war can be considered the exclusive property of a single family or clan."

Thrr-gilag pressed the tip of his tongue against the roof of his mouth, keeping his mouth firmly shut. The Zhirrzh alien-specialist community was a reasonably small group, and he could name at least three Cakk'rr experts right off the end of his tongue who would be capable of working with the Mrachanis. Clearly, putting a Dhaa'rr on the group was a political decision, not a scientific one.

"The Kee'rr still protest," Hgg-spontib said in the tone of one who knows a lost battle when he's lost it. "And what of Searcher Thrr-gilag?"

"The Dhaa'rr insist on a full investigation," Cvv-panav put in before the Prime could answer. "The escape of the Human—the Human-Conqueror—must be properly examined."

"Your insistence is premature," the Prime told him. "An inquiry board is examining all the records from Base World Twelve. Until they come to a decision, Searcher Thrr-gilag will be permitted to observe all proceedings involving the Mrachani aliens."

"But not to speak to them," Cvv-panav insisted.

"Proper protocol will of course be followed," the Prime said. "He may offer questions through Searcher Nzz-oonaz." He looked at Thrr-gilag. "Do you accept these limitations?"

As if he had a real choice. "I do," Thrr-gilag said, a flush of shame twitching through his tail. Svv-selic had let Too'rr domination of this mission slip from his grasp by letting the Human prisoner get too close to the Elders' pyramid. Now Thrr-gilag's mistake had similarly lost the speakership for the Kee'rr clan.

How long would it be, he wondered, before Nzz-oonaz made his mistake and Cvv-panav demanded that Gll-borgiv and the Dhaa'rr take charge? He doubted it would be very long.

"You look as if you have something else to say, Searcher," Cvv-panav said, an edge of challenge to his voice.

"No," Thrr-gilag said, resolutely turning away. Arguing any of this would just give them an excuse to throw him off the mission completely. "With the Overclan Prime's permission, I'd like to leave the complex for a time."

"What of the aliens?" the Prime asked. "If they should awaken, you'd be needed."

So at least the Prime still thought of him as a useful part of the group, even if Cvv-panav didn't. That was something, anyway. "If our shipboard experiences are a guide, they should sleep at least four or five tentharcs," Thrr-gilag said.

"Very well," the Prime said. "You may leave, but I don't want you more than a few hunbeats away from this room. And be certain to update your location with the servers at the Overclan shrine."

"I obey," Thrr-gilag said. He turned away, easing through the crowd toward the door—

"One other thing," the Prime's voice said quietly from beside him.

Thrr-gilag looked over, a bit startled. He hadn't realized the Prime had followed him. "Yes, Overclan Prime?"

"There are certain things you and your group are aware of that have not been released to the general Zhirrzh public," the Prime said.

Thrr-gilag winced. Yes; Prr't-zevisti. "I understand fully," he assured the Prime. "I'll be careful not to say anything outside the complex."

"I'm sure you understand the sort of thing I'm talking about," the Prime went on as if he hadn't spoken. "Stories that would spread rumors and fear. Panic, even, particularly among those who are unaware of the full scope of the countermeasures Warrior Command is taking." He gazed hard at Thrr-gilag. "And I don't refer only to those outside the Overclan complex."

Thrr-gilag frowned at him. What in the eighteen worlds was the Prime getting at?

And then, abruptly, he got it. CIRCE. The Humans' ultimate weapon. Long ago disassembled, according to the captured Human recorder, with its components scattered among several planets of their empire for safekeeping. If they were allowed the time to collect those components and reassemble them once more into a functioning weapon . . .

The Prime was still studying his face. "You understand," he said.

"Yes," Thrr-gilag said, his tongue flicking in a shiver. He understood, all right. If even a hint leaked out at this point that their enemies had a weapon against which there might not be any defense at all . . .

He looked sharply at the Prime, the other's almost offhanded comment suddenly registering. *Not only those outside the Overclan complex* . . . "May I inquire," he asked carefully, "who among the Zhirrzh are aware of this aspect?"

"I am," the Prime said. "So are a handful of the supreme commanders at Warrior Command, the former Overclan Primes, and perhaps thirty other high-security Elders. Plus your alien-study group, of course."

Thrr-gilag pressed his tongue hard against the inside of his mouth. "And the Overclan Seating?"

The Prime didn't flinch. "It would not be advisable for them to know as yet."

"I see," Thrr-gilag murmured. Suddenly it all made sense, this mad rush to throw beachheads and encirclement forces at the Human worlds. Warrior Command wasn't looking for territory to conquer; it was trying desperately to capture or entrap one or more of CIRCE's components before the Humans could gather them together.

And in the meantime the Overclan Prime was trying equally hard to prevent Zhirrzh society from exploding into hysterical terror at the thought of the potential genocide facing them. And if that meant hiding the truth from even the Overclan Seating, then that was what they were going to do.

"You understand the situation," the Prime said. "I could lock you and the others away somewhere, but that would attract unwelcome attention and questions. So for the time being you're free to move about; but be assured that if you tell anyone about this thing, you and your whole family will suffer greatly. Do you understand?"

"I do," Thrr-gilag managed. "And if I may say so,

Overclan Prime, there's no need to make threats. I understand as well as you the need to avoid a panic."

"Just so long as we understand each other," the Prime said. "Where exactly will you be going right now?"

"Just to get something to eat," Thrr-gilag said. "There's a place nearby called the Lapper's Paradise I thought I'd try."

"Very well," the Prime said. "But I meant what I said about staying close to the complex. These Mrachani aliens may hold the key to our survival against the Human-Conquerors."

Survival. Previous Overclan Primes throughout history, facing other aggressive alien races, had spoken not of survival but of victory. Or so the histories said.

But then, none of their other alien enemies had ever had a weapon like CIRCE. "I understand," Thrr-gilag said quietly. "I'll be close."

3

The Lapper's Paradise, Thrr-gilag had once heard, claimed to be the largest and best patronized full-service tavern in all of the eighteen worlds. He didn't know whether that was literally true, but certainly the establishment had both the floor space and the population base to take a good slash at the title. Located just across the main public thoroughfare that ran past the west side of the Overclan complex, the Paradise drew from the Speakers and aides of the Overclan Seating as well as from the population of Unity City itself, a population made up largely of the Overclan family members who served as the complex's permanent staff. From the way the crowd was packing into the tavern, it looked as if a goodly slice of that population was already there. Drinking, eating, and talking.

And worried sick. Thrr-gilag could hear the fear in the nervous laughter; could see it in the serious faces huddled together across tables; could smell it in the glycerol- and sweat-scented air.

Somewhere out there, in the blackness of space, the Humans were waiting. Powerful, deadly, and ruthless . . . and gathering for war.

Thrr-gilag sipped at his drink, looking around the tavern and listening to snatches of passing conversations as he marveled once again at the incredible speed of information flow that the Zhirrzh culture was capable of. He'd done his searcher thesis on general information dissemination among the cultures of the four known alien races, and in none of them had he found anything to compare with this vast informal network of Elders—one reason, his thesis had concluded, that the Zhirrzh had always been able to defeat the spacefaring races who attacked them.

But the Human empire was far larger than anything the Zhirrzh had faced before. And if the Humans had an Elder network of their own . . .

"Thrr-gilag?" a voice called from behind him.

Thrr-gilag turned around. Beckoning him over from a small group seated together around one of the tables was Nzz-oonaz. Picking up his drink, Thrr-gilag slid off his bar couch and went over. "Thought that was you," Nzz-oonaz said, indicating an empty couch across the table from him. "Join us?"

"Sure," Thrr-gilag said, easing past the other Zhirrzh and seating himself. "I'm surprised to find you here—I'd have thought you'd be standing over our prisoners."

"They're sleeping quite soundly," Nzz-oonaz said. "I decided I could risk leaving for a while." His tongue flicked sourly. "Besides, Gll-borgiv seems to have things well under control."

"Taking over, is he?"

"He's trying," Nzz-oonaz said. "Him and the whole

Dhaa'rr clan, from Speaker Cvv-panav on down. Actually, I'm half-inclined to let them have the mess. See how far *they* can get with it."

Thrr-gilag looked around the group. All of them were young members of the Overclan staff, he saw now, wearing the jumpsuits and insignia threads of assorted service positions within the complex. An admiring entourage of overawed youngsters? Or were they a quiet protector escort, here to make sure no one mentioned the name CIRCE? "From what I've heard of Speaker Cvv-panav, he'd probably enjoy the challenge," he commented.

"I'm sure he would," Nzz-oonaz said with a grimace. "Right up to the point where it rose up and strangled him." He took a sip from his cup. "I don't like this, Thrr-gilag. None of it. Especially this whole Mrachani business."

"Anything specific?"

"The whole thing strikes me as just a little too simplistic," Nzz-oonaz said. "They fire on the Cakk'rr ship with Elderdeath weapons but completely ignore my question as to why. They sleep practically the whole way back from Base World Twelve—which conveniently keeps them from having to answer any questions, you'll note—coming out of it just long enough to let us know they speak the Human language. We get here, and again they come up just long enough to deliver a plea for help before dropping back down again. You'd think that after four fullarcs they'd be healing and getting stronger, but you wouldn't know it from their behavior or metabolic readings."

Thrr-gilag thought about that. The complete lack of communication with the Mrachanis during the trip here had bothered him, too. "Still, it's not completely unreasonable," he said. "Without a biochemical/metabolic baseline, there's really no way to know how bad their injuries are."

Nzz-oonaz grunted. "Yes. Again, how convenient for them."

"You think they're spies for the Human-Conquerors, Searcher?" one of the Overclan youths asked.

"That's one possibility," Nzz-oonaz said. "Another is that they're fish lures, sent here to spin us this tale of a subjugated people eager to recruit allies. We go to their aid, and they promptly turn around and slice us in the neck. We've certainly done that sort of thing often enough to each other."

For a few hunbeats no one spoke. Thrr-gilag sipped at his drink, listening to the swirl of other conversations as he looked around the tavern. It was a mixed lot there this postmidarc, with little if any attention being paid to the old traditional standards of social and clan stratification that used to be the norm of Zhirrzh society. Construction and maintenance workers, professional people like searchers and advocates, even a scattering of warriors from the Unity City bases—all sitting or standing and drinking together. Over and through it all floated a mobile cloud of Elders, listening or joining in the conversations or just watching. Some scrutinized the unseemly mixing of social strata with undisguised disapproval; others watched the eating and drinking with wistfulness or equally undisguised envy.

Mostly, though, their expressions seemed to match those of the physicals around them. Like everyone else, the Elder community was worried.

"Perhaps we're being too cynical," another of the Overclan youths at the table said. "Perhaps the Mrachanis are being completely sincere. I can see where these Human-Conquerors would be pretty terrifying to everyone."

Thrr-gilag looked at the grim expression on Nzz-oonaz's face. *If you only knew the half of it,* he thought silently at the youth. "I'm sure we'll find out firsthand about that soon enough," he said aloud. "Speaking of Human attacks, Nzz-oonaz, has anyone been able to confirm yet whether the warcraft that hit the pyramid on Study World Eighteen were the same ones that hit us five tentharcs later?"

"I doubt it," Nzz-oonaz said. "From what I've heard, the pyramid on Study World Eighteen had mostly construction and structural engineer types aboard, there to study the ruins of that city. They didn't have any actual alien specialists along."

Thrr-gilag nodded heavily. Which meant there'd been no one there with the training to sort out the fine details of a specific alien's face or body type or stance, or who could memorize the unintelligible wing markings on an alien warcraft. "Typical," he said to Nzz-oonaz.

"You got that right," Nzz-oonaz grunted. "Bored Elders falling all over each other looking for something to do, but no one thought about putting an alien specialist's *fsss* cutting out there."

Thrr-gilag flicked his tongue. "Backsight is always so much clearer," he reminded the other. "Any idea which clan was running that pyramid?"

"No idea," Thrr-gilag said. "Probably one of the ones who think alien studies are beneath the dignity of a proper Zhirrzh. You know: 'The proper study of Zhirrzh is Zhirrzh,' and all that."

Abruptly, an Elder appeared, his torso coming partway through the tabletop. "Searchers Nzz-oonaz and Thrr-gilag," he said, his faint voice barely audible over the background noise. "Urgent message: you're both needed at the medical center."

"The Mrachanis?" Nzz-oonaz asked as he and Thrr-gilag scrambled to their feet.

"Yes," the Elder said. "Their metabolic readings have suddenly dropped. Searchers Gll-borgiv and Svv-selic think they may be dying."

"Get me some readings," Nzz-oonaz ordered, starting across the crowded tavern. "And tell Svv-selic to rig life-support gear."

"I obey," the Elder said, and vanished.

They headed for the door, the Overclan youths who'd been at their table forming a traveling wedge that cleared the way in front of them. They were just passing the end of the bar when the Elder returned. "Blood absorption readings on both aliens have dropped fifteen percent from their sleep levels," he reported. "Respiration has slowed and become erratic; galvanic response and brain-function activity are down twelve percent; cellular metabolic readings have dropped eight percent. Life-support equipment is in place and is being connected. Searcher Svv-selic has ordered four units of premarin colatyin for both aliens."

"Warn him to be careful," Nzz-oonaz said. "Overloading alien systems with untested drugs could kill them right here and now."

"I obey," the Elder said, and vanished.

They'd made it to the tavern's outer door by the time he returned. "There's been no response to the premarin," he said. "Six units of propodine miantoris are now being prepared for injection. Searcher Svv-selic says there's no choice now but to risk using these drugs."

Nzz-oonaz swore grimly under his breath. "Tell him we're on our way," he said as the group hurried out beneath the dark postmidarc clouds. "Let me know immediately if there are any signs of allergic reactions."

"I obey."

He disappeared. "Come on," Nzz-oonaz said, pointing Thrr-gilag to the left. "I've got a priority vehicle over here, a fast one. We can be there in three hunbeats."

Thrr-gilag nodded. "Let's hope it's enough."

It wasn't. They were across the public thoroughfare and speeding down the access tunnel toward the Overclan complex when the Elder brought the news that both aliens were dead.

They spent nearly a tentharc debriefing the technics who'd been on duty and analyzing every nuance of the events that had led up to the Mrachanis' deaths. Afterward came the autopsies—four more painstaking tentharcs' worth—which all four searchers sat in on. After that came more discussions, more analysis, and more study, stretching through the latearc.

By the time they were summoned to the Overclan Prime's private conference room, a tentharc after a gloomy sunrise, Thrr-gilag was as exhausted as he'd ever been in his life. And as discouraged.

"The summation line is that we simply don't know why they died," Nzz-oonaz said as he concluded their all-too-brief report. "It could have been a result of their injuries, the sudden upsurge of a disease organism they picked up during their short time on Base World Twelve, or some preexisting condition. Or something else entirely."

"Let me understand," the Prime said, his voice dark. "Our single most promising source of information about the Human-Conquerors, as well as a possible key to gaining some allies in this war. And you can't even tell me how they died."

"I'm sorry," Nzz-oonaz said, his voice quavering slightly beneath the combined glare of the Prime and the four speakers facing them. "We'll continue our studies, of course. But without a baseline for the species, it's unlikely we'll learn much more than we have already."

"I see," the Prime said. For a few beats his gaze swept the four searchers arrayed before him, visually castigating all of them with equal severity. "Let's hear your recommendations. Yes, Searcher Svv-selic?"

"We know where the Mrachani homeworld is," Svv-selic said. "I suggest we send a delegation there to return the bodies of their envoys, and to open direct communication with them."

"Communication with a race who fired on the Cakk'rr with Elderdeath weapons?" Hgg-spontib scoffed.

"The Speaker for Kee'rr has a valid question," the Prime said. "Have you an answer, Searcher?"

"Of course I'm not suggesting we send an unarmed envoy," Svv-selic said. "But I would remind the Overclan Prime that the Mrachanis are a subjugated race. Presumably everything they know about us would have come filtered by the Human-Conquerors' own biases. Their attack on the Cakk'rr ship might in that case have been nothing more hostile than a simple panic response."

Thrr-gilag glanced at Nzz-oonaz, their conversation at the Lapper's Paradise running through his mind. "I didn't think trained diplomats were supposed to panic," he murmured.

He thought he'd spoken quietly enough for only Nzz-oonaz to hear. He was wrong. "You have a comment, Searcher Thrr-gilag?" Cvv-panav spoke up.

Thrr-gilag grimaced. But it was too late to back out now. "I was wondering, Speaker, if perhaps this whole Mrachani contact might have been a very carefully staged deception."

"Staged by whom? The Human-Conquerors?"

"Or by the Mrachanis themselves," Thrr-gilag said. "I

ask the Overclan Prime and the Speakers to remember that we know virtually nothing about this race."

"I disagree," Svv-selic said. "There were several references to the Mrachanis in the Human-Conqueror recorder that the Too'rr survey ship salvaged from the space battle. It was clear from those references that they were subservient to the Human-Conquerors."

"With all due respect to Searcher Svv-selic, I would challenge any assertion that the references in the recorder could be considered clear," Thrr-gilag said. "Particularly unclear, to my mind, is the relationship of the Humans to other races within their sphere of influence."

"With a title of 'Conquerors Without Reason'?" Svv-selic countered. "Come on, Thrr-gilag. The name says it all."

"A name that was given them by the Mrachanis," Thrr-gilag reminded him. "All that does is turn the argument back into a circle."

"Do I understand you correctly, Searcher Thrr-gilag?" Cvv-panav demanded. "Are you actually defending the Human-Conquerors?"

Thrr-gilag forced himself to meet the Speaker's glare. "I defend the principle that conclusion should follow only from factual information, Speaker for Dhaa'rr," he said. "The Humans—"

"The Human-Conquerors attacked a group of four survey ships, Searcher," Cvv-panav bit out. "Need I remind you that they also attacked your group on Base World Twelve? What more in the way of factual information are you looking for?"

"They were rescuing one of their own on Base World Twelve," Thrr-gilag insisted doggedly. "Would the Zhirrzh have done less under similar circumstances?"

"And what of the Elderdeath weapons used on Study

World Eighteen?" Hgg-spontib put in. "Or the killing of Prr't-zevisti on the Human-Conqueror world Dorcas?"

"Well, Searcher?" the Prime prompted.

Thrr-gilag swallowed. "I agree, Overclan Prime, that these are strong indications of Human barbarism. But my personal experience with the Human prisoner Pheylan Cavanagh doesn't appear to fit the pattern. His escape attempt, for example. Once aboard the Mrachani space-craft, he no longer needed either the technic or me for protection against the warriors outside. Yet he raised nei-ther of us to Eldership, though with his superior muscula-ture he could have easily done so."

"Perhaps he didn't feel he could afford to take the time," the Prime suggested.

Thrr-gilag flicked his tongue in a negative. "No. You've seen the records—those hands and arms could break a Zhirrzh neck with a single twist."

"Then he thought he'd have further need of you," Cvv-panav said impatiently. "I submit, Overclan Prime, that this discussion is a waste of time. Whatever the minor specifics of the Human-Conqueror ethos, it's abundantly clear they're a highly dangerous threat to the Zhirrzh peo-ple. We must seize all opportunities that present them-selves, with speed and determination."

For a handful of beats the room was silent. Then, al-most reluctantly, the Prime nodded. "I'll instruct Warrior Command to prepare a small group of ships for an expedi-tion to the Mrachani homeworld," he said. "Searcher Nzz-oonaz, you are hereby appointed as speaker of the mission."

Cvv-panav shifted on his couch. "With all due respect, Overclan Prime—"

"I presume," the Prime continued, ignoring the other, "that you'll wish Searchers Svv-selic and Thrr-gilag to accompany you"—he paused, just long enough to make the point—"and Searcher Gll-borgiv, as well."

Nzz-oonaz glanced at Thrr-gilag, a guardedly sour expression on his face. Thrr-gilag returned the look, careful not to say anything this time that the Speaker for Dhaa'rr could pounce on. Gll-borgiv was competent enough, he supposed, but he'd hardly have put the other's name on top for a job of such critical importance as this. Even with Cvv-panav determined to keep this in the Dhaa'rr clan, there were far better choices he could have made. Klnn-dawan-a, for obvious example—

Thrr-gilag pressed his tongue hard against the top of his mouth. No, of course the Speaker wouldn't have chosen Klnn-dawan-a. Not if she'd been the best alien specialist in all eighteen worlds. Not after the mess Thrr-gilag had made of things on Base World 12.

"With the approval of the Speakers?" the Prime said, glancing around the room. "Very well, then. How long will you need to prepare, Searcher Nzz-oonaz?"

"That depends partly on what peripheral equipment and personnel Warrior Command and the Overclan Prime decide to send along," Nzz-oonaz said. "Probably six to eight fullarcs."

"Very well," the Prime said. "The mission will leave from the warrior landing field outside Unity City in eight fullarcs. Between now and then a small group of diplomats and warriors will be chosen who will accompany you."

"Chosen with the assistance of the Overclan Seating, I presume?" Cvv-panav put in. "And with its approval?"

An odd sort of expression passed across the Prime's face. "Of course, Speaker," he said softly. "Of course."

4 Thrr-mezaz frowned at the Elder floating in front of him. "Yes, we've been getting bits and pieces already about this diplomatic mission to the Mrachanis," he said. "Excuse my ignorance of politics, my brother, but the whole thing strikes me as a little premature."

The Elder nodded and vanished. Shifting on his couch, Thrr-mezaz looked out the window at the Human-Conqueror village and the swaying plant life beyond its borders. At first he'd rather liked the idea of having a premade headquarters to move into on Dorcas, even one of alien design and manufacture. But that comfortable feeling had eroded considerably over the past eleven full-arcs. Aside from occasional harassing raids, the Human-Conquerors were still sitting mostly silently out there in their mountain stronghold.

Far too silently. The only logical explanation was that they were preparing a major counteroffensive.

And when that assault came, Thrr-mezaz had the feeling that his Zhirrzh were going to feel badly exposed here in their borrowed dwellings. Perhaps he should try one more time to persuade Supreme Ship Commander Dkll-kumvit to let him disperse his warriors into the wooded areas surrounding the village. It would be less convenient, but far more concealed.

The Elder reappeared. " 'I don't think it's all that premature,' " he quoted Thrr-gilag's words. " 'The Humans are an extremely dangerous threat. We need to learn as much about them as we can, and the quicker the better. I just hope this mission is the right way to go about it.' "

"It sounds like you're not all that eager to go," Thrr-mezaz suggested. "Is anything specifically wrong?"

The Elder nodded again and was gone. Reaching to his desk, Thrr-mezaz activated his reader and called up the most recent update from the encirclement warships orbiting the planet. Another small Human-Conqueror spacecraft had come into the system about twenty hunbeats ago, too far away for the Zhirrzh warships to reach before it left again. It had sent laser communications at the planet, though, obviously intended for the Human-Conqueror stronghold. The messages had been unintelligible; the language experts and translators were still trying to decipher them.

The Elder returned. " 'I'm not exactly wild about going, naturally. But what bothers me most is that the Speaker for Dhaa'rr has insisted on Gll-borgiv going as Dhaa'rr alien specialist. With the unquestioning acquiescence of the Overclan Prime, I might add.' "

Gll-borgiv; Dhaa'rr. The name didn't mean anything

to Thrr-mezaz. "Is this Gll-borgiv incompetent?" he asked.

He was rereading the report for the second time when the Elder returned. " 'Not incompetent as such, but nowhere near the best the Dhaa'rr have. Klnn-dawan-a could slice circles around him on her worst fullarc, just to name one.' "

Thrr-mezaz had to smile at that one. "There wouldn't be any personal bias mixed into that assessment, would there?" he asked blandly.

" 'None at all,' " the somewhat indignant answer came back a hunbeat later. " 'I've seen Klnn-dawan-a at work. She's a highly capable searcher.' "

And even if she wasn't, Thrr-mezaz suspected, Thrr-gilag would defend her abilities just as passionately. Love was like that. "Maybe she's just too far away from Oac-canv or too embroiled in some other study right now," he soothed. "That could be why the Speaker for Dhaa'rr didn't pick her."

" 'She's on Gree studying the Chig,' " the answer came back. " 'That's only a fullarc's spaceflight away. I guess what bothers me most is that my part in the fiasco on Base World Twelve may have influenced Speaker Cvv-panav's decision. It feels like the Dhaa'rr are trying to put as much distance as possible between them and me, even if it means sending less than their best to the Mrachanis.' "

Thrr-mezaz slid his tongue gently around the inside of his mouth. "Well, don't go all paranoid before you absolutely have to," he advised his brother. "Don't forget that the main reason you were assigned to this mission in the first place was that you were the only Kee'rr alien specialist close enough to Base World Twelve to get there before the Human-Conqueror prisoner arrived. Decisions get made for lots of different reasons."

The Elder nodded and vanished. Reaching to his reader, Thrr-mezaz called up the reports of the last four intrusions by Human-Conqueror spacecraft and arrayed them side by side. Four intrusions in two fullarcs, three of them in the past fullarc alone. It was surveillance, all right; surveillance and communication with the Human-Conquerors in the mountains. But in preparation for what?

Whatever it was, he doubted he was going to like it.

The Elder reappeared. " 'I suppose you're right. And I suppose I'd better let you get back to your work, too. Are you doing all right?' "

"No worse than any warrior does in enemy territory," Thrr-mezaz said dryly. "It comes with the ranking threads. But we get by." He hesitated. "Incidentally, were you planning to see Mother while you're on Oaccanv?"

The pause this time was longer, and Thrr-mezaz was picturing a puzzled frown on his brother's face when the Elder finally returned. " 'I was hoping to see her and Father both. Why? Is anything wrong?' "

"She's been having some problems," Thrr-mezaz said evasively, wishing he hadn't had to bring this up. Thrr-gilag had been with that archaeology group on Study World 15 half a cyclic ago when the whole problem really started, and it hadn't been something either he or their father, Thrr't-rokik, had wanted to trust to the gossiping of the Elder communications network. But his brother deserved to know that things there weren't right before he walked in on it. "She's moved, for one thing. I wasn't sure you knew that."

" 'No, I didn't,' " the reply came back. " 'When was this?' "

"About thirty fullarcs ago," Thrr-mezaz said. "She's in a little house just south of Reeds Village now."

Another long pause. " 'But I was talking to her right

around that time, Thrr-mezaz. That was just before I was grabbed and taken to Base World Twelve to meet with the Human prisoner. She never mentioned anything about a move.' "

Thrr-mezaz sighed. "You can ask her about it when you see her," he said. "Father can give you directions to her new house. And some of the details about the move."

He'd expected another long pause, but the answer came back with only the usual delay. Clearly, Thrr-gilag had picked up that this was something private and not to be discussed via an Elder pathway. " 'All right. You be careful, my brother. Much as I'd like to see you, I'd just as soon you not arrive at the family shrine while I'm visiting.' "

"I'll be careful," Thrr-mezaz assured him. "You too, especially on this new expedition of yours."

The Elder was back a hunbeat later. " 'I will,' " he said. " 'Farewell, my brother.' "

"Farewell, Thrr-gilag," Thrr-mezaz said with a sigh. "You may release the pathway, Communicator," he added.

"I obey." The Elder vanished, returning quickly. "The pathway is released, Commander. Will there be anything more?"

"Not right now," Thrr-mezaz said. "Return to your observation duties."

A flicker of distaste might have crossed that transparent face. "I obey," he said, and vanished.

"But not happily," Thrr-mezaz murmured, turning back to his reader. A dazzling bit of understatement, really; and under the circumstances, he could hardly blame the Elders for their anger with him. They'd been brought along to serve as communicators, information pipelines between the Dorcas expeditionary force and home. Having them double as sentries had been a flick-of-the-beat idea of Thrr-mezaz's, partly a response to the limited number of warriors he'd been given and partly because it had seemed like such a good idea.

No one else had thought so, even back then. Now, with Prr't-zevisti gone, the Elders were half a beat away from open revolt, putting pressure on him to pull the pyramids back inside the perimeter, and undoubtedly making the same demands of the Overclan Seating and Warrior Command.

Thrr-mezaz sighed. No, it wasn't paranoia on Thrr-gilag's part to think the Speaker for Dhaa'rr was trying to distance his clan from the Thrr family. Between Thrr-gilag's mistakes on Base World 12 and Thrr-mezaz's own fiasco here, he wouldn't be surprised if the Kee'rr-clan leaders themselves decided to throw the family out.

And the consequences of all this were likely to hit his younger brother far more personally and deeply than Thrr-gilag had yet realized. Or at least more deeply than he was letting on.

With an effort Thrr-mezaz sliced the thought away. Thrr-gilag was his brother; but right now even the needs and future of his family must be subordinated to the task facing him here on Dorcas. Optimistic official statements to the contrary, Thrr-mezaz himself had a strong sense that this was the opening round in a long and potentially devastating war.

And in that kind of situation the actions of a simple ground-warrior commander on a minor enemy world could prove as momentous as anything else that happened across the vast reaches of space.

He pulled up a map of the land surrounding their appropriated Human-Conqueror village; and he was just settling down to search for a good place to move his encampment when the clanging of the alarm split the silence.

"Alert!" he shouted unnecessarily to the warriors in the command/monitor room, jabbing at the alarm to mute it. An Elder appeared in front of him. "Have all communicators report on enemy activity," he ordered, getting up from his couch.

"I obey," the Elder said, vanishing.

One of the warriors poked his head around the door into the office. "Signal from the *Imperative,* Commander," he called. "An attack force of seven midsized Human-Conqueror warcraft have entered the system. They'll be in combat range of the encirclement forces in approximately six hunbeats."

Four Elders appeared. "We find no indications of Human-Conqueror movement, Commander," one of them reported.

"There will be," Thrr-mezaz told them, heading for the door. "Have everyone spread out to the full range of their anchorlines and keep moving around. And don't watch only in the direction of the mountains—the Human-Conquerors are tricky. Let me know the instant you spot anything."

The command/monitor room was buzzing with activity. For a few beats Thrr-mezaz paused in the doorway, surveying his warriors, giving special attention to the movements of their tails. But there were no panic spins. Untried for the most part before this expedition, the beachhead attack and Human-Conqueror harassment were rapidly hardening them into combat veterans. Above them, hovering silently out of the way, a half-dozen Elders waited to run Thrr-mezaz's orders out to the perimeter warrior teams, the protector units at the four pyramids, and anyone else who was out of the optronic direct-communication circuit they'd set up within the village. The Elders themselves were unlikely to panic, fortunately. All were combat veterans, mostly from wars fought two and three generations ago against other alien enemies.

Small and inexperienced, the Dorcas expeditionary force nevertheless had good potential. Thrr-mezaz could only hope it had gathered together enough of that potential to stand against whatever was about to happen. "Report," he said, stepping into the room.

"All ground defense systems energized and standing ready, Commander," one of the warriors said. "Warrior patrols are moving to their perimeter jump points."

"We have a direct laser link now with the shipboard monitor cameras," another added.

"Good," Thrr-mezaz said. Supreme Ship Commander Dkll-kumvit and his warriors would undoubtedly be too busy to talk to him, but this way he'd at least be able to observe the space battle. "Offer them good luck, then maintain silence unless they address you."

"I obey, Commander," the warrior said, turning back to his monitor.

"So," the quiet voice of Second Commander Klnn-vavgi said from beside Thrr-mezaz. "You think this is it?"

"You mean their main counteroffensive?" Thrr-mezaz flicked his tongue in a negative. "No. What we have here, Second, is little more than a probe. A few warcraft, a simultaneous air assault, perhaps some ground warriors thrown in for good measure. A test of our strength, or of their ability to befuddle us with multiple opponents."

"Maybe." Klnn-vavgi looked around the room at the monitor stations. Thinking, perhaps, of the warriors' lack of experience. "I hope you're right."

"No, you've got that backward," Thrr-mezaz advised him dryly. "You're supposed to hope I'm *wrong*. That way

I'll be demoted in disgrace, and you can settle down to revel in the glory of command."

"There are several highly impolite words that would reflect my opinion of such glory," Klnn-vavgi said tartly. "As far as I'm concerned, you're the right Zhirrzh for this particular hot seat, and clan politics be damned."

Thrr-mezaz smiled. There was loyalty to one's family, to one's clan, to one's warrior unit. And then there was friendship, which could supersede them all. "Thank you, my friend," he said. "I hope you feel the same way when Speaker Cvv-panav offers you my job."

"He already has," Klnn-vavgi said. "I told him what I just told you. Shouldn't we be getting the Stingbirds into the air?"

For a pair of beats Thrr-mezaz stared at him, the other's question barely registering. He'd meant that crack about Cvv-panav to be facetious, a slightly disparaging comment on the Speaker's fondness for throwing Dhaa'rr political weight around. To find out that Cvv-panav had already been trying to do exactly that . . .

"Commander?" Klnn-vavgi prompted.

With an effort Thrr-mezaz brought his attention back to the task at hand. As Klnn-vavgi had already said, clan politics be damned. "No," he said. "We're leaving all our aircraft right where they are."

Klnn-vavgi's midlight pupils contracted noticeably. "Commander, if I may recommend—"

"We're leaving them where they are, Second," Thrr-mezaz repeated, glancing up at the group of silent Elders above him. They'd heard the whole exchange, of course, which probably meant that in a couple of fullarcs the Elders of all eighteen worlds would know that the Speaker for Dhaa'rr had tried to have him replaced. Should make for some interesting discussions. "Seriously, Klnn-vavgi, it's really our best strategy," he continued. "Our ground defenses should be adequate to handle anything they have except those two Copperhead warriors. I want to hold the Stingbirds in reserve against the fullarc that we find a way to deal with those."

"Excuse me, Commander," an Elder said, leaving the hovering group and moving in front of him. "I have to say that I stand with Second Commander Klnn-vavgi in recommending we lift the Stingbirds. This looks disturbingly like the same entrapment situation the Chig used against us in the Battle of Ko Roaddo. I was there, in a ground force consisting of—"

"The Battle of Ko Roaddo was nothing like this," Thrr-mezaz interrupted, resisting the urge simply to tell him to shut up and get back to his post. If he had a tentharc's leave for every time some Elder insisted on giving him sage advice based on out-of-date experience, he'd be retired with high honors by now. "For one thing, these aren't Chig. For another, the Copperhead warriors are too valuable for their commander to waste."

"You don't know that he thinks that way," the Elder argued. "It wouldn't necessarily be wasting them, either. If the Copperhead warriors would give him victory, he'd be a fool not to use them."

"And if he does send them in," a second Elder added, moving in to back up his associate, "they'd be here before we could even get the Stingbirds off the ground."

"A victory down here would be meaningless as long as the encirclement is intact over his head," Thrr-mezaz said. "He must surely know that."

"I still stand with Second Commander Klnn-vavgi," the first Elder insisted.

"Good," Klnn-vavgi put in. "Because Second Commander Klnn-vavgi stands with his commander. The decision has been properly made; the order has been duly given. Now return to your duties."

Glowering, the two Elders moved back to the communicator group. "Thank you," Thrr-mezaz muttered.

"They mean well," Klnn-vavgi muttered back. "For whatever that's worth. You're right, though: their commander is surely smart enough not to risk his Copperhead warriors. Certainly not while our encirclement denies him replacements for them."

"Which is really the key point here," Thrr-mezaz said. "If our warships lose their phase of the battle, those Copperhead warriors are indeed likely to make an appearance. We'll have to keep close watch on that."

"Agreed," Klnn-vavgi said grimly. "So it's all up to Supreme Ship Commander Dkll-kumvit."

Thrr-mezaz glanced around the monitors. "There should be plenty for all of us to do."

"Commander?" one of the warriors called. "The Human-Conqueror warcraft have reached the encirclement. All warships are engaging."

"Acknowledged," Thrr-mezaz said, moving forward a few steps for a better view of the monitors. The Human-Conquerors had launched their explosive missiles, with their fighter warcraft following close behind. The Zhirrzh warships were responding with laser fire, targeting first on the missiles and second on the fighter warcraft. "What about their Elderdeath weapons?" he asked.

"No sign of them, Commander," the warrior said. "Not from either the warcraft or the missiles."

"Odd," Klnn-vavgi murmured. "You'd think they'd use those right from the start to try to cut off our communications. That's certainly what they did against the survey ships."

"Book Lesson Number One," Thrr-mezaz said. "The

enemy will seldom accommodate your preconceptions of him. Stay alert; the ground commander could launch his attack anytime."

The words were barely out of his mouth when an Elder appeared. "They're coming, Commander," he said. "Three aircraft approaching from the southwest. Treetop height; range approximately fifteen thoustrides."

"Have someone keep watch on them," Thrr-mezaz ordered. "Are the warriors at the south and west jump points ready?"

The Elder vanished, reappearing a few beats later. "All three teams are ready," he reported.

"Tell them to stand quiet," Thrr-mezaz said. "They're not to attack without orders unless they're in immediate danger. Detail two Elders to run liaison and communication for each team; the rest will maintain surveillance."

"I obey," the Elder said, and again vanished.

"Alert the ground defense stations," Thrr-mezaz ordered the warrior at the appropriate monitor. "Prepare to repulse enemy aircraft."

"I obey, Commander."

"You're expecting them to send ground warriors in behind the aircraft?" Klnn-vavgi asked.

"I think there's a good chance they will," Thrr-gilag said. "That's why I ordered the perimeter warriors to stand quiet. No point in blatantly giving away their positions by firing on the aircraft."

"Especially since they probably wouldn't hit them anyway," Klnn-vavgi agreed. "I wonder how they were able to move those aircraft that far from the mountains without the encirclement warships spotting them."

"Slowly and carefully, no doubt," Thrr-gilag said. "Now that we know they can do that, we'll have to watch for it."

"Commander, laser scan has picked up the aircraft," one of the warriors spoke up. "Defenses ranging on them."

"They've veered off," someone else said. "Cutting back around—" He threw Thrr-mezaz a sharp look. "Heading directly for the southern pyramid."

"All ground defenses open fire," Thrr-mezaz ordered. "Communicator: probable air attack on southern pyramid. Order guards there to fire at will on enemy aircraft."

"I obey," one of the Elders said, and vanished.

"Everyone keep sharp," Thrr-mezaz warned the others, his eyes skipping across the monitors. "They've got something else under their tongues. Bet on it."

An Elder appeared. "Southern-pyramid guards have opened fire on the enemy aircraft. No apparent damage."

"The pyramid itself?"

"The aircraft don't seem to be firing." The Elder disappeared, was back three beats later. "Enemy aircraft have passed over the pyramid and left. Still without firing."

"Keep close watch," Klnn-vavgi said. "They may be back."

"I obey, Second Commander."

The Elder vanished; and as he did so, another popped into view. "Five enemy ground warriors have been spotted, Commander," he said, his tone edged with apprehension. "Two thoustrides northeast of the northern pyramid."

"Show me," Thrr-mezaz ordered, stepping over to a monitor that showed an aerial view of the village and surrounding terrain.

"Here," the Elder said, pointing a transparent tongue at a low ridge that ran roughly east to west a few thoustrides north of the village. "They're following behind this ridge," he added, tracing out a westward line.

"Heading for the pyramid, you think?" Klnn-vavgi suggested.

"Or else trying to use that ridge and those others as cover for an approach on the village." Thrr-mezaz frowned at the overview monitor, flicking his tongue out thoughtfully. "Or else . . ."

"Signal from Supreme Ship Commander Dkll-kumvit," one of the warriors called. "The Human-Conquerors have launched a group of fighter warcraft away from the battle, heading toward the planet surface."

"How far away are they?" Thrr-mezaz asked, crossing to him.

"Approximately eight thousand thoustrides," the warrior said. He indicated them on his monitor, a somewhat jumpy picture obviously being fed directly from one of the *Imperative*'s optical viewers. "They're cutting down and away from both us and the Human-Conquerors' mountain stronghold."

"Going to drop straight to the surface and come in at low altitude from there," Klnn-vavgi muttered.

"And if they reach the lower atmosphere, the warships' lasers aren't going to be able to get them," Thrr-mezaz agreed. "Has Supreme Ship Commander Dkll-kumvit detailed a warship to intercept them?"

"The message didn't say," the warrior said. "But they may not be able to spare one right now."

Thrr-mezaz felt his tail speed up slightly as he studied the monitors. The warrior was right; the encirclement forces were taking a beating. Despite the Zhirrzh laser defenses, far too many of the Human-Conqueror missiles were getting through, their powerful concussive blasts sending devastating shock waves straight through the nearly indestructible ceramic hulls and into the more delicate structures and equipment within. Enough of this kind of pummeling, and the Zhirrzh warships would be turned to hard-shelled jelly.

Still, the prognosis was hardly desperate. Even as the Zhirrzh warships suffered under the Human-Conquerors' battering, their attack lasers were steadily ripping away at the softer composite metal hulls of the enemy warcraft and cutting a swath through the swarm of fighter warcraft. "Signal to Supreme Ship Commander Dkll-kumvit," he said. "Urgently request that he detail one of his warships to attack the Human-Conqueror fighter warcraft before they reach atmosphere. Second, order the Stingbirds to lift for interception."

"I obey, Commander," Klnn-vavgi said, stepping over to the Stingbird monitor.

Thrr-mezaz turned back to the *Imperative*'s monitor; and as he did so, a half-dozen laser flashes lanced out toward the fighter warcraft diving toward the surface. "Supreme Ship Commander Dkll-kumvit seems to have acceded to your request, Commander," the warrior said. "The *Requisite* is dropping to intercept."

Another salvo of laser fire lanced out. Thrr-mezaz frowned hard at the monitor, wishing he had a better view of what was happening. "Communicator, have one of the Elders go straight up to his anchorline limit," he ordered. "I want to know if he can see anything."

"I obey."

"The Stingbirds are in the air," Klnn-vavgi reported, stepping back to Thrr-mezaz's side. "Anything on the fighter warcraft?"

"The *Requisite* is attacking them," Thrr-mezaz told him. "I've ordered an Elder to his anchorline limit to see if he can see anything."

Klnn-vavgi snorted gently. "If they get that close, we're already in trouble."

"True," Thrr-mezaz conceded. "Still, five thoustrides straight up should give him considerably less atmosphere to have to look through. He might at least be able to catch a glimpse of the *Requisite*'s laser fire. Stay on this one for me, Second. If those warcraft make it to the surface, we're in trouble."

"Right."

Thrr-mezaz moved over to the overview monitor. "Communicator, get me an update on those ground warriors."

An Elder appeared. "They appear to be changing direction," he reported, pointing to a spot. "They're behind this ridge now, moving slightly north of west."

Thrr-mezaz frowned at the monitor. "Are you sure?"

"Yes, Commander."

"Get me a confirmation."

The Elder vanished, was back a half-dozen beats later. "Confirmed," he said, jabbing his tongue at the monitor again. "This is their position, and they're moving this direction."

"Thank you," Thrr-mezaz murmured, moving his tongue thoughtfully back and forth inside his mouth. Confirmed . . . only it didn't make any sense.

"Commander, the *Requisite* reports all the approaching Human-Conqueror fighter warcraft are out of the air," Klnn-vavgi called. "Either destroyed outright or crashed and presumed destroyed. I have two Stingbirds on their way to the projected crash site to confirm."

Thrr-mezaz felt some of the tension leave his tail. At least that threat had been neutralized. "Acknowledged, Second. Have two more standing ready as backup if enemy aircraft head that direction. And warn them to keep sharp. If the Human-Conquerors think they can salvage anything from the wreckage, we might see those Copper-head warriors after all."

"Right." Klnn-vavgi murmured an order to the warrior at the Stingbird monitor, then came over to join Thrr-mezaz. "Looks like the main Human-Conqueror attack force is preparing to disengage, too. What's left of them, anyway." He gestured at the overview monitor. "What are the ground warriors doing?"

"What they're mostly doing is not making any sense," Thrr-mezaz growled. "At last report they were here, moving along behind this ridge."

Klnn-vavgi frowned. "Where are they going?"

"Good question," Thrr-mezaz agreed. "They're not really getting any closer to either the northern pyramid or the village."

"Could this be the only route with adequate cover?" Klnn-vavgi suggested doubtfully.

"No," Thrr-mezaz said. "That's the whole point: it's not. This ridge here—see it? Leads almost due southwest, right over to this group of hills. At least as much cover as they've got now, and they'd end up in a line-of-sight position over the village. Or they could follow this other ridge over here and make their way to the pyramid."

"Maybe they're just lost," Klnn-vavgi sniffed. "Shall I send a couple of Stingbirds to chase them away?"

Thrr-mezaz gazed at the monitor, trying to think himself into the aliens' footsteps. All right. If they were heading for either the village or the northern pyramid, they weren't doing a very good job of it. Could they have merely been part of the Human-Conquerors' feint, like the aircraft that had overflown the south pyramid? Something else to keep the Zhirrzh ground warriors occupied while those reinforcement warcraft tried to sneak in?

Or was that merely what they were hoping he would

think? Could the aircraft—maybe even the fighter war-craft—have actually been the distraction for the ground mission? Were they even now making their way toward some important objective, something outside the village itself?

"They had two high-power Elderdeath weapons operating when we first arrived," Thrr-mezaz said, tapping the shoulder of the warrior at the monitor. "Show me where those were."

"Yes, Commander," the warrior said, fingers and tongue flicking across the keyboard. A beat later two flashing spots appeared superimposed on the view, one at the northern edge of the village, the other on a hill a few thoustrides west of it. "The heavy air-assault craft destroyed both of them at the beginning of the invasion," the warrior added.

"Yes, I know," Thrr-mezaz said. But the Human-Conquerors had already demonstrated that they had small, portable Elderdeath weapons on hand. If they had another of the high-power versions hidden out there some-where . . .

"Do you want me to send the Stingbirds?" Klnn-vavgi prompted.

Thrr-mezaz flicked out his tongue. Time for a command decision . . . and a command gamble. "No," he said. "Let's let them go a little farther. See if we can figure out where they're going."

He sensed the flick of Klnn-vavgi's tail. "I'm not sure that would be a wise idea," the second commander said. "We've already seen that some of their explosive weapons don't rely on line of sight. If we let them get too close, they could do considerable damage."

"I realize that," Thrr-mezaz said. "I think it's worth the risk."

"Commander, if I may suggest—"

"Commander, the enemy warcraft are withdrawing," one of the warriors called.

Thrr-mezaz looked over at the *Imperative*'s optical-viewer feed in time to see the last of the Human-Conqueror warcraft flicker away. It was over, at least for now. "See if you can find out how extensive the damage to our warships was," he instructed the warrior.

"Yes, Commander," the other acknowledged. "It'll probably take a while, though—they're going to be busy up there. Just a beat . . . Commander, the *Imperative* reports that there was a series of laser-communication signals to the surface just before the Human-Conquerors withdrew."

Final messages. Or final orders. "Understood," Thrr-mezaz said. "Keep a close watch; the Human-Conquerors may have a second wave on its way."

"I don't think so," Klnn-vavgi said. "The ground warriors seem to have given up."

Thrr-mezaz turned to find an Elder hovering beside Klnn-vavgi. "Are you sure?"

"They've moved back to this point, Commander," the Elder said, indicating a spot. He vanished, reappeared—"They're here now. Moving back the way they came."

And moving pretty quickly, if the Elder was marking their position correctly. "Check and see if they're carrying anything they didn't have before," he instructed the Elder. "Or whether they seem to have left anything behind."

"I obey," the Elder said, vanishing. A handful of beats later he was back. "No to both questions," he said. "At least nothing larger than hand-sized. Do you want us to try to make a closer examination?"

"No need," Thrr-mezaz said. The Elders wouldn't have had a detailed list of what the Human-Conquerors had carried in, anyway. "Looks like they've aborted their mission. Whatever it was."

"There's still plenty of time to hit them before they get to the mountains," Klnn-vavgi pointed out. "With the Stingbirds or either of the two teams of ground warriors we've got on their flanks. Shall I give the orders?"

Gently, Thrr-mezaz rubbed his tongue against the inside of his mouth. Tactically, of course, the Second Commander's suggestion was certainly the thing to do. Every enemy warrior destroyed was one less warrior to threaten their beachhead. Plus the intangible but inevitable damage it would inflict on Human-Conqueror morale.

And if they hit the ground team now, before they got another half thoustride away, the Zhirrzh warriors would have the advantage of instant targeting and tactical information from the Elders anchored at the north pyramid. It would be a chance to prove to the skeptics, from Supreme Ship Commander Dkll-kumvit all the way up to Warrior Command, that using Elders as sentries this way was a sound and practical military tactic. A way finally to silence the rumblings of criticism and contempt that had been circling his head ever since the theft of Prr't-zevisti's *fsss* cutting.

Yes, he could easily destroy them. But if he did, they might never try this again. Whatever it was they were trying . . .

"No," he told Klnn-vavgi. "Let them go."

The low buzz of conversation around them vanished into silence. "Excuse me?" Klnn-vavgi asked carefully.

"We're letting them go," Thrr-mezaz repeated, turning away from the monitor. "We'll have the Elders watch them, of course, and I'll want both the ground warriors and the Stingbirds standing ready. But as long as they continue to head away from the village and the pyramids, we don't attack."

Klnn-vavgi cleared his throat. "With the Commander's permission—"

"They were up to something out there, Second," Thrr-mezaz said. "Something important. I want to make sure they feel secure enough to try it again."

"Understood," Klnn-vavgi said, his tone making it clear that he didn't understand at all. "What are you all sitting around for?" he added, throwing a quick glare around the room at the warriors watching them. "We have damage assessments to make, Stingbirds to service, and warriors to redeploy. And the Human-Conquerors might still decide to fight over the wreckage of those fighter warcraft. Get busy."

The warriors turned back to their monitors. Klnn-vavgi glared at them another couple of beats, then stepped to Thrr-mezaz's side. "This is risky, Thrr-mezaz," he said quietly. "And I don't mean just from a tactical stand-point. I hope you know what you're doing."

"So do I," Thrr-mezaz agreed. "History will have to pass the final judgment."

"That won't stop a thousand clan Speakers from writing their own versions of it."

"They'll be doing that whatever decisions I make at this point," Thrr-mezaz said. "The Thrr family is in polit-ical trouble, and there are going to be a lot of Zhirrzh scrambling to capitalize on that. That's the nature of poli-tics."

"I suppose so," Klnn-vavgi said reluctantly. "It really shouldn't be allowed in wartime, though. I just hope Warrior Command has enough stiffening not to cave in to the whims of the Overclan Seating."

"I think they do," Thrr-mezaz said, sliding his tongue thoughtfully across the roof of his mouth. "There's been something different about Warrior Command these past few fullarcs. They've become more serious than I've ever heard them before."

"You know, I've been thinking the same thing," Klnn-vavgi said slowly. "The first few fullarcs after the survey ships were attacked, everything coming out of Warrior Command was all bright and brisk and businesslike. Cheerful, even, as if they were really looking forward to taking on this new challenge. And then suddenly it all changed."

Thrr-mezaz nodded. The messages and orders had suddenly become terse and grim, and Warrior Command had begun scrambling together new expeditionary forces to throw at the new enemy.

And so there they sat, underequipped, overvulnerable, trying to hold on to a barely tenable beachhead on a clearly minor Human-Conqueror world, while similarly underequipped and overvulnerable expeditionary forces did the same on other Human-Conqueror worlds.

Why?

"They know something, Klnn-vavgi," Thrr-mezaz said quietly. "Something they've learned about the Human-Conquerors that's got them scared. Something they can't or won't tell us."

"Could be." Klnn-vavgi snorted under his breath. "Then again, maybe some genius there has only just gotten around to counting and realized we're eighteen worlds against the Human-Conquerors' twenty-four."

"Maybe," Thrr-mezaz said. "If the data in that Human-Conqueror recorder can be believed, anyway. Personally, I'm not convinced the thing wasn't a deliberate deception. Planting a recorder loaded with disinformation would be just the sort of thing a devious conqueror race might do. Maybe this mission to the Mrachanis isn't so premature after all."

"The Mrach—? Oh, right. Those new aliens. That mission's confirmed to fly, then?"

"That's what I hear," Thrr-mezaz said. "I want you to keep close track of the Stingbirds heading out to the warcraft wreckage. It's still possible the ground warriors were nothing but an attempt to distract us."

"Maybe." Klnn-vavgi looked back at the overview monitor. "What do you think they were really up to?"

"I don't know," Thrr-mezaz said. "But I can't help noticing that that's the same general area they were in when they took Prr't-zevisti's cutting."

"Interesting point," Klnn-vavgi said slowly. "I'd assumed they were there that time to get a look at the pyramid. You think there's something hidden out there that they want?"

"Or else they're trying to plant some non-line-of-sight weapon in position," Thrr-mezaz said. "Or trying to gain access to an underground supply or tunnel system. All we know for sure is that it's important to them." He flicked his tongue. "And I don't want them waiting until they've gathered so much strength that we won't have a hope of stopping them."

Klnn-vavgi snorted. "Under the circumstances, I hardly think that's likely."

"Unfortunately, circumstances seldom stay constant for long," Thrr-mezaz countered dryly.

"Point," Klnn-vavgi conceded. "All right, I'll go watch the Stingbirds. What about you?"

Thrr-mezaz looked back at the monitor. "First, I want to make sure those ground warriors really do leave. After that . . . I think I'm going to get the Elders started on a thorough search of that area. See if we can get to whatever the enemy's looking for before they do."

5 It was quiet in the big metal room. Amazingly quiet, distressingly boring, and very, very lonely. An ideal sort of place, Prr't-zevisti had long since decided, for meditative remembrance and reflective thought.

And such thoroughly positive pastimes as berating himself for having done such a mallet-headed thing in the first place.

It had seemed like a good idea at the time, or at least no worse than everything that had gone before it. The first mistake had been a group one, with enough blame for everyone to get his fair share: no one had noticed that group of Human ground warriors until they were practically on top of the northern pyramid. The Zhirrzh warriors had done their best, but without a timely warning from the Elders their response had been unfocused and far too late. The Humans had reached the pyramid; but instead of destroying it, they'd simply poked around, broken into Prr't-zevisti's niche and taken his *fsss* cutting, and moved on.

His cutting. Hovering at the edge of the lightworld, Prr't-zevisti gazed down at the thin slice of tissue sitting there in its tiny sealed box. It had been taken from his *fsss* organ a little over seventeen cyclics ago, but he still remembered that event as vividly as if it had just been last fullarc. The procedure had been brand-new at the time, only a couple of cyclics old, and most of Prr't-zevisti's friends had sworn up and down that they'd never let a technic take a blade to their *fsss* organs. But Prr't-zevisti had always had a reckless streak to him, and the prospect of getting to flit between two different areas instead of being stuck in just one had been highly intriguing. A little thought, a little boredom—a little goading from his friends—and he'd had his name put on the list.

Letting the Human warriors get to the pyramid had been their first mistake. The second had merely compounded it. Instead of redoubling their efforts to destroy or defeat the enemy, the Zhirrzh warriors had shifted their focus to merely driving the attackers back into the mountains.

At the time, of course, no one had thought of it as a mistake. With Prr't-zevisti's *fsss* cutting bouncing ignominiously around in some Human's combat bag, an illplaced shot by the Zhirrzh warriors could have vaporized the cutting and sent him snapping unceremoniously back to his main *fsss* anchorpoint at the Prr-family shrine. The Elders would certainly have pressured Commander Thrrmezaz not to take such a risk, a point of view Prr't-zevisti himself would definitely have supported if he hadn't been so quickly taken out of direct range of the discussion. Besides which, considering why Commander Thrr-mezaz had put the communicators' pyramids outside the village in the first place, he'd probably had some crazy notion of Prr't-zevisti serving as a spy at the enemy mountain stronghold.

He'd kept a low profile during the first couple of tentharcs of his captivity, staying deep in the grayworld where he couldn't see and could hear only through his *fss* cutting. Stoically enduring the Humans' discomforting and occasionally painful manipulation of the cutting.

Though none of it had been nearly as discomforting as the cutting process itself had been, seventeen cyclics ago. There was no way to apply an anesthetic, of course, and even though they'd used a cold-knife, a fair amount of pain had necessarily made it through to him. Far more sickening, at least to him, had been what the whole procedure had looked like. He'd seen other preserved *fss* organs when he was a physical and had known that the preservation technique had left a thin, hard shell around the exterior of the small, finger-shaped organ. What he hadn't realized until the cutting operation was that either time, or those same preservatives, had turned the interior of the *fss* into a fluid, jellylike substance. It oozed slowly around the knife as the healers cut, trickling down the side of the *fss* like some sort of extra-thick *kavra*-fruit juice. Like something dead and decaying, even though he knew intellectually that it was fully alive and vibrant. He'd watched in morbid fascination, a combination of shocked disgust and stubborn pride preventing him from looking away, as they finished their cut and turned the parts right side up to minimize and contain the leakage. They'd applied a new treatment of more modern preservatives, sending an odd sort of double tingling sensation through him. Both sections had skinned over; the healers had announced the cutting a success; and as the disgust and pain had faded into disinterest and fatigue, Prr't-zevisti had wandered off.

The Humans had eventually lost interest in his cutting, too. And as darkness fell and the aliens settled down for the latearc, Prr't-zevisti had come up to the edge of the lightworld again and begun to poke around.

But he'd underestimated the enemy's cunning. The area where his cutting had been taken was absolutely crammed full of metal: metal weapons, metal tools, even what appeared to be metal packaging. Like every Elder, he knew that refined metal could not be breached; what he hadn't properly appreciated until then was that the effect went far beyond the actual physical space occupied by that metal. Each piece seemed to throw the grayworld equivalent of a shadow, a sharply defined area shaped exactly like the shadow that would have been created by a light source at his *fss* cutting. A shadow as impenetrable as the metal itself. Obviously having to do with his anchorline, though he was rather surprised he'd never heard of this effect before.

And as he was picking his way carefully through the area, his full attention on the metal and the shadows, the Humans had sprung their trap.

He was standing there in the darkness—he or she; Prr't-zevisti still didn't know which. Standing there waiting for him to make his appearance . . . and even as Prr't-zevisti had belatedly noticed him, the Human had let out a shriek of discovery and triumph that had echoed through his mind a half-dozen beats after he'd dropped frantically back into the grayworld.

For a while he'd stayed there in the haze, unwilling to come up and risk being seen again. Silly, of course— irrational, even; trying to hide himself in the grayworld while his *fss* cutting sat open and unprotected in Human hands. Presently, he'd heard voices and felt movement and, bracing himself, had come back up.

To find a Human carrying his *fss* cutting toward a room-sized box rising above the shorter stacks around it. A thick-walled box, with an equally thick door, furnished with lights and a long table and shelves stacked high with equipment.

A room made entirely of metal.

There'd been a room very much like it back on the Dhaa'rr homeworld of Dharanv, he remembered. Once the cutting had been pronounced viable, the healers and technics had offered to take his *fss* into that room and take a second cutting from it. The metal, they'd pointed out, would force him to anchor to the just-completed cutting, blocking all pain and discomfort from the *fss* itself away from him. They'd been rather enthusiastic about the whole idea, a fact that had struck him as rather suspicious. He'd satisfied the requirements of pride and curiosity, and had no intention of being someone's experimental animal, and had politely declined.

But the Humans hadn't asked his permission to put him in their metal box. Nor were they likely to do so. And once his cutting was inside it, he'd be well and truly trapped there.

He'd been gone in an instant, stretching out and upward to the full length of his anchorline, sweeping across the foreshortened hemisphere that was all the surrounding piles of metal had left him, searching frantically for the anchorpoint-sense that would have shown he had a clear path back to safety at the Prr-family shrine. But nothing. He'd scanned the stars, wondering what the chances might be that Dorcas's rotation would bring the Dhaa'rr ancestral world of Dharanv into range in the handful of beats it would take the Humans to reach the box. But the stars were difficult to see from even the closest edge of the lightworld, and the constellations there were too different from those of home. He'd flicked back to the cutting—nearly to the metal box now—back to his anchorline limit; back to the cutting—just inside the door now, instantly shrinking his available angular range to practically zero—one last time along the anchorline—

And even as he'd shot back to the cutting, the door had swung shut with a deep and hollow boom.

Prr't-zevisti had gone over the scene probably a thousand times since then, wondering what he could have done that would have saved him from this. Should he have paid more attention when he'd first started looking around, putting more effort into avoiding detection? Should he not have dropped down into the grayworld, hiding like a frightened child, after he'd been spotted? Seventeen cyclics too late, of course, but should he have allowed the technics to take that second cutting? Another cutting, nestled in a pyramid on another of the eighteen worlds, might have been open to him.

Or should he perhaps have taken the ultimate gamble? Should he have simply stayed at the length of his anchorline and let the Humans close the metal on his *fss* cutting?

It was a thought that had occurred more and more frequently to him these past few fullarcs, and it was a thought that had never yet failed to send a chill through the core of his being. The anchorpoint effect of the *fss* organ had been known among the Zhirrzh since prehistoric times, whereas the double-anchorpoint of a *fss* plus a *fsss* cutting had become practical only twenty cyclics ago. Barely enough time for the Zhirrzh people to become comfortable with the idea; far too little for a situation even remotely similar to this one to have come up. It was possible, he supposed, that if he'd let them cut him off from his *fss* cutting, he would simply have hung out there in space until the Prr-family shrine had cleared the shadowing metal and he'd been drawn back home.

It was possible. But in Prr't-zevisti's opinion, it was vanishingly improbable. It was far more likely that, like an Elder whose *fss* was destroyed, he would simply have died.

Would have died.

Which was really why this whole line of thought was so unnerving to him. The fact that he was even thinking such things implied a desperation far out of proportion to his situation. Eight fullarcs of imprisonment should not be enough to lead anyone to thoughts of suicide.

From across the room came a muffled clang. Prr't-zevisti started, darting across to the upper corner by the door and dropping deeper into the grayworld. The door clanged again and swung open, revealing two Humans.

Prr't-zevisti was outside like a shot, easing past the stacks of metal and out into the open air. The sun was shining brilliantly out of a clear blue sky as he stretched out to the length of the anchorline. Maybe this time Dharanv and the family shrine would be within reach.

But no. The anchorpoint-sense wasn't there. Either he was being absurdly unlucky here, or else the piles of metal combined with the angles of Dorcas's rotational and orbital movement had managed to create a permanent shadow in Dharanv's direction. And unless he was willing this time to risk death . . .

He was back to his *fss* cutting well before the Humans shut the door, sealing themselves and him inside the metal room. He drifted up into his corner again, hiding himself in the mist of the grayworld, a fresh shiver running through him. *That* was what bothered him about this, he suddenly realized. Not the fact that he was contemplating his own death, but that the decision was never really over and done with. Each and every time the Humans opened that door, the choice and the risk were again before him. The question of whether this time a slim chance at freedom was worth the probable risk of death.

He didn't want to die. A fatuous statement, really; he didn't suppose anyone ever really *wanted* to die. The First Eldership War of a thousand cyclics ago had been sparked by that reluctance: the common Zhirrzh demanding the same right to this postponement of death that their clan and family leaders were already enjoying. The desire to maintain and continue one's life was probably as close to a universal instinct as was possible to get.

Zhirrzh warriors had the knowledge of Eldership to comfort them through the dangers of war. Did the Human warriors, he wondered, have anything similar?

Across the room one of the Humans was saying something. Cautiously, Prr't-zevisti eased up toward the lightworld again. The Humans were standing beside the torn and barely recognizable body of the Zhirrzh warrior that had occupied the center of the room since shortly after Prr't-zevisti's cutting had been brought in. At first he'd assumed the mutilation had been the result of some barbaric attempt at torture, and had hated the Humans for it. Only as he'd watched them work had he grudgingly decided it was probably more likely a medical dissection on the body of a Zhirrzh who'd been raised to Eldership in battle.

But this fullarc they weren't working on it. Instead they were carefully maneuvering it into a long translucent bag they'd apparently brought in with them. They finished the job, using some kind of sealing strip to close the bag, and together lifted the body to a rolling table. With one of the Humans at either end, they pulled it across the room.

The one in front opened the door, and they began to pull the table outside.

They were taking the body away. And when it was gone, they would be leaving Prr't-zevisti there.

All alone.

"No," Prr't-zevisti whispered to himself, a ripple of panic flickering through him with more intensity than he'd felt from any emotion in the seventy cyclics since being raised to Eldership. To be sealed in here alone— maybe forever—without even the Human's occasional visits to break up the monotony . . .

And in that beat he finally recognized the truth that he'd been trying to avoid ever since his capture. The truth that there were indeed some situations worse than facing the dark and frightening unknowns of death.

And it was time at last to make the final decision.

He eased to the top of the doorway and rose to the edge of the lightworld, nearly trembling as the panic turned to a grim resolve. All right. He would do it. As soon as the Humans had their burden all the way out, he would go. And this time he wouldn't come back. No matter what. The back wheels of the table dropped to the ground outside with a muffled thud; bracing himself, Prr't-zevisti moved around the corner—

And abruptly stopped. Off to one side, accompanied by two more Humans, was a second rolling table with another Zhirrzh body laid out on top of it. The first table cleared the doorway; without losing a beat, the other Humans began pulling the second table inside.

Prr't-zevisti retreated back to his corner again, the panic and resolve draining away and leaving only fatigue in their wake. Fatigue, and the painful recognition that he was indeed near the end of his rope here. If he didn't find something to keep his mind occupied, he was never going to make it through this.

But what could he do? Run through the memories of his life? No. He'd done that often enough during the dull times on Dharanv. Here it would only depress him. Try to replay favorite books or poems or movies? No; he didn't have nearly that good a memory for such details. Hold imaginary conversations with his friends and family and descendants? Hardly. Borderline insane, and any kind of insane was exactly what he didn't need right now.

Or should he finally quit all this whining and self-pity and get busy doing his job?

He looked down, feeling a mixture of embarrassment and frustration, as one of the Humans closed the door with its unsual muffled clank. Yes, he'd been a warrior once, serving both the Dhaa'rr clan and the Overclan Seating with honor and distinction. And warriors of the Dhaa'rr clan had never been known for neglecting their duty. But that had been a long time ago, back when he was a physical living in the lightworld. He was an Elder now, with all the limitations that came with it. What in the eighteen worlds could he do?

The Humans had moved to either side of the table, speaking quietly to each other as they laid out a neat row of surgical instruments. *All right,* Prr't-zevisti told himself. Maybe he couldn't fight like a traditional warrior. But he was in the middle of enemy territory, with the enemy apparently unaware that he was still there. That had to be good for *something*.

All he had to do was figure out what it was. And in the meantime he would set himself to becoming better acquainted with the Humans' language.

Moving to a spot beside the room's ceiling light source, Prr't-zevisti came up as close to the lightworld as he dared.

He'd had a short but intense briefing on the Human language by the Elders from the Base World 12 group before the expeditionary force had hit Dorcas, plus a fifteen-fullarc course in the Etsijian language way back before he'd landed with the expeditionary forces in that war. Minimal fluency, equally minimal linguistic expertise, but he'd once been fairly good with languages. At least it gave him somewhere to start.

One of the Humans reached a hand to a small black box on one corner of the rolling table. "Doctor-Cavan-a," it said, its voice echoing faintly from the walls. "(Something) fifteenth, twenty-three-oh-three. Assist (something) by (something) (something). Prepare (something) for second (something) on (something) (something)."

Doctor-Cavan-a. A startlingly Zhirrzh-type name, even down to the -a female suffix. Coincidence? Undoubtedly. Still, it gave Prr't-zevisti his first solid verbal anchor to these aliens. And, paradoxically perhaps, it somehow made him feel not quite so lost and alone here. Maybe these aliens could be understood, after all.

Settling in, gazing down on the enemy as they began carving up another of his people, he began to listen.

6

For a while it had looked like Thrr-gilag's hopes of visiting his parents were going to evaporate without effect or trace. Shortly after the decision to send an expedition to the Mrachanis, the Speaker for Dhaa'rr had insisted—"strongly recommended" had been the words he'd used—that none of the study group be allowed even to leave the Overclan complex, let alone head off on a four-thousand-thoustride journey across Oaccanv. A fairly worthless recommendation, in Thrr-gilag's opinion, since none of the searchers would have much to do until the ships and supplies had been gathered together.

Still, the Overclan Prime had seemed inclined to listen to the Speaker's argument; and it was to Thrr-gilag's surprise, therefore, when he reversed himself at the last beat, stipulating only that Thrr-gilag be back at the complex at least a fullarc before the expedition was scheduled to leave.

Five hundred cyclics ago, when the Overclan Seating was first established, the trek from Unity City to the Kee'rr clan's ancestral territory would have been a serious and difficult journey. Two major mountain ranges lay between them, as well as the ancestral territories of forty to fifty other clans. Clans whose suspicion toward outsiders had always been high, who with the carnage and devastation of the Third Eldership War fresh in their minds would have been even less hospitable toward strangers than usual. The last thing any of them would have believed was that a time of peace was even possible, let alone near at hand.

But it had happened. They'd pulled it together, all of them: the clan and family leaders first, the common Zhirrzh afterward. The Third Eldership War had been Oaccanv's last, and within two hundred cyclics even minor border skirmishes had all but disappeared. It had taken a special breed of Zhirrzh, Thrr-gilag had always believed, to have created such a future from the ashes of war. A unique group of visionaries, drawn together by destiny and necessity alike, who had risen above the traditional patterns of the past and found a way to bring the rest of the Zhirrzh race along with them.

Gazing out the window of the suborbital transport, Thrr-gilag stared at the lush green landscape beneath them. And wondered if, even with those same visionaries available to advise them, any Zhirrzh leaders since that time would have been able to pull off such a miracle.

The transport put down at the landing field outside Citadel, once the main stronghold city of the Kee'rr and still the clan's political and cultural center. The Thrr-family territory and shrine were three hundred thoustrides farther on, perched on the edge of a line of hills between two small branches of the Amt'bri River. A supply transport was getting ready to leave Citadel for the region; with a little fancy wordwork and judicious waving of his Overclan-complex pass, Thrr-gilag was able to talk himself aboard. Ten hunbeats later they were in the air.

"Heading home, eh?" the pilot commented as he brought the transport to its cruising altitude and leveled off. He was a middle-aged Zhirrzh, with age wrinkles around his eyes and an interesting crack-scar on his mouth. His tunic threads placed him as a member of the Hgg, the same family the current Speaker for Kee'rr belonged to. "Getting out of the fast pace for a little while, eh?"

"A very little while," Thrr-gilag told him. "I have to be back in Unity City in a few fullarcs."

"Ah," the pilot said, throwing him a speculative look. "I hear the Overclan Seating's going crazy back there over this Human-Conqueror thing. You involved with any of that?"

"The whole Zhirrzh race is involved with it," Thrr-gilag said, marveling yet again at the sheer speed of the Elder information network. Less than a single fullarc since the Overclan Prime had coined the term *Human-Conqueror,* and here was a pilot on a minor supply run four thousand thoustrides away already using it.

"Involved right up to our tonguetips, from what I've heard," the pilot agreed darkly. "My grandfather was telling me about it last fullarc. Vicious warriors, nasty weapons, plus lots of Elderdeath stuff they're not shy about using. You know anything about that?"

"I've heard some of those same rumors," Thrr-gilag said evasively, wishing he knew exactly how much information the Overclan Seating had officially released to the general public. The last thing he wanted to do was toss more rumors into the general mix, especially considering the trouble he was already in. "Was your grandfather with one of the survey ships?"

"No, but he got it pretty straight," the pilot said. "One of his old co-workers has a friend who'd talked directly to the first cousin of an old warrior friend of one of the Elders on the mission."

"Sounds pretty straight, all right," Thrr-gilag conceded. If the Elders were talking, it was all over the eighteen worlds by now, official release or not. "I wouldn't panic just yet, though. We've got some pretty good weaponry, too, you know."

"I suppose," the pilot said. "I just hope we haven't sliced off more than we can eat here. This isn't just three planets' worth of Chig this time, you know."

"The war wasn't exactly our idea," Thrr-gilag reminded him, a twinge of almost-guilt tugging at him. Pheylan Cavanagh's insistence that the Humans hadn't started it . . . "Don't forget, they fired first."

"Yeah, that's what they say," the pilot said doubtfully. "Course, they might say that anyway."

"I suppose that's possible," Thrr-gilag murmured, turning to look out the window and putting his own doubts resolutely out of his mind. In a couple of tentharcs, with a little good luck, he'd know the truth about that battle.

The Kee'rr clan's ancestral territory extended across most of the fertile Kee'miss'lo River valley, from the river delta nearly to its source in the Phmm'taa Marshes. With few if any natural barriers to protect their land against outside aggression, the Kee'rr clan had been forced by necessity to become the dominant military power in the region. Political power had inevitably followed, bringing the Kee'rr up against neighboring clans in the ever-shifting patterns of alliance and betrayal and conflict that had formed the backdrop to much of Zhirrzh history. The political clashes had necessitated still more military might, which had created more political clashes, and so on.

Most of the clan and family leaders from that age had perished when their *fsss* organs had been destroyed in the Second and Third Eldership Wars. Thrr-gilag had often wondered what they would have thought of the changes their successors had created.

He smiled sourly to himself, thinking back to the passengers on that suborbital transport. Members of fifty different clans, traveling freely and without restriction to and from Kee'rr territory. No, the old clan leaders wouldn't have liked this new Oaccanv at all. They probably would have reacted rather violently to the whole idea, in fact.

Was that the same social structure the Humans were now living under? Had their attack on the Zhirrzh been a reflection of the same single-minded desire for territory that had driven the Zhirrzh themselves during Oaccanv's feudal period?

"Where exactly you heading this fullarc?" the pilot asked into his musings.

"To the family shrine, to see my father," Thrr-gilag told him, turning back around. "Then out to Reeds Village to visit my mother."

"Reeds Village?" the pilot echoed, frowning at Thrr-gilag. "That's way over in, what, Frr family territory?"

"That's right," Thrr-gilag said.

There was a short pause, with the other clearly waiting for further explanation. But Thrr-gilag remained silent, and after a few beats the pilot turned back to his controls with a shrug. "All right. Well. I'll go ahead and drop you off at the Thrr shrine, then."

"You don't have to do that," Thrr-gilag said. "I can take the rail over from Cliffside Dales."

"It's no problem," the pilot insisted. "There's a landing field just outside the predator fence gate—I'll put you down there, and you can walk right in. At least it'll save you the rail trip one direction."

"I appreciate the offer," Thrr-gilag said. "But you have a schedule to meet, and I can't let you—"

"Yes, you can," the other said firmly. "Like you said, we're all in this together. I served my stint with the Etsijian encirclement force when I was younger; I want to do my bit on this one, too."

It was a little under half a thoustride from the predator-fence gate to the Thrr-family shrine itself, its towering shape partially blocked by the darker bulks of the twin protector domes that sat on either side of the ceramic-pebbled path ten strides in front of it. Twenty or more Elders popped into view at one point or another as Thrr-gilag walked toward it, looking at the visitor with expressions ranging from hopefulness to suspicion to simple curiosity. One or two of them—probably members of his branch of the family, though Thrr-gilag didn't recognize them offhand—greeted him by name before leaving. The rest simply peered at his face, decided he wasn't there to visit them, and vanished.

He was perhaps five strides from the domes when the one on the left slid open a door and a tall Zhirrzh carrying a laser rifle stepped into view. "Stand fast," he said, "and speak your name."

"I obey the Protector of Thrr Elders," Thrr-gilag gave the ritual response, stopping beside the rack of *kavra* fruit that stood beside the path. "I am Thrr-gilag; Kee'rr."

"Who will prove your goodwill and intentions?"

"I will," Thrr-gilag said, taking one of the *kavra* and slicing it with his tongue. The ancient ceremony of trust, with the equally ancient exception: the protector of the shrine did not reciprocate.

"And who will prove your right to approach?"

"My father will," Thrr-gilag said, dropping the *kavra* into the disposal container beneath the rack. Like much of Zhirrzh tradition, this whole shrine routine had come under attack lately, its mostly youthful critics ridiculing it as a wasteful and meaningless throwback to Oaccanv's violent history. Personally, Thrr-gilag had always found a certain sense of comfort and security in the ritual. "Thrr-rokik—sorry," he interrupted himself. His father was an Elder now, with the Elder suffix added to his family name. "Thrr't-rokik; Kee'rr."

A flicker of a smile crossed the protector's face. It was probably a mistake he heard all the time. "Advance, Thrr-gilag," he said, lifting the muzzle of his rifle to point to the sky. "And welcome. It's good to see you again."

"It's good to be back, Thrr-tulkoj," Thrr-gilag said, stepping up to him and gripping his arm. "I do seem to get home less and less frequently these fullarcs."

"You can't blame anyone but yourself for that one," Thrr-tulkoj pointed out, mock-seriously. "You pick a career that requires you to travel, and this is what happens."

"Now, let's not start that all over again," Thrr-gilag said, mock-warningly. The whole question of career choices had been the subject of many a long and earnest discussion when he and Thrr-tulkoj had been growing up. Over the cyclics it had evolved into something of a personal joke between them. "Anyway, it's not the travel so much as the long delays at the far end."

"Yes, well, I wouldn't know much about that," Thrr-tulkoj said. "I don't think I've gone outside Kee'rr territory three times in the past two cyclics."

"You're not missing much," Thrr-gilag assured him. "There have been plenty of times sitting in a field shelter waiting for an alien storm to blow over when I wished I'd chosen a protector's job instead."

"You'd never have made it," Thrr-tulkoj said decisively. "You're too good at thinking. And too rotten at shooting."

"Thank you so very much." Thrr-gilag looked over his friend's shoulder at the shrine. "How's he doing?" he asked quietly.

"Not too bad, really," Thrr-tulkoj said. "It's a shock, of course, for almost everyone. Takes a lot of getting used to, and of course he's only been at it for half a cyclic. But with an illness, at least, he was more or less prepared for the change. It's the ones who get unexpectedly raised to Eldership in sudden accidents who seem to have the hardest time of it."

"Yes," Thrr-gilag murmured, an edge of guilt prodding him. He really should have spent more time with his parents—should have made the time, no matter what the hectic schedule of his career. His brother, Thrr-mezaz, had certainly managed it, despite the responsibilities and demands that came with being a warrior. "How's my mother handling it?"

"Well, that's a different story entirely," Thrr-tulkoj said, his tongue flicking oddly. "But I think you'd better hear that from your father."

Thrr-gilag's tail twitched. So he'd been right: there had indeed been something behind Thrr-mezaz's words in that last conversation. "I see. Well, I'd better go call him, then."

"Stop back before you leave," Thrr-tulkoj invited, stepping back into the shelter of the dome. "Maybe we can find time to get caught up on things before you head off-planet again."

"We can certainly try," Thrr-gilag agreed. "I can't make any promises, though—my schedule's going to be pretty tight."

"Sad," Thrr-tulkoj said, flicking his tongue in mock-disappointment. "You young people growing up and leaving home . . ."

"Thank you, grandfather, and I'll see you later," Thrr-gilag said dryly, stepping between the domes and walking toward the shrine. Thrr-tulkoj, of course, would be seeing Thrr-gilag the whole time if he wanted to, as would whoever was playing backstop in the other dome. One of the best-kept secrets about shrine-defender domes was that, once the door was closed, they became perfectly transparent from the inside.

Easy to see through, and equally easy to fire through. Criticism of tradition there might be out there, but Elders didn't take many chances with the defense of their *fsss* organs.

Up close, a family shrine was even more impressive than it was at a distance. Nearly nine strides tall—three times taller than the smaller cutting pyramid they'd had on Base World 12—it was dotted with upwards of forty thousand niches. Thrr-gilag had no idea which of them was his father's, but it really didn't matter. Right up beside the shrine like this, all the Elders would be able to hear his voice, carried directly to them through their *fsss* organs. "Thrr't-rokik?" he called. "It's Thrr-gilag."

There was a flicker, and his father was there in front of him. "Hello, my son," he said, his voice faint but with its well-remembered warmth. "It's good to see you."

"And you, my father," Thrr-gilag said, the remnants of

his guilt washing away in a sudden surge of emotion. His father; and yet, not really his father. His father as fragile spirit, a voice and faint image of what he'd once been, his physical body long since consigned to the fire.

His father as Elder.

Thrr-tulkoj had been right. This was going to take a lot of getting used to.

"You're looking well," Thrr't-rokik said. "I'd heard you were on Oaccanv; I'd rather expected you would get in touch with me sooner."

"I'm sorry," Thrr-gilag said. "I've been rather busy."

"So I hear." His father eyed him closely. "I also hear that not all has been going well for you."

"No." Thrr-gilag glanced up at the shrine towering above him. "That was one of the things I wanted to discuss with you."

"Well, as it happens, I'm free for the postmidarc," Thrr't-rokik said with a smile. "Shall we walk over to the bluff overview?"

To the bluff, and away from the unavoidable eavesdropping that would take place beside the shrine itself. "Certainly," Thrr-gilag said, turning and heading across the grass.

The overview was relatively modest, as such things went: a slight rise leading up to the predator fence, with the land then dropping off steeply into a rocky bluff just outside the fence. Past the edge of the bluff Thrr-gilag could see one of the minor tributaries of the Amt'bri River as it wended its casual way through the wooded plain below. Beyond the woods, some of the higher towers of the Hlim-family city of Hlimni's Glen were visible.

"The Thrr leaders are talking again about putting up a new shrine," Thrr't-rokik commented. "I've been trying to talk them into locating it down there in the woods, close enough that we could hear the river."

"They'll never do it," Thrr-gilag said. "Not that close to a river. Too much risk of flood damage."

Thrr't-rokik sniffed. "Flood damage. The Amt'bri hasn't flooded in probably two hundred cyclics. But you're right, too many people would be afraid. Sometimes I think Elders are the most timid creatures in existence."

"You can't really blame them," Thrr-gilag shrugged. "When you're that close to the unknowns of death, I suppose it's natural to try to hold on as tightly as you can."

"Perhaps," Thrr't-rokik sighed. "Personally, I think that being terrified of taking the most minuscule of chances is no way to live."

Thrr-gilag looked off across the valley. "We're certainly taking chances now," he said. "Every one of us."

"Yes," Thrr't-rokik agreed quietly. "The Human-Conquerors. You've seen them up close, Thrr-gilag. What do you think?"

"Of the Humans, or of our chances against them?"

"Either. Both."

Thrr-gilag pressed his tongue against the top of his mouth. "I don't know, Father. I really don't. They're fearsome and dangerous enemies—there's no doubt about that. But at the same time there are things about them that don't seem to fit together. Large inconsistencies in their aggressiveness level, for one thing."

"They're aliens, after all," Thrr't-rokik reminded him. "Their reasons for doing things don't have to be the same as ours."

"True," Thrr-gilag said. "But there's one other possibility: that the Humans aren't the vicious warmongers we've been led to believe."

Thrr't-rokik frowned. "What are you talking about? They attacked first."

Thrr-gilag turned again to look down at the river. "Unless the Overclan Seating and Warrior Command were wrong about that."

He could feel his father's gaze on him. "You mean mistaken?"

"Or just wrong."

For a long beat the rustling of the trees below was the only sound. Thrr-gilag kept his eyes on the valley and river, not daring to see what his father's expression might be. "You realize what you're saying," Thrr't-rokik said at last. "You're accusing the Overclan Seating of deliberately starting a war. And of then lying to the Zhirrzh people about it."

"I know," Thrr-gilag said. "Are you saying our leaders are incapable of lying?"

Thrr't-rokik snorted. "Hardly. Still, people generally lie for specific purposes. For personal gain, or to evade punishment or other trouble. What motivation would the Overclan Seating have to lie about a Human-Conqueror attack?"

"I don't know," Thrr-gilag said. "But I also can't simply dismiss the eye-witness testimony of the Human Pheylan Cavanagh. And he was apparently convinced that the Zhirrzh ships fired first."

Thrr't-rokik snorted. "You accuse your own leaders of lying yet assume a vicious would-be conqueror would tell you the truth?"

"I know it seems backward," Thrr-gilag conceded. "But he hung strongly to his story the whole time he was our prisoner. Longer than I would expect someone who knows he is lying would do."

For another few beats Thrr't-rokik was silent. "You're not just telling me all this to hear my opinions on the subject. What is it you want?"

Thrr-gilag braced himself. "Two of those survey ships were Kee'rr. I was hoping you could arrange for me to talk to one of the Elders who was aboard."

"I was afraid that was it," Thrr't-rokik said heavily. "Do you have any idea of the penalties involved with that sort of unauthorized communication?"

"I'm willing to take the risk," Thrr-gilag said.

"I wasn't thinking of your risk," Thrr't-rokik retorted icily. "I was thinking of the other Elder's. If Warrior Command caught him talking privately about sensitive warrior matters, they could summarily take his communicator position away from him. Are you willing to have that on your conscience?"

"Not really," Thrr-gilag said, feeling ashamed that that aspect hadn't even occurred to him. With *fsss*-cutting techniques had come an exponential explosion in the number of jobs available for Elders, everything from the simple participation in interstellar communication pathways to the more demanding professional roles of planetary explorer or searcher assistant. But such jobs still numbered only in the low billions; and with well over three hundred billion Elders clamoring for some way to fill their time, the permanent loss of a job was not a threat to be taken lightly. "I'm sorry. I should have thought about that."

There was another pause. "This is very important to you, isn't it, my son?" Thrr't-rokik asked, his voice gentle again.

"Yes," Thrr-gilag said. "And worth a fair amount of risk. But for me, not for someone else."

Thrr't-rokik sighed, a whisper against the background breezes. "Wait here. I'll see what I can do."

He vanished. Thrr-gilag leaned against the predator fence, gazing out again at the woods and river. The woods, the river, and the never-ending problem of what to do with the ever-growing number of Elders.

On one side it could be seen as a simple problem of storage. The shrine towering behind him had enough niches for forty thousand *fsss* organs, and it had taken the Thrr family nearly two hundred cyclics to fill it to capacity. Another shrine, wherever it was put up, would probably do them for two centuries more.

But on the other side it was an incredibly complex issue, a problem that sliced through to the very soul of Zhirrzh culture. In generations past all Zhirrzh had lived comfortably together, with Elders moving freely through the homes and lives of their children and grandchildren and great-grandchildren. For many of the Elders that was the way it had always been and thus the way it should continue to be.

But nothing ever remained the same, not even with the weight of a thousand cyclics of tradition bearing down on it. And as the basic underlying conception of Zhirrzh society was changing, so too was the view of the Elders' role in it.

There was a flicker and Thrr't-rokik was back, another Elder at his side. "This is my son, Searcher Thrr-gilag," Thrr't-rokik said, gesturing to Thrr-gilag with his tongue. "He was one of the alien-research group studying the Human-Conqueror prisoner. This"— he gestured to his companion—"is Bvee't-hibbin, a distant cousin of your mother's line. He's one of the communicators aboard the *Far Searcher*."

Thrr-gilag felt his tail speed up. One of the four survey ships that had been in that first contact with the Humans. "Honored to meet you," he said.

"Yes," Bvee't-hibbin said, running an obviously critical eye over Thrr-gilag. "So you're the one. Perhaps you don't care, Searcher, but I consider you personally responsible for the fact that one of my great-great-nephews has arrived prematurely at the family shrine."

"Yes, I know," Thrr-gilag said, wincing again with painful memory of his failure. "Seven others were also raised to Eldership in the Humans' attack."

"Did you know as well that he is still without sanity?" Bvee't-hibbin demanded. "Seven fullarcs since his arrival, and he's still twisted in shock. Seven fullarcs; and no one will predict for his family when he'll be recovered."

"You can hardly blame Thrr-gilag for that," Thrr't-rokik put in gently. "Base World Twelve is two hundred fifty light-cyclics from Oaccanv. Drawn from such a distance, it was inevitable that his initial anchoring would be severely traumatic. It's the price we pay for our expansion to the stars."

The anger drained from Bvee't-hibbin's face, leaving only weariness behind. "Perhaps it's too high a price, Thrr't-rokik," he said with a whisper of a sigh. "Perhaps some fullarc we'll stretch too far and condemn new Elders to a madness that will never end."

"Perhaps," Thrr't-rokik said. "But that limit is still well beyond our current knowledge. If it exists at all. For myself, I have a great faith in the strength and resilience of the Zhirrzh spirit."

"Perhaps." Bvee't-hibbin seemed to draw himself together again. "I'm told you have questions, Searcher Thrr-gilag. What is it you wish to know that only I can tell you?"

"I spent a great deal of time with the Human prisoner, Communicator," Thrr-gilag said. "It was his contention that the Zhirrzh ships, not his, were the aggressors at the battle."

Bvee't-hibbin snorted. "And you believe an alien instead of your own leaders?"

"I want to make sure no mistake has been made," Thrr-gilag countered.

"Then listen and believe, Searcher Thrr-gilag," Bvee't-hibbin said bluntly. "I was there . . . and the Human-Conquerors most certainly attacked first."

"You're sure of that?" Thrr't-rokik asked.

"When a warcraft sweeps focused Elderdeath weapons across your *fsss* cutting, it can hardly be mistaken for anything else," Bvee't-hibbin snapped. "And you'd both better hope you never have to feel that kind of pain yourselves."

His gaze drifted away. "It never stopped," he said, his voice almost too soft to hear. "Never. Their warcraft blanketed the whole region with the pain, their explosive missiles drove focused cones of it ahead of them—even after they were defeated and their warcraft burned to dust, they didn't let up the attack."

He looked up out of the memories at Thrr-gilag. "All except your prisoner. Alone of all of them he voluntarily shut off his Elderdeath weapon. That was what caught our commanders' notice in the first place. That, along with the fact that he was trying to move his spacecraft out of the battle region. Our ship commanders interpreted that as evidence of below-average aggression and decided to take him for further study."

His mouth twisted. "You saw how well that decision turned out."

Thrr-gilag nodded, a bitter taste beneath his tongue. So

that was that. Pheylan Cavanagh had indeed known about the Elderdeath weapons—obviously, since he'd shut his off. And he'd been lying about it the whole time. "I see," he murmured.

"Was there anything else?" Bvee't-hibbin asked.

"No," Thrr-gilag said. Pheylan Cavanagh had lied to him. Somehow he still couldn't believe it. "Thank you, Bvee't-hibbin. I and my family are in your debt and your family's."

"I wouldn't commit your family to too much if I were you," Bvee't-hibbin suggested, the first hint of humor peeking through his stiff manner. "Particularly not with the trouble you're in right now. I wish you good luck, though. If only for the honor of the Kee'rr."

"Thank you," Thrr-gilag said dryly. "I'll do my best not to let the Kee'rr down."

"Farewell." Bvee't-hibbin nodded and vanished.

"Does that set your fears at rest?" Thrr't-rokik asked.

"I suppose," Thrr-gilag said reluctantly. "Now if I could just answer the question of whether or not the Humans have Elders of their own."

"Yes, I heard about the stir you caused in the Overclan Seating with that suggestion," Thrr't-rokik said. "Do you really believe that might be true, or were you just trying to carve a slice out of their complacence?"

"I certainly wasn't trying to slice anything," Thrr-gilag said. "Whether there's any truth to it, I really don't know."

"Their use of Elderdeath weapons doesn't necessarily mean anything," his father pointed out. "All the alien races the Zhirrzh have encountered have attacked us that same way, and yet none of them have had Elders."

"I know," Thrr-gilag said. "But there's more. The fact that they used the Elderdeath weapons directly against the study group's pyramid on Study World Eighteen, for example, implies they knew what they were doing. Plus that *fsss*-sized incision in the Human prisoner's lower torso, which has yet to be explained. That was one of the reasons I didn't want him killed during his escape attempt, by the way. If they have Elders, that would merely have sent him back home."

"Yes," Thrr't-rokik said thoughtfully. "And of course there was the theft of Prr't-zevisti's *fsss* cutting from the Dorcas beachhead."

Thrr-gilag felt his tail twitch. "So that one's gotten around, too."

"You weren't expecting it to?" his father countered. "That was not a wise thing for you to talk about, Thrr-gilag."

"I know," Thrr-gilag sighed. "Certain members of the Overclan Seating were none too happy about it, either."

"More unhappy than you know," Thrr't-rokik said darkly. "I'm starting to hear rumors that the leaders and Elders of the Dhaa'rr are beginning to reconsider their approval of your bond-engagement to Klnn-dawan-a."

Thrr-gilag stared at him, his midlight pupils contracting to slits. "They can't do that," he protested. "They've already agreed to it."

"I know," Thrr't-rokik said. "But between your trouble on Base World Twelve and your brother Thrr-mezaz's role in the loss of Prr't-zevisti, the Dhaa'rr are furious with the whole Thrr family. And considering how unenthusiastic most of the Elders were about allowing a Dhaa'rr and Kee'rr to bond in the first place . . ." He flicked his tongue in a negative.

Thrr-gilag pressed his tongue hard against the inside of his mouth. He'd suspected from the start that it was his mishandling of things that had kept the Dhaa'rr leaders from assigning Klnn-dawan-a to the Mrachani study group, settling on the vastly less competent Gll-borgiv instead. But this was a blow he had somehow never anticipated. "Has there been any official action yet?" he asked.

"Not that I've heard of," Thrr't-rokik said. "I take it you're going to try to head it off?"

"You take it right," Thrr-gilag said, the shock of betrayal beginning to give way to an icy anger. He and Klnn-dawan-a had had to fight uphill once already against the Elders—from both their clans—and these stupid antiquated prejudices against interclan bonding. Now, it seemed, they were going to have to do it all over again. "I have to get in touch with Klnn-dawan-a right away. Let her know what's going on."

"I suggest you speak with her in person," Thrr't-rokik warned. "If the Dhaa'rr Elders find out you know, they're likely to push the clan leaders all the harder."

"Yes, I know," Thrr-gilag said. "The problem is, she's out on Gree with a group studying the Chig. That's a two-fullarc round trip right there."

"Is your timing that tight?"

"It's reasonably tight, yes," Thrr-gilag said. "But it's what I've got, and I'll just have to make do." He hesitated. "You haven't said what the response of Klnn-dawan-a's immediate family has been."

"I haven't heard anything one way or the other about them," Thrr't-rokik said. "But unless you hear otherwise, I'd suggest you assume they're still behind you. Klnn-dawan-a's family are good people." He paused. "And of course it goes without saying that your own immediate family will support you."

"Thank you," Thrr-gilag said. "That helps."

"It supplies some emotional support, at any rate," his

father said. "I only wish one of our two families had more political pull with our respective clans. A lifetime of work in ceramics design does not exactly heap up huge piles of favors. Especially with—"

He broke off, flicking his tongue in an oddly impatient gesture. "You'd better get moving if you're going to make it to Gree and back," he said, his voice suddenly brisk. "If you have time, stop back and see me before you go off to whatever the Overclan Seating has scheduled next for you. I presume you know that you don't have to come all the way out here to speak with me, by the way. As long as you're within a hundred thoustrides of the shrine, you can call Thrr-tulkoj or one of the other protectors on the direct-link and they can send me to wherever you are."

"I know," Thrr-gilag assured him. "And one way or the other, I promise I'll talk to you after I get back from Gree."

"Good. In the meantime I have friends with access to Unity City. I'll see what other information I can dig up."

"All right," Thrr-gilag said. "You know, you really ought to consider having a cutting taken. You could get yourself a niche in a pyramid near Unity City and watch all this political stuff directly instead of having to sift through rumors."

Again his father's tongue flicked oddly. "No, I don't think so," he said. "Not now. Tell me, are you going to see your mother before you go?"

"I'd planned to," Thrr-gilag said, frowning at the abrupt change of topic. "Thrr-mezaz told me she'd moved out to Reeds Village?"

"Yes," Thrr't-rokik said. "About thirty fullarcs ago. You were out on Study World Fifteen during the preparations;

and then this whole Human-Conqueror thing came up, and you were rushed out to Base World Twelve."

"Yes, I've been busy," Thrr-gilag said, studying his father's transparent face. "Hardly out of touch, though. What is it you and Thrr-mezaz aren't telling me?"

Thrr't-rokik looked away. "Perhaps it would be best if you spoke with her for yourself," he said. "If you have time, that is. This matter with Klnn-dawan-a should take precedence."

"My family takes precedence," Thrr-gilag told him firmly. "I'll make the time."

It was only a five-hunbeat walk to the rail stop near the shrine. Three cars were waiting there on the siding; climbing into the first, Thrr-gilag fed in his value number and keyed for the main nexus at Cliffside Dales. The car beeped its acceptance and eased onto the main rail, and they were off.

There was a flicker, and an Elder appeared in front of him. "You are Thrr-gilag; Kee'rr?" he asked.

"Yes," Thrr-gilag said.

"I was told you wanted information on space-flight schedules," the Elder said briskly. "When, and to where?"

"As soon as possible," Thrr-gilag said, wondering what had taken the travel communicator so long to get out there to him. He'd put in the request with Thrr-tulkoj before leaving the shrine. "Destination is the planet Gree."

"Gree?" The Elder seemed taken aback. "That's a Chig world."

"There are indeed large numbers of Chig on it," Thrr-gilag agreed. "Along with a few hundred Zhirrzh in about fifty study groups."

The Elder sniffed. "The proper study of Zhirrzh

is Zhirrzh," he said primly. "What anyone thinks they're going to find on a planet full of aliens I'll never know."

"I'm sure you won't," Thrr-gilag said, not trying overly hard to hide his disgust. With Human forces gathering against the Zhirrzh like storm clouds over a field of grain, it should be blindingly obvious that the ability to understand alien cultures was going to be of critical importance in the fullarcs ahead. Obviously, there were still Zhirrzh too stupid to understand that. "Just check the schedule for me, please."

The Elder sniffed again and was gone. Thrr-gilag turned back to the window, running the numbers through his mind. One fullarc each way to Gree; six and a half until he needed to check in again with Nzz-oonaz and the rest of the Mrachani study group. That left barely four and a half fullarcs to try to get all this straightened out.

He gazed at the scenery going past outside, a twinge of guilt tugging at him. He really ought to call the Overclan before he headed off-world this way. The Overclan, or at the very least Nzz-oonaz. Let someone in authority know where he was going and what he was doing.

But if he did that, Speaker Cvv-panav would almost certainly find out about it. And he'd either summarily cancel Thrr-gilag's trip or else push the Dhaa'rr clan leaders to move even more quickly on their repudiation of his bond-engagement to Klnn-dawan-a. Or both.

Besides, there was no reason why anyone in Unity City would need him for the next few fullarcs. The Mrachani bodies weren't going to need any more examination, and Nzz-oonaz surely had the study group's end of the upcoming voyage under control. And if for some reason he needed help, Gll-borgiv and the Dhaa'rr would be more than happy to assist.

And anyway, Thrr-gilag would be back well before the time he'd been told to return. No, best just to keep it quiet.

With a flicker the Elder was back. "A warrior supply flight leaves for the Gree encirclement forces in seven tentharcs," he growled. "It'll be lifting from the warrior field at Pathgate; flight time approximately nine tentharcs. Do you wish a place reserved for you?"

"Please," Thrr-gilag said, holding out his identification card and, for good measure, his Overclan-complex pass.

"Um," the Elder said, peering at the cards. "The reservation will be made in your name. Payment is due one tentharc before departure."

"I understand," Thrr-gilag said. A hundred cyclics ago, right after the first credit/debit system had been set up, Elders had carried value numbers directly between buyers and sellers. But as the system had expanded, someone had belatedly realized that Elders who could handle whole sections of a conversation should have no trouble at all memorizing a few strings of numbers. A handful of dishonest Elders had been caught proving it—to the tune of nearly half a million in fraudulent purchases and fund transfers—and that had been that. "Thank you."

The Elder sniffed one last time and was gone. "You're welcome," Thrr-gilag murmured, settling tiredly back against the railcar couch. Seven tentharcs before lift. Plenty of time to get to Reeds Village first and see his mother.

And to find out what was going on out there that neither his father nor his brother would tell him about.

He sighed. It was unfair. It really was. This looming war against the Humans was enough trouble for anyone to have to handle. To throw in family and personal crises on top of it was asking far too much.

But the crises were there, and they were on his shoulders, and he would just have to deal with them as best he could. Settling back on his couch, he closed his eyes against the light filtering through the postmidarc clouds and tried to get some sleep.

7 The tissue analyzer beeped notice that it had finished its work, the gentle tone almost lost amid the continual snap-flapping of the shelter walls. Laying down her stylus, Klnn-dawan-a got up from her couch and headed over to the analyzer, eying the shaking walls warily as she walked. The wind outside had been increasing steadily for nearly half a tentharc now, with no sign that it was planning to modulate anytime soon. If the storm didn't pass in another tentharc or two, they could say farewell to the latearc's sampling run.

"Getting pretty noisy out there," her assistant Bkar-otpo commented from across the shelter, his tone sounding a little uneasy. "How strong do these winds get, anyway?"

"Don't worry, we'll be all right," Klnn-dawan-a told him, shutting the analyzer back to standby and keying for a datalist. "These shelters can handle anything Gree's likely to throw at us. At least this time of cyclic."

"Yes, I've heard stories about those equinox storms," Bkar-otpo said. "You ever been in one of those?"

"A couple of times," Klnn-dawan-a said. The datalist came up, and she ran a quick eye over the numbers. Promising; definitely promising. Maybe this time they'd finally hit the proper window for the genetic-ring transmutation. "I wouldn't want to be in a field shelter during one, but a perm building stands up to them just fine."

"It must still be pretty impressive—"

"It's wonderful and exhilarating both," she interrupted gently, stepping over to him and holding out the datalist. "File this into the recorder, would you? And then run up a comparison between it and the other samplings."

"I obey, Searcher," he said briskly, all business now as he took the datalist and pulled his couch up to the recorder. "Will we be taking another set of samplings this latearc?"

"Assuming the wind dies down, yes."

"I've been wondering about that," Bkar-otpo said doubtfully. "Even at the best of times, Chigin whelps can be pretty unpredictable. No telling what this storm will do to their dispositions."

"We'll be fine," Klnn-dawan-a assured him, focusing her attention again on the wind. Was it marginally less violent than it had been a few hunbeats ago? Possibly. "I'm going to take a quick look outside, see if I can spot the edge of the storm."

"You want me to go with you?" Bkar-otpo asked, half standing up.

"No, I'll be fine," she said. "I won't be going very far."

"I could call an Elder to go with you," he persisted, his hand hovering near the signaler control.

"I'll be fine," she said firmly. "You just get busy with that comparison, all right?"

He seemed to sigh. "I obey, Searcher," he said again, and turned reluctantly back to the recorder.

Klnn-dawan-a stepped to the shelter door and began unfastening the catches, mentally shaking her head and wondering yet again what exactly she was going to do about Bkar-otpo. Fresh out of school, studious and earnest as all get out, he was the totally stereotypical searcher assistant.

With, unfortunately, what looked like the beginnings of a strong crush on her.

She was holding on to the grips tightly as the door came open, but even so, the wind nearly ripped it out of her hands. Maneuvering out into the blast, she sealed the door behind her. Gree's sun was long gone below the horizon, and for a beat she stayed where she was beside the shelter as her lowlight pupils widened to compensate for the darkness. A few beats later, with the rocky ground now adequately visible, she headed off between the cluster of wind-buffeted shelters toward the edge of the shallow hollow the group had set up in.

The simplest thing to do, of course, would be to arrange for Bkar-otpo to be transferred to one of the other three Dhaa'rr study groups on Gree. It would give him time to forget her and maybe latch on to someone who wasn't ten cyclics older than he was and already bond-engaged. If she did it properly, chances were good that he'd never even guess that she'd been behind the transfer.

The problem was, he might. And if her own experiences when she was nineteen were anything to go by, that would be devastating to him. Klnn-dawan-a had always considered herself a rather plain sort of person when she was growing up: average in appearance and personality, considerably less than average in conversational ability and family status. Her intellect had been sharp enough, certainly, but she'd never found that to have much in the way of appeal to the people around her. It wasn't until she'd discovered her love of alien studies and the close-knit group of people who felt likewise that she'd really begun to feel at home. By the time her friendship with Thrr-gilag had begun to grow into something stronger, she'd been strong enough herself to take the chance of getting hurt.

Bkar-otpo, unfortunately, wasn't anywhere near that stage yet. Nevertheless, it was clear that she was going to have to do something, and soon. The bond-engagement threads she always wore weren't deterring him in the slightest; neither were her attempts to work Thrr-gilag's name into the conversation every chance she got. Apparently, she was just going to have to come out point-blank with it.

And then, maybe, she'd get him transferred.

She'd reached the edge of the hollow now and the predator fence that protected the encampment. The wind was stronger here, with a tangle of eddies and crosscurrents that seemed determined to knock her off her feet. Bracing herself against a shoulder-high rock, she put her hands up to protect her eyes and peered out across the sky.

Good luck was with them. The cloud formations that indicated the edge of the windstorm were clearly visible between the rolling foothills directly ahead and the taller mountains rising beyond them. Ten hunbeats—twenty at the most—and the winds should begin settling down. Should be no problem for her and Bkar-otpo to get out to the Za Mingchma farm and take their tissue samples on schedule.

She shifted her position against the rock, letting her

gaze drop to the foothills themselves. The lights of perhaps fifty Chigin houses were visible through the tight mesh of the predator fence, the homes scattered unevenly up and down the slopes of the hills and even part of the way up the sheer face of the mountain behind. Farm families, most of them, working hard to coerce a living from the thin soil and thin air up here. Aloof to the Zhirrzh study group for the most part, but at least not openly hostile the way the valley and city residents always seemed to be.

Klnn-dawan-a frowned, her gaze pausing on one of the plots of land. The fence surrounding the whelp enclosure looked wrong, somehow. She stared hard at it, feeling her lowlight pupils widening to full enlargement. The landscape brightened slightly. . . .

There it was: a thick tree branch, apparently blown there by the wind, leaning against the middle of the enclosure fence on one side and holding it partially pinned to the ground.

She fumbled out her caller from the survival pack fastened around her waist, her view of the landscape ahead changing again as her darklight pupils expanded to pull in the heat radiance that surrounded all homoiothermal creatures. The tips of the houses' chimneys and the smoke pouring from them took on a gentle glow; larger, more diffuse images appeared inside the enclosures of the nearest yards: whelps, huddled together against the wind or else prowling their circuits in mindless defiance of the elements.

In the enclosure with the downed fence there was nothing.

"Terrific," Klnn-dawan-a muttered under her breath, half turning to aim the caller at the top of the white cutting pyramid in the center of the Zhirrzh encampment. The brilliant darklight beam lanced out, and over the wind she faintly heard the clang as the alarm mounted to the pyramid's top went off in response. She turned back around again, peering out into the darkness—

An Elder appeared in front of her. "Yes, Searcher?"

"The fence at the Ca Chagba farm has been breached," she shouted over the wind. "The whelps have gotten out. I'm going to go look for them. Tell Director Prr-eddsi, and ask him to send someone to help me."

"Not a good idea, Searcher," the Elder shouted back. "Especially not in a storm like this. They could get vicious."

"I'll be all right," Klnn-dawan-a assured him. "I've been to the Ca Chagba farm several times—the whelps know me as well as they know any Zhirrzh. I don't think they'll bother me."

"They're not going to be able to smell you in this wind," the Elder objected. "It's too big a risk."

"It's not that big a risk," Klnn-dawan-a said firmly. "Regardless, I'm taking it. Oh, and tell Prr-eddsi he should send someone to alert the Ca Chagba family, too. There's a good chance they don't even know their whelps are missing. Go on, get going."

"I obey, Searcher," the Elder said reluctantly. "Don't go far; I'll have an escort for you in a beat."

He vanished. Moving out of the limited shelter of the hollow, Klnn-dawan-a slid the caller back into its survival-pack pouch and pulled out her stinger. The whelps might or might not bother her, but there were other dangers roaming the mountains out there. Keying the weapon on, feeling the reassuring vibration against her palm as its energy capacitor filled, she opened the gate in the predator fence and stepped outside.

"Searcher?" an Elder's voice called faintly in her ear. "We were told to come help you."

"All right," Klnn-dawan-a said, glancing around at the pale shapes. Good; Prr-eddsi had assigned three of them to her. That would help. "We're searching for missing Chigin whelps," she told them. "I want two of you to start quartering the area. Pay particular attention to gullies, the lee sides of rock formations, and other wind-protected areas. You"—she gestured to the third, a fairly recently raised Elder named Rka't-msotsi-a—"stay with me. Keep an eye out for predators."

The other two Elders acknowledged and vanished. "Where are we going?" Rka't-msotsi-a asked.

"We'll start at the creek," Klnn-dawan-a told her, taking a bearing on one of the houses and pointing ahead and to the left. "That section where the cut's particularly deep. Stay close."

She headed off, struggling to keep her balance in the wind, hoping that Prr-eddsi would be willing to send some of the other Zhirrzh to help in the search. Elders were fine as communicators, but as hunters or trackers— particularly at latearc—they left a lot to be desired. Unfortunately, chances were good that Prr-eddsi would do nothing but stay where he was. For all his genius with alien languages, the director was about as timid a Zhirrzh as Klnn-dawan-a had ever seen.

"Searcher?" Rka't-msotsi-a's voice called faintly in her ear. "I checked ahead, and I think I may have spotted them. There's something, anyway, in that cut you mentioned down by the creek."

"Good," Klnn-dawan-a said, passing over the fact that she'd given Rka't-msotsi-a explicit instructions to stay with her. "How many were there?"

"I'm sorry," Rka't-msotsi-a said, a tinge of bitterness and self-reproach in her voice. "I couldn't tell."

"That's all right," Klnn-dawan-a hastened to assure her. Rka't-msotsi-a had been raised to Eldership only a cyclic ago, the result a drudokyi attack elsewhere on Gree, and she was still coming to grips with these new limitations that had been imposed on her. And of course she'd been only thirty-four cyclics old when it had happened, barely five cyclics older than Klnn-dawan-a. That had to make it even more difficult. "Let's go take a look."

They headed off, Klnn-dawan-a straining to keep both her lowlight and darklight pupils as wide-open as possible and to keep watch in all directions. Rka't-msotsi-a, she knew, had been mauled badly by the drudokyi before her injuries had raised her to Eldership, and Klnn-dawan-a had no desire to suffer through something like that herself. Perhaps the whole unpleasantness surrounding that event explained some of Director Prr-eddsi's timidness, too, especially regarding Gree's animal life. He'd been right there with Rka't-msotsi-a when it had happened. . . .

Off to their right, something moved behind a rock formation. "Searcher!" Rka't-msotsi-a snapped. "There!"

"I've got it," Klnn-dawan-a said, her stinger tracking that direction. Something alive, all right, and certainly big enough to be a Chigin whelp. Trouble was, it could be any of a number of other things, too. Including a drudokyi. "Go get a closer look. See if you can tell what it is."

"I'll try," Rka't-msotsi-a said tightly. She flicked toward the rock, vanishing as she passed through it toward the creature behind. Klnn-dawan-a waited, holding her breath. . . .

And then Rka't-msotsi-a was back. "It's a drudokyi," she hissed.

Klnn-dawan-a's tail twitched violently. "Are you sure?"

"I'm sure," Rka't-msotsi-a said, her voice trembling. "I'm sure. It's a big one, too."

"All right, don't panic," Klnn-dawan-a said, glancing quickly around her. "At this time of latearc there's a fair chance it's already fed. Let's just ease away and head for the creek."

There was no answer. "Rka't-msotsi-a?"

But the Elder was gone. "Terrific," Klnn-dawan-a muttered, looking around again as she began carefully backing away. She could dispose of the animal over there, certainly; on full power the laser beam from her stinger would vaporize a slender line through hide and muscle and bone, the explosive expansion of the resulting gas creating a hydrostatic shock wave that would instantly incapacitate and then kill the creature. The problem was that, despite Rka't-msotsi-a's identification, Klnn-dawan-a herself wasn't totally convinced the skulking creature was indeed a drudokyi. If not—if it was instead one of the missing whelps—then killing it without provocation could easily wipe out the vanishingly small amount of goodwill the Zhirrzh study group had so painstakingly built up with the Chigin community here. Best if possible just to get out of its way.

She took another step back; and as she did so, the mass behind the rock shifted position a little. Klnn-dawan-a raised the stinger warningly. . . .

"Left!" Rka't-msotsi-a's voice shrieked in her ear.

Klnn-dawan-a spun around. From out of nowhere a second darklight-glowing image had appeared, bearing down on her with the speed and power of a double-wide railcar.

Her thumbs jerked spasmodically against the stinger's triggers, sending a brilliant slash of laser fire cutting through the air as she tried desperately to swing the weapon around to bear on this new threat. The light blazed into her dilated lowlight and darklight pupils, stabbing agony into her eyes and head and plunging everything else around it into terrifying darkness. Desperately, she swung the stinger back and forth, not sure she was even aiming in the right direction, hearing the roar of the drudokyi over the wind, feeling the click as the stinger shifted to autokill mode, smelling the drudokyi and the exotic Gree air and her own fear—

The drudokyi slammed into her, knocking the stinger from her grip and driving her backward to the ground. She gasped in pain, the predator's weight and heat settling on top of her, crushing her against the cold rocks. Dimly, she felt herself slashing again and again into the thick hide with the edges of her tongue. . . .

And then, quite suddenly, the weight was gone. Klnn-dawan-a opened her eyes—she hadn't realized until then that she'd closed them—to find a group of Zhirrzh crouching over her. "Are you all right?" Bkar-otpo asked anxiously, dropping to the ground beside her and taking her arm. "You're—Director Prr-eddsi, she's covered in blood!"

"It's all right," Klnn-dawan-a gasped, patting his hand reassuringly as she struggled to get air back into her body. "I'm all right. It's the drudokyi's blood, not mine."

"Are you sure?" Prr-eddsi asked from her other side.

"I'm sure," Klnn-dawan-a said. "I think it must have been dead before it even reached me."

"That may well be," Prr-eddsi rumbled. "It's still only by immensely good luck that you're not an Elder by now."

"I know," Klnn-dawan-a said, a shiver running through her as she took stock of herself. Her face and torso were sticky with warm drudokyi blood, a stickiness that was rapidly turning to ice in the cutting wind. Her head still throbbed with the aftereffects of those blinding laser flashes, her whole body ached from that fall to the ground, and her tongue tingled with fatigue and the acrid tastes of the drudokyi's hide and blood and her own poison.

But she hadn't been raised to Eldership, and her body was still whole. She had indeed had immensely good luck.

"I'm glad you agree," Prr-eddsi growled. "I trust the lesson will find a permanent home with you. You should never, ever, go out into a dangerous situation alone. If Rka't-msotsi-a hadn't alerted us when she had, that other drudokyi would most likely have gotten to you before we did."

So that was where Rka't-msotsi-a had disappeared to just before the attack. "Believe me, I won't do it again," Klnn-dawan-a said. "I was just worried about the missing whelps."

"The whelps would have stood a considerably better chance against a pair of drudokyis than you did," Prr-eddsi countered, a shade less gruffly. "Anyway, they're fine. They're down by the creek. We've alerted the Ca Chagba family—some of them have gone down to herd them back."

"Good." Klnn-dawan-a pushed herself up and onto her left side. Her tail, freed from where it had been pinned beneath her leg, decided it was going to hurt, too. "Then I presume the sampling is still on for this latearc."

"You can't be serious," Bkar-otpo objected, clutching at her arm again. "After what you've just been through—?"

"Do be quiet, Bkar-otpo," Prr-eddsi said, running a critical eye over Klnn-dawan-a. "Are you really going to feel up to that, Searcher?"

"I'm fine," Klnn-dawan-a said, getting all the way to her feet and peering up at the sky. The wind was still pretty fierce, but the edge of the storm was markedly closer than the last time she'd looked. "Besides, we're at a critical point in the ring transmutation. We can't afford to miss even a single sampling right now."

"All right," Prr-eddsi said. "If you're sure you can handle it. But you take the time first to get cleaned up. And I mean *really* cleaned up. You walk into a whelp enclosure smelling of drudokyi, and you won't get a chance to put this latearc's lesson into practice. Bkar-otpo, escort her back to the encampment. And then start getting the sampling equipment together."

The wind had died down to a bare whisper by the time Klnn-dawan-a eased open the gate of the enclosure surrounding the Za Mingchma farm. "Hello?" she called gently in the Chigin language as she and Bkar-otpo slipped inside. "Anyone home?"

"I don't see them," Bkar-otpo muttered nervously. "You suppose something's wrong?"

"I doubt it," Klnn-dawan-a said, looking around as her tail sped up with uncomfortable anticipation. She certainly hoped nothing was wrong, anyway. The drudokyi attack had taken more out of her than she'd realized, and all she really wanted to do right now was go back to her shelter and curl up in bed where she could ache in peace. The last thing she needed was a confrontation—any kind of confrontation—with a Chig.

"Then where are they?" Bkar-otpo demanded.

"They're probably just—there they are." Klnn-dawan-a

pointed as the group of whelps came silently toward them around the side of the house. "They were just staying out of the wind," she added, bracing herself as she stepped forward and offered the back of her hand. Certainly the whelps had seen the two of them often enough; but as Bkar-otpo had pointed out earlier, the storm wouldn't have done their moods any good. If they got it into their limited minds that the family's grant of safe passage no longer applied to these particular intruders . . .

The lead whelp trotted up to Klnn-dawan-a and sniffed delicately at her outstretched hand, and for a beat he rumbled deep in his throat. Then, flattening his ears and nostrils back again, he trotted away.

Carefully, Klnn-dawan-a let out her breath. "See?" she said. "No problem. Come on."

The three chrysalises were fastened to the south side of the farmhouse, huge tangled masses of silky threads spun by the whelps that were now secreted within them—whelps in the process of metamorphosing from mindless animals that guarded the farm into the full sentience of adult Chig.

"Gives me the creeps every time I think about it," Bkar-otpo muttered as Klnn-dawan-a knelt down beside the first chrysalis and opened her sampling kit.

"I don't see why it should," Klnn-dawan-a replied, selecting a probe and a tissue sampler. Using the probe to pull away some of the silk, she eased the slender needle of the sampler into the chrysalis mass. "In some ways it's parallel to our own transition from physical to Elder."

"Maybe that's what bothers me about it," Bkar-otpo said, producing a probe of his own and pulling some of the chrysalis silk back out of Klnn-dawan-a's way. "The parallels with the way the Chig treat their whelps."

Klnn-dawan-a flicked her tongue in a negative. "Now you've lost me."

"Well, just think about it a hunbeat," Bkar-otpo said. "The Chig treat their whelps like animals—"

"They are animals."

"You know what I mean. They could at least keep them in a storage outbuilding or something instead of leaving them unprotected in the open like this. You know how many of them die from exposure and predator attack before they even reach metamorphosis stage?"

"A fair number," Klnn-dawan-a conceded.

"A fair number? You call seventy percent a fair number? And that's up here. I hear the death rate's even higher in the cities, where the whelps from different families are always fighting with each other."

"These are Chig, Bkar-otpo," Klnn-dawan-a reminded him. The tip of the sampler needle touched something solid: the whelp body sleeping within. Carefully, trying not to move the tip, she touched the button on the end, feeling the slight vibration as the tiny suction driver inside the device began the task of drawing fluids and soft tissue into the sampler's collection tube. "You can't judge aliens by Zhirrzh ethical standards."

"Maybe not," Bkar-otpo growled. "But we can certainly judge Zhirrzh by Zhirrzh standards. And I sometimes think the Elders use us physicals the same way the Chig adults use their whelps."

Klnn-dawan-a threw him a frown. "What's that supposed to mean?"

Bkar-otpo sighed. "I don't know," he said. "All I know is that we seem always to be giving up stuff for the Elders. I guess I shouldn't have said anything."

"No, I don't think you should have," Klnn-dawan-a agreed shortly. "And before you start talking such nonsense again, I suggest you think about all the ways the Elders contribute to Zhirrzh society. From interstellar communications all the way down to saving me from those drudokyis a tentharc ago."

"Yes, Searcher," Bkar-otpo muttered. "I will."

The sampler stopped vibrating, indicating that the tube had been filled to its designated level. Carefully, Klnndawan-a eased it out of the chrysalis, wondering what all that had been about. But it was probably nothing. Bkarotpo was only nineteen, after all, and youth was always rebelling against something. This was probably nothing more than that.

At any rate, Zhirrzh youth psychology wasn't her concern. Chigin metamorphosis was; and there were still eleven tissue samplings yet to be done this latearc. Snugging the first sampler back into its niche in her kit, she pulled out the second and got back to work.

8 Thrr-gilag's railcar switched direction at the main Cliffside Dales station, shifting onto a northward line that led all the way across the flat Kee'miss'lo River valley and ultimately into the Ghuu'rr-clan territory in the hills beyond. Once, while still back in school, Thrr-gilag had ridden this line all the way to its end, just to be able to say he'd done it. For this trip, though, he would be going less than a tenth of that distance. Just ninety-five thoustrides, as the halkling flew, to the small Frr town of Reeds Village.

The sun was glinting through the clouds near the horizon by the time the railcar pulled onto the siding and let him out. According to his father, his mother was living out in the farmland two thoustrides south of town in a small reddish house with white edging and a large vymis tree growing beside the roadway.

A house that Thrr't-rokik himself had of course never seen. Reeds Village was 115 thoustrides from the Thrr family shrine, fifteen thoustrides out of Thrr't-rokik's anchor range. The more Thrr-gilag had thought about that fact, the more ominous it had loomed in his mind. Something had caused his mother to move such a deliberate distance away, and he wasn't at all sure he was going to like the reason.

The darkness of latearc was filling the sky by the time he reached the house, which stood alone at the edge of the farmland, looking just the way his father had described it. Stepping up to the door, he knocked.

"Why, hello, my son."

Thrr-gilag jumped, turning to his left toward the voice. His mother Thrr-pifix-a was kneeling in a small garden beside the house, almost invisible in the gloom. "Hello, Mother," he said, starting toward her and letting his low-light pupils dilate. She looked reasonably good: a couple of cyclics older than he remembered her, but strong and alert and capable. "Sorry I didn't notice you there."

"That makes us even, then," Thrr-pifix-a said, easing to her feet. "No, that's all right." She waved Thrr-gilag's hand away as he moved forward to help her. "I can manage. Sorry if I startled you; I didn't notice you myself until you knocked. I was trying to get the last of my seeds planted before it got too dark to see. I'm afraid my low-light vision isn't all it used to be. Not to mention my hearing."

"Next time I come by so late, I'll be sure to whistle," Thrr-gilag promised lightly, touching his tongue gently to her cheek. "So what are you planting this cyclic?"

"Flowers, mostly," she said, taking his arm and returning the kiss. "Plus a few vegetables. The home-grown ones always taste so much better than mass-cultivated, don't they? Goodness, I must look terrible. Please excuse me—I didn't know you were coming."

"I tried sending you a message," Thrr-gilag said, eying his mother closely. "The communicator said you wouldn't accept it."

"Oh, I don't talk to Elders much anymore," Thrr-pifix-a said equably. "Have you eaten?"

"Ah—no, not recently," Thrr-gilag said, frowning down at her. "Is there some reason you don't talk to Elders?"

"Well, as long as your timing has worked out so well, we might as well put you to work," Thrr-pifix-a said. "I'll get you started on dinner while I go clean up. Come, I'll show you to the kitchen."

The meal was, for Thrr-gilag, a strange and rather discomfiting experience. On the one side, it was a warm, comfortable reunion with his mother, a time for food and conversation after too many cyclics of hurried neglect as he flew back and forth across Zhirrzh space studying alien races and artifacts. But even as he tried to relax in the warmth of family love, he couldn't ignore the taste of apprehension at the back of his tongue. Thrr-pifix-a was his mother; and yet, somehow, she wasn't. She had changed, in a way Thrr-gilag couldn't seem to get a grip on.

And she wouldn't talk about it. That was the most disturbing part of it. Every attempt he made during dinner to reintroduce her comment about Elders—every delicate probe he floated as to why she'd left home and come out here to the edge of a tiny Frr village—all were deftly deflected and instantly buried under a new flurry of news about distant cousins or friends.

So they sat and ate and talked . . . and it was only as

the meal drew to an end that Thrr-gilag caught the new look on his mother's face and realized that she hadn't been ignoring the issue at all. She had, instead, been postponing it.

Until now.

"Well," Thrr-pifix-a said, setting down her utensils and getting carefully up from her meal couch. "That was excellent, Thrr-gilag; thank you. You must be getting a lot of practice in cooking out there on all those study worlds."

"Actually, you'd be surprised at how little cooking we try to get by with out in the field," Thrr-gilag confessed, stepping around the table and taking her arm. "And the meals out there certainly suffer for it. Why don't you go sit down in the conversation room while I get the dishware cleared away?"

"The dishware can wait," Thrr-pifix-a said, her voice quiet and serious. "Let's go sit down together, my son. We need to talk."

The conversation room was tiny, less than half the size of the one in their old house. "Small, isn't it?" Thrr-pifix-a commented, looking around her as she eased down onto one of the couches. "Nothing like the house I raised you and your brother in. Or the house I was raised in myself, for that matter."

"The size of the house isn't important," Thrr-gilag said. "As long as you're happy."

"Happy." Thrr-pifix-a looked down at her hands. "Well. I'm sure you've talked with your brother. And . . . others. What have they told you?"

"Absolutely nothing," Thrr-gilag said. "I didn't even know you'd moved until a few fullarcs ago."

She looked up at him again, and he felt his tongue stiffen against the side of his mouth. Here it came. "It's really very simple, Thrr-gilag," she said softly. "I've come to the conclusion—and the decision—that I don't wish to become an Elder."

Thrr-gilag stared at her, his heart thudding out the beats as an unreal sort of silence filled the room. Had she really said what he thought he'd heard her say? His own mother? "I don't understand," he managed at last.

She smiled slightly. "Which part don't you understand? Eldership, or my not wanting it?"

"I'm glad you're not taking this lightly or anything," Thrr-gilag shot back with a force that startled him. "Mother, what in the eighteen worlds are you thinking of?"

"Please." Thrr-pifix-a held up a hand. "Please. This isn't some bright new idea I dreamed up last latearc and haven't properly thought through. Nor is it the product of insanity or a broken mind. This decision has grown gradually, with a great deal of thought and study and meditation behind it. The least you can do is hear me out."

Thrr-gilag took a slow breath, willing his tail to calm its dizzying spin. No wonder Thrr-mezaz hadn't wanted to talk about this through a communicator pathway. "I'm listening."

Thrr-pifix-a looked around the room again. "I know it's rather a cliché, my son, but the older I get, the more I've begun to realize that it really is the smaller things in life that make that life worth living. The taste of one's food; the delicate smell of flowers or rainfall or the sea; the touch of a loved one's hand. Things we all too often seem to take for granted. I know I did when I was your age. But not anymore. My senses are fading—have been fading slowly for a long time now. I can't see or hear nearly as well as I used to, or taste or smell."

She lowered her gaze to her hands again. "I can still

touch. But with all too many of my old friends, touch is no longer possible."

She looked up at him. "Eldership isn't life, Thrr-gilag. That's the long and the short of it. It may be a shadowy illusion of life—a wonderfully clever imitation, even. But it's not real life. And I've enjoyed life too much to settle for an imitation."

Thrr-gilag seemed to be having trouble breathing. "But there's no alternative, Mother. Without Eldership there's nothing afterward but . . ."

"Death?" Thrr-pifix-a said gently. "It's all right, you can say it."

"But you can't do that."

"Why not?" she asked. "Zhirrzh did it all the time, you know, until we learned how to remove and preserve *fsss* organs. Millions of Elders were summarily thrown into the great unknown during the various Eldership Wars. Even now some are lost each cyclic to accidents or the simple weight of age of their *fsss* organs. Eventually, we'll all have to face death."

"Eventually, maybe," Thrr-gilag said. "But not now. Not while you're still—" He broke off.

"While I'm still what?" Thrr-pifix-a asked. "Young? Capable? Able to impart the wisdom of my cyclics to my descendants?"

"All of those," Thrr-gilag insisted. "And more. We need you, Mother. More than that, we want you. How can you think of taking yourself away from us?"

She looked him straight in the eye. "How can you think of demanding that I stay?"

There was no answer to that. Only an ache deep within Thrr-gilag, an ache that had no words. "Couldn't you at least give it a try?" he asked at last. "Perhaps it's not as frightening as you think."

Thrr-pifix-a flicked her tongue in a negative. "I'm not frightened, Thrr-gilag. You've missed the point entirely if you think that. I know what the grayworld is like—I've heard all the descriptions and talked to many Elders. If anything, all the fear lies on the other side, with the unknowns and uncertainties of death. It's simply a matter of not wanting to live the way an Elder must."

"But you can't make that kind of decision without giving it a try," Thrr-gilag persisted. "You can't."

"But I have to," Thrr-pifix-a said. "Don't you see? If I wait until I've been raised to Eldership, I'll have lost my chance to decide otherwise."

Thrr-gilag stared at her, sudden realization sending a jolt from his tongue straight through to his tail. "Mother, what are you talking about?" he asked carefully.

"I'm sure it's obvious," she said. "The only way I can avoid Eldership is to go retrieve my *fsss* organ from its niche at the family shrine. And to destroy it."

Thrr-gilag took a careful breath, the room seeming to tilt around him. "Mother, you can't do that," he said, hearing in his voice the tone of one explaining something to a very young child. "Tampering with a *fsss* organ is a grand-first felony."

"But it's my own *fsss*," she pointed out. "Taken from my own body. Why shouldn't I be able to do what I want with it?"

"Because you can't," Thrr-gilag said. "That's all there is to it. It's the law."

"Oh, come now," Thrr-pifix-a said, tilting her head in that peremptory way Thrr-gilag always associated with her challenges to his schoolwork answers. "Just because something is a law doesn't mean it's right. A thousand cyclics ago it was illegal for anyone except clan and family leaders to have their *fsss* organs removed at all."

"I'm familiar with Zhirrzh history, thank you," Thrr-gilag said. "But you can't use arrogant stupidities in our past to justify breaking the law now."

"I'm not trying to justify anything, Thrr-gilag," Thrr-pifix-a said tiredly. "There's no challenge to the law itself in this—I'm sure it was written for good reasons by Zhirrzh who were intent on doing the right thing. All I want is the right to choose for myself. And I should have that right. All Zhirrzh should."

Thrr-gilag closed his eyes. "Who have you told all this to?"

"This part? Just you. Though your brother may have recognized on his own where the track was leading."

"And father, too?" He opened his eyes. "Is that why you moved out of his anchorline range? So he wouldn't have a chance to try to talk you out of it?"

Thrr-pifix-a stood up and stepped over to one of the windows. "Your father is gone, Thrr-gilag," she said, almost too softly for him to hear. "What's left out there at the shrine is not the Zhirrzh I bonded to and worked beside for forty-eight cyclics. I left home because the reminders of what I'd lost were too much to bear."

"I understand," Thrr-gilag said, a twinge of her same ache tugging at him. He'd felt it himself at the shrine: talking to the Elder his father had become was not the same as having his father there beside him. Not really. "I wish I knew what I could say that would make it better."

Thrr-pifix-a turned back from her contemplation of the darkness outside. "I know. And I thank you for caring." She made an attempt at a smile. "I wish *I* knew what to say to keep you from worrying about me the way you are right now."

"You could say you'll think about this idea of yours some more," Thrr-gilag suggested. "You could say that you understand that this loss is still fresh, and that you'll give it more time to heal before you do anything drastic."

"How about if I just say I'll put you up for the latearc?" she countered, the smile more convincing this time. "With a promise of breakfast at the other end? I won't even make you cook this time."

Thrr-gilag sighed. "I'm sorry, Mother, I wish I could. But I've got to get going. I have to leave for Gree in a few tentharcs."

"Gree?"

"Yes. Klnn-dawan-a's there with a study group."

"Ah," Thrr-pifix-a said. "I should have known. Please give her my best when you see her. I hope you two find the time to be bonded soon. While I'm still around to come to the ceremony."

"Yes," Thrr-gilag murmured, frowning at the unconcerned look on his mother's face. Could it be that she didn't know about the Dhaa'rr threat to revoke the bond-engagement?

No, of course she didn't know. She wasn't talking to Elders anymore. "We'll try to accommodate you," he said. "Look, I really have to go. But you take care. And . . . keep thinking about all of this. All right?"

"I will," she promised, stepping over to kiss him farewell. "You think about it, too. And take care of yourself."

"Sure. I'll talk to you when I get back. I love you, Mother."

"I love you, my son."

The walk back to the rail seemed longer, somehow, than the earlier walk in the other direction. Colder, too, in the chilly latearc air. Thrr-gilag plodded mechanically along, oblivious to the silent, starlit world around him. And tried to think.

It was a waste of effort. There were too many questions, too many potential crises facing him and his loved ones. And no solutions to any of them.

Should he tell his father what Thrr-pifix-a had planned? Or if not him, should he tell Thrr-tulkoj? Surely the Zhirrzh charged with protecting the Thrr family shrine would want to know of this kind of threat. And it was almost certainly Thrr-gilag's legal duty to report it to *someone*.

But on the other side, it had been only half a cyclic since Thrr't-rokik had been raised to Eldership. If this attempt to run away was really nothing more than an expression of her grief and her struggle to adjust, reporting it would do nothing but cause more trouble for everyone. And shame to go along with it.

Or should Thrr-gilag himself have tried harder to talk his mother out of the whole thing? Canceled his trip to Gree, perhaps, and spent more time with her? Maybe it was loneliness that was driving it, or a cry for help and support?

Maybe he should have told her about the threat to his bonding with Klnn-dawan-a. It would have given him an opening to suggest that she should bury such radical thoughts for now in favor of family solidarity, as well as reminding her of the advantages Elders had in obtaining knowledge and information.

No. Thrr-pifix-a didn't care about information and knowledge. She cared about her garden, and her cooking, and her edgework, and her family. And Eldership would take three of those away from her.

He sighed, a startling sound in the stillness of the latearc. No, there was nothing more he could do about this. Not right now. Maybe when he got to Gree and had a chance to talk with Klnn-dawan-a, the two of them might be able to come up with something.

He picked up his pace, the weariness lifting a little from his spirit. Yes; Klnn-dawan-a. Together, the two of them would find some way to resolve this mess. All of it.

They had to.

9

The small transport glided in from the western sky, circling the area once before touching smoothly down onto the Dorcas-village landing field. For a few beats the screech of the reversers mixed in with the roar of the engine noise as the pilot braked against the transport's momentum. The craft slowed to a crawl, the roar and screech fading together into a dull rumble. Turning again, much more ponderously now that it was on the ground, it began a leisurely circle back to where Thrr-mezaz and Klnn-vavgi waited.

An Elder appeared in front of Thrr-mezaz. "They're down, Commander," he reported. "The Elders' initial postflight check on the engines shows all systems normal."

"Very good," Thrr-mezaz said. "Inform all perimeter

warriors to stand down to secondary-alert status. And have the Stingbirds recalled from their escort zones."

"I obey, Commander," the Elder said, and vanished.

"Well, here we go," Thrr-mezaz commented, glancing at Klnn-vavgi. "You ready, Second?"

"Not really, no," Klnn-vavgi said. "To be perfectly honest, Thrr-mezaz, this whole thing makes me nervous. There's no reason I can think of why Dkll-kumvit should need to come all the way down here just to talk to us. That's what he's got direct laser links for."

"Maybe he just wants to overview our defensive setup for himself," Thrr-mezaz said.

"He can do a blame sight better overview from orbit than he can from down here," Klnn-vavgi said. "Anyway, he's a ship commander. You ever known a ship commander who voluntarily came down on the ground?"

Thrr-mezaz shrugged. "There's always a first time."

"You believe that if you want to, Commander," Klnn-vavgi growled. "I say he's got a hummer with him, and that we've got some bad news coming."

The transport rolled to a stop in front of them, a landing ramp unfolding from its side as its doorway slid open. Dkll-kumvit was waiting at the top, and even before the ramp had completely settled into place, he was on his way down.

"Good postmidarc to you," Thrr-mezaz said as the other reached the ground. "I'm Commander Thrr-mezaz; Kee'rr. This is Second Commander Klnn-vavgi; Dhaa'rr."

"Commander Thrr-mezaz; Second Commander Klnn-vavgi," Dkll-kumvit acknowledged. "I'm Supreme Ship Commander Dkll-kumvit; Ghuu'rr."

"Honored, Supreme Ship Commander Dkll-kumvit." Thrr-mezaz gestured, and the three warriors waiting with the *kavra* fruit stepped forward.

The ritual was quick and perfunctory, all the more so here in the middle of a war zone. "I have some matters to discuss with you, Commander," Dkll-kumvit said when they were finished. "Have you a place where we can speak in private?"

"Certainly, Supreme Commander," Thrr-mezaz said, carefully keeping his emotion out of his voice. A private talk . . . and that pouch riding on Dkll-kumvit's waist was just the right size for a hummer. Klnn-vavgi had called it, all right. "This way, please."

A hunbeat later the three of them were in Thrr-mezaz's office, the door securely closed behind them. "The following is official Warrior Command business," Dkll-kumvit called into the air, pulling the expected hummer from his waist pouch. "For the ears of the commander and second commander alone."

He set the hummer on the desk and turned it on, and an intrusive, pulsating tone filled the room. "Is that setting all right, Commander?" he asked Thrr-mezaz.

"It's fine," Thrr-mezaz said, not entirely honestly. Hummers were highly effective at masking normal speech from the diminished hearing capacity of Elders, and were thus useful in situations where Elder eavesdropping was unacceptable for one reason or another. The Elders themselves, who hated being left out of things, had tried on at least five occasions to get the Overclan Seating to institute a total ban on the devices. They'd failed all five times, vowing each time to try again.

It was, in Thrr-mezaz's opinion, a great deal of fuss and fury over nothing. Despite their apparent advantages, hummers were unlikely ever to come into common use for the simple reason that the same sounds that interfered with Elder hearing also rattled the brains of everyone within earshot. Some Zhirrzh were so sensitive that they became physically ill; for most others a reasonably short exposure wasn't much of a problem, though even with them there was a fair chance of winding up with a headache for a tentharc or two afterward.

Thrr-mezaz himself fell somewhere between those two extremes, and he was pretty sure Dkll-kumvit knew it. The supreme ship commander's use of the device anyway was an unpleasant underscoring to the seriousness of the visit.

"I expect you're both wondering what this visit is all about," Dkll-kumvit said, leaning back into his couch. "To be honest, I'm not sure I understand myself all of what's going on. But I'm getting some disturbing rumblings; and since you two are the Zhirrzh on the firing line, I wanted to give you as much advance warning as possible."

Thrr-mezaz glanced at Klnn-vavgi. Something special from the Human-Conquerors? "What sort of rumblings, Supreme Commander?"

"Political ones, of course," Dkll-kumvit grunted, making a disgusted noise in the back of his throat. "Even in the middle of a war you can never seem to lose the politics." He looked hard at Thrr-mezaz. "Especially politics pertaining to or emanating from Elders. And right now, Commander, you are the Zhirrzh they want most on the hot seat."

Thrr-mezaz grimaced. "Prr't-zevisti."

"You got it," Dkll-kumvit agreed. "Many of the Elders consider you responsible for his death."

"Actually, Supreme Commander, there's no real proof that he's dead," Klnn-vavgi put in. "Considering all the metal the Human-Conquerors use, it's entirely possible that they simply have him trapped up there."

"Unlikely," Dkll-kumvit said. "But I suppose it's possible. Still, at this point it almost doesn't matter what's actually happened to him. The fact is that Prr't-zevisti has vanished; and the political reality is that you, Commander Thrr-mezaz, are going to be held accountable."

Klnn-vavgi snorted. "With your permission, Supreme Commander, I'd like to say that that's not only ridiculous but also unfair. This is a war zone, not a student field trip. A million things happen out here that can't be anticipated or controlled by anyone."

"I agree completely, Second Commander," Dkll-kumvit said dryly. "Unfortunately, I'm not the one you need to convince. And if you'll permit me a certain degree of speculation, I would suggest that your presence here as second commander is part of the reason the Dhaa'rr Elders are stirring this particular pot so strongly. I suspect they're hoping to use this Prr't-zevisti business as a lever to get you promoted to command on Dorcas."

Klnn-vavgi hissed in contempt. "I've already had that offer. I told Speaker Cvv-panav that I wasn't ready for this command, and that I didn't want it."

"I applaud your loyalty, Second Commander," Dkll-kumvit said. "As well as your assessment of your experience and capabilities." His tongue flicked sourly. "Unfortunately, clan Speakers like Cvv-panav never let such trifles as common sense stand in the way of what they want. No disrespect to your clan intended, Second Commander."

"None taken, Supreme Commander," Klnn-vavgi assured him. "I have no illusions as to the purity and nobility of any clan leaders, including my own."

"What exactly is the gist of the Dhaa'rr argument?" Thrr-mezaz asked. "That I had no business putting the pyramids and their *fsss* cuttings outside our defense perimeter in the first place?"

"That's basically it, yes," Dkll-kumvit said. "They also claim that after Prr't-zevisti's cutting was captured, you did little or nothing to intervene."

"Do they note that my own Elders strongly advised me to hold back?" Thrr-mezaz countered. "Out of concern that Prr't-zevisti's *fss* cutting would be destroyed if we attacked?"

"Or that Prr't-zevisti himself had the option of returning to his family shrine at any point along the way?" Klnn-vavgi added. "I would suggest that that gives him a fair amount of the blame for whatever's happened to him."

"As I've already said, Second Commander, this is politics, not logic," Dkll-kumvit said quietly. "All I came here for was to make you aware of the situation as it currently exists. Whatever moves are made next will be directed at Commander Thrr-mezaz. It'll be up to him to deal with them."

"I appreciate the warning, Supreme Commander," Thrr-mezaz said. "I'll try not to let any of this interfere with the smooth operation of this beachhead."

"I'm sure you won't, Commander." Dkll-kumvit gestured at the village-area map on the wall. "So. Anything new on your search efforts north of the village?"

"Not yet," Thrr-mezaz said. "The Elders have completed their examination of the surface and are starting to look underground."

"Hard work, that, even for Elders," Dkll-kumvit commented. "There are always annoying little veins of metal ore that get in the way down there. I take it they've examined the rocks and trees as part of their surface search?"

"Yes." Thrr-mezaz nodded. "Quite thoroughly."

"Um," Dkll-kumvit rumbled, gazing at the map again.

"You really think that Human-Conqueror warrior team was trying to get to something out there?"

"I wouldn't have the Elders searching if I didn't," Thrr-mezaz said.

"And if they don't find anything?"

"I'll ask your permission to move the pyramid to a new area and continue the search," Thrr-mezaz told him. "Whatever's out there, the Human-Conquerors seem to consider it important. I wouldn't want to treat it any less so."

"Well, I hope you're right," Dkll-kumvit said. "A success here could prove highly important. In more than just matters of war."

Thrr-mezaz nodded. A significant warrior success that followed directly from his placement of the pyramids outside the perimeter would go a long way toward deflating the arguments of his political opponents. "I understand, Supreme Commander," he said. "If there's something out there the Human-Conquerors want, we'll get to it first."

"Good." Dkll-kumvit stood up. "Then I suppose I'd best get back to the *Imperative* and let you get on with your work. Never know when the Human-Conquerors will try their hand at another attack, and I'd hate to be stuck here on the ground while my warships fight it out up there."

He reached for the hummer; paused. "One other thing, Commander," he said. "I've heard back from Warrior Command on my request for reinforcements. It's been denied."

Thrr-mezaz looked at Klnn-vavgi. "The whole request?"

"The whole request," Dkll-kumvit confirmed. "No new warships for me; no new ground warriors for you. And no heavy air-assault craft for either of us."

Thrr-mezaz grimaced. So much for any attacks on the Human-Conquerors' mountain stronghold, then, at least for the foreseeable future. The expeditionary force had included just two of the heavy-weapon air-bombardment craft, a tenth of the number that should have been assigned for this sort of invasion. Dkll-kumvit had argued strongly against the decision, protests that had been ignored by the parsimonious strategists at Warrior Command. The result had been both inevitable and crippling: both air-assault craft had been destroyed within the first tentharc of the invasion. "Did they give you any reasons?" he asked Dkll-kumvit.

"All they would say was that they had nothing to spare right now," the supreme commander said.

"What about the veterans' reserves?" Klnn-vavgi asked. "Have they started calling them up yet?"

"I asked about that," Dkll-kumvit said. "I'm still waiting for an answer." He hesitated. "I have heard, though—strictly unofficially and not to be repeated—that Warrior Command has already launched expeditionary forces onto two more Human-Conqueror worlds. And that they're planning to attack three more worlds within the next few fullarcs."

Thrr-mezaz stared at him. Five more beachheads, before their first three target worlds had even been pacified? "Excuse me, Supreme Commander, but that strikes me as a bit . . . premature."

"*Insane* was the word I used, Commander," Dkll-kumvit said heavily. "I don't know what in the eighteen worlds they're thinking of back there. I can only assume they have some good reason for it."

Thrr-mezaz looked at Klnn-vavgi, their brief discussion just after the last Human-Conqueror attack flashing to mind. The conversation where they'd speculated that

Warrior Command had learned something about the Human-Conquerors that had them scared. "Perhaps they've altered their threat assessment," he murmured.

"Perhaps," Dkll-kumvit said. Reaching to the desk, he picked up the hummer and shut it off. "I just hope they aren't getting overconfident," he added into the sudden silence. "This isn't going to be like taking on four planets' worth of Isintorxi, you know."

Thrr-mezaz looked at Klnn-vavgi again. "No," he said. "Somehow I don't think overconfidence is going to be a problem."

The latearc darkness had fallen, masking the village in a sort of watchful gloom. Shifting position on his couch, Thrr-mezaz stared out the window of his office, squeezing his hands against the sides of his head and the dull pain throbbing there. A headache, generated by Dkll-kumvit's hummer. And by Dkll-kumvit's words.

Behind him the door slid open. "Commander?" Klnn-vavgi called.

"Come on in, Second," Thrr-mezaz said, gesturing him over. "I'm just sitting here in the dark."

"Yes, I can see that," Klnn-vavgi said, stepping in and letting the door slide shut behind him. "Any particular reason why?"

"Headache," Thrr-mezaz said. "Or trying to think, or basic fear of the light. Take your pick. Any report from our intrepid search party?"

"Well, the major news is that the Dorcas topground has metallic ore veins in it," Klnn-vavgi said dryly. "Vast numbers of them, judging by the number and volume of the complaints I've been getting. The Elders aren't happy at all with this assignment."

"This is a war," Thrr-mezaz snapped, abruptly sick and

tired of the Elders and their attitude. "In case they've forgotten, let me remind them that wars do not involve large shares of personal happiness. I get any more of this whining—about anything—and I'm going to send the whole batch of them back to their shrines. They can sit there and watch the clouds go by for the rest of eternity for all I care. You got that?"

"Yes, Commander," Klnn-vavgi said, his voice stiff and formal. "I'll make sure the Elders understand."

For a few beats the room was silent. Thrr-mezaz squeezed his hands against his headache, the sudden flare of anger burning down again into tiredness. "All right, then," he said more calmly. "Aside from complaints, did they have anything to report?"

"Not yet," Klnn-vavgi said. "But they've covered only about ten percent of the area. This part's going to be slower than the above-ground search."

"I know," Thrr-mezaz said, turning back to the window. What was the Human-Conqueror commander doing up there, he wondered, secure behind his explosive missiles and his Copperhead warriors? Was he staring out into the darkness, too, wondering and worrying about what his enemy was doing? Or was he instead poring over maps and timetables with his warriors, confidently planning their next expedition to the mysterious objective to the north?

In any given arena, at any given time, one side or the other always had the initiative. Or so Thrr-mezaz had been taught. Which side, he wondered, had it here?

"Commander?" Klnn-vavgi asked tentatively.

Thrr-mezaz gave his head one last squeeze and dropped his hands back to the desk. "Enough is enough, Klnn-vavgi," he said, keying on his reader and pulling up one of the overview maps that the orbiting warships had made up. "We've been sitting on our hands here for eleven fullarcs now, letting the Human-Conquerors make all the moves. It's time we took some of the initiative ourselves."

"You going to petition for more heavy air-assault craft?"

"I had in mind something with higher odds of success," Thrr-mezaz said. "What do we know about the approaches to the Human-Conquerors' stronghold?"

"Well, we know there aren't any easy ones," Klnn-vavgi said, coming around to his side of the desk where they could both see the reader. "Are we talking about an attack direction here?"

"Not necessarily," Thrr-mezaz said. "Or rather, not yet. What we need first is to find out more about the place."

"I don't know how we're going to do that," Klnn-vavgi said, flicking his tongue in a negative. "We'd never get a Stingbird in close enough. Not with those Copperhead warriors waiting there like hungry halklings."

"What if we go on foot?"

"That's not much better," Klnn-vavgi said, leaning over the desk and keying the reader for an overlay. "There are only a handful of passable approaches—you can see where they're marked. The Human-Conquerors have sentry points guarding all of them."

"True," Thrr-mezaz said, studying the map. "But those posts have probably been set up to keep anyone from getting through into the stronghold itself. There's no particular reason we have to go in that far."

Klnn-vavgi frowned down at him. "You're not thinking about using the Elders, are you?"

"Why not? They're perfect for this kind of scout work."

"As I recall, that was one reason we let the Human-

Conquerors leave with Prr't-zevisti's cutting," Klnn-vavgi reminded him. "You're not going to get a lot of volunteers to try it again."

"I'm in command here, and I don't have to ask for volunteers," Thrr-mezaz reminded him mildly. "Besides, the main problem with Prr't-zevisti was that we let the Human-Conquerors in on the transport end of the operation. This time we'll do it all ourselves."

Klnn-vavgi rubbed thoughtfully at the corner of his mouth. "I don't know, Thrr-mezaz," he said slowly. "That's pretty rough country to tackle on foot. And unless we can talk Dkll-kumvit out of one of his ten-thoustride-range Elders, we're going to have to get the pyramid within five thoustrides of something useful. That's going to put us uncomfortably close to one or the other of those sentry points, and I somehow doubt a nice shiny white pyramid would go unnoticed."

Thrr-mezaz grimaced. Klnn-vavgi was right, of course, on all counts. And given the current political realities, Dkll-kumvit probably wouldn't go out on soft sand like this for him. Particularly not with something involving an Elder. "Then there's no way around it," he said. "We're just going to need a cutting with a longer anchor range. If we can't get it from Dkll-kumvit—"

He broke off, an odd thought suddenly striking him. "Is there any particular reason why we need to lug a whole pyramid up there?" he asked slowly. "We're only talking about one, maybe two cuttings here. Why not just put them in some kind of small predator-proof container and carry it on up?"

Klnn-vavgi's midlight pupils narrowed in astonishment. "You aren't serious," he said. "You mean just throw an Elder's *fsss* cutting into a box like it was an order of fresh produce or something? Come on, Thrr-mezaz—you think you have trouble with the Elders *now,* you try even suggesting something like that. They'd be screaming for you to be staked out for the savagefish before you could blink twice."

"All right, forget it," Thrr-mezaz growled. Traditions were fine in their place, but the fastidious and inflexible adherence to them could sometimes be a complete pain in the throat. "Then we're back to finding ourselves a cutting with a longer range. I wonder if Warrior Command would be able to furnish us with one."

Klnn-vavgi snorted. "I don't see why not," he said sourly. "Look at all they've saved on warriors and equipment for us."

"Right; we'll appeal to their sense of guilt," Thrr-mezaz said. "I'll go ahead and put in a request. All they can say is no."

"And they probably will." Klnn-vavgi frowned at the reader. "Before you do that, maybe we ought to try talking to your brother. He might have some idea why the Human-Conquerors would be poking around out there."

"I doubt it," Thrr-mezaz said. "As far as I know, his study group didn't get any detailed information on Dorcas."

"No, but he knows a lot about the Human-Conquerors themselves," Klnn-vavgi said. "Anyway, it can't hurt to ask him."

"I suppose not," Thrr-mezaz said reluctantly. After that conversation with Dkll-kumvit this postmidarc—and his own little outburst a few hunbeats ago—he wasn't exactly eager to trust a private family conversation to a pathway of possibly hostile Elders. Still, he couldn't avoid it forever. "Communicator?" he called.

There was a short pause, and then an Elder appeared. "Yes, Commander?"

"A pathway to the Overclan Seating. I want to speak with the location server on duty."

The Elder nodded and vanished. Klnn-vavgi stepped back around the desk and was just settling onto his couch again when the Elder returned. " 'I am the location server for the Overclan Seating,' " he said. " 'Speak, Commander Thrr-mezaz.' "

"I need to locate my brother, Searcher Thrr-gilag; Kee'rr," Thrr-mezaz said. "He's currently working with an alien-study group under Overclan Seating supervision."

The Elder nodded and left.

And stayed gone. "Interesting," Klnn-vavgi murmured as the beats rolled slowly by. "You think they've lost track of him?"

"Could be," Thrr-mezaz said. "Thrr-gilag has a tendency to wander off without telling anyone where he's going. Drove my mother crazy when we were growing up."

The Elder returned. " 'I do not have a current location for Searcher Thrr-gilag; Kee'rr,' " he said. " 'I will keep trying and will alert you if contact is established with him.' "

"I see," Thrr-mezaz said. "Thank you. Farewell."

The Elder vanished, returned. "The pathway is released, Commander. Will there be anything else?"

"Yes," Thrr-mezaz told him. "Open a pathway to my father, Thrr't-rokik; Kee'rr. He's at the Thrr family shrine near Cliffside Dales."

"I obey," the Elder said, and vanished.

"You suppose he's being kept incommunicado?" Klnn-vavgi suggested. "Something connected with that mission to the Mrachanis?"

"Could be," Thrr-mezaz agreed. "Let's try a couple more things before we give up."

The Elder reappeared. " 'It's good to hear from you, my son,' " he said. " 'How are you?' "

"I'm fine, Father," Thrr-mezaz said. "I need to talk to Thrr-gilag, and I'm having trouble locating him. Do you have any idea where he might be?"

The Elder vanished, returned. " 'He visited me here at the shrine last fullarc. He then went to see your mother, and after that he was to board a spacecraft for Gree to see Klnn-dawan-a.' "

"He's going to Gree?" Thrr-mezaz frowned. "I'd have thought the Overclan Seating would want him to stay close to Unity City."

" 'Really? He didn't say anything about that. Something having to do with his studies?' "

"More or less," Thrr-mezaz said evasively. Semiofficial details of the Mrachani expedition had been circulating through secure warrior pathways for a good fullarc now, but that didn't mean the news had been released to the general public yet. Chances were good it hadn't, in fact, and that it wasn't going to be. "Do you happen to know which flight he went out on?"

" 'No, but I can find out. Is this a carnival, or what?' "

Thrr-mezaz smiled tightly. *Carnival*—private family code for a vitally important matter, derived from the seriousness with which he and Thrr-gilag had treated such things when they were children. "It could very well be a carnival, yes," he agreed soberly. "Both for him and for me."

" 'I understand, my son. If you can hold on to the pathway a hunbeat, I'll see what I can find out.' "

"Yes, please do," Thrr-mezaz said.

The Elder vanished. "A carnival?" Klnn-vavgi asked,

tilting his head as he looked at Thrr-mezaz. "Interesting terminology you Kee'rr have."

"It's private family slang," Thrr-mezaz told him. "And don't give me a hard time about it—I'll bet you had plenty of goofy slang when you were growing up."

"I beg your pardon, Commander," Klnn-vavgi said, with feigned indignation. "There was nothing goofy about it. *Floogy* and *gritch* were perfectly good words—"

The Elder reappeared. " 'Sorry to be so long,' " he said. " 'He's on the warrior supply ship *Ministration,* which left Oaccanv about three tentharcs ago.' "

"Thank you, my father. I appreciate it."

" 'You know I'm always here to help you, Thrr-mezaz. Take care of yourself, and I'll talk to you soon. Farewell.' "

"Farewell." Thrr-mezaz nodded to the Elder. "Release the pathway, and open another to the *Ministration,*" he ordered.

"I obey."

"I don't think the Overclan Seating's going to be happy about his charging off to Gree," Klnn-vavgi commented.

"Probably not," Thrr-mezaz conceded soberly. "Unless they've already dropped him from the mission."

"That's possible," Klnn-vavgi agreed. "Considering the likely pathway, though, you probably shouldn't ask him about it."

"I wasn't planning to."

The Elder appeared. " 'Hello, Thrr-mezaz. This is a surprise.' "

"And I know how much you've always liked surprises," Thrr-mezaz said dryly, glancing at his armwatch and belatedly doing a quick time conversion. "I'm sorry—you were probably asleep, weren't you?"

" 'Yes, but don't worry about it,' " the answer came back. " 'I can sleep next cyclic. What's up?' "

"Just one quick question," Thrr-mezaz said. "Our Human-Conquerors here have been trying to get into an area north of our encampment. There's nothing obvious out there they might want, and no particular tactical advantage that I can see to the location. I was wondering if you might have some idea what they might be up to."

The Elder nodded and vanished.

Once again the beats rolled by. "You suppose he's fallen back asleep?" Klnn-vavgi asked.

"I don't know," Thrr-mezaz said, frowning out the window. Either Thrr-gilag had indeed fallen asleep, or else he was thinking very hard about the question.

Or else he already knew the answer and was trying equally hard to phrase his answer carefully . . .

The Elder returned. " 'I can't tell what they might want up there,' " he said. " 'But I'm sure you'll want to keep on top of the situation. You certainly don't want the Humans making a carnival out of this whole thing.' "

Thrr-mezaz felt his midlight pupils narrow. A carnival. "I understand, Thrr-gilag," he said, trying to keep his voice steady. "We'll watch ourselves. You, too."

" 'I will,' " the reply came back. " 'Farewell, my brother.' "

"Farewell." Thrr-mezaz nodded to the Elder. "You may release the pathway. That will be all for now."

"I obey," the Elder said, and vanished.

"Well, that was interesting," Klnn-vavgi said, standing up and stepping toward the door. "I'm not sure how informative it was, but it was interesting. If that's all, I think I'll be getting back to my quarters."

"Go ahead," Thrr-mezaz said. "Before you go, though, I want to apologize for blowing up at you a few hunbeats ago. This sitting around here like wounded nornins is starting to get to me."

Klnn-vavgi smiled lopsidedly. "Don't worry about it, Commander. I'll see you next fullarc."

He left, the door sliding closed behind him. With a tired sigh Thrr-mezaz resettled himself on his couch and closed his eyes. A carnival. Not something Thrr-gilag would have just accidentally said. Not a word he would have used lightly.

Which meant that his suspicions had been right. There was something about this war and the Human-Conquerors that Warrior Command wasn't telling anyone.

And Thrr-gilag knew what it was. *I can't tell you what they might want*, he'd said. Innocently and deceptively worded, but Thrr-mezaz knew his brother better than that. Thrr-gilag knew what the secret was but had obviously been forbidden to talk about it.

And some part of that secret—whatever it was—was right here on Dorcas.

And it was suddenly more imperative than ever that the Zhirrzh find out what was going on up there in the mountains. Which meant getting a warrior inside, or an Elder in close.

Or maybe, just maybe, they already had an Elder in close. . . .

Thrr-mezaz flicked his tongue restlessly, trying to think it through. In its own way it was a wildly audacious idea, and certainly not one that was going to go down well with anyone else involved. And even he had to admit the odds of success were extremely low.

But if it worked, it would be worth whatever grief they threw at him over it. Well worth it. "Communicator?"

The Elder appeared. "I thought you were finished, Commander," he said, his tone just short of a grumble.

"You have somewhere else you want to be?" Thrr-mezaz countered. "I want a pathway to the recorder of the Prr family shrine on Dharanv."

The Elder blinked. "The Prr family shrine?"

"That's right," Thrr-mezaz said. "Go on—it's getting late here and I want to get to sleep."

"I obey," the Elder said, the bemused look on his face vanishing along with the rest of him.

Thrr-mezaz turned back to his reader and the overview map. All right. What they needed was a spot out of view of the Human-Conqueror sentry points. . . .

The Elder was back. " 'I am fourth assistant recorder for the Prr family shrine,' " he said. " 'Speak, Commander Thrr-mezaz; Kee'rr.' "

"I'm inquiring about the *fsss* organ of Prr't-zevisti; Dhaa'rr," Thrr-mezaz said. "What has been the disposition of it?"

The Elder vanished, reappearing a hunbeat later. " 'The *fsss* organ you refer to remains untouched in its niche. Why would you think it would be otherwise?' "

"Excellent," Thrr-mezaz said. "Then I would like to request formally that a new cutting be taken from it as soon as possible. A cutting which will then be sent to me here at the expeditionary force beachhead on the Human-Conqueror world of Dorcas."

The Elder stared at him, looking stunned. "Commander?"

"Just deliver the message," Thrr-mezaz said.

The Elder gulped. "I obey, Commander," he said, and disappeared.

Thrr-mezaz flicked his tongue in a grimace and resettled himself again on his couch. The wait this time was likely to be a long one.

He was right. It was nearly four hunbeats before the Elder returned. " 'This is a most irregular request, Commander Thrr-mezaz,' " he said. " 'Most irregular indeed. One might almost say it was illegal; one would certainly say it was a violation of generations of Zhirrzh tradition.' "

"Nevertheless, I make it," Thrr-mezaz told him. "I believe that it would be in Prr't-zevisti's best interests, as well as aiding in our war efforts against the Human-Conquerors."

"But Prr't-zevisti is dead," the Elder frowned.

"The Prr family doesn't seem convinced of that," Thrr-mezaz pointed out. "Otherwise, why keep his *fss* organ intact? Deliver the message—let's see what they say."

"I obey," the Elder sighed, and vanished.

The pause this time was nearly as long as the previous one had been. " 'I cannot grant such a request, Commander. It is not within my authority to do so.' "

"Then I suggest you confer as quickly as possible with your family and clan leaders," Thrr-mezaz said, putting an edge in his voice. "If Prr't-zevisti is still alive, this could be his best chance at survival. Possibly even his only chance."

" 'I will do as you ask,' " the reluctant answer came back.

"I thank you for your efforts," Thrr-mezaz said. "I'll expect a quick response."

" 'I will do what I can.' " The Elder paused. "Commander, if you'll pardon a personal observation, this is not going to make you any friends among the Dhaa'rr."

"No, I expect I already have all the friends among the Dhaa'rr I'm ever going to," Thrr-mezaz said. "Unless the recorder has something else, you may release the pathway. And this time I *am* finished for the latearc."

"I obey," the Elder said, his tone that of one disappointed with his commander, and vanished.

Reaching to his reader, Thrr-mezaz keyed it off, stretching tired muscles in arms and shoulders. Let the Elder be disappointed with him. Let the whole expeditionary force be if they wanted to. Winning this war was the overriding consideration here. Nothing else mattered.

Getting up from his couch, he crossed the office to the door. The next move was with the Dhaa'rr and the Prr family. He could only hope they were taking the war as seriously as he was.

10

It was a long ride by rail from Reeds Village to the Thrr family shrine. Long enough for the sunlight glinting through the railcar window to have burned away premidarc mists and wispy clouds to blaze brilliantly down through the uncustomary cloudless sky. Long enough, as Thrr-pifix-a gazed out the window, for her faint reflection on the glass to be replaced by an equally faint shadow.

Long enough, certainly, for her to have changed her mind about what she was planning to do. But she hadn't. And as she walked down the path toward the towering white pyramid, she realized that that fact meant her decision was indeed final.

The choice was made. She would not become an Elder.

Ahead, the door into the leftmost protector dome slid open, and Thrr-tulkoj stepped out, laser rifle in hand. "Stand fast," he said, "and speak your name."

"I obey the Protector of Thrr Elders," Thrr-pifix-a said, nodding politely. Thrr-tulkoj was an old friend of Thrr-gilag's, but the ritual nevertheless had to be observed. "I am Thrr-pifix-a; Kee'rr."

"Who will prove your goodwill and intentions?"

"I will," she said, picking out one of the *kavra* fruit from the rack and slicing it. The first time she'd ever done this, she remembered, she'd almost dropped the *kavra* at the sharp and bitterly strong taste of its poison-neutralizing juice. Now, with the slow fading of her senses, the fruit seemed depressingly bland.

"And who will prove your right to approach?" Thrr-tulkoj asked.

"Why, you will, of course," Thrr-pifix-a said, smiling at him as she dropped the *kavra* into the disposal container. "How are you, Thrr-tulkoj?"

He smiled back, a combination of patience and wry humor in his expression. "I'm fine, Thrr-pifix-a," he said. "Come on, now—you know there's a protocol to be followed here."

"Oh, but I did follow it," Thrr-pifix-a said. "I'm not here to talk to any specific Elder, you see. So you're the one who has to prove my right to approach."

Thrr-tulkoj frowned slightly. "Ah," he said. "Well, all right, then. Advance, Thrr-pifix-a, and state your purpose here."

"I just wanted to come and watch for a while," she said, glancing up at the shrine as she stepped forward. "See what the Elders do here, maybe join in a conversation or two. Just . . . see what it's like."

"I understand," Thrr-tulkoj said quietly. "Is there anything I can help you with?"

"No, thank you," she said. "I can manage."

"All right," he said. "Feel free to take your time. I'll be here if you need me."

He stepped back inside the guard dome, propping his weapon against the inside wall. Thrr-pifix-a waited until the door had sealed shut behind him; then, taking a deep breath, she headed toward the shrine. There were something like forty thousand niches there, identified only by number. But that wouldn't be a problem: the certificate she'd been given at the hospital when she was ten cyclics old had been carefully preserved in the memories book her mother had begun for her two fullarcs after her birth. She could find her *fss* . . . and then all she would need would be a few beats of privacy.

The numbers carved beneath each of the niches were small and difficult to see in the glare of the sunlight. She peered at some of the ones at eye level as she started walking slowly along the near wall of the shrine. 27781— too low. 29803—still too low, but going the right direction. 31822 . . . 33850 . . . 35830 . . .

And there it was, at waist height just before the shrine's edge. 39516: her niche. And resting there inside it . . .

For a handful of beats she gazed through the mesh screen at the *fss* that had been surgically removed from behind her brain so many cyclics ago. Such a small and fragile thing, it seemed to her. So unlikely a thing to have been the driving force behind so much of Zhirrzh history.

But it had. And unless she completed what she'd set out to do this fullarc, it would continue to drive her own history as well. For a long, long time.

Heart thudding in her chest, her tail spinning like a foamed-ceramic mixer, she fumbled with suddenly trembling fingers at the mesh door's release catch. It came open with a explosive *snap* that seemed to echo across the landscape. She glanced quickly around at the protector domes, her tail spinning faster than ever, sure that they must have heard that.

But neither Thrr-tulkoj nor anyone else was in sight. Taking a deep breath, she turned back to the niche and lifted the now loosened door—

And without warning a figure stepped around the corner of the shrine, and a hand darted across to lock around her wrist. "I'm sorry, Thrr-pifix-a," Thrr-tulkoj said quietly, taking another step and capturing her other wrist. "You know you can't do that."

"What are you talking about?" Thrr-pifix-a demanded, her voice quavering with shock and frustration despite her best efforts. "I just wanted to look at it."

"Come on," the protector said, pulling her courteously but firmly away from the shrine. Holding her there with one hand, he resealed the mesh door she'd opened. "Come on," he said again, shifting to a hold on her upper arm and guiding her back along the path toward the domes. "I'll take you back to the rail, all right?"

Thrr-pifix-a looked ahead down the path at the glistening mesh of the predator fence, the bitter taste of failure mixing with the *kavra* juice on her tongue. Just like that, her one chance was gone. "Please, Thrr-tulkoj," she whispered. "Please. It's my *fsss*. My life. Why can't I do what I want?"

"Because the law says so," he reminded her gently. "Along with hundreds of cyclics of Zhirrzh history."

"Then they're wrong. The law and history both."

"Perhaps," Thrr-tulkoj said. "It wouldn't be the first time tradition and reality had gotten out of step. But my job isn't to make law here. Just to enforce it." He looked sideways at her. "Maybe you should try talking to the family and clan leaders. Present your case to them."

Thrr-pifix-a flicked her tongue in a negative. "They

wouldn't listen to me. An old female, without any status or political standing?"

Thrr-tulkoj shrugged. "You never know. Maybe there are others out there thinking the same thing who just haven't had the nerve to talk about it. Anyway, you're not nearly as status poor as you seem to think. What with Thrr-gilag out studying the Human-Conquerors and Thrr-mezaz out fighting them, the family leaders owe you at least a serious hearing. And don't forget, as soon as Thrr-gilag and Klnn-dawan-a are bonded, she can probably talk to the Dhaa'rr clan leaders for you, too."

Thrr-pifix-a sighed. "Perhaps," she said.

But he was wrong, and they both knew it. No clan leaders were going to take the time to hear the babbling plea of an old female. Not even if they weren't in the middle of a war.

It was a long ride back home to Reeds Village. And seemed even longer.

The last page of the last report rolled up off the display, and with a tired sigh the Overclan Prime turned off his reader. So the initial battles were over. The fourth and fifth Zhirrzh beachheads were now established on Human-Conqueror worlds, with encirclement forces on guard overhead. Two more expeditionary forces were preparing even now to lift off the main staging areas on Shamanv and Base World 11, bound for two other Human-Conqueror worlds, with five more groups being assembled from across the eighteen worlds. The reports coming in from captured territory were fairly glowing with success and victory. From all appearances the Zhirrzh counterattack against this new alien threat was going perfectly.

The Prime knew better. The Zhirrzh forces were in fact teetering on the edge of disaster.

The Prime sighed again, leaning back on his couch and staring morosely up at the overview star chart projected on his office wall. The Zhirrzh people didn't realize it, of course. Probably most of the clan Speakers didn't, either. But Warrior Command knew. And so did he.

Because the Human-Conquerors weren't just sitting there accepting their defeats. They'd been taken by surprise, perhaps, by the vigor of the response to their attack on the Zhirrzh survey ships. But that wouldn't last. Already they were gathering their strength and striking back, more often than not with devastating results. The huge Nova-class warcraft mentioned in the captured recorder had made their appearances, as had the awesomely deadly Copperhead warriors. So far all the attacks had been beaten off, but at a steep price. The Kalevala encirclement forces were down to two combat-ready warships; the Massif forces were completely helpless. If the incredibly tough ceramic hulls hadn't disguised the internal damage, the Human-Conquerors would undoubtedly have been back already to finish the job. As it was, the warriors and technics had some breathing space to try to effect repairs.

But they wouldn't have long. These were the Humans. The Conquerors. They would soon be back.

And unless the beachheads had succeeded in locking a critical component away from them, the next time they came, they might have CIRCE with them.

The Prime cursed softly under his breath as he gazed up at the star chart. They were spread too thin. That was the real summation line here: they were spread too cursedly thin. Worse, they were concentrated in the same general part of the Human-Conqueror empire, the sections denoted as Lyra and Pegasus Sectors. The enemy knew where to find them and could bring all their forces to bear with a minimum of logistical trouble.

What the Zhirrzh needed was something to shake up the enemy, something to diffuse their focus. A bold strike into some other area of their empire, perhaps. Maybe even one of their more populous central worlds: Celadon, Prospect, Avon, or even Earth itself. It would be a risk, but a reasonably minimal one as long as they kept the strike brief. With warships impossible to track through the tunnel-line of stardrive, it would be a trivial matter to sneak across the Human-Conqueror empire to whatever world the Zhirrzh warriors chose to hit. At that point the uncertainties would be due mainly to the unknown defenses they'd find at the other end.

"Overclan Prime?" a faint Elder voice came in the silence.

The Prime looked up, stiffening to a respectful posture. Not just an Elder, but one of the twenty-eight Overclan Primes who had gone before him. "Yes, Eighteenth?" he said.

"Your private chambers, if you please," the Eighteenth said shortly. "There are matters we need to discuss."

"Certainly," the Prime said, a twinge of concern flicking through him as he stood up from his couch. The Eighteenth was about as imperturbable a personality as former Primes ever got. For him to be troubled meant something decidedly unpleasant was in the works.

To the average Zhirrzh the Overclan complex was generally seen as a triumph of cooperation, a monument to openness and honesty between the clans. Cooperation there might be, at least after a fashion; the openness, however, was little more than a cleverly structured illusion. The main Overclan Seating chamber itself was open enough, certainly, accessible to Elders from two family shrines and a dozen of the smaller cutting pyramids. But only the chamber itself was accessible. The two office buildings, with their offices, conference rooms, and other work areas, had been carefully positioned to be just out of range of all of them.

Only the two Overclan pyramids located in the Seating chamber itself had access to the entire complex. And it was regarding those that the cleverest stratagem of all had been created. On the vast open area between the chamber building and the two office buildings was a memorial display of some of the most powerful and deadly war machines the Zhirrzh had created throughout their long and violent history. A highly impressive display, too, with long-range cannon, fighter aircraft, and over twenty of the siege and battle machines that had rolled destruction and death across the battlefields of the three Eldership Wars. A mute reminder of what life on Oaccanv had been like before the creation of the Overclan Seating.

That was what the visitors to the memorial saw. What they didn't see was that two of the siege machines were made entirely of metal. Metal that cast shadowlike spaces which the Elders from the main Overclan family shrine could not enter.

The secure conference room in the Speakers' office building lay nestled in one of those shadows. The Overclan Prime's private chambers lay in the other.

The existence of those carefully positioned shadows was a closely guarded secret, known only to the Prime and certain of the Overclan Speakers. And only the Prime knew that the two inaccessible areas were not, in fact, *entirely* inaccessible.

The former Primes were waiting when he arrived in his chambers—all twenty-eight of them, in fact, by a quick count as the Prime sealed the door behind him. Another sign that this matter was something serious. "I greet the former Overclan Primes," he said, stepping over to his couch and sitting down. "To what do I owe the honor of this assembly?"

"To a looming crisis," the Twelfth growled. "A crisis which, if not dealt with quickly and decisively, could conceivably rip apart the very fabric of Zhirrzh society."

"Really," the Prime said, eying the set expression on the other's transparent face. The Twelfth, he knew, was inclined to be overly dramatic, as well as seeing crises and disasters beneath every stone. Still, this seemed beyond even his usual pessimism. "Is there general consensus on this?"

"The Twelfth perhaps overstates the case a bit," the Twenty-second said. "But—"

"I overstate nothing—"

"But he is correct," the Twenty-second said, raising his voice, "in saying the problem must be dealt with quickly."

"Then let me hear it," the Prime said, moving to take control of the discussion. Having five hundred cyclics' worth of leadership experience in the same room, he'd long ago discovered, was not nearly as useful or productive as he'd once thought it would be. Vastly different personalities from vastly different eras, yet with the same compelling strength of will that had gained each of them the position of Overclan Prime in the first place. All convinced on one level or another that they should still have a say in the management of the eighteen worlds. "Which of you first heard about this crisis?"

"It was I," the Seventh spoke up. "From one who was once Speaker for Kee'rr, now anchored at the Thrr family shrine with a cutting at the third pyramid of Unity City. You are, I believe, familiar with the Thrr family of the Kee'rr. One of its sons, Searcher Thrr-gilag, was the incompetent fool who allowed the Human-Conqueror prisoner to escape."

"I know Searcher Thrr-gilag, yes," the Prime said. "I'm not prepared to judge him incompetent. Certainly not on that basis."

"He should at least have made sure the prisoner died," the Seventh sniffed. "The Zhirrzh warriors of my time knew to do that much."

"Yes, he could have done that," the Prime agreed. "And in doing so might have found himself and his entire group raised to Eldership by the Human-Conquerors."

"It is hardly a dishonor to be raised to Eldership," the Twentieth bristled.

"It is when we need their hands right where they are," the Prime countered. "If they'd all been raised to Eldership, who would have cared for the injured Mrachani prisoners until the *Diligent* could arrive? More important, who would have been there to stop the Human-Conqueror warriors from landing and gathering up all of the Base World's records? Are you that anxious to see enemy warcraft flying over Oaccanv?"

"Calm down, Prime," the Eighteenth soothed. "No one's going to blame a searcher for not acting like a warrior under fire. Speaking of Thrr-gilag, were you aware that he'd left Oaccanv?"

The Prime frowned. "No, I wasn't. When was this?"

"Early this premidarc, apparently," the Eighteenth said. "The Overclan location server didn't realize he was missing until Thrr-gilag's brother, Commander Thrr-mezaz, called to set up a pathway to him. It took the location server several tentharcs to track him to a warrior supply ship bound for Gree."

"For Gree?" the Fifteenth asked. "What in the eighteen worlds is he going there for?"

"He's bond-engaged to a searcher working there," the Prime sighed. "Searcher Klnn-dawan-a; Dhaa'rr. I should have thought of that—it was in his file."

"I was under the impression that you were going to hold all the Mrachani-expedition members here in the complex," the Seventh said.

"Searcher Thrr-gilag asked for permission to visit his parents," the Prime said. "I granted it."

"Along with permission to leave the planet?"

"Nothing specifically was said either way," the Prime said. "I wasn't expecting him to leave Oaccanv; but actually I can't see any particular harm in it."

"Really," the Twelfth growled. "A Zhirrzh who holds full knowledge of CIRCE, and you can't see the harm in letting him wander around untended?"

"Calm down," the Prime said. "It's all right. He won't say anything."

"Can you be certain of that?" the Twelfth demanded. "Absolutely certain?"

"Yes, I can," the Prime said firmly. "As I've already said, I've read his file. Carefully. A graduate in alien studies with exceptionally high marks, his behavior and deportment since childhood have been equally exceptional. Granted, he's young and obviously somewhat inexperienced, but he's neither foolish nor impulsive nor careless. More to the point, he appreciates as well as you how devastating a premature disclosure of CIRCE's existence would be. He won't say anything."

"Trust is a noble quality for an Overclan Prime to possess," the Seventh said contemptuously. "It can also be his downfall. May I suggest that we at least arrange for all future communications from this Thrr-gilag to be routed through our communicators here at the complex?"

The Prime waved an impatient hand. "If it would make you feel better, go ahead."

"Thank you," the Seventh said frostily, and vanished.

"Interesting," the Eighteenth commented, eying the Prime thoughtfully. "All that about Thrr-gilag—I daresay it sounded rather like a prepared speech."

"Not preparation; familiarity," the Prime corrected him with a grimace. "As it happens, I've already fought the same battle with the Speaker for Dhaa'rr. Twice, actually. I must say I'm getting a little tired of it."

"Understandable," the Eighteenth said. "I only hope this young searcher is worthy of your trust."

"He's worthy of more than just trust," the Prime growled. "I've seen his file and read his reports, and it's clear to me that he has an exceptionally good mind for alien cultures and behavior. And we're going to need every bit of such insight in this struggle against the Human-Conquerors."

"True," the Fourteenth put in. "Besides which, if he's planning to talk, it's already too late to stop him."

The Seventh reappeared. "The pathway watch is set," he said, throwing one last glare at the Prime. "May we get back to the immediate issue at hand now?"

"Please do," the Prime said, gesturing polite invitation.

"Very well," the Seventh sniffed. "It concerns Searcher Thrr-gilag's mother, Thrr-pifix-a. Earlier this fullarc she traveled to the Thrr family shrine and attempted to steal her *fsss* organ." His eyes bored into the Prime's face. "Apparently, she wishes to refuse Eldership."

"I see," the Prime said. "And?"

The Seventh frowned. "What do you mean, *and?* Surely you can see the implications."

"Did she succeed?" the Prime asked.

"No," the Seventh said. "The chief protector of the shrine was suspicious and stopped her in time."

"Then, no, I don't see the implications." The Prime shrugged. "We get crazed fanatics all the time who try to steal their *fsss* organs."

"Which is precisely where the problem lies," the Eighteenth said impatiently. "Thrr-pifix-a isn't a crazed fanatic —that's what makes her so dangerous. She's a simple, quiet, reasonable old female; nothing more, nothing less. A reasonable person who has nevertheless decided that she would prefer death to Eldership."

"I'm sorry, but I still don't see the problem," the Prime said. "What are you afraid of—that she'll go off and create some wide-scale protest movement against Eldership?"

"Exactly," the Twenty-second said. "Not that she'll do it on her own, necessarily, but that she could become the flash point for such a movement."

"There are philosophical aspects to this, you see," the Eighteenth added. "Aspects that go beyond her particular case."

"Correct," the Twelfth said. "And those aspects—"

"Please," a quiet voice said.

The other Elders felt instantly silent, and the Prime stiffened with respect as the Elder who'd spoken left the group and came toward him. Not just another former Prime, but the First. The Zhirrzh who'd been chosen as their world's last hope by the clan leaders assembled together on that final smoking battlefield of the Third Eldership War. The Zhirrzh who'd stood stoically before them and been stripped forever of all family and clan ties. The Zhirrzh who'd accepted the awesome task of turning generations of hatred and mistrust into first an armistice and then a lasting peace. And who had succeeded.

The First seldom spoke at these gatherings. When he did, they all listened.

"Perhaps you do not see, Twenty-ninth," he said in that same quiet voice, "because you regard the past from too great a distance. You see history as events that happened to other Zhirrzh instead of as a force that has not only molded our society but also strongly influenced the ways in which we think. The three Eldership Wars were, at their core, wars over rights: the rights of common Zhirrzh to have their *fsss* organs preserved as their leaders already had; the rights of Elders to have their *fsss* organs protected from deliberate or accidental destruction; the rights of Elders and physicals alike to living space, without one group being displaced to make exclusive room for the other."

The Prime nodded. Yes; and that last conflict was one that was beginning to lift its ugly head again. "I understand, First," he said.

"Good," the First said. "Then consider for a hunbeat what Thrr-pifix-a is really asking. She is asking for Eldership to no longer be a right, but a privilege."

The Prime frowned. That was an angle that hadn't even occurred to him. "I see what you're saying," he said hesitantly. "But can't something like Eldership be both a right and a privilege?"

"In theory, certainly," the First said. "In actual practice, though, it never remains in such balance for long. The Twenty-second is quite right in fearing that other, more radical Zhirrzh will seize upon Thrr-pifix-a's case, twisting it into an attack on Elders and Eldership generally." He gestured to the Second. "It happened twice during my son's tenure as Overclan Prime."

"And once during mine," the Ninth put in.

"And during mine, as well," the Sixteenth added.

"There's no need to list them all," the First said. "The point is that this is not uncharted territory. It's a threat that has raised itself time and again throughout Zhirrzh history, threatening to erode the sense that Eldership is an absolute right that cannot be altered or taken away. If you allow individual Zhirrzh to refuse Eldership, the inevitable result will be Zhirrzh claiming the right to make that same decision not for themselves, but for others. Never mind the lack of a logical connection; it's been demonstrated time and again that that is the direction in which such thinking evolves. The only way to keep that from happening is to make sure we never take that first step."

"And so the very idea must be suppressed," the Prime said.

"Yes," the First agreed solemnly. "As quickly as possible. As ruthlessly as necessary."

"I see," the Prime said, a shiver running through him as he looked around the room. He'd never heard even rumors of such incidents—he, the Overclan Prime of the Zhirrzh people. A ruthless suppression, indeed. "And you're convinced that suppression is the only way? All of you?"

"Do you doubt our word?" the Twelfth demanded, the pitch of his voice dropping imperiously. "Our combined experience alone—"

"Please," the First said again. "Of course we can't guarantee that this is the only way, Twenty-ninth. No one can. But at the very least, any such movement against Eldership would be a serious distraction for the Zhirrzh people. And we cannot afford even a beat of distraction. Not now. Not as we battle for our survival against these conquerors."

"No, I suppose not," the Prime murmured. "Very well.

You've presented the problem. Have you likewise prepared a solution?"

"We have," the Sixteenth rumbled. "The problem arises not because of what this Thrr-pifix-a wants but because of what she is: a common, reasonable, respectable person. As you yourself said, there are crazed fanatics all the time who don't want Eldership."

"Yes," the Prime said grimly. He saw where this was going now, all right. "And therefore what we need to do is prove Thrr-pifix-a to be as crazed as any of the rest of them."

"I take it from your voice that you don't approve," the Twenty-eighth suggested.

The Prime looked him square in the face. "No, Father, I don't," he said bluntly. "I don't like using the office of Overclan Prime this way. It feels far too much like an abuse of the power I've been granted."

"Then perhaps you should resign," the Twelfth snapped. "An Overclan Prime who's afraid of his power is of no use at all to the Zhirrzh people."

"Or perhaps he's all the more valuable to them," the Prime snapped back. "Correct me if I'm wrong, but wasn't it the abuse of personal power that has led to most of our wars?"

"Well stated," the Eighteenth said approvingly. "But as it happens, the abuse of personal power—not yours—is a second problem that you're currently facing. Our proposal is that you solve both of these problems with the same knife."

The Prime frowned at him. "I'm listening."

"It's really quite simple," the Twelfth said. "You have on the one side Thrr-pifix-a of the Kee'rr clan, who wishes to decline Eldership. On the other side you have Speaker Cvv-panav of the Dhaa'rr, whose ambition is clearly to build his clan's power beyond even the height of its old political dominance." He eyed the Prime. "This latter, I presume, is not news to you."

"Hardly," the Prime assured him sourly. "Cvv-panav sees himself as the head of a new Dhaa'rr empire."

"And because of that he must be made to stumble," the Twelfth said. "Not to fall, but to stumble. Here is what we propose."

The twenty-nine of them talked long into the latearc . . . and in the end the Prime reluctantly gave in. At the least, he told himself, it would reduce the distractions that were being created by Speaker Cvv-panav's drive for power, allowing all of them to concentrate more fully on their war of survival.

And if it hurt an old, harmless female . . . well, perhaps that was the price that had to be paid.

The price of Zhirrzh survival. And of the Prime's own education regarding the painful duties that sometimes came with power.

11 The door to the metal room swung open, the muffled clang bringing Prr't-zevisti out of one of the dreamy mental wanderings that seemed to pass for sleep among Elders. He eased to the edge of the lightworld as a single Human came into the room and flicked on the light.

Good luck was with him: it was the Human called Doctor-Cavan-a. A Human who, bearing a Zhirrzh female-style name, ironically enough did indeed seem to be a female. The Humans had been doing a lot of re-arranging in this room lately, moving the shelves around and changing what was being stored on them, and as a result Doctor-Cavan-a hadn't been around much. To Prr't-zevisti's annoyance, too—his inspections of the Humans who came in here were necessarily slow and stealthy, and there were still a number of areas of Human anatomy that he hadn't yet been able to get to. Most notably that organ in the lower abdomen that some young searcher on Base World 12 had speculated might be a Human equivalent of the Zhirrzh *fss* organ. Not that anyone seriously believed it was.

But at any rate, she was back. Now, with a little more good luck, maybe she'd stay put for a while.

Doctor-Cavan-a went to one side of the room and pushed a small box a half stride farther into a corner, then turned and gestured a hand toward the door. "All right," she said. "Bring it in."

There was a grunted response, a clink of metal on metal, and the front end of a large tablelike slab with thick side supports appeared in the doorway. A very different sort of table from the ones the two Zhirrzh bodies had been dissected on, Prr't-zevisti noted. This one had several indentations and clamps scattered around its upper surface, apparently deliberately positioned. The rear edge flowed up into a ridge with small apertures and various controllike devices set into it. Not an autopsy examination stand, this, but more like some alien version of a searcher's laboratory table.

Abruptly, a twinge of low-level pain lanced through him. Prr't-zevisti tensed, forcing himself to keep quiet. An Elderdeath weapon again, its beam impinging on his *fss* cutting sitting there in its box on one of the shelves. It had been happening more and more frequently lately, and Prr't-zevisti still hadn't decided whether it was a deliberate attack against him or merely a side effect of some general weapons testing.

One thing was certain, though. Despite Supreme Ship Commander Dkll-kumvit's efforts at the beginning of this invasion, the Humans clearly still had access to Elderdeath weapons. Maybe not as powerful or long-range as the two the heavy air-assault craft had knocked out, but undoubtedly just as dangerous at close range. A potentially vital discovery, and he could only hope he would be able to find a way out of here with it before Commander Thrr-mezaz's warriors launched their attack on the place.

Assuming, of course, the attack ever came. Prr't-zevisti had heard disturbing rumors before his capture that Warrior Command was preparing expeditionary forces against more of the Human worlds, forces that were supposedly going to be launched before the current beachheads were anything but minimally secured.

It was a strategy that made no sense at all to Prr't-zevisti, even given how admittedly out-of-date his own warrior training and experience were. But if true, it might explain why Thrr-mezaz hadn't yet moved against the Humans' stronghold. The warriors had lost both of their heavy air-assault craft and several of their Stingbirds in the initial invasion, and without adequate reinforcements an attack would be nothing less than lunacy cubed.

The two other Humans finished rolling the table into the room and left, leaving the female Human alone inside. The door swung shut behind them, and as it did so, the nearby Elderdeath weapon stopped.

Doctor-Cavan-a opened a drawer in one of the table's thick side supports and withdrew two unfamiliar pieces of equipment, setting them side by side on the table. One had a thin cable attached; taking the end of the cable, she inserted it into one of the apertures in the raised edge and flicked a switch. There was a soft hum; and with it came a new low-intensity flicker of Elderdeath sensation.

Prr't-zevisti tensed, expecting the worst. But the level stayed where it was, a sort of mental humming well below any sort of pain threshold. More like the sun-sense he remembered from childhood, now that he thought about it: the ability to locate the sun even through heavy clouds.

A sense that, like all Zhirrzh children, he'd lost the fullarc after his tenth birth anniversary. For him that had been the most traumatic part of the whole *fsss*-removal operation, more upsetting than the anesthetic or the wooziness or even the ten fullarcs of bandaged ache at the back of his head. It had been like going a little blind, and not even his parents' assurances that it would be ultimately worthwhile had been any real consolation.

Impatiently, he sliced away the thought. He was there to study the Humans, not to sit around endlessly reminiscing like some old Elder with nothing better to do. The Human female was making some adjustments to the device, but though the sun-sense altered subtly, it never approached anything remotely painful. Perhaps the Humans had miscalculated the threshold of Elderdeath pain. Or perhaps they thought they could annoy him into submission.

The Human female touched the small black box, at its customary place on one corner of the table. "Doctor-Cavan-a," she said. "(Something) eighteenth, twenty-three-oh-three."

Prr't-zevisti eased as close to the lightworld as he dared, straining to understand. The Human-language briefing he'd been given before coming to Dorcas had turned out to be more complete than he'd first realized, and he'd picked up a surprising number of new words in the past three fullarcs just by watching and listening. But it took concentration, and even so there were any number of words that still eluded him.

"Begin (something) secondary (something) work on the Zhirrzh (something) sample," the Human female continued. "I'll start with a first (something) (something) analysis." She stepped away from the desk—

And to Prr't-zevisti's sudden horror reached toward the

shelf and picked up the box containing his *fsss* cutting. Carrying it back to the table, she opened it.

He was back in the grayworld in an instant, dropping deep into the darkness. Running the only way he could, knowing full well the whole time how utterly useless and childish it was. As long as he was anchored here, whatever pain Doctor-Cavan-a chose to apply to his cutting would instantly be transmitted to him. "I'm take (something) a three (something) sample," he heard Doctor-Cavan-a say. There was a twinge, an almost-felt stab of almost pain—

And then, nothing. Only the background sun-sense.

"Sample take (something)," Doctor-Cavan-a continued. "Looks good. I'm put (something) it into the (something)."

Cautiously, suspiciously, Prr't-zevisti eased back to the edge of the lightworld. Doctor-Cavan-a was bent over one of the instruments, peering into a rectangular tube. His *fsss* cutting was back in its box beside the instrument, apparently untouched.

He frowned, moving over for a closer look. No; he was wrong. The once-smooth circular edge of the cutting now showed a tiny gap. The sample, apparently, that Doctor-Cavan-a had mentioned.

He looked back at her. She was still peering into the tube, but from his new vantage point he could now see glimmerings of light from inside it. A hooded display, he decided, and moved beside her for a look.

It was all he could do to stifle a gasp of amazement. He'd seen Zhirrzh cellular structure through microscopes before, certainly—there'd been whole classes devoted to such things back when he was in school. And certainly there'd been tremendous advances since then; as recently as a cyclic ago he'd seen a demonstration of an awesome new microscope that Warrior Command had commissioned from a group of searchers and technics. They'd hailed it at the time as a triumph of Zhirrzh ingenuity and expertise.

This one left it in the dust.

It was nothing short of astonishing. In the center of the display were a group of *fsss* cells, sharper and clearer than he'd ever seen them. Superimposed on them were multicolored rings and curves and lines, with other multicolored symbols scattered around the edges. Some of the symbols had lines linking them to various parts of the cell, while others scrolled like words on a reader display. Even as he watched, one of the lines created a small square at its tip, the image inside the square magnifying to fill the display. One of the secondary nuclei, Prr't-zevisti tentatively identified it. More symbols, rings, and lines appeared. A hunbeat later another of the small squares formed, and the microscope zoomed in on a portion of the secondary nucleus's edge.

A microscope and analysis machine both. Half the size of the best the Zhirrzh could come up with for a microscope alone.

Slowly, Prr't-zevisti moved back from the Human female, a sense of stunned dread replacing his earlier astonishment. He'd heard the reports from the *Far Searcher,* had seen firsthand some of the bits and pieces of technology that had been scavenged from the wrecks of those Human warcraft. But aside from the recorder and a few parts of the Human prisoner's private spacecraft, it had all been damaged and nonworking. Odd arrangements of metal and unknown materials, more curiosities than anything else.

They'd seen the results of Human technology. Now Prr't-zevisti was getting a look at the technology itself.

He'd suspected the Zhirrzh were in trouble. He hadn't realized until now just how much trouble they were in.

"Interest (something)," the Human female said. "A surprise (something) amount of (something) and (something) activity in the (something) cells. Far too much for something that's supposed (something) to be dead. I'm start (something) with the (something)."

With an effort Prr't-zevisti pulled his thoughts away from the growing darkness of his fears. All right; so the Humans were formidable opponents. But, then, so were the Zhirrzh. Other alien races had tried throughout history to conquer or destroy them, and all had failed. The Humans would fail too.

And everything he learned here would help toward that ultimate victory. Easing his face through the outer skin of Doctor-Cavan-a's back, ready to drop into the grayworld if she turned around, he continued his study of her alien body.

12

"There it is," the transport pilot said, gesturing ahead and to the right. "In that hollow, up against that big rock face. See it?"

"Yes," Thrr-gilag said, peering down at the motley assortment of field shelters with a mixture of nostalgia and embarrassment. Nostalgia, because it looked just like the training expeditions they'd all gone on back when they'd been students. Embarrassment, because he hadn't realized until that beat just how much better than this he'd been faring lately. His Human-prisoner study group on Base World 12 had had top-mark laboratory and living facilities; even the archaeological expedition he'd been with on Study World 15 had had warrior-style perm buildings for their encampment.

Clearly, funds for studying the Chig were distributed with a somewhat less lavish hand.

"We're only going to be here about a tentharc," the

pilot said as he circled around toward the more or less flat stretch of ground that seemed to serve as the expedition's landing field. "We weren't actually scheduled to make this supply run for another few fullarcs. You're welcome to fly back up to the encirclement warships with us when we leave."

"I appreciate the offer," Thrr-gilag told him. He had no idea how he could possibly get through everything he wanted to discuss with Klnn-dawan-a in a single tentharc. But the pilot was right: it was indeed a long way back up to the encirclement warships orbiting overhead. "Let's see how things go, all right?"

"Fine by me," the pilot shrugged. "Hang on—this can get a little bumpy."

Bumpy was hardly the word for it; but they made it without injuries and with no direct evidence of structural damage to the transport. Unstrapping stiffly, thankful that the study group's director had had the sense not to set up on the absolute *top* of the mountain, at least, Thrr-gilag made his way back to the doorway and opened it.

Three young Zhirrzh were waiting a short ways past the end of the landing ramp: typical eager-eyed student-searcher-assistant types, probably there to help the transport's crew unload the supplies. Thrr-gilag hardly noticed them. He certainly didn't give them any thought.

Standing in front of them, at the foot of the ramp, was Klnn-dawan-a.

"Hi," she breathed, favoring Thrr-gilag with one of those special smiles of hers as he walked down the ramp. "The Elders told me you were coming. I'm glad you're here."

"So am I," Thrr-gilag said, hearing a sudden slight trembling in his voice. With all that had happened lately, he'd almost forgotten how much he'd missed her. "I'm afraid I can't stay very long, though," he added as he reached her.

"I didn't expect you'd be able to," Klnn-dawan-a said regretfully as she looked up at him. "Still, even a little time is better than nothing."

"Yes," Thrr-gilag said, his hands trembling a little as he took her hands and squeezed them tightly. The strictures of propriety, not to mention the presence of the student assistants standing there three strides away, forbade the kind of greeting he really wanted to give her. He hoped they'd be able to find some time alone before he left.

Klnn-dawan-a, he could tell, was thinking along the same lines. "I was rather surprised to hear from the Elders that you were on your way down," she commented, taking his arm and turning them toward the encampment. "I'd assumed your work with the Overclan Seating would be taking all your time." She lowered her voice. "Especially with your group about to head out on a new expedition."

Thrr-gilag frowned at her. He'd been under the distinct impression that the Mrachani mission was going to be kept a fairly close secret. "How in the eighteen worlds did you hear about that?"

"Never underestimate the ingenuity of a trained searcher," Klnn-dawan-a said dryly. "As it happens, Director Prr-eddsi has had several long conversations back to Oaccanv in the past couple of fullarcs. Very serious, very secret—secure Warrior Command pathways and all that."

"And you just happened to be sort of leaning up against the shelter wall at the time?"

"Me?" Klnn-dawan-a asked with a good imitation of hurt pride. "I recoil at the very thought. No, Prr-eddsi brought me into the discussion at one point, and the word *Mrachani* came up. Then someone mentioned Nzz-oonaz's name, and the rest fell into place pretty quickly. Obvious, really—your people are certainly the current experts on everything regarding the Human-Conquerors and their territory."

Thrr-gilag grimaced. Human-Conqueror. The term had even made it out here. "They're hardly my people anymore," he told Klnn-dawan-a. "I've been demoted."

"I gathered as much," Klnn-dawan-a said quietly. "I'm sorry."

"My own fault," Thrr-gilag told her. "Apparently, the rule is you kill prisoners rather than let them escape."

She eyed him. "Do I detect a trace of bitterness?"

"More strong indignation than bitterness," Thrr-gilag told her. "And mostly on your behalf, actually. Speaker Cvv-panav pressured the Overclan Prime into putting a Dhaa'rr in the group; and because he was mad at me, he picked Gll-borgiv instead of you."

Klnn-dawan-a shrugged. "Gll-borgiv's not all *that* bad."

"He's still nowhere near as good as you."

"I appreciate the vote of confidence," she said. "Still, I don't really think you should take the blame for my missed chance at glory."

Thrr-gilag looked at the encampment ahead. At the predator fence, the shelters . . . and the white tip of the pyramid sticking up over them. That was something else they hadn't had on those training expeditions ten cyclics ago. No *fsss* cuttings with anchored Elders there to act as communicators.

Or to listen over your shoulder, whether you wanted them there or not. "Is there someplace where we can talk privately?" he asked Klnn-dawan-a.

"I'm sure we can find one," she said, her tone faintly amused. "I thought you didn't have much time."

"I'm not talking about that," Thrr-gilag said, feeling his tail speed up with both anticipation and a faint embarrassment. "I mean, not that I don't want to be close—but that's not what I meant. I meant talk. Really talk."

"Oh," she said, frowning up at him. She followed his line of sight to the pyramid. "Well . . . sure. I've been wanting to check out some of the farms around the other side of the ridge, anyway. And that would give me a chance to show you what we're doing here. Let's go see if Prr-eddsi will let me take out one of the floaters."

Ten hunbeats later they were in a floater, heading out from the encampment. Thrr-gilag waited until they were well outside the Elders' five-thoustride anchorline limit, and then told Klnn-dawan-a the bad news.

She listened in silence. "You're sure about this?" she asked when he'd finished.

"I don't know if you can ever be sure about Elder rumors," Thrr-gilag said, gazing out at the rocky Gree landscape flowing by beneath them. "All I know is that my father thought it was solid enough to warn me."

"Yes," Klnn-dawan-a said, her face set in hard lines as she stared out through the windscreen. "I notice that no one bothered to tell *me* about any of this."

"Maybe none of your Elders here have heard the rumors," Thrr-gilag suggested diplomatically.

She threw him a scornful look. "Oh, come on, Thrr-gilag. You get a rumor started anywhere in the eighteen worlds, and every Elder's going to hear about it. You know that better than I do—you wrote your searcher thesis on it. Our Elders here know, all right. They've just decided not to tell me about it."

Thrr-gilag shrugged uncomfortably. "I suppose you can hardly blame them. All your Elders here are Dhaa'rr, after all. They're probably less thrilled than even your leaders about having me in the clan."

"Well, that's just plain stupid," Klnn-dawan-a said angrily. "Stupid and unfair. No one can possibly blame you for the Human-Conqueror attack on your base—everyone agrees they were out looking for your prisoner. And as for your brother, so he's using his communicators as sentries. So what? We use our Elders here for that sort of thing all the time."

"Except that your pyramid's safely inside a predator fence," Thrr-gilag pointed out. "His aren't. Anyway, that's not really what they're mad at him about."

"They can't blame him for Prr't-zevisti, either," she said firmly. "I know he was my clan and I should be sorry he's dead; but what happened to him was at least as much his own fault as it was Thrr-mezaz's. No one ordered him to stay with his cutting—he could have gone straight to his family shrine and stayed there."

"Unless there's a link between the cutting and the main *fsss* organ we don't know about," Thrr-gilag said doubtfully. "Maybe if you destroy a *fsss* cutting, the Elder dies whether he's anchored there at the time or not."

"No," Klnn-dawan-a said. "Don't forget, it took them at least thirty cyclics of trying before they figured out how to take successful *fsss* cuttings. If the destruction of a cutting section killed the Elder outright, then every Elder whose *fsss* was experimented on back then would have died. They didn't."

"You're right," Thrr-gilag said, a small fraction of the weight lifting from his shoulders. "I hadn't thought about that. Still, I doubt it's going to make much difference to the Dhaa'rr Elders."

"No, of course not," Klnn-dawan-a bit out. "Prr't-zevisti's death is a convenient excuse for the clan leaders to back out of something they didn't want to allow in the first place." She sighed, some of the anger and toughness seeming to drain out of her. "Oh, Thrr-gilag. What are we going to do?"

"We're not going to give up," Thrr-gilag told her. "That much is for sure. The only question is how to fight back."

"Yes," Klnn-dawan-a murmured, her pupils narrowed with thought. Thrr-gilag gazed sideways at her, smiling despite the seriousness of the whole situation. A beat ago her anger and indignation had dissolved almost instantly into depression and the hint of defeat; and now that too had promptly changed again to determination. Many of her friends and colleagues, he knew, found this rapid mood processing of hers to be intimidating. Personally, he found it rather endearing. "All right," she said. "What have we got? The clan leaders have already given permission for our bonding, so to renege now is to break their word. That makes them look bad unless they can show really good reasons. So what we have to do is show that their reasons are totally inadequate."

"We can point out how antiquated these prejudices are, too," Thrr-gilag suggested. "We've had open territorial borders for a hundred cyclics now—strictures on interclan bonding ought to be obsolete, too."

"Right—let's toss in a little shame and embarrassment," Klnn-dawan-a agreed. "I just wish one of our families had more political leverage. We'd stand a better chance if we could get some of the other clans interested in this, even just as observers."

"Yes," Thrr-gilag said, feeling a little shame of his own. He'd had that leverage once, after Svv-selic was demoted and he'd been made speaker of the Base World 12 group. And had proceeded to lose all of it. "You know, it occurs to me that there were a couple of times when the Overclan Prime seemed to be on my side. Making minor decisions in my favor against Speaker Cvv-panav. But I don't suppose that really counts for anything."

"I doubt it," Klnn-dawan-a said. "The Overclan Prime doesn't like the Dhaa'rr much—he'd rule against Speaker Cvv-panav just to keep in practice. Besides, this is too much an internal clan matter for him to stick the Overclan's tongue into it."

For a few hunbeats neither of them spoke. The floater glided smoothly over the rocks and ridges, its air cushion dampening out the smaller bumps and turning larger ones into gentle parabolic arcs. Ahead, the ground sloped toward a creek in the distance; beyond the creek the terrain turned sharply upward again, culminating in more of the towering, white-capped mountains.

"Uh-oh," Klnn-dawan-a muttered.

"What is it?" Thrr-gilag asked as the floater abruptly turned to the right.

"A Chigin whelp," Klnn-dawan-a said, pointing ahead toward the creek. "Over there."

"I see it," Thrr-gilag nodded. The whelp was standing stock-still beside a pile of boulders this side of the creek, its ears standing stiffly up, its full attention on the approaching floater. "You think it's lost?"

"Well, it certainly shouldn't be out here all by itself," Klnn-dawan-a said. "It could be the lead or tail of a grazing party, though. Let's take a closer look, see what family it belongs to."

"How do you tell them apart?" Thrr-gilag asked.

"Mountain families glitter-tag their whelps," Klnn-dawan-a explained. "Those little flashes of light at the edges of their ears—there; see it."

"Yes," Thrr-gilag nodded. "Do you know all the patterns?"

"Most of them," Klnn-dawan-a said. "We're going to have to get pretty close, though. You game?"

"I don't know," Thrr-gilag said dubiously. "I was under the impression that solitary Chig whelps weren't all that safe to approach."

"So the book says," Klnn-dawan-a agreed. "Our own studies indicate that that applies mainly to solitary whelps on their own family's territory. Solitary whelps on neutral territory seem to be actually less unpredictable than larger groups."

"The exact opposite, in other words, of how the book says they're supposed to behave."

"On home territory, anyway. You got it."

"Great," Thrr-gilag said. "Just how good are these studies of yours?"

"Oh, the studies are all wonderful, of course," Klnn-dawan-a said, slowing the floater down to a drifting crawl. The whelp was still standing there, still staring at them. "It's only the conclusions you ever have to worry about. No, seriously, I'm sure we'll be okay. Still, you'd better get the stinger out of the survival pack under the seat. Set on low, please; we don't want to really hurt it."

"If you say so," Thrr-gilag said, pulling the pack out and digging the stinger out of its pouch. He turned it on, grimacing at the vibration of filling energy capacitors. He'd never liked these things, not since his first time on the target range with one. They were awkward to hold, impossible to aim, and utterly absurd looking for something that was supposed to be a weapon. Thrr-mezaz, who dealt with real warrior laser weapons all the time, had laughed himself silly the first time he'd seen one. "So what's the plan?"

"I'll bring us as close to the whelp as I can without spooking it," Klnn-dawan-a said. "Then I'll go the rest of the way on foot, and you can cover me while I try to get a look at the glitter tag. Sound good?"

"Sounds terrible," Thrr-gilag retorted. "What if you're wrong about the whelp being dangerous?"

"Well, one of us has to get close," Klnn-dawan-a pointed out reasonably. "And you don't know the first thing about Chigin glitter-tag patterns."

"I could describe it to you."

"Now you're being silly, dear," Klnn-dawan-a chided. "All right, I think this is about as close as we can get. Everybody out."

The floater settled to the ground and the two of them got out. Stinger in hand, Klnn-dawan-a started slowly toward the whelp, talking soothingly to it as she walked. Thrr-gilag crouched down beside the floater, resting his arm on the curved beak plate, keeping his own stinger trained on the whelp. A motion off to the left caught the edge of his eye, and he flicked a glance that direction—

And froze. "Klnn-dawan-a?" he called quietly. "I think you'd better stop. Take a look to your left."

She paused and turned her head. Thrr-gilag couldn't see her face, but the sudden increase in her tail motion told him all he needed to know.

There were eight of them standing there: eight Chig, all in the unmistakable mottled dark-green metal semiarmor of hunter-warriors. Grouped around them on both sides were perhaps twenty whelps. The whole crowd was gazing unblinkingly at the two Zhirrzh . . . and they did not look friendly.

"Just take it easy," Klnn-dawan-a said softly to Thrr-gilag. "No fast movements. Those aren't toys they're holding."

Thrr-gilag nodded, feeling his own tail speed up. He hadn't even noticed the repeating crossbows until that beat, their shapes blending into the blotchy coloration of the semiarmor behind them. Forbidden by the Zhirrzh to possess high-technology weapons, the Chig had come up with these little gems instead. And they were most emphatically not toys. "What do you want me to do?" he murmured. "Should I try to take them out?"

"Not unless you want your bonding to be with an Elder," Klnn-dawan-a said tartly. "Just stay put and let's see what they want. And whatever you do, *don't* point your stinger at them."

The Chig were moving toward them, weapons at the ready, the whelps scampering chaotically around their feet. The group crossed the stream, and as they approached the floater, the lead Chig gestured sharply to Klnn-dawan-a with his crossbow. *"Bkst-mssrss-(cough)-vtsslss-(cough)-hrss-vss-chlss,"* he said.

"Mrss-zhss-(cough)-hvssclss'frss-sk-(cough)," Klnn-dawan-a replied, waving her empty hand back toward Thrr-gilag.

"Bkst-mssrss-(cough)," the Chig said.

Klnn-dawan-a nodded and started walking slowly backward toward the floater. "What did you say?" Thrr-gilag asked. "Did you tell him we weren't going to hurt the whelp?"

"I don't think they particularly care about the whelp," Klnn-dawan-a said, her voice tight. "We're the ones they're interested in."

Thrr-gilag looked at the aliens' faces. "I don't like the sound of that."

"Neither do I," Klnn-dawan-a said, backing up against the floater. "These aren't mountain people, Thrr-gilag.

Look at those whelps—no glitter tags. They're from one of the cities."

Thrr-gilag felt his tail speed up a little more. Five of those repeater crossbows were now pointed directly at the two Zhirrzh. "Aren't they a little far from home?"

"A good hundred fifty thoustrides at least," she said. "Possibly farther."

The leader and two of the others were standing together, gazing at the Zhirrzh and muttering among themselves. "I thought they weren't allowed to travel long distances," Thrr-gilag said.

"They're not," Klnn-dawan-a said. "But most of the warriors who used to enforce those restrictions have been pulled off Gree."

She spoke in the Chigin language again. The three Chig paused in their discussion, the leader saying something in reply. Klnn-dawan-a spoke again, and for a hunbeat the conversation went back and forth. Then the Chig said something sharp sounding and turned his back on the Zhirrzh. The other two Chig followed suit, the three of them resuming their muttered conversation.

Thrr-gilag took a careful breath. "So what's going on?"

"You're not going to believe this," Klnn-dawan-a said. "Apparently, they're a war party."

Thrr-gilag craned his neck to look at her profile. "They're *what?*"

"A war party. Or maybe a justice party—they use the same word for both. He says they're here to punish the mountain people for collaborating with us."

Thrr-gilag looked at the five Chig guarding them. At the semiarmor, the metal crossbows, the slender crossbow bolts.

At the long, unusually slender feathering and tips on those bolts . . .

"No," he murmured to Klnn-dawan-a. "I don't think so. Look at the feathering on those crossbow bolts. They look to me just about the right size to slip through the mesh of a predator fence."

Klnn-dawan-a stiffened. "You're right," she breathed. "They must be going for our encampment. But that's crazy."

"I agree," Thrr-gilag said, looking carefully around. "But they must have good reasons. Or what they consider to be good reasons."

He frowned, suddenly aware of the stinger he still held loosely in his hand. The Chig hadn't disarmed them . . . and only slowly did it dawn on him that they probably didn't realize the stingers were weapons. Most likely they assumed the devices were hand recorders—the size and shape were just about right for that.

Which meant the Zhirrzh had an advantage their opponents didn't know about. The question was how to use it. If he could quietly bring the stinger up to firing position, then whip it quickly around . . .

He looked at their guards again, the surge of excitement fading into reality. No. Not unless he wanted to wind up at the family shrine and send Klnn-dawan-a to hers along with it. "What do you suppose they're waiting for?" he asked.

"I was wondering that myself," Klnn-dawan-a admitted. "They've got us; they've got the floater. I'd think they would want to get going before—"

She broke off. From somewhere nearby something gave a warbling yowl, the sound echoing across the mountains. The stray whelp, almost forgotten beside its pile of boulders, howled back in reply. "Uh-oh," Klnn-dawan-a muttered. "I think we're about to get some more company."

Thrr-gilag looked around. Two of the five Chig who'd

been guarding them were moving up beside the leader and his two friends, their crossbows pointed in the direction the yowl had come from. "More Chig?"

"More Chig. Keep quiet—this could get tricky."

Thrr-gilag had no time to wonder what she meant by that. Directly ahead, three Chig topped a small rise, a half-dozen whelps following along behind them.

"Grazing party," Klnn-dawan-a identified them. "I was right; the whelp had just gotten separated from them."

For a beat the newcomers paused as they caught sight of the group gathered together beside the creek. Then, hefting their own crossbows, they continued on down the hill.

They came to within three strides of the armored leader before stopping. *"Sk-(cough)-ssst-tssmss-(cough)-mts-os-mss,"* one of the newcomers said, gesturing toward the Zhirrzh with the slender tentacles edging his mouth. *"Sk-pss-mtss-hrss'mss-(cough)-kss."*

The leader of the war party answered in kind. One of the other newcomers spoke and was answered. "What are they saying?" Thrr-gilag whispered.

"I'm not entirely sure," Klnn-dawan-a answered. "They're talking much faster than I'm used to. But it sounds like the warriors want the grazing party to join them. The grazing party is refusing."

Thrr-gilag looked at the three Chig, an odd feeling of warmth rippling through him. "They're on our side?"

"Hardly," Klnn-dawan-a said shortly. "They just don't want to risk bringing reprisals down on themselves."

The warm feeling evaporated. "Oh."

"Don't take it personally," Klnn-dawan-a advised. "There aren't any Chig anywhere who really like us."

Typical bad losers, in other words. All the more contemptible given that they were the ones who'd started the war in the first place. "So why are they still talking?"

Klnn-dawan-a shrugged. "The war-party leader is still trying to talk the others into coming along. The others just want to get their whelp back and go home."

The conversation droned on. Thrr-gilag found himself studying the two different crossbow styles: the multishot repeaters carried by the war party, the much simpler two-shot models of the mountain Chig. If it came to a fight . . .

But it wouldn't. As Klnn-dawan-a said, none of the Chig liked the Zhirrzh. All they were talking here was varying degrees of hatred. "I wish they'd give it up," he muttered. "Let the grazing party go and get on with it."

"I know," Klnn-dawan-a agreed, her voice frowning. "It's almost as if they were stalling."

Abruptly, she stiffened. "Of course they're stalling," she said. "They're worried about the warships."

Thrr-gilag felt his midlight pupils narrow. Of course—the Zhirrzh encirclement forces. Five warships filled with the best high-power monitoring telescopes in existence. Orbiting slowly over the Gree landscape, watching everything that happened there. "Are any of them overhead right now?"

"I don't know," Klnn-dawan-a said. "I don't know the orbit pattern."

"I'll bet the war party does," Thrr-gilag said, thinking furiously. That must have been what the three Chig were discussing just before the grazing party showed up: whether or not they were in view. The last thing they would want at this point would be for the orbiting warriors to see them kidnap a pair of Zhirrzh. Or, worse, to see them raise those same Zhirrzh to Eldership.

And the fact that they were still talking would imply

the group was under at least one of those distant telescopes right now. . . .

Klnn-dawan-a must have sensed something from his posture. "What is it?" she asked, half turning to frown at him.

"Just thinking," Thrr-gilag muttered, glancing up at the occasional fish-scale clouds scattered across the otherwise clear sky. The Chig eye, if he remembered correctly, was supposed to be incapable of seeing the darklight laser frequencies that Zhirrzh stingers operated at. If he eased his stinger to point straight up and fired it . . .

"What are you thinking?" Klnn-dawan-a asked.

"About trying to call for help," Thrr-gilag told her. All right. The laser, he knew, would sizzle the water in the air as the beam passed through it, producing secondary radiations within the Chigin vision range as well as a certain amount of sound. But in bright sunlight, and with the wind blowing strongly off the mountains and across the stream toward them, there was a fair chance that both the light and the sound would go unnoticed. Particularly with the bulk of the Chig attention on the grazing party.

"Thrr-gilag, are you crazy?" Klnn-dawan-a hissed. "You want to make Elders out of both of us?"

"Quiet," he hissed back, not daring to look at the three Chig still guarding them. All right. He didn't remember very much of the flash-code he and Thrr-mezaz had memorized back when they were children, but every Zhirrzh knew the old three-two-three emergency signal. Carefully, trying not to let the movement show, he turned the stinger to point straight up between him and Klnn-dawan-a. Taking a deep breath, he keyed for full power and adjusted his thumbs on the triggers—

And with a crack of a supersonic shock wave, a Zhirrzh transport shot over the hilltops and blazed past overhead.

One of the Chig screeched, a high-pitched howl that dug like knives into Thrr-gilag's ear slits. An instant later he found himself sprawled on the ground, his legs having collapsed ignominiously beneath him. With one hand he was gripping Klnn-dawan-a's jumpsuit, dragging her bodily down beside him; with the other hand he still clutched his stinger. All around him the air was alive with the thunder of the transport, the sizzling of laser shots, the sharp multiple snap of crossbow threads. The Chig and their whelps were howling madly; and over all of it he could hear Klnn-dawan-a screaming something. Pulling her tightly against him, he fired his stinger, sweeping it blindly around them. There was a crack of stressed ceramic as the beam caught the side of the floater—a sudden stab of pain slashing across the side of his head—the stinger swinging randomly toward the ground as he flinched away from the pain—

And then a new roaring sound abruptly joined the pandemonium around them. A sizzling roar, followed instantly by a violent, blinding rush of dense steam.

Unexpectedly, certainly without planning on his part, the beam from his stinger had found the creek. Bracing himself, squeezing his eyes shut against the scalding cloud, Thrr-gilag kept firing.

The Chig were still howling, but the howl had taken on a note of desperation. Buffeted and burned by the wind-driven steam, their enemies effectively shrouded from view, they must have known they had lost. But still they fought, until all the howls had been silenced.

And Klnn-dawan-a's desperate, pleading scream was all that was left.

The battlefield, once Thrr-gilag was finally able to get a good look at it, was horrifying.

Dead Chig and whelps littered the ground, some with their limbs twisted at bizarre angles, all crisscrossed with the blackened lines of laser burns. A group of Zhirrzh moved back and forth across the carnage, going silently about the grim task of collecting the dead.

And at one edge of it stood Klnn-dawan-a. Her face as dead as those of the Chig.

She didn't look up as Thrr-gilag stepped over to her. "Hey," he said softly, touching her shoulder. "You all right?"

"They killed them all," she said, her voice as dead as her expression. "All of them. Even the grazing party."

Thrr-gilag nodded. "I know."

"The grazing party wasn't even doing anything," she said. "They weren't bothering anyone."

"I know," Thrr-gilag said again with a sigh. That wasn't how the transport's pilot and Director Prr-eddsi were going to report it, of course. That much he'd been able to figure out from the snatches of conversation he'd heard while the healer had patched up his head wound. Prr-eddsi was going to report it as a coordinated Chig attack, with a violent but necessary Zhirrzh response.

Thrr-gilag and Klnn-dawan-a knew better. Not that anyone was likely to listen. Or was likely to care.

"We're finished here," Klnn-dawan-a said, looking slowly across the bodies. "Our chrysalis studies, our whelp examinations—all of it. Gone, just like that. The Chig up here will never trust us or cooperate with us again."

"Maybe," Thrr-gilag agreed. "But if the warship hadn't spotted us when it did and sent the transport over, we'd be Elders by now. You think that would have left your relationship with the Chig in any better shape?"

"No," Klnn-dawan-a conceded. "Certainly not after the reprisals were finished with." She turned and looked at him, wincing as her gaze came to rest on his bandage. "I'm sorry, Thrr-gilag. I didn't even think to ask about your wound."

"Oh, it's all right," he assured her. "And I'm fine. A near miss by a crossbow bolt, they tell me."

"More near than miss," she said, a flicker of life coming back into her face as she touched the bandage with gentle fingers. "You sure you're all right?"

"I'm fine." He looked back at the transport. "I don't mean to be callous or anything, but I'm going to have to leave soon, and we still haven't got anywhere on our problem. You have any idea of what levers we can use against the Dhaa'rr leaders?"

Klnn-dawan-a took a deep breath, visibly extricating herself from her emotional tangle about the Chig slaughter. "I don't know," she said. "I can't think right now."

"I understand," Thrr-gilag said. "I can probably stay a little while longer."

"No, you'd better head back while you can," Klnn-dawan-a said, flicking her tongue in a negative. "We won't have any chance at all if you show up late at Unity City. I'll talk to my family and friends. See if we can come up with something."

"All right," Thrr-gilag said. "Just try to be careful which Elders you use as your pathway."

"Searcher Klnn-dawan-a?" a voice called.

Thrr-gilag turned to see the transport pilot standing at the top of the landing ramp. "Yes?" Klnn-dawan-a called.

"Call for you, Searcher," the pilot said. "Direct laser link from orbit."

Frowning, Thrr-gilag followed Klnn-dawan-a back to the transport and up the ramp. "Here she is," the pilot said, keying a switch on a small communications board just inside the hatchway and gesturing to it. "All yours, Searcher."

He moved a few strides away as Klnn-dawan-a stepped up to the board. "This is Searcher Klnn-dawan-a."

"Searcher, this is the third commander of the *Perseverance*," a voice said. "We've received a priority message from the Dhaa'rr Leadership Council indicating that you're to be brought immediately to Dharanv."

Klnn-dawan-a threw Thrr-gilag a startled look. "For what reason?"

"The message didn't specify," the third commander said. "You'll have one tentharc to make preparations, at which time the transport currently at your encampment will bring you to orbit. We'll leave for Dharanv as soon as you're aboard."

"Understood," Klnn-dawan-a said. "I'll be ready."

"Very good. *Perseverance* out."

There was a click, and the communication went quiet. "I'm coming with you," Thrr-gilag murmured.

"They may not be willing to take you along," Klnn-dawan-a murmured back.

"I don't care if they're willing or not," Thrr-gilag said firmly. "We go together, or we don't go at all. Anyone makes a stink about it, and I'll raise noise all the way up to the Overclan Prime."

"All right." Klnn-dawan-a squeezed his hand tightly. "I didn't really want to go alone, anyway."

The pilot stepped over to them. "I've been ordered to take you to orbit, Searcher," he said to Klnn-dawan-a. "If you'd like, I can take you back to the encampment right now, instead of waiting for the group outside to finish up. That would give you a little more time to pack."

"Thank you," Klnn-dawan-a said. "You'll have room for Thrr-gilag, too, won't you?"

The pilot looked at Thrr-gilag, a hint of uncertainty crossing his face. He was Dhaa'rr, and the word had come down from above; and all at once, it seemed, the easy informality that had let him juggle his schedule so that he could give Thrr-gilag a lift was gone.

But only for a beat. "Sure, no problem," he assured them. "Go ahead forward and get strapped in. I'll go tell Director Prr-eddsi what we're doing, and then we'll be off."

Great, Thrr-gilag thought to himself as he and Klnn-dawan-a made their way toward the front of the transport. Off to face the Dhaa'rr leaders and Elders. All of them looking for a rock-hard reason to nullify his bond-engagement to Klnn-dawan-a. Like a group of crazed Chig whelps, waiting for their prey to make a fatal mistake . . .

He frowned suddenly. Chig whelps. Dangerous in packs; safer and less violent as individuals.

Just like Humans?

"What is it?" Klnn-dawan-a asked.

"I don't know," Thrr-gilag said slowly. "Maybe nothing. Or maybe I've just found the key to the Humans' behavior."

"Really? What is it?"

Thrr-gilag flicked his tongue in a negative. "Let me think about it a little longer. Can you get copies of all your studies?"

"I've already got them," Klnn-dawan-a said. "They're back at the encampment."

"Bring them along," Thrr-gilag told her. "Especially anything having to do with biochemical behavior triggers in Chig whelps."

But that wouldn't be enough, he knew. It might give them an idea of the direction to look in, but it wouldn't prove anything. The only proof would be if he could find similar behavior triggers in the Humans' biochemistry.

And for that they'd need to get hold of another Human.

"I don't like that look," Klnn-dawan-a said into his thoughts. "It worries me."

"It's all right," Thrr-gilag said, grimacing as he patted her hand. "I'm just thinking about how I'm going to ask my brother for a favor."

"A big favor?"

Thrr-gilag sighed. "You wouldn't believe it if I told you."

13

"Overclan Prime?" the Eighteenth said, his voice seeming to come out of nothingness in the darkened room. "The Speaker for Dhaa'rr is on his way."

"Thank you," the Prime said, laying his stylus down beside the gently glowing reader monitor and swiveling his chair to face the door of his private chambers. "Was he seen?"

"Not since he left the Speakers' office building," the Eighteenth said. "I don't think he's seen us, either."

"Make sure you keep it that way," the Prime warned him. "Especially here. Everyone who knows about this room and its secrets is also under the impression that no Elders at all are positioned to reach it."

"We won't be seen," the Eighteenth assured him. "Good luck."

The Prime took a deep breath, settling his thoughts. A

few beats later there was a quiet knock at the door. "Come," the Prime called.

The door swung open to reveal a dark figure, silhouetted against the brighter corridor light behind it. "You wished to see me, Overclan Prime?" Speaker Cvv-panav said.

"Yes, Speaker," the Prime said. "Please; sit down."

Cvv-panav moved inside, closing the door behind him. "Your lighting seems to have failed," he commented dryly as he stepped into the circle of pale light from the reader monitor and sat down on the visitor couch. "Careless of the maintainers."

"I find darkness to be conducive to thought," the Prime said. "Tell me, have you heard the news from Gree?"

"What news would that be?" Cvv-panav asked evenly.

"News about Searcher Thrr-gilag; Kee'rr," the Prime said. "Bond-engaged to a daughter of the Dhaa'rr. I understand there was an incident a few tentharcs ago that has certain members of your clan speaking rather highly of him. Something about quick thinking under pressure."

"Utter nonsense," Cvv-panav spat. "And you know it as well as I do. I doubt Thrr-gilag had any intention whatsoever of hitting that creek with his stinger beam. If he was aiming at anything—and I doubt even that—it was at one of the Chig. What happened out there was pure good luck, nothing more."

The Prime shrugged. "Perhaps. Still, he *did* hit the water; and all who were there agree that the cloud of steam was a significant factor in a quick Zhirrzh victory. I've seen the sort of crossbow bolts the Chig use—a few properly positioned shots could easily have taken out something as lightly armored as a shipping transport. Two of their four laser cannon had already been disabled, in fact, when Thrr-gilag made his move. And, of course, he also pulled Klnn-dawan-a down out of danger. All in all, a reasonably impressive display. Particularly for one not trained as a warrior."

"If you asked me here to rub my tongue in Kee'rr triumphs, Overclan Prime, then I would ask permission to be excused," Cvv-panav growled. "If instead you have a point to make, kindly make it. It's very late, and my time is valuable."

"My point is quite simple, Speaker," the Prime said. "Whatever the contributions of good luck or accident, the fact is that Thrr-gilag has come out of this incident with considerably more personal prestige than he had going in. Particularly among those Dhaa'rr who were facing into the Chig crossbows. It occurs to me that the last thing you might want right now is for a member of the Thrr family to have his reputation enhanced."

For a long beat Cvv-panav was silent, his expression unreadable. "Interesting conjecture," he said at last. "Have you a suggestion to go along with it?"

"A suggestion and an offer both," the Prime said. "I submit that what you really want right now is an excuse to call of the bond-engagement of Thrr-gilag to Klnn-dawan-a. How would you like to obtain evidence that Thrr-gilag's mother is both insane and criminal?"

Cvv-panav straightened slightly on his couch. "Is she?"

"No, not really," the Prime said. "But I believe that such an illusion can be created. She has in fact taken the first steps for us: she has apparently decided that she doesn't wish to accept Eldership."

"I see," Cvv-panav said. "That would be the insanity part, I presume. What about the criminal part?"

"That will stem from her hiring someone to steal her

fss organ from her family shrine," the Prime said. "Stolen so that she may destroy it."

"Really," Cvv-panav said. "And how would she go about finding someone willing to do this for her?"

"Obviously, she would have no idea how to do so." The Prime smiled tightly. "Which is why the Dhaa'rr will offer her their services."

Cvv-panav's eyes flicked around the room, as if reassuring himself that this room and conversation were completely private. "If this is some sort of joke, it's in extremely poor taste," he said calmly. "The Dhaa'rr do not rob shrines. Not for Kee'rr or anyone else."

"Oh, she wouldn't know they were Dhaa'rr," the Prime assured him. "She wouldn't know anything about them at all. Not even that they were robbers for hire."

"Then why bring the Dhaa'rr into it? Why not stage the entire deception yourself?"

"Because there's no one in the Overclan capable of handling such a delicate operation," the Prime told him. "At least none whom I could implicitly trust. Certainly none who could quietly vanish afterward to, say, the wilds of Dharanv without anyone noticing. Without evidence and with no one around she can identify, no one will believe Thrr-pifix-a's story."

There was another beat of silence. "It's still nothing more than a tasteless joke," Cvv-panav said. "But I'll allow myself to be amused. Tell me more."

"Again, it's quite simple," the Prime said. "You'll send two or three of your people to Thrr-pifix-a's home near Reeds Village. People close to you, of course, whom you can implicitly trust. They'll represent themselves as members of some fictitious organization that advocates Eldership as a private and personal choice, and will offer to retrieve her *fss* from the shrine and bring it to her. They will do so; and as soon as they've left her, warriors under Overclan authority will move in, recovering the *fsss* and charging her with grand-first theft."

"Risky," Cvv-panav grunted. "Even without any substantiation, there would be some at a public hearing who would wonder about her story."

"Which is why there won't be any hearing," the Prime nodded. "The warriors will move in quickly enough to prevent any damage to her *fsss,* circumventing the most serious charges. After that—" He gestured vaguely. "I thought that as a compassionate gesture you might be willing to use your influence with the Overclan to arrange for the charges to be quietly dropped."

"In exchange for an equally quiet cancellation of the bond-engagement?"

"Exactly."

"Interesting," Cvv-panav murmured, stroking the side of his face thoughtfully. "You spoke of an offer."

"Obviously, you'd want no witnesses to this transaction," the Prime said. "Thrr-pifix-a lives alone, and in an isolated area, but of course one must always consider the Elders. Fortunately, there's only one shrine—that of the Frr family—whose Elders have access to the region around Thrr-pifix-a's house. On the chosen latearc I'll have one of my chief subordinates moderate an open debate on some issue of vital interest to the Elders—a possible increase in the number of cutting pyramids, perhaps, or some news about job opportunities. The debate will be held in Kee'rr territory, within easy range of both the Frr and Thrr shrines. That should guarantee your privacy at both the theft and delivery ends of the operation."

"Perhaps." Cvv-panav eyed him. "An interesting suggestion, Overclan Prime, and an even more interesting offer. It's clear what the Dhaa'rr would gain. Now tell me what the Overclan would gain."

The Prime shrugged. Here came the tricky part: convincing Cvv-panav that all this by itself was enough of a reason for him to get involved. "The Overclan would gain in two ways," he said. "First, it would neutralize Thrrpifix-a and her dangerous ideas before they have a chance to spread. That's the overwhelming reason I want her discredited, and as quickly as possible."

"I doubt anyone's going to pay much attention to her," Cvv-panav sniffed. "Certainly not in the middle of a war."

"On the contrary: the middle of a war is precisely when such ideas find their widest audience," the Prime countered. "With the public watching dozens of young warriors being raised to Eldership every fullarc—and watching all of them suffer the lengthy disorientation of long-distance anchoring shock—some are bound to call into question the basic relevance and usefulness of Eldership. The last thing we can afford is to have the focal point of a simple, reasonable old female asking for the right to decline Eldership on her own."

"Perhaps," Cvv-panav said. "It still seems unlikely to me."

"Trust me: there are numerous historical precedents," the Prime told him. "I won't go into details. And second, I would consider my assistance on this as the purchase price for enhanced Dhaa'rr cooperation with our campaign against the Human-Conquerors."

Cvv-panav's face darkened. "You accuse the Dhaa'rr of working crossways to the Zhirrzh war effort?"

"Not exactly crossways," the Prime said. "But you have your own interests; and they do not always mesh with mine. Or with those of the Zhirrzh people as a whole."

Cvv-panav smiled. "You're still upset about my insistence that the Dhaa'rr be represented on the upcoming Mrachani mission, aren't you?"

"To be honest, yes," the Prime said, allowing a touch of annoyance to creep into his voice. "That was against all standard protocol, and we both know it. There are also your various political machinations over at Warrior Command as you try to slice through established warrior authority structures to suit yourself and the Dhaa'rr. Totally unacceptable at any time; potentially disastrous in time of war. Plus there's your continuing pressure on the Overclan to grant you—and you alone—restricted information on warrior operations."

"Some of which should not be nearly as restricted as you seem to think," Cvv-panav said pointedly.

"You're entitled to your opinion," the Prime said. "Such decisions will nevertheless remain with Warrior Command and me. And I would expect you to accept that authority as part of this bargain."

Cvv-panav stroked the side of his head again. "I don't know, Overclan Prime. You ask a great deal in return for the cancelation of a single distasteful bond-engagement."

"Perhaps," the Prime said. "I suppose you'll just have to decide how distasteful the bond-engagement really is. And how distasteful it would be for the rest of the Dhaa'rr leaders and Elders."

A hint of a wince crossed the other's face. Small, brief, but unmistakable . . . and in that flicker of emotion the Prime knew he'd won. Even Speaker Cvv-panav, ostensibly the most powerful member of the Dhaa'rr clan, could not escape the pressure and influence of his own Elders. Elders who were in many cases as anchored to their own long-past eras and customs as they were to their family shrines. "You drive a hard bargain, Overclan Prime," the

Speaker said. "I'll agree to this much: I'll suspend my efforts to have competent warrior commanders replaced by Dhaa'rr subordinates, and I'll furthermore stop demanding full briefings on restricted war information. Will that be sufficient?"

"I think so, yes," the Prime said. "Let me know when you'll be ready to move."

"I can let you know right now," Cvv-panav said. "It'll be in two fullarcs."

"Really," the Prime said, somewhat taken aback. "So soon?"

"You're the one who said this should be done as quickly as possible," Cvv-panav reminded him. "I have people on hand right here who can handle my part of the operation and then disappear for a while." He smiled slyly. "Unless, of course, you're going to have trouble setting up your open Elder debate so quickly."

The Prime smiled back. "Hardly. I'll have the announcement made within the tentharc."

"Good," Cvv-panav said, nodding politely as he stood up. "Two fullarcs from now, then."

"I'll look forward to hearing how it went."

"I'll be sure to give you a proper briefing," Cvv-panav said dryly as he stepped to the door. "Good latearc, Overclan Prime."

"Good latearc, Speaker Cvv-panav."

The Speaker left, closing the door behind him, and for a few beats the room was silent. "An interesting character," the Eighteenth's voice commented into the darkness.

"*Interesting* is hardly the word I'd use," the Prime growled, glaring at the closed door.

"Arrogant, perhaps?" the Twenty-fifth suggested. "Or slippery?"

"Much closer," the Prime agreed. "You notice how he

appeared to accept both of my conditions without actually giving in on either of them?"

"Certainly," the Eighteenth said. "Only competent warrior commanders are henceforth immune from his politics. With their competence being defined by him, of course."

"And no more demands for full briefings means he can still clamor for private briefings," the Eleventh put in.

"Or simply ignore the Overclan briefing process entirely and concentrate his investigations at Warrior Command," the Seventh added.

"That won't gain him anything," the Twenty-eighth rumbled. "Warrior Command knows as well as we do what releasing knowledge about the CIRCE weapon could do to Zhirrzh society."

"Yet they also know we can't keep it under cover forever," the Fourth said quietly. "Eventually, the truth will leak out."

"But not until we've fought the Human-Conquerors to an impasse," the Prime said firmly, cutting off the impending debate. "We need only control access to any one of the CIRCE elements to make the weapon useless to them."

"The trick being to know when we've done that," the Twenty-second muttered. "Otherwise, we risk spreading our resources so thin that they're all but useless."

"We can do only what we can," the Eighteenth said philosophically. "At any rate, this should at least eliminate the added distraction posed by Speaker Cvv-panav and his inconvenient curiosity. You can be ready in two fullarcs, Overclan Prime?"

"Easily," the Prime assured him. "The debate is already planned. All I need to do is announce the time and place.

And I've already spoken to my warriors about the other part of it."

"Good," the Eighteenth said. "Then we have nothing to do except wait."

"Yes," the Twenty-second said darkly. "And hope that the Human-Conquerors will be as easy to deal with as Speaker Cvv-panav."

14 The cliff face loomed above them, stark and blank and dirty-gray in the blazing sunlight. And a good thirty strides straight up. "I don't know, Commander," Warrior First Vstii-suuv said, shading his eyes as he looked up at the cliff. "Looks a bit tricky."

"Not to mention pretty exposed," Warrior Third Qlaa-nuur added.

"It is both of those," Thrr-mezaz agreed, gazing up at the cliff. "All in all, I'd prefer a more reasonable route myself. The question is, is one available?"

"One that doesn't expose us to direct view from the Human-Conqueror sentry positions?" Vstii-suuv asked.

"Yes."

Vstii-suuv looked up at the cliff again, measuring it with his eyes. Thrr-mezaz watched him, wondering if he should just give up on this and get the three of them back to the village. He'd persuaded Supreme Ship Commander Dkll-kumvit to authorize this little trip up the mountain by calling it a dry run; but unless and until he could get another *fsss* cutting from either Warrior Command or the Prr family, this wasn't much more than a refresher course in rock climbing.

Still, right now none of them had much else to do. Between their own village encampment and the Human-Conqueror mountain stronghold, the war on Dorcas had settled into a basic halkling-nornin standoff. The Zhirrzh might as well try being the halkling half of the game for a change.

"Well, if it's a choice between climbing here or being shot at by Human-Conqueror sentries, I guess I'd go for the climb," Vstii-suuv decided, shrugging the coil of rope off his shoulder.

"Of course, once we're above the tree line, we can have both at once," Qlaa-nuur muttered.

"If the Human-Conquerors spot us, these trees aren't going to provide a lot of cover anyway," Thrr-mezaz pointed out. "Let's get to it."

"Right," Vstii-suuv said, handing Thrr-mezaz the coil of rope and checking to make sure it was secured to his climbing harness. "I'll take lead; Qlaa-nuur, you're on anchor. Let's go."

He stepped to the cliff face, dug fingers and toe-boots into small crevices, and started nimbly up. Thrr-mezaz played the rope out behind him, waiting for his own turn to start climbing and wondering for the thousandth time what in the eighteen worlds he was doing out here. Yes, he was one of exactly three Zhirrzh in the Dorcas expeditionary force who had done any rock climbing at all; and yes, the first rule of mountaineering was that three climbers was the absolute minimum for any halfway safe climb.

But his limited recreational climbing hardly put him in the same class with these two members of the Aree'rr clan, who'd practically grown up scaling mountains. Inevitably, he was going to slow them down . . . and here, in the shadow of Human-Conqueror weapons, that kind of handicap could easily wind up raising all three of them to Eldership.

And he didn't want to become an Elder. Not yet. There were still too many things he wanted to do, places he wanted to see, experiences that would require his physical self to fully and properly appreciate. Sometime in the vague and distant future, certainly, he would be ready for that stage of life. But not now. Not yet. If he had any sense, he would abort this and head back to the relative safety of the village.

"All right," Qlaa-nuur said. "Go ahead, Commander."

"Right." Snapping Vstii-suuv's rope into the friction grab rings on his harness, Thrr-mezaz took a deep breath and started up the cliff face.

It wasn't as slow going as he had feared. Vstii-suuv had been liberal with his expansion pitons, scattering them around within easy climbing distance of each other. Three strides up, Thrr-mezaz came on one in crumbling rock that was already loosening; pulling a replacement from his harness, he slid its slender tip into a nearby crack and sliced through the protective cover with the edge of his tongue. There was a gentle hiss as the foamed-ceramic interior of the tip, exposed to air, began to swell up inside the crack, filling the empty space as it hardened. A few beats later, with the piton now a virtual extension of the rock, he locked in the rope and continued on.

"Certainly a change from the encampment, anyway," Qlaa-nuur commented from just beneath him.

Thrr-mezaz looked down. Predictably, the more experienced Aree'rr had caught up with him. "Almost like a vacation," he agreed, turning back around and concentrating on his climbing, reminding himself not to be pressured into rushing this.

Qlaa-nuur was obviously of the same opinion. "Careful and steady, Commander," he warned. "We're not in any particular hurry here."

"Right," Thrr-mezaz said. "You two are very good at this."

"Lots and lots of practice," Qlaa-nuur said. "In my case, much of it against my parents' wishes."

Thrr-mezaz stopped to set another expansion piton, wondering what sorts of things like this he and Thrr-gilag might have done as children to drive their parents crazy. Offhand, he couldn't think of any. "Well, according to the orbital terrain maps, this cliff is the last real challenge between here and the top," he reminded Qlaa-nuur. "And once we get to the other side of this ridge, we should be within four thoustrides of the edge of the Human-Conquerors' stronghold. A good place to put a ten-thoustride cutting, assuming we can get Warrior Command to send us one."

"Or maybe a little something from Prr't-zevisti's *fsss*," Vstii-suuv muttered.

"What was that?" Thrr-mezaz asked, looking up at him.

"Nothing, Commander. Watch out—the rock right here is a little crumbly."

"Understood," Thrr-mezaz murmured, stifling a sigh. Two and a half fullarcs now after presenting his request to the Prr family recorder, the story had gotten out to the entire Dorcas ground force. Most of them, like the Elder who'd carried the initial message, were thoroughly scandalized at the very idea of his asking for a cutting from an

Elder presumed dead, especially an Elder from a different clan. Some, like Vstii-suuv, were offended enough to hint at it to his face.

It was just as well, he reflected, that Klnn-vavgi had kept the second part of that latearc idea to himself. If his warriors knew that he'd suggested putting a *fsss* cutting out in the wilds without a shrine or pyramid around it, he'd probably wind up with an open mutiny.

"Commander?" Qlaa-nuur's voice was very quiet.

"Yes?" Thrr-mezaz said, looking down at him again.

Qlaa-nuur was gazing to the side, away from the cliff. "We've got company."

A sinking feeling in his throat, Thrr-mezaz turned to look. Knowing all too well what he would see.

And he was right. Hovering there on its jet stream, its beak and weapons turned pointedly to face them, was a Human-Conqueror aircraft.

"Hold it up, Vstii-suuv," Thrr-mezaz called softly to the lead, his eyes on the aircraft, the sinking feeling turning into a dark and hopeless certainty. Halfway up a cliff face, pinned there by ropes and pitons and a twenty-stride sheer drop to the ground below, their position was about as devoid of options as it could be. A single salvo with those lethal projectile weapons, and all three Zhirrzh would be back at their respective family shrines.

A soft curse floated down from above: Vstii-suuv, becoming suddenly aware of the situation. "What now, Commander?" he asked. "Should we try to get in the first shot?"

"Not much chance of that," Thrr-mezaz said, keeping his own voice quiet. Though what good silence and stealth were going to do them right then he couldn't imagine. "We're right in his sights—he could cut us to worm food before we could even begin to get our weapons unslung."

"What do you suppose he's waiting for?" Qlaa-nuur muttered from beneath him.

"Checking to see if there are more of us around, maybe," Thrr-mezaz said. "Or trying to locate our transport. Or just keeping us pinned here until the ground warriors arrive."

Vstii-suuv swore again. "I'm not going to be a Human-Conqueror prisoner, Commander. I'd rather go to my shrine right now."

"Let's not do anything drastic just yet," Thrr-mezaz advised him, leaning his head back and trying to gauge the distance remaining to the top of the cliff face. If he and Qlaa-nuur could somehow distract the Human-Conquerors long enough for Vstii-suuv to make a quick surge for the top . . .

But no. Not a chance. There were still ten strides yet to cover, all of it too steep for anything but a cautious advance. A single misstep along the way—

He frowned. For a pair of beats he thought he'd seen something up there. A flicker of movement, up among the shadows of the trees atop the cliff. Something that might have been a trick of the light, or a glimpse of Human-Conqueror ground warriors.

Or a Zhirrzh Elder.

"Commander?" Qlaa-nuur asked. "What are we going to do?"

For another few beats Thrr-mezaz continued to gaze at the top of the cliff. But whatever he'd seen up there didn't return. If it had been real in the first place. "We're going to start down," he told the others. "Slow and easy, not reaching for any weapons, nothing that looks like a threat. Vstii-suuv, you'll pop the rope free from the upper pitons as you pass them. We'll go about ten strides down; and then, about ten strides up from the bottom, we're all going to let go and do a flat-out drop. With good luck that may take them by surprise. Any questions?"

The question was obvious, too obvious for either of the other two to bring it up. The friction grabs built into expansion piton rings were designed precisely for the purpose of protecting climbers by slowing down dangerous falls of that sort. But it was fairly certain that the pitons' designers hadn't assumed that three climbers would all be falling at the same time. If they overstressed the grabs too far, there was a fair chance the Human-Conquerors would be able to just leisurely stroll up and cart them off on stretchers.

But under the circumstances it was the best chance they had. And all of them knew it. "All right, then," Thrr-mezaz said, taking a careful breath. "Nothing to be gained by waiting. Let's get to it."

The door to the metal room swung open, clanging dully against its stop. Hovering in his corner, Prr't-zevisti eased up to the edge of the lightworld to see what was happening.

The Human female Doctor-Cavan-a had returned. Back to do more experiments on his *fss* cutting.

"Terrific," he muttered to himself. Doctor-Cavan-a had spent a good two tentharcs in here last fullarc, taking samples here and digging with metal probes there; never really hurting him but never very far from that threshold, either. And always with those low-level Elderdeath emissions in the background, just to keep him distracted and annoyed.

And now she was back. To do more cutting and digging and probing? Or had they finally decided to go all-out with the Elderdeath weapons? It occurred to him that they might have deliberately let him run loose in here, allowing him to learn their language in preparation for a proper and almost certainly painful interrogation. . . .

He frowned, his apprehensions coming to a puzzled stop. Doctor-Cavan-a wasn't moving over to her laboratory worktable. Nor was she going to any of the shelves for equipment or supplies, nor was she looking outside as if waiting for someone else to come in behind her. She was just standing there in the doorway, looking around the room.

Cautiously, dropping back to the darkness of the grayworld, Prr't-zevisti left his corner and eased to the door beside her, coming back to the edge of the lightworld to take a look. A handful of other Humans were in sight outside, but none of them seemed to be heading toward the metal room.

He looked back at Doctor-Cavan-a, wondering if she had simply paused for thought or meditation before beginning her work. But she was still standing in the doorway looking around the room. Steadily, methodically, as if searching for something.

Or for someone.

Prr't-zevisti felt a chill run through him. He'd been right. They did indeed know he was in here.

But then why was she searching for him with the door open? Daring him to leave, with perhaps some sort of trap waiting for him?

Prr't-zevisti grimaced. Fine; he was game. He was getting tired of the metal room, anyway. Carefully, trying to look every direction at once, he headed out along his anchorline. Some of the equipment piles in the cave area outside had disappeared since his last time out there, but aside from that he couldn't see much change. Bright sunlight poured in from outside the rock overhang, throwing brilliant glints from some of the metal devices near the edge.

So far, no traps. Looking back once to assure himself that Doctor-Cavan-a wasn't in the process of closing the door, he headed out into the light. Across the deep cut directly below the cave he went, through the tops of the trees growing on the opposite side, across another gap to the top of another ridge—this the one with a sheer cliff face on the other side of it—a few strides farther on to the end of his anchorline, back again toward the cliff—

And jolted to an abrupt stop, a rush of shock rippling through him. There, working their way up the cliff face, were three Zhirrzh warriors. Among them, Commander Thrr-mezaz himself.

And approaching stealthily from around the far side of one of the hills, still out of the warriors' sight, was a Human aircraft.

"Look out!" Prr't-zevisti shouted as loudly as he could. "Commander Thrr-mezaz, Zhirrzh warriors—look out!"

It was no use. The warriors were a good twelve strides down from him, much too far away to hear an Elder's faint voice over the restless mountain winds. Prr't-zevisti dropped toward them, knowing that the effort would be futile. He was right: he got barely a stride before bumping up sharply against the shadow created by the underside of the distant metal room. "Look out!" he shouted again, all but screaming now. But still they continued on, making their laborious way up the cliff—

"Well?"

Prr't-zevisti was shooting back along his anchorline almost before the quiet Human word had had a chance to register. That voice had spoken near his *fsss* cutting; and if Doctor-Cavan-a was about to close the door, it would be his death unless he immediately got back inside. He crossed the hills—darted back beneath the mountain overhang—noted almost without conscious thought as he passed that the door was still wide-open—and came to a halt back in the relative safety of the metal room.

Directly in front of Doctor-Cavan-a and another Human. Both of whom were looking straight at him.

Prr't-zevisti was deep in the grayworld in an instant. But too late. "There!" Doctor-Cavan-a's voice said, faint and distant. "Did you see it?"

"Yes," the other Human voice said. "Very (something) indeed."

Prr't-zevisti moved over to his preferred corner of the metal room, cursing himself for his carelessness. He was in for it now, all right. Whether Doctor-Cavan-a had ever known for sure that he was there, she definitely knew now. And unlike the last time he'd been seen by the Humans, this time they had him well and properly trapped. He eased back to the edge of the light-world. . . .

To find both Humans again gazing right at him. "You —Zhirrzh—at the other end," the other Human said, pointing a hand at him. "Can you hear me?"

Prr't-zevisti dropped back into the grayworld, cursing his carelessness and stupidity. "It's gone again," Doctor-Cavan-a's voice came via his *fsss* cutting.

"Maybe," the other Human said. "Maybe not. Zhirrzh, this is (something) (something) (something), commander of the Human (something) forces. I wish to speak to your commander."

My commander's climbing a cliff into your ambush, Prr't-zevisti thought bitterly, hugging the illusory safety of the grayworld and hating his vulnerability. And his helplessness.

"I don't understand, (something)," Doctor-Cavan-a's voice murmured. "If this is the end of a (something), why can't they hear?"

"I'm sure they (something) can," the Human commander said. "They just aren't answer (something). Keep an eye out—I'm go (something) to check with the (something)."

There was the sound of a footstep on metal. Prr't-zevisti found a different corner and eased back to the edge of the lightworld. The Human commander was walking toward the door, probably intending to close it.

And suddenly Prr't-zevisti snapped out of his frozen paralysis. There were Human forces closing in on Zhirrzh warriors out there, and he had to make one final effort to warn them. Darting past the Humans and out of the room, he shot back to the cliff.

The Zhirrzh were still there, but they were no longer climbing. They were hanging from the cliff face by their ropes, looking at the aircraft now hovering in full view in front of them.

Prr't-zevisti cursed again, a fresh sense of helplessness flooding through him. Surely there was something he could have done. Something he still could do. He looked around desperately, trying to come up with an idea. Trees, soil, the cliff face itself—

But nothing. Nothing that an Elder could touch. Nothing that an Elder could do.

And then there was an irresistible nudge at his side. The door to the metal room, being swung closed against his anchorline.

He was back in an instant, trembling with the reaction of too many shocks and emotions piled too quickly on top of each other. Doctor-Cavan-a was still there, her eyes searching for him, as he dropped into the grayworld.

A muffled clank penetrated into the darkness from his *fsss* cutting: the door, slamming shut. Prr't-zevisti stayed where he was, aching with the image and memory of those three young Zhirrzh out there facing sudden Eldership. For a hunbeat nothing happened. Then, with another clank, he heard the door open and shut again. "They're start(something) down," the voice of the Human commander said. "Probably go (something) to make it before the (something) team gets to them."

"What are you go(something) to do?" Doctor-Cavan-a asked.

"Unless they keep come(something), I'm go(something) to let them go," the Human commander said. His voice, Prr't-zevisti noted, was growing louder, as if he were moving closer to the *fsss* cutting. "I'd like to find out what they want (something) here. (Something), we (something) them to try it again."

"You don't think it was just (something)?" Doctor-Cavan-a said.

There was a gentle click: the lid of the box holding his *fsss* cutting being opened. "No," the Human commander said, so close now that Prr't-zevisti could feel the puffs of warm air from his breath. "No, I think it had some(something) to do with this thing. Try (something) to position themselves where they could (something) with it, perhaps."

"The (something) idea?"

"Why not? All we really know about their tech (something) is that it's (something) different from ours."

"But here in the (something) (something)? I thought it block (something) all (something)."

"(Something), yes. Maybe that's why the others out there were climb(something). Try (something) to get into range." The commander exhaled loudly, his breath tickling uncomfortably across the *fsss* cutting. "This is the key, Doctor-Cavan-a. Right here. I know it is. You any closer to figure (something) out what it is?"

"It's (something) (something)," Doctor-Cavan-a said. "That much I know for sure. It's also (something) with (something) and (something). But the really interest (something) part, at least from a (something) point of view, is that the hard (something) is hard only on the outside. The rest of it is soft and even somewhat (something) active."

"What do you mean, (something) active?" the commander asked. "It's dead. How can it be (something) active?"

"I haven't the (something) idea," Doctor-Cavan-a said. "But here's the other interest(something) part of it. When you take a new sample, the outer (something) slowly hard (something) up again. It must be trigger (something) by (something) to air."

"But then we're not talk (something) any kind of ordinary (something)," the commander said. "This is a more active (something)."

"Right," Doctor-Cavan-a said. "Though what sort of (something) could do that, I don't know."

"And (something) active in the (something)," the commander murmured. "Interest (something). Very interest (something)."

He stopped talking, and for a few beats there was nothing but the sound and feel of his breath on Prr't-zevisti's *fsss* cutting. "Well, keep at it," he said at last, his breath and voice turning away. "At the (something), it's about all we have to go on."

"I know," Doctor-Cavan-a agreed. "I'll get back to work right away."

"I (something) you wait a few (something) first," the

commander said, his voice accompanied by the sound of the metal door opening. "If the Zhirrzh out there decide to (something), we may have other (something) work for you."

He left, closing the door behind him. Carefully, choosing a different corner this time, Prr't-zevisti eased back to the edge of the lightworld.

Doctor-Cavan-a was standing beside the shelves, gazing down at the *fsss* cutting in its box. "What are you for?" she asked softly. "Why do the Zhirrzh take you out of their (something)?"

For a pair of beats Prr't-zevisti was almost tempted to answer her. They had him trapped, and at this point they surely knew that. There really wasn't a lot to be gained by skulking around pretending he wasn't there.

But he stayed quiet. His long-past warrior training, perhaps, and those dire warnings about the dangers of voluntary communication and cooperation with the enemy. Or maybe it was just the irrational hope that they didn't really *know* he was trapped there.

Because once they knew they had him trapped, there would be no reason for them not to start a serious interrogation. Accompanied by their Elderdeath weapons.

Doctor-Cavan-a picked up the box and moved it to the worktable. Prr't-zevisti watched her, wincing with the always unpleasant anticipation of the unknown. He'd never felt a real Elderdeath weapon, but the histories were very clear about the catastrophic effects their use had had on Zhirrzh culture. The first—and last—Elderdeath weapons had been created by the Svrr family of the Flii'rr clan at the height of the Second Eldership War eight hundred cyclics ago. All sides of the war had called on the Svrr to halt their use of the weapons, which had only a minor dizzying effect on warriors but which could be lethal to

Elders and children. But the Svrr had refused. Ultimately, when the war was over, that refusal had cost the family its existence.

The Zhirrzh had never used the weapons again. But every alien race they came upon had done so: deliberately, viciously, and without a twinge of conscience. Every race, from the Chig to the Isintorxi and now to the Humans.

A twinge make him jerk. Doctor-Cavan-a, taking yet another sample from his *fsss* cutting. But that would end soon enough. Eventually, he knew, she would get tired of these preliminaries.

And then the real interrogation would begin. Prr't-zevisti could only hope he would find death before he betrayed his people.

They'd all made it down to the ten-stride height Thrr-mezaz had specified without the Human-Conquerors making any move. And it was time for the Zhirrzh to make theirs.

"All right," Thrr-mezaz said, glancing down at the tree- and rock-littered terrain below them. "Here we go. Vstii-suuv, you'll go first, pulling Qlaa-nuur and me down along behind you. If the Human-Conquerors think the fall was accidental, it might gain us a few extra beats. Take it whenever you're ready, and try not to hit us too hard on your way down."

"Right," Vstii-suuv said. "Here goes."

There was a sudden flurry above him, a brief shower of broken stone; and then Vstii-suuv shot past, one foot caroming off Thrr-mezaz's left shoulder along the way. The rope snapped tight at Thrr-mezaz's harness, yanking him away from the cliff face. He managed to miss Qlaa-nuur as he fell—bounced painfully against the cliff with the same sore shoulder—twisted half over as he clawed at the rock to try to get himself vertical—

And then one foot hit the ground, and he was fighting a losing battle for balance. He dropped to one knee, falling over on his side and rolling awkwardly back again to his knees. "Report," he snapped, fumbling for the rope and release rings with one hand as he unslung his laser rifle with the other.

"I'm all right, Commander," Vstii-suuv said, breathing heavily. "Just a little winded."

"Same here," Qlaa-nuur said. "Those friction grabs work better than I thought."

"Good," Thrr-mezaz said, getting up into a crouch and looking around. Still no ground warriors in sight, though in a wooded area like this that didn't mean much. Now, if the Zhirrzh could just get in the first shot against the Human-Conqueror aircraft before it swooped around the trees for a clear shot and shredded all three of them. He looked up into the sky—

To find that the aircraft hadn't moved.

Thrr-mezaz frowned up at it. It was still right there, bits of it visible through the trees. Still hovering in the same spot. Not making any attempt at all to attack.

"Commander?" Vstii-suuv hissed urgently. "Shall we take it down?"

Thrr-mezaz looked around them again. No ground warriors; no further air support that he could see; the one aircraft on the scene inexplicably not moving to attack position. It was as if—

As if the Human-Conqueror commander was letting them go.

He took a deep breath. "Hold your fire," he told the two warriors. "Keep your weapons ready, but I don't think we're going to need them. They're letting us go."

"Letting us go?" Qlaa-nuur echoed, looking around. "I don't believe it."

"No, they just haven't reacted yet," Vstii-suuv agreed tightly. "This is our one chance, Commander. I strongly recommend we take it."

Thrr-mezaz looked back up at the aircraft, an eerie feeling pricking at the base of his tongue. The Human-Conqueror commander was letting them go. Just as he himself had allowed that Human-Conqueror ground-warrior team to escape four fullarcs ago north of the village.

"Hold your fire," he told the others. "That's an order." He took one last look around and started down the steep slope. "Come on, let's get back to the transport."

They didn't believe him, of course. Neither of them did. Not until they were airborne again with no sign of pursuit.

Vstii-suuv was the first to put it into words. "I don't believe it," he said, staring out the back of the transport at the Human-Conqueror aircraft, still on guard, fading into the distance behind them. "They let us go. Why in the eighteen worlds would they do a thing like that?"

"Maybe as a payback for our not slaughtering their ground warriors when we had the chance," Thrr-mezaz suggested.

"With all due respect, Commander, that's highly dangerous thinking," Qlaa-nuur growled. "These aren't civilized beings we're talking about here. They're vicious barbarian killers. Ascribing Zhirrzh-like characteristics to them will do nothing but tempt us into blocked-street thinking."

"Perhaps," Thrr-mezaz said. "Perhaps not. They have a highly advanced technology; they must have a certain degree of civilization to go along with it. And if appreciation toward an enemy is beyond them, then perhaps their commander let us go for the same reason I let his warriors go: because he wants to find out what we were doing out there. Maybe that will also induce him to let us get back inside his territory. Assuming, of course, that we're able to get a new cutting from Warrior Command."

"Or from the Dhaa'rr," Vstii-suuv murmured, his voice thoughtful.

Thrr-mezaz looked at him, frowning in mild surprise. Vstii-suuv had been decidedly hostile about the whole Prr't-zevisti cutting idea back on the climb. Yet he'd now brought the subject up on his own. And not as a prelude to an argument, either, from the tone.

And then he understood. "You saw it," he said. "Didn't you?"

"I think so," Vstii-suuv admitted. "You did, too?"

"About the same as you," Thrr-mezaz nodded. "I saw something. I'm not sure what."

"What are you talking about?" Qlaa-nuur asked. "What did you see?"

"Maybe nothing," Vstii-suuv said hesitantly. "Maybe —well, maybe Prr't-zevisti."

Qlaa-nuur looked back and forth between the two of them. "Are you sure?"

"No, we're not sure at all," Thrr-mezaz told him. "Which is why I don't want either of you telling anyone else about this. Most won't believe us; the rest will assume we're spinning the story for political reasons."

"We are going to do *something*, though, aren't we?" Vstii-suuv asked.

"Oh, you can bet on that," Thrr-mezaz assured him. "One way or the other, we're going to get back up there and find out what's going on."

Vstii-suuv straightened a little. "We'll be ready whenever you want us, Commander," he said, his voice brisk and professional. "You can count on us."

And he could, Thrr-mezaz realized. He really could. The reluctant warriors who'd flown up there with him— the even more reluctant and distrustful climbing companions who'd hurried down the mountain behind him under the hostile eyes of the Human-Conquerors—those two were gone. With even a hint of a possibility that Prr't-zevisti might still be alive, they had suddenly turned instead into staunch allies.

But then, the Aree'rr clan had always had a long and proud warrior tradition. And Prr't-zevisti had once been a warrior.

Whether that tradition and their newfound enthusiasm would survive another trip into the heart of enemy territory was something else again. Thrr-mezaz would just have to hope the Dhaa'rr leaders would give them all an opportunity to find out.

15

There were two Zhirrzh standing there when Thrr-pifix-a answered her door: young males, dressed in conservative outfits, smiling cordially yet with a serious undertone to their expressions.

As near as she could remember, she'd never seen either of them before. "Yes?" she said.

"Good postmidarc to you," the taller, slightly older of the two said. His voice matched his smile: friendly, yet serious. "We're looking for a lady named Thrr-pifix-a; Kee'rr."

"I'm she," Thrr-pifix-a said. Door-doors, probably, here to try to sell her something she didn't need at a price she couldn't afford. But that was all right. She'd already finished her garden work for this fullarc, and she always enjoyed the mental challenge of a good argument over someone's sales spiel. "And you?"

"Call me Korthe," he invited. "This is Dornt, my associate. May we come in?"

Thrr-pifix-a looked at them, the first twinges of uneasiness tugging at her. First names only, with no indication of family or even clan. Certainly not door-doors, then. Certainly not casual visitors of any sort. "I'm really rather busy—"

"It's all right," the younger Zhirrzh, Dornt, assured her. "Really. We're here to help you with your problem."

"What problem is that?"

"We'd prefer to discuss it indoors," Korthe said. "May we come in?"

Thrr-pifix-a took a careful breath. They could be robbers or undesirables of any sort; and if so, she would be foolish to let them past her doorway. But on the other side, considering her age and her isolation out here, robbers would hardly need to ask her permission to get inside. More likely, they were just some sort of religious cultists. "All right," she said, stepping aside. "The conversation room is straight ahead."

They all went in and sat down on the couches. "Now," Thrr-pifix-a said, looking between them. "What's all this about?"

"Another hunbeat, please," Dornt said, fiddling with a small device he'd pulled from a waist pouch. "We want to make sure this conversation is private. There."

Thrr-pifix-a frowned, straining to hear. There was a new sound in the room, one that her failing ear slits could just barely pick up. A sort of high-pitched humming sound.

"Excellent," Korthe said, his earlier smile completely submerged in seriousness now. "We know you're busy, Thrr-pifix-a, so with your permission we'll get directly to business. Have you ever heard of an organization called Freedom of Decision for All?"

She'd called it, all right: religious cultists. "No, I don't believe I have."

"I'm not really surprised," Korthe said. "We're still fairly new to this area of Oaccanv. And certainly the various clan and family leaders who do know about us are working hard to keep us quiet. Very simply, FoDfA is composed of people who, just like you, believe strongly that each and every Zhirrzh should have the right to choose whether or not to accept Eldership."

Thrr-pifix-a frowned at him. "I'm sorry. What did you say?"

"You heard correctly," Korthe said. "We believe Eldership should be your own personal choice. No one else's."

Thrr-pifix-a took a deep breath, a rush of surprise and an odd sense of relief flooding through her. So she wasn't alone in this. Thrr-tulkoj had been right: there were indeed others who believed the same way she did. "You don't know how it feels to hear you say that," she said quietly. "I thought I was the only one."

"Hardly," Korthe said with a faint smile. "Our organization consists of over two million Zhirrzh."

Thrr-pifix-a felt her midlight pupils narrow in surprise. "Two *million?*"

"Two million," he confirmed. "And that doesn't count those sympathetic to our philosophy who for one reason or another don't want to join. Rest assured, Thrr-pifix-a; you have plenty of company out there."

"How else do you think we knew about you?" Korthe shrugged. "We have information sources all over the eighteen worlds."

"And," Dornt added quietly, "we stand ready to assist you in putting your choice into action."

"That's very kind of you," Thrr-pifix-a said. "And I'd certainly appreciate any help you can give me. I've tried talking to the family leaders, but the clan leaders have so far refused even to grant me a hearing—"

"Excuse me, Thrr-pifix-a," Korthe interrupted gently. "But I don't think you quite understand. Our group doesn't focus on advocacy or negotiation. We concentrate on, shall we say, more direct methods."

Thrr-pifix-a frowned, looking back and forth between them. "What do you mean?"

"You seem a straightforward person," Korthe said. "Allow me to be equally so. What we propose to do is retrieve your *fsss* organ from your family shrine and deliver it here to you. Where you may do with it whatever you choose."

For a long beat Thrr-pifix-a stared at him, replaying that sentence over and over again in her mind. "You're not serious," she said at last. "You mean . . . *steal* my *fsss* organ?"

"Why not?" Dornt shrugged. "You tried to do the same thing just three fullarcs ago, didn't you?"

"Yes, but that was me," Thrr-pifix-a said. "My risk, for my gain. I can't ask you to commit such a crime for me."

"You don't have to ask," Dornt said. "We're volunteering."

"Besides, you prejudice yourself when you use the word *steal*," Korthe added. "In actual fact your *fsss* was stolen from *you*, back when you were ten. It doesn't belong to the Kee'rr clan or the Thrr family. It belongs to you."

Thrr-pifix-a felt her tail twitching nervously. The same argument—many of the same words, in fact—that she'd used in trying to persuade Thrr-gilag to her point of view a few fullarcs ago. But to hear it being argued in her own home by total strangers was more than a little disconcerting. "What about the risks?" she asked. "I'm sorry to keep coming back to this, but you're talking about committing a major crime here. And for no gain for yourselves."

"On the contrary," Korthe said. "We stand to gain a great deal: an incredible measure of freedom for all Zhirrzh. The family and clan leaders know perfectly well what they're doing—why else would they have such heavy guard around the shrines? It's the common people who don't know or don't understand what's been done to them. Every time we of FoDfA take action like this, we're injecting another tiny bit of awareness into Zhirrzh culture. Eventually, we'll prevail . . . and then we all win."

Thrr-pifix-a nodded slowly. It still felt odd. All of it did. But they were here, and they were offering their help.

And it was for certain that she would never be able to do it on her own. "How would you go about it?" she asked. "How exactly, I mean."

"That's nothing you need to worry about," Dornt soothed her. "We'll handle all the details."

"No, that's not what I meant," Thrr-pifix-a said, flicking her tongue in a negative. "I meant would you have to hurt anyone to do it. Because I wouldn't be able to accept that. The chief protector at our shrine, Thrr-tulkoj, is a personal friend of my son's—"

"Now, what did Dornt just say?" Korthe said, his tone mildly reproving. "Didn't he say you didn't need to worry about such things?"

"I'll worry about whatever I choose to worry about, thank you," Thrr-pifix-a snapped. "And unless you can promise me right now that there'll be no danger to the shrine's protectors, you can just pack up and leave."

"Please," Korthe said, holding up a hand. "Thrr-pifix-a; please. We understand your concerns, but you protest far more than necessary. Of course we'll guarantee that no one will be hurt. Our whole philosophy of respect for the rights and dignity of individual Zhirrzh would be meaningless if we didn't."

"If you're assured of nothing else this postmidarc, be assured of that," Dornt added earnestly. "When we bring your *fsss* to you, it will not be at any cost to anyone else."

"I'll hold you to that," Thrr-pifix-a warned.

"Of course," Korthe said. "Then it's decided."

And suddenly Thrr-pifix-a realized that it was. Somehow, without her making a real conscious decision, it was indeed decided. "All right," she said, hearing the defiance of uncertainty in her voice. "Yes. It's decided. When?"

"Next latearc," Korthe said, gesturing to Dornt and standing up. "We can let ourselves out."

"Wait a beat," Thrr-pifix-a frowned as Dornt also stood. "*Next* latearc? As in just over a fullarc from right now?"

"I see no advantage in waiting," Korthe said. "Do you?"

"Well . . . no. No, I suppose not," Thrr-pifix-a conceded reluctantly. "It just seems so sudden."

"Suddenness is a great ally," Dornt said. "Especially against the sluggishness of a layered leadership structure."

"But I was just caught trying to take it myself," Thrr-pifix-a pointed out. "Won't they be expecting me to try again?"

"They might be expecting you," Dornt said, smiling faintly. "They certainly won't be expecting us."

Thrr-pifix-a swallowed. "And no one will be hurt?"

"There will be no need for violence of any sort," Dornt said quietly. "Trust us on that. We have many methods, and many contacts."

"It'll be all right, Thrr-pifix-a," Korthe added. "Really it will. Please try not to worry. We'll be back before you know it."

His face turned serious. "And then your future will be in your hands, and in your hands alone. As it should be."

They left . . . and for a long time after the door closed behind them, Thrr-pifix-a just sat there in her small conversation room. Wondering if her decision, so quickly and strangely made, had been the right one.

And wondering, too, at the sudden uneasiness simmering inside her.

16

The end of the wave front disappeared behind the massive sea rock that sat fifty strides out into the ocean, its base lapped by the white-tinged blue-green water. For a beat nothing happened; then, abruptly, the edge of the rock seemed to explode into a burst of white froth as the wave smashed into it. The wind caught the froth, curving it partway around the rock, changing grayish stone to black where it hit. The froth itself turned into a fan of rivulets and tiny impromptu waterfalls as the water ran down the rock and returned to the sea.

Thrr-gilag took a deep breath, savoring the sharp-salty air as he gazed past the sea rock and tried to guess which of those incoming lines of white-capped wave fronts would be the next spectacular splash. And tried not to think of what might be happening, without him, back there in the Klnn family hall.

"Composing poetry?" a familiar voice called from behind him.

Thrr-gilag turned. Dressed in full formal Klnn family attire, Klnn-dawan-a's brother Klnn-torun was making his careful and precise way across the last few strides of rock-strewn beach that separated them. "What makes you think I'd be composing poetry?" Thrr-gilag called back over the roar of the waves.

"I thought you were the sort of person who might do that sort of thing," Klnn-torun said. "Especially standing here looking out at the ocean."

"Typical Klnn smugness," Thrr-gilag said. "What makes you think the hills and streams of the Thrr family territory can't compare with this puny ocean of yours?"

Klnn-torun frowned slightly. "Can they?"

Thrr-gilag smiled, flicking his tongue in a negative. "Not a chance."

"Ah." Klnn-torun's face cleared. "I didn't think so. You had me worried, though."

Thrr-gilag looked back at the sea rock, just in time to catch a minor wave splash at its edge. "How about you?" he asked. "You ever write poetry about the ocean?"

"Not really," Klnn-torun said. "I tried a few times, back when I was younger. But I could never come up with anything that sounded any good. I guess my mind just doesn't work that way."

Thrr-gilag shrugged. "To tell you the truth, neither does mine."

"Oh, come on." Klnn-torun frowned. "What about those three poems you wrote for Klnn-dawan-a right after you two met?"

Thrr-gilag eyed him suspiciously. "She didn't let you see those, did she?"

"Oh, no, she just read me some of the highlights,"

Klnn-torun assured him. "Really, I thought they were very good. Smooth and quite poetic."

"I'm glad I fooled you," Thrr-gilag said, snorting gently. "Truth is, I sweated blood over those things and still never really got them the way I wanted. I'm just glad they caught her attention before I had to write too many more of them. I'm still half-convinced she started seeing me out of sheer pity."

"Hardly," Klnn-torun said with a faint smile. "No, she was most impressed by them. And by you, too, of course."

"Not half as impressed as I was of her," Thrr-gilag murmured, looking over his shoulder. The Klnn family meeting hall towered back there behind him, its rock-faced walls blending almost seamlessly with the bluff on which it had been built. Klnn-dawan-a was up there right now, standing before the family and clan leaders. Trying to win them over the way she had won over her brother and parents.

And trying to do so all alone. They hadn't allowed Thrr-gilag in; nor had they allowed Klnn-torun or her parents or any of her closest friends to stand with her. There was nothing any of them could do but sit in the waiting gallery or wander around outside, wondering what was happening in the chambers and waiting for the family leaders to summon them back in. The whole stupid, outdated single-trial procedure—

"I heard about your father's being raised to Eldership half a cyclic ago," Klnn-torun said. "I'm sorry I wasn't able to attend his welcoming ceremony. We were right in the middle of a sudden influx of shahbba beetles, and we needed everyone we had to drive them off."

"That's all right," Thrr-gilag said, feeling a fresh twist of old guilt. "As it happens, I didn't make it, either. I was out on an archaeology dig when it happened, and with our extremely limited transportation arrangements I just wasn't able to get back."

"Yes, Klnn-dawan-a once missed an uncle's ceremony the same way," Klnn-torun said. "How's Thrr't-rokik adapting to life as an Elder?"

"Reasonably well, I think," Thrr-gilag said. He nodded toward the ocean. "Though his biggest goal these fullarcs seems to be to try to get a shrine set up near the Amt'bri River so that he can hear running water. Imagine what he'd want if he saw this."

"I don't have to imagine," Klnn-torun said grimly. "The Dhaa'rr leaders are already up to their tongues in demands to allow cutting pyramids along the seashore."

"Really," Thrr-gilag said, looking around. Aside from the Klnn family hall, there were only a handful of other buildings visible. "I guess I'm surprised it isn't a solid wall of shrines already."

"Actually, you'd never get shrines themselves put up here," Klnn-torun told him. "Salt air has always been considered too dangerous to *fsss* organs for anyone to risk putting an actual shrine near the shore."

"Ah," Thrr-gilag said, nodding his understanding. "But that's not such a problem when all you're dealing with is cuttings."

"Right," Klnn-torun said. "And the more this cutting idea has caught on, the louder the demands have become."

Thrr-gilag looked back at the ocean. "Well, at least here on Dharanv you have a whole planet's worth of territory to spread out over. Those of us whose clan centers are still crammed together on Oaccanv don't have that same advantage."

"Maybe," Klnn-torun said. "But even here it's not as easy as you might think. All the most popular and spectacular sites are already owned, either by families or individuals. Many of the spots have been extensively developed."

"And none of the owners want bored Elders hanging around looking over their shoulders."

"You got it." Klnn-torun stroked pensively at the side of his face. "You know, Thrr-gilag, to be perfectly honest, I'm beginning to worry about all this. Starting to wonder if things may be getting out of hand."

"How so?"

"Well . . ." Klnn-torun hesitated. "Have you ever studied Zhirrzh history? Really studied it, I mean?"

Thrr-gilag shrugged. "I had the usual courses, plus a few," he said. "Nothing extensive."

"I studied it quite a bit," Klnn-torun said. "Especially the Eldership wars."

"Really." Thrr-gilag eyed him. "I wouldn't have thought of you as the warfare-studying type."

Klnn-torun shrugged. "Just because I try to avoid conflict in my own dealings doesn't mean I shouldn't be interested in reading about it. In fact, I'd venture to say that a desire to avoid conflict would give a Zhirrzh an extra incentive to learn about its causes."

"And logically so," Thrr-gilag agreed. "So what cause of conflict from history are we talking about here?"

Klnn-torun looked back up at the Klnn-family hall. "Are you aware that it was exactly this same competition between Elders and physicals for territory that sparked the Third Eldership War?"

Thrr-gilag frowned, thinking back to his own history courses. "Well . . . it wasn't *exactly* the same situation. For one thing, we were all stuck on Oaccanv back then. Now we've got seventeen other worlds to spread out on."

"Which I presume is the main reason it's taken us five

hundred cyclics to reach this point again instead of the three hundred we got between the Second and Third Wars," Klnn-torun pointed out. "But there's another factor now that's been added into the mix. Back then people were much more used to having Elders around them all the time, their presence woven into the fabric of their lives. Now, suddenly, our culture seems to be obsessed with privacy and solitude—obsessed to the point of hostility, sometimes. We don't want anyone too close to us; we especially don't want Elders close to us. There's increasing pressure to put shrines and cutting pyramids way out somewhere where they can't reach cities or even major towns. At least on Dharanv the areas that are inaccessible to Elders are being developed at a tremendous rate. It doesn't make any sense."

"Actually, it does," Thrr-gilag said thoughtfully. "What you're seeing here is an underlying cultural shift. Five hundred cyclics ago people generally stayed their whole lives in one spot, with the only Elders around being those from their own family. Familiar, friendly, comfortable. Now, with all this cross-territory and interstellar mobility we've picked up over the past hundred cyclics or so, you can never know who's nearby or who might be watching over your shoulder. That makes people nervous. People who are nervous long enough often start getting hostile and resentful."

"You're right," Klnn-torun said thoughtfully. "I hadn't thought about that."

"Well, I've had a little more training in all this cultural stuff," Thrr-gilag told him. "Plus the fact that I live that way myself more than you do. Living and working with your family's old orchards, you're much more connected to the way Zhirrzh culture used to be."

"Yes, I see that," Klnn-torun said. "Oh, and that's

another factor: with all these new cutting pyramids the Elders themselves are also less connected to the family lands than they used to be." He frowned. "Actually, that might make my point even more valid."

"That point being?" Thrr-gilag asked.

Klnn-torun's tail twitched. "That it seems to me the Elders have a great deal to gain from a war of conquest against the Human-Conquerors."

Thrr-gilag stared at him, the magnificent ocean scenery abruptly forgotten. "What do you mean?"

"Well, think about it," Klnn-torun said. "Every planet we're able to take from the Human-Conquerors is one more world the Elders have to expand into. More variety, more scenery—more room in general."

"You aren't seriously suggesting anyone would start a war over *scenery,* are you?"

"No, of course not," Klnn-torun said. "At least, not specifically for scenery. But we're talking territory, and that's always been one of the big driving forces behind conflict. And don't forget, what Elders want even more than scenic places to live is something to do. Every new world opens up that many more jobs for them, from communication pathways on up."

Thrr-gilag looked back up at the Klnn family hall behind them, thinking about the world he and Klnn-dawan-a had just come from. When the Zhirrzh and Chig had run into each other two hundred cyclics ago, the Chig had had colonies in two other star systems and had begun the exploration of two others. The subsequent war had pushed them back to their home world of Gree, guarded ever since then by Zhirrzh encirclement forces.

And their other four colonies were now part of the eighteen worlds. With thousands of Zhirrzh, and dozens of cutting pyramids scattered across them.

"I know it sounds unbelievable," Klnn-torun said into his thoughts.

"Well, yes, it does," Thrr-gilag said. "For one thing, you have to assume a massive conspiracy to make it work, with virtually *every* Elder in on it. You have to admit that's pretty unlikely."

"Under normal circumstances, certainly," Klnn-torun said. "We all know how fast information and rumors percolate through the Elder community. But there are times when a particular bit of information is controlled by a bare handful of Elders. Klnn-dwan-a's study group on Gree is a good example. She told me that despite the fact that your father had already heard about the threat to your bond-engagement, her own Elders hadn't said a word to her about it. You had to fly out personally and tell her."

Thrr-gilag looked out at the ocean, his suddenly contracted pupils not really seeing any of it. The whole philosophical basis of this war was that the Humans were an aggressive conqueror race who had deliberately and ruthlessly fired on four peaceful Zhirrzh survey ships with Elderdeath weapons. And the sole source of that assertion was the statements of the eight Elder communicators who'd been aboard those survey ships.

Thrr-gilag had heard their statement firsthand from Bvee't-hibbin back on Oaccanv. He'd assumed then that the Elder could have no possible reason to lie about it.

But what if Klnn-torun was right? What if Bvee't-hibbin had had a reason to lie? What if the Human prisoner Pheylan Cavanagh had been telling the truth about that battle?

What if the Zhirrzh had in fact started this war?

"You're very quiet," Klnn-torun prompted.

Slowly, Thrr-gilag forced his mind back on track. Was Klnn-torun thinking along these same lines? Probably. An orchard-tender wasn't exactly a prestigious profession, but Klnn-torun was considerably smarter than the usual stereotypes would suggest. Should Thrr-gilag tell him about that conversation with Bvee't-hibbin? And perhaps also about Pheylan Cavanagh's claims?

But neither of them had any proof of all this . . . and there were Elders up there at the Klnn family hall who could easily be listening in on this conversation. "It's an interesting speculation," he said instead. "And I'll certainly concede that there are probably Elders here and there who slant things or even some who tell outright lies. But I'm afraid I can't buy any suggestion that there's a conspiracy of Elders out there. Even a small conspiracy."

"I see." For a long beat Klnn-torun seemed to be studying his face. Then, with deliberate casualness, he turned back to look at the ocean. "Well, you're the expert on cultures, I suppose. You'd know best."

"Um," Thrr-gilag said noncommittally, looking at the ocean himself and wishing like blazes he knew what Klnn-torun was thinking right now. Was he taking what Thrr-gilag had just said at face value? Or was he simply playing along with what he perceived to be a subtle, between-the-lines concurrence with his conspiracy theory?

An Elder appeared. "Klnn-torun?" he called, his voice faint over the noise of the waves. "You are summoned to the hall."

"I understand," Klnn-torun said. "What about Thrr-gilag?"

A faint flicker of disgust crossed the Elder's face. "He can come, too," he said grudgingly. "But be quick about it, both of you. They're waiting."

He vanished. "Don't let him rattle you," Klnn-torun advised Thrr-gilag as the two of them started back across the rocky beach. "If they've just called us, they can hardly have been waiting very long."

"Yes," Thrr-gilag said, his tail spinning hard even in the cool sea air. This was it. The judgment of the family and Dhaa'rr clan leaders on him and Klnn-dawan-a.

"Thrr-gilag; Kee'rr?" a voice murmured in his ear.

Thrr-gilag turned, leaning his head to the side to try to focus on the Elder hugging close at his side. A female, no one he recognized. "Yes?"

"Shh!" she said urgently before vanishing.

"What was that?" Klnn-torun asked, turning to look at him.

"Ah—nothing," Thrr-gilag said, frowning to himself as he glanced around. Clearly, that Elder wanted to talk to him, and to him alone. Something having to do with Klnn-dawan-a? "Look, why don't you go on ahead," he told Klnn-torun. "I'll catch up in a hunbeat."

Klnn-torun looked puzzled, but he nodded. "All right," he said. "Don't be long."

He headed off, hunching forward a little as he labored uphill through the sand. Thrr-gilag glanced around, then stepped over into the lee side of a sea-grass-coated boulder and waited.

He didn't have to wait long. A few beats later the Elder was back. "I'm sorry for this," she said, her face a mirror of rapidly shifting emotions. "Really, I am. Actually, I shouldn't even be talking to you—I mean, you're not even Dhaa'rr, and—"

"It's all right," Thrr-gilag interrupted soothingly. "Besides, anything that concerns Klnn-dawan-a is something I have a right to know about."

The Elder blinked in surprise. "Klnn-dawan-a? This isn't about Klnn-dawan-a. It's about Prr't-zevisti."

Thrr-gilag drew back a little toward his boulder. "I see," he said carefully.

"No, you don't," the Elder said, her face and voice flashing sudden anger and frustration. "You don't understand at all. Or maybe you don't even care that they're going to take away his last chance. His very last chance. Don't you care about that?"

"Hold it," Thrr-gilag protested, holding up a hand. "Just wait a beat, please. I'm afraid you've lost me. Who are you, and who's trying to take away whose last chance?"

The Elder closed her eyes briefly. "My name is Prr't-casst-a. I'm Prr't-zevisti's wife. The one who was lost on the Human-Conqueror world of Dorcas."

"Yes, I know who he was," Thrr-gilag said with a quiet sigh. So Prr't-zevisti's wife was here. Probably one of those sitting in judgment on him and Klnn-dawan-a. Terrific.

"Not *was,*" she snapped, her face flashing the anger and frustration again. "Not was. Is! He's not dead, Thrr-gilag. I know he isn't. He can't be."

Thrr-gilag winced. "Look, Prr't-casst-a, I know how you feel. But—"

"Just be quiet," she cut him off. "Be quiet, and listen to me. The Dhaa'rr leaders have decided to call final rites for Prr't-zevisti three fullarcs from now. Including the ceremony of fire."

A shiver ran through Thrr-gilag. The ceremony of fire: the ritual of destruction of a dead Elder's *fsss* organ. It didn't happen all that often anymore, but when it did, it was always traumatic for those involved. The final act of farewell to one who would never be seen again . . .

He frowned suddenly, the timing here belatedly catching up with him. "Wait a hunbeat. Final rites already? It's been only, what, ten fullarcs or so?"

"Twelve," Prr't-casst-a said. "That's all. Just twelve full-arcs since he's been seen."

"That doesn't seem nearly long enough," Thrr-gilag said. "Certainly not to make a final declaration of death. What reason are the clan leaders giving for it?"

Prr't-casst-a waved a hand helplessly. "They invoked some ancient law of the Dhaa'rr. Something obscure that laid out fifteen fullarcs without contact as being the proper waiting period."

"Doesn't seem long enough," Thrr-gilag said again, trying to remember if he'd ever heard of the Kee'rr having anything similar in their legal structure. But he couldn't. "Must be really ancient, though. Before preservation methods were even halfway reliable."

"That's exactly right," Prr't-casst-a agreed. "I asked one of my family to look it up. He couldn't find it in any legal documents created since the time the Dhaa'rr moved off Oaccanv onto Dharanv."

Which made the law at least 350 cyclics old. Hardly the sort of law invoked twice a fullarc as a matter of course. "So why are they doing it?"

"I don't know," Prr't-casst-a said, a look of pain and helplessness settling onto her face. "They won't tell me anything. The servers just repeat the law to me, and say that the ancient traditions of the Dhaa'rr must be maintained. The clan leaders won't talk to me at all."

"There's probably more than just tradition at work here, then," Thrr-gilag said grimly. "Sounds to me like something political."

"I think you're right," Prr't-casst-a said. "That's why I came to you. You're not of Dhaa'rr politics. And yet you must care about the Dhaa'rr—otherwise, why would you bond with a Dhaa'rr? But I don't have much time. Prr't-zevisti doesn't have much time. Can you do anything to help us?"

Thrr-gilag looked at her agitated face, feeling a wave of understanding for this part of his mother's fear of Eldership. To be alive and aware, yet so fundamentally powerless.

But Thrr-gilag was hardly in a position to do anything himself.

But how could he just refuse her?

"I'll try," he sighed. "I'll do whatever—well, I'll try."

"Thank you," Prr't-casst-a breathed. Already she seemed calmer. "What will you do first?"

"First thing we need is a better idea of what's really going on," Thrr-gilag told her, glancing across the beach. Klnn-torun was nearly to the first line of scrub plants, dotting the sand a few strides beyond the high-water mark. "I've got an idea, but right now I have to get to the meeting hall and hear what the Klnn and Dhaa'rr leaders have decided to do about Klnn-dawan-a and me. Do you have a cutting nearby?"

"No, my family shrine is near a town thirty thoustrides inland from here."

"All right," Thrr-gilag said. "Let's set it up this way. Half a tentharc after the hearing is over, we'll meet back here on the beach."

"There's a small cave over in that headland," Prr't-casst-a suggested, pointing to a rocky finger of land jutting out into the waves a couple hundred strides down the beach. "It would give you a little shelter, at least."

"Sounds good," Thrr-gilag agreed. "We'll meet at the cave. Now, the next part's up to you. Between now and then, you'll need to find me a secure pathway to my brother. Commander Thrr-mezaz, commanding the ground warriors on Dorcas."

"I can do that," Prr't-casst-a said. "Yes, I can do that."

"And I mean *really* secure," Thrr-gilag warned. "The fewer Elders who are in on this conversation, the better. And they all have to be good friends of yours, who can be trusted not to let anything we say slip out to anyone else. If the Dhaa'rr leaders get wind that you're talking to me about this, it'll be the end of any chance for Klnn-dawan-a and me."

"Oh," Prr't-casst-a said, suddenly looking stricken. "I hadn't even thought about that. I'm sorry. I—I don't—"

"It's all right," Thrr-gilag soothed her. "Just be sure the pathway is secure."

"It will be," Prr't-casst-a said. "I promise on my life. It will be. I . . . thank you, Thrr-gilag."

She vanished. "You're welcome," Thrr-gilag murmured to the ocean breezes. Already he didn't like the feel of this whole thing, and particularly not the assumption that he was going to get involved any deeper in it.

But it wouldn't hurt to discuss the situation with Thrr-mezaz. He might have some information, maybe even some ideas.

In the meantime, one crisis at a time. Bracing himself, he headed across the beach toward the Klnn-family hall.

Prr't-casst-a had described their rendezvous point as a cave. To Thrr-gilag's mind it was much less a cave than it was a small carved indentation in the rock facing the ocean. It was also damp, noisy, and smelled of rotting sea grass.

But the waves that continually lapped at the opening would help insure that no one disturbed their conversation, while the noise of those same waves would pretty well guarantee that no Elders would be able to eavesdrop unnoticed.

Prr't-casst-a was already waiting when Thrr-gilag and Klnn-dawan-a arrived. So was her pathway.

So, to Thrr-gilag's surprise, was Thrr-mezaz. "I hope I didn't keep you waiting, my brother," Thrr-gilag said after they'd exchanged greetings. "I wasn't intending the pathway to be opened until I got here."

He nodded to Prr't-casst-a. "Go ahead," he prompted.

"Oh. Yes," she said, and vanished.

"I doubt she's ever done either end of a communication before," Klnn-dawan-a commented, looking around the cave.

"She'll pick it up," Thrr-gilag assured her. "I'm more worried about the security of this pathway of hers." He looked around the cave, too. "Or that one of the leaders up there will get curious and send an Elder down to investigate."

"I doubt anyone will be bothering with us right now," Klnn-dawan-a said. "The way they were talking—"

Prr't-casst-a reappeared. " 'No problem, my brother,' " she quoted. " 'It's latearc here, and I wasn't doing anything constructive anyway. Just trying to figure out what your Human-Conquerors might be up to.' " Prr't-casst-a frowned in concentration. "Just a beat . . . oh, right. 'But first things first. What happened with you and Klnn-dawan-a and the hearing?' "

"A thorough anticlimax," Thrr-gilag said. "They gave Klnn-dawan-a the full spectrum of questions, threw about a half spectrum at me, and then said they'd think about it for a few more fullarcs."

Prr't-casst-a nodded and vanished. "I didn't get a chance to ask you if you were able to read anything from them," Thrr-gilag commented to Klnn-dawan-a.

"Nothing I'm sure of," she said. "I get the feeling that the Klnn leaders themselves have no real problems with our bonding, but that they feel they have to submit to the wishes of the Dhaa'rr leaders."

"Interesting," Thrr-gilag said. "I got the impression that both the Klnn and Dhaa'rr leaders were instead being pushed by their Elders."

There was a flicker, and Prr't-casst-a was back. " 'Well, I suppose it's better than a straight-out no,' " she said. " 'Now. What's all this about?' "

"We have a problem here," Thrr-gilag said. "I've learned that the Dhaa'rr leaders are planning final rites for Prr't-zevisti, including the ceremony of fire. I suppose my question is whether you've found conclusive proof out there that he is in fact dead."

Prr't-casst-a's face was pinched with quiet agony, but she vanished without a word. "You think that's what's happened?" Klnn-dawan-a asked.

"It's either that or something political," Thrr-gilag said. "I haven't been able to come up with any other options."

Klnn-dawan-a shivered, hugging herself against the cold and damp. "It's frightening to think about people playing politics with other people's lives."

Thrr-gilag pressed his tongue hard against the top of his mouth, his thoughts flicking back to his conversation with Klnn-torun. "Yes," he murmured. "It is."

Prr't-casst-a reappeared . . . and even before she began to speak, Thrr-gilag knew something had happened. The fear that had been on her face when she left had been replaced by something hard and cold. " 'The situation out here has changed, all right,' " she said. " 'But it has nothing to do with any evidence of death. What's happened is that I've petitioned the Prr family to send me a second cutting from Prr't-zevisti's *fss* organ.' "

Thrr-gilag threw a startled look at Klnn-dawan-a. "A second cutting? What for?"

"Wait a beat, there's more," Prr't-casst-a said. "Mm— 'It occurred to me that if Prr't-zevisti was trapped somehow up in the Human-Conqueror stronghold, then our best chance of getting him out would be to move another cutting into range nearby.' "

"That's going to be a little tricky, isn't it?" Thrr-gilag asked. "Hauling a pyramid up a mountain isn't exactly easy."

Prr't-casst-a vanished. When she returned, there was yet another new expression on her face. " 'Actually, I had something else in mind,' " she quoted, her voice tight but firm. " 'I was thinking—and you and Prr't-casst-a would need to talk about this—that instead of using a pyramid we could perhaps just put the cutting in a small airtight and predator-proof container.' "

Klnn-dawan-a muttered something under her breath. Thrr-gilag frowned at Prr't-casst-a, trying without success to read her expression. "What do you think, Prr't-casst-a?" he asked.

"It's a terrible idea," she said, her voice trembling. "Completely and utterly disrespectful. A violation of everything civilized that the Dhaa'rr and the Prr have ever stood for." She seemed to brace herself. "But if it's the only way to get Prr't-zevisti back . . . then, yes, let's do it."

Thrr-gilag looked at Klnn-dawan-a. "Don't look at me," she said, holding up her hands. "It's not my decision to make."

He nodded and turned back to Prr't-casst-a. "All right, my brother, we're agreed on this end," he said. "Assuming you can get the Prr family to get you that cutting."

"But what if he can't?" Prr't-casst-a protested. "The

Dhaa'rr leaders only have to wait three more fullarcs. After that they're going to destroy his *fsss.*"

Thrr-gilag grimaced. Three fullarcs from now. The same time he and the alien study group were scheduled to leave Oaccanv for the Mrachani homeworld. "Doesn't give us much time."

"Certainly not enough time to bring pressure on the Prr family," Klnn-dawan-a put in. "Unless that's not what we're talking about here."

Thrr-gilag looked at her, an unpleasant feeling running through him. "What do you mean?"

She gestured to Prr't-casst-a. "Prr't-casst-a, why don't you go get the message started," she said. "Tell him that you agree to his idea about how to handle the cutting."

"All right," Prr't-casst-a said.

She vanished. "You want to tell me what you've got in mind?" Thrr-gilag asked Klnn-dawan-a.

"I think you know as well as I do," she said. "If the Dhaa'rr leaders are bound and determined to destroy Prr't-zevisti's *fsss,* the three of us aren't going to have much chance of convincing the Prr family to stand up to them. Certainly not with just three fullarcs to do it in."

"And actually, I've only got one fullarc before I have to leave," Thrr-gilag agreed. "So what are the alternatives?"

Klnn-dawan-a shivered again. "I see only one. We're going to have to take the cutting ourselves."

Prr't-casst-a was back before Thrr-gilag could think of anything to say. " 'Good,' " she quoted Thrr-mezaz. " 'I know how hard this is going to be for all of you, especially Prr't-casst-a. I'm not all that thrilled about it myself. But I think it's Prr't-zevisti's only chance. I'll try to get the Prr family moving on this.' "

"Good," Thrr-gilag said. He looked at Klnn-dawan-a

—"But I think we'd better have an alternative plan ready. Just in case."

Prr't-casst-a frowned slightly, but she nodded and disappeared. "Do you have any idea what you're suggesting?" Thrr-gilag asked Klnn-dawan-a. "None of us is exactly qualified to take *fsss* cuttings."

"It's not supposed to be all that hard anymore," Klnn-dawan-a said. "Not with modern preservation methods. There's not so much of that internal liquefaction that made those first cuttings so difficult."

"A great cheer for progress," Thrr-gilag growled. "Unfortunately, that's not going to help us a bit. Prr't-zevisti's *fsss* wasn't treated with modern preservatives, remember?"

Klnn-dawan-a winced. "You're right."

"And that means cold-knives and a compressed argon atmosphere and all the rest of it," Thrr-gilag went on. "And something to seal the cut end before everything leaks out, and a healer qualified to do that sort of work. Not to mention the whole trick of sneaking a *fsss* out of its niche and then sneaking it back in afterward."

"I didn't say it would be easy," Klnn-dawan-a snapped, glaring at him. "I just said it was our only chance."

Thrr-gilag glared back. But she was right. Except that it was Prr't-zevisti's only chance.

Prr't-casst-a reappeared. " 'I think I understand—' " She paused. "Are you all right?" she asked, looking back and forth between Thrr-gilag and Klnn-dawan-a.

Thrr-gilag sighed. "Sure," he said, laying a hand on Klnn-dawan-a's shoulder. "Just a little difference of opinion. What did Thrr-mezaz say?"

"Right. 'I think I understand what you're saying. Good luck, and keep me informed. Farewell.' "

"Farewell, Thrr-mezaz," Thrr-gilag murmured, an odd sensation tingling at the base of his tongue. That last message from Thrr-mezaz had sounded suspiciously rushed. Could there be some trouble with the Humans?

Prr't-casst-a was still waiting. "Go ahead and release the pathway," Thrr-gilag instructed her. "Remind them we may be needing them again later."

She nodded and vanished, returning a few beats later. "They've all agreed to stand ready. What now?"

"We need ideas," he told her. "Let's go off and think, and plan to meet back here in, say, three tentharcs. Or as close to here as we can manage," he added, glancing at the encroaching waves again. "Oh, we'll also need to know where exactly Prr't-zevisti's niche is. Can you get the number for us?"

"He's right beside me," Prr't-casst-a said, bittersweet memories crossing her face. "We were moved to adjoining niches after we were bonded."

A different system from the one the Kee'rr used. "Good," he said. "That will help. All right, then. Three tentharcs from now."

"Yes," Prr't-casst-a said. "Again, I thank you. Both of you."

"Sure," Thrr-gilag said. "Go on, get going."

"So what are we going to do?" Klnn-dawan-a asked as they picked their way carefully between the waves and left the cave.

"I don't know," Thrr-gilag confessed. "But we'll come up with something."

17 "The *Imperative* picked it up about three hunbeats ago, Commander," the warrior at the monitor said tightly. "There it is—right there."

"I see it," Thrr-mezaz nodded, peering closely at the monitor. As always with direct laser links, the image was a little fuzzy. But it was clear enough to see that the spacecraft slowly drifting toward Dorcas was not of Human-Conqueror design. "What do they make of it?"

"It'll have to get a little closer before they know for sure," the warrior said. "But their preliminary analysis indicates that it's very much like the design of the spacecraft the Cakk'rr captured at Cataloged World Five Ninety-two."

Thrr-mezaz grimaced. "A Mrachani spacecraft."

"Or at least Mrachani designed," the warrior nodded. There was a sound behind Thrr-mezaz, and he turned as Klnn-vavgi stepped up beside him. "Anything happening out there, Second?" he asked.

"No, so far everything's quiet," Klnn-vavgi reported. "All perimeter warrior teams are on alert, and I've got all the Elders out at their full anchorline limits watching for trouble."

For all the good that would do. Elder eyesight wasn't all that terrific in broad sunlight; at latearc it was even less so. "And there's nothing stirring at the Human-Conqueror stronghold?"

"Nothing we can spot." Klnn-vavgi gestured to the image on the monitor. "You think our visitor might not be expected?"

"I don't know," Thrr-mezaz said. "To be honest, none of this Mrachani business makes any sense to me."

Klnn-vavgi shrugged. "I don't think it's all that hard to understand. The Mrachanis are a subject race under Human-Conqueror domination, and they want us to help them."

"Yes, that's what they say," Thrr-mezaz agreed. "Question is, is that really what they're about? Look at the chronology a hunbeat. We've got our first sighting of a Mrachani spacecraft about half a cyclic ago by a Cakk'rr survey ship that was poking around Cataloged World Five Ninety-two. They went back there about fifteen fullarcs after that first brush with the Human-Conquerors and found another spacecraft, which promptly opened fire on them with Elderdeath weapons."

"And was just as promptly shot back at," Klnn-vavgi said. "Injuring the crew and requiring some patchwork to make it flyable again."

"Allegedly injuring the crew," Thrr-mezaz reminded him. "Last I heard, the Overclan healers still weren't sure it was the Cakk'rr counterattack that injured them. But here's where it gets interesting. The Cakk'rr put a couple of warriors aboard the Mrachani spacecraft and were escorting it to Base World Twelve when they got a scream for help from the Elders on Study World Eighteen. The warships diverted that direction, leaving the Mrachani spacecraft to go on alone, and got to Study World Eighteen just in time to chase some Human-Conqueror warcraft away."

He touched his thumbs together for emphasis. "Which meant the Mrachani spacecraft was all alone when it reached Base World Twelve. Which means that if Thrr-gilag's Human-Conqueror prisoner had succeeded in getting it off the ground, there would have been no Zhirrzh warships anywhere nearby that could have stopped him."

"Interesting," Klnn-vavgi murmured. "Come to think of it, it occurs to me that those Copperhead warriors didn't show up until the prisoner had failed to lift the spacecraft. Almost as if they knew he'd failed."

"Right," Thrr-mezaz nodded. "And the fact that they were there at all either means they were flooding the whole region with warriors looking for him—in which case we should be seeing a lot more Human-Conqueror warcraft than we have so far—or else they knew exactly where to look. Put it all together, and it starts sounding suspiciously like a coordinated effort."

"Could be," Klnn-vavgi said. "That would mean the Mrachanis would have had to transmit the Base World Twelve vector to the humans before they left Cataloged World Five Ninety-two. And transmitted it in some way the Cakk'rr couldn't detect."

"An X-ray laser, perhaps," Thrr-mezaz said. "Or something simpler: a visual flash-code at an angle where the Cakk'rr warships and Elders couldn't see it."

"There's one other possibility," Klnn-vavgi said slowly. "It could be that the Human-Conquerors have managed to crack the age-old problem of tracking spacecraft in the tunnel-line."

Thrr-mezaz looked at the image on the monitor, an eerie tingling running through him. Thrr-gilag had half-jokingly suggested the same thing, just after the attack on Base World 12. The concept was impossible, and provably so, and he'd said so at the time.

But the Human-Conquerors had already demonstrated that their technology was different from that of the Zhirrzh. If they had found a way to do the impossible . . .

"Commander?" one of the warriors called. "Message from Supreme Ship Commander Dkll-kumvit. He requests your presence immediately aboard the *Imperative* for a full-force commanders' meeting. A transport will pick you up in fifteen hunbeats."

"Acknowledge the order," Thrr-mezaz told him, the eerie feeling growing stronger. Something was up with this, all right. "Better get a couple of Stingbirds in the air, Second."

"Right," Klnn-vavgi said, gesturing the order to the warrior at the appropriate monitor.

"And keep a sharp watch on the mountain," Thrr-mezaz added quietly. "If the Mrachanis and Human-Conquerors are working together, this might be a good time for them to attack."

"The device they dropped is still drifting slowly toward us," the commander of the *Requisite* said, jabbing his tongue at one of the monitors in the *Imperative*'s strategy room. "Still apparently attached to the Mrachani spacecraft itself via a long cable. The searchers and Elders on the scene report that it appears to be a slightly different version of the recorder device found in the wreckage of the Human-Conqueror warcraft after that first battle. The message visible on the monitor is in the Human-Conqueror language. We've set up a direct-link back to the *Requisite*'s interpreter and should have something shortly."

"A Human-Conqueror recorder," one of the other ship commanders commented. "Odd way to communicate."

"Not all that odd," Supreme Ship Commander Dkll-kumvit rumbled, stroking the side of his face. "Rather inventive, in fact. Don't forget, they have no way of knowing what frequencies our direct-link lasers use."

"Unless they were able to learn that from the escaped Human-Conqueror prisoner," one of the other ship commanders said tartly, throwing a meaningful look at Thrr-mezaz.

Thrr-mezaz ignored the gibe. "The question is, Supreme Commander, can we believe whatever it is they have to say?"

"That is indeed the question," Dkll-kumvit agreed. "Fortunately, I suppose, it won't be up to us to decide. Warrior Command and the Overclan Seating will be in that particular hot seat. Have the Elders been able to learn anything?"

"Nothing useful," the *Requisite*'s commander said. "Most of the spacecraft's outer hull is metal, and those sections made of other materials usually have metal behind them." The console in front of him twittered— "We have a translation of the Mrachani message," he announced. "Coming through now."

Thrr-mezaz looked at his monitor. The message that scrolled across was very brief.

> We are the Mrachanis. We are not your enemies.
> Please do not attack us. Please allow us to speak
> directly with you.

"Not much there that we're going to have to worry about believing or not believing," one of the ship commanders remarked. "Pretty straightforward."

"True," Dkll-kumvit agreed, rubbing the side of his face again. "Communicator?"

The Elder hovering overhead dropped closer. "Yes, Supreme Commander?"

"Message to Warrior Command. Advise them of the situation and request instructions."

"I obey," the Elder said, and vanished.

"We should have their response in a few hunbeats," Dkll-kumvit said, looking around the strategy room. "Until then I suggest you all adjourn to the war room, where you can monitor events more closely." His gaze stopped on Thrr-mezaz. "Commander Thrr-mezaz, you might as well return to your encampment. I'll keep you company here until your transport is ready."

"I obey, Supreme Commander," Thrr-mezaz said.

The rest of the ship commanders collected their datalists and equipment and left. "Interesting turn of events," Dkll-kumvit said when he and Thrr-mezaz were alone. "Why do you suppose the Mrachanis came here, instead of to one of the other beachheads we've established?"

Thrr-mezaz shrugged. "Convenience, perhaps. Or maybe privacy."

"What do you mean, privacy?"

"Well, except for that one brief raid and the survey ship visits that led up to it, the Human-Conquerors have left Dorcas pretty much alone," Thrr-mezaz pointed out. "If the Mrachanis are the conquered race they claim to be, this would be a logical place to contact us without running into their conquerors."

"You say that as if you don't really believe it," Dkll-kumvit commented. "Do you think the Mrachanis are lying?"

"I think it's a definite possibility," Thrr-mezaz said. "The apparent abandonment of Dorcas by the Human-Conquerors could be a ruse, with the Mrachanis being sent in to try it a different way."

"That's certainly possible," Dkll-kumvit said. "There's another possibility, of course. From Warrior Command's analysis of the data in the captured recorder we've been assuming that the Human-Conquerors are dominated by a single clan, the NorCoord. But there's no reason why the Mrachanis have to be so monolithic."

"So what we could have here might be two different clans at work," Thrr-mezaz said, nodding thoughtfully. "One working for the Human-Conquerors, the other not."

"Or else they're both working against the Human-Conquerors but also against each other," Dkll-kumvit said. "All you have to do is study Zhirrzh history to see how complicated this sort of thing can get."

Thrr-mezaz looked at the monitor and the Mrachani message still displayed there. "I'd recommend, Supreme Commander, that you make sure all these possibilities are passed on to the Overclan before the Mrachani mission leaves Oaccanv."

"I intend to." Dkll-kumvit looked up as the Elder reappeared. "Yes?"

"Message for you, Supreme Commander," the Elder said. " 'Warrior Command to Supreme Ship Commander Dkll-kumvit. Mrachani prisoners are to be held at Dorcas until suitable arrangements can be made for their interrogation. Under no circumstances are they to be brought aboard any of the encirclement warships or sent on to other Zhirrzh worlds.' "

"Understood," Dkll-kumvit said. "How long are these arrangements likely to take?"

The Elder nodded and vanished. "So much for putting a few warriors aboard their spacecraft and sending them on to Oaccanv," Dkll-kumvit commented.

"Yes," Thrr-mezaz agreed. "It sounds as if Warrior Command is having their suspicions, too."

"That's a proper part of their job," Dkll-kumvit pointed out. "The question then arises of what exactly we're supposed to do with the Mrachanis in the meantime."

The Elder reappeared. " 'We anticipate a delay of only a few fullarcs,' " he quoted. " 'We do not wish a repeat of the Base World Twelve incident.' "

"Understandable," Dkll-kumvit said, looking at Thrr-mezaz. "It does, however, leave me in a somewhat awkward position. I concur that we don't want them aboard our warships. But I also don't like the idea of leaving them aboard their own spacecraft, with access to unknown equipment and weaponry."

Thrr-mezaz nodded, suppressing a grimace. It was obvious now why Dkll-kumvit had invited him up here to this meeting. Obvious, too, why the supreme commander had asked him to stay behind for this private chat after sending the other ship commanders off to the war room. "I'm sure that Warrior Command has considered all such possibilities, though," he said. "Shall I volunteer now to take them down to my encampment, or should I wait for an official order?"

Dkll-kumvit smiled wryly. "I suppose you might as well volunteer," he said. "Provided, of course, that you can make sure they're kept away from Zhirrzh technology."

"That won't be a problem," Thrr-mezaz said. "There are several Human-Conqueror buildings we aren't using, one of which in particular would be easy to guard. We'll put them in there."

"Accessible to Elders?"

"Yes," Thrr-mezaz said. "It's a sort of storehouse, with a metal frame and metal in the doors, roof, and window covers. But the rest is all wood. We can also make it comfortable enough to hopefully not offend them in the event they really *are* ambassadors of goodwill."

"Good point," Dkll-kumvit grunted. "A possibility we're going to have to keep in mind." He hesitated, and in his face Thrr-mezaz could see the stipulations of preestablished policy battling with his basic concern for his warriors. "I won't shred words for you here, Commander," he said. "This whole thing could be very dangerous, both to you and the beachhead in general. If you're right, and the Mrachanis are up to something, it could put your ground force in serious danger. As supreme commander on the scene, I can overrule Warrior Command's instructions on this."

"I appreciate that, Supreme Commander," Thrr-mezaz said. "And I thank you for the offer. But being in danger is part of our job, after all." He flicked his tongue. "Besides, I'm curious to see what the Human-Conqueror reaction will be to a Mrachani spacecraft landing inside our encampment."

"It should be interesting," Dkll-kumvit agreed heavily. "Very well, then." He gestured to the Elder. "Inform Warrior Command that the Mrachani spacecraft will be landing in the Zhirrzh beachhead on Dorcas."

"I obey," the Elder said, and vanished.

"Well, that's it, then," Dkll-kumvit said, getting up from his couch. "Better get back to your encampment, Commander, and prepare to receive visitors. Your transport's standing ready for you."

"I obey," Thrr-mezaz said, standing up with him. "Is there anything else about all this I should know?"

"Nothing that's not obvious," Dkll-kumvit said. "A communicator relay pathway will be set up before the Mrachanis arrive at the encampment, with continuous contact between Dorcas and Warrior Command to be maintained during all interactions with them. You may ask general questions concerning their purpose here, but I'll be the only one authorized to perform a complete and formal interrogation. Unless the Overclan decides to send an official alien-studies team—that part's still being worked out. And, of course, the same policy concerning the Elders is to be observed with these aliens as it was for your brother's Human-Conqueror prisoner: they're not to be given any reason to suspect the Elders' existence or presence."

"I understand," Thrr-mezaz said.

"Good," Dkll-kumvit said. "Then good luck, Commander. And be careful."

It was another tentharc before the alien spacecraft came swooping in from the west, its engines making a strange twittering drone sound as it came into earshot. Ahead of it flew one of the *Requisite*'s transports; on either side were a pair of Thrr-mezaz's Stingbirds. All of the beachhead's aircraft were in the sky, watching tensely for the move Thrr-mezaz half expected the Human-Conqueror commander to make.

And at one point an enemy aircraft did indeed appear, drifting almost casually to a point near the edge of the extended air perimeter the Stingbirds' positions had defined. But the aircraft flew back without threat or challenge, disappearing again into the Human-Conqueror stronghold. The Copperhead warriors, thankfully, did not appear at all.

Thrr-mezaz was waiting as the Mrachani spacecraft came down, a translator-link firmly planted in his ear slits, a similarly linked optronic speaker on his shoulder. This spacecraft was much larger than the one the Cakk'rr had tangled with near Cataloged World 592, he saw, and as it rolled toward him, he wondered uneasily what sort of weaponry it carried. If its true mission was to get into the Zhirrzh encampment and try to obliterate it . . .

But the spacecraft rolled to a stop without incident in the center of the circle of light formed by the spotlights the technics had rigged. A hatchway and ramp appeared in one side; and as Thrr-mezaz stepped to the foot of the ramp, two aliens appeared at the top and started down.

The reports regarding the first Mrachani spacecraft had arrived at the Dorcas encampment the previous fullarc, so Thrr-mezaz had some idea what to expect. Even so, the Mrachanis were somthing of a shock. Roughly Zhirrzh-sized, they were slender creatures, with heads and necks coated in short fur like some kind of small animal. Their faces were flat, much closer in appearance to Human-Conqueror design and arrangement than to Zhirrzh faces. They looked harmless, even friendly.

Except that one of their kind had already opened fire on a Zhirrzh ship. It wouldn't hurt to keep that thought in mind.

The Mrachanis reached the foot of the ramp and started speaking. Thrr-mezaz waited, catching an occasional word here and there from his brief and hurried studies of the Human-Conqueror language, until the translation began to come through his translator-link. "We bring greetings to the Zhirrzh people. I am Lahetti-las, representative of the Mrach people. We are not your enemies. We are your friends. We wish to discuss the possibility of working together against our common enemy, the *Mirnacheem-hyeea*."

"I see," Thrr-mezaz said. That *Mirnacheem-hyeea* thing had been in the Overclan Seating report. Conquerors Without Reason, the other Mrachani had translated it: the Human-Conquerors. "I am Thrr-mezaz; Kee'rr," he told them, gesturing to the waiting warriors. Three of them stepped forward and handed *kavra* fruit to Thrr-mezaz and the two Mrachanis. Thrr-mezaz sliced his and waited.

The aliens' response was interesting, and far different from the one Thrr-gilag had observed back on Base World 12 from the Human-Conqueror prisoner. Whereas Phey-lan Cavanagh had simply shown that his tongue wasn't like those of the Zhirrzh and had offered the *kavra* back, the two Mrachanis seemed bound and determined to du-plicate Thrr-mezaz's action. Their tongues were as un-equal to the task as the Human-Conqueror's had been, but they had a go at it anyway. Using the clawlike exten-sions of his fingers, Lahettilas struggled to dig a short and rather shallow groove in the *kavra*'s skin, while the other alien did likewise with his teeth. Thrr-mezaz watched their efforts with mild interest, trying to decide whether he preferred their attempts to act like Zhirrzh or Pheylan Cavanagh's more honest and straightforward acceptance of his limitations.

It took another hunbeat, but eventually the Mrachanis seemed to decide that they had satisfied whatever honor was inherent in this ritual. Thrr-mezaz handed his *kavra* back to the warrior, and the aliens did likewise. "Now,"

Thrr-mezaz said, lowering his hands to drip the remainder of their accumulated juice onto Dorcas's soil, "let us speak. You offer the Zhirrzh your assistance. Tell me why you believe we need such assistance."

His shoulder speaker gave the translation. Thrr-mezaz watched the aliens closely, noticing the sudden stiffening of their fur. A reaction to his question? Lahettilas spoke again—"Surely the Zhirrzh cannot stand alone against the Humans," the translation came. "Surely not against the weapon CIRCE."

Thrr-mezaz frowned. CIRCE? There hadn't been any reference to a weapon called CIRCE in any of the reports he'd read. "The Zhirrzh have mighty weapons, too," he said, wondering if he should ask about this CIRCE thing or pretend he knew all about it. "Perhaps instead we should—"

"Commander Thrr-mezaz!" a thin voice snapped. Thrr-mezaz looked up, to see an Elder hovering directly over the two aliens. "You are to halt this line of questioning immediately."

It was obvious from the way the Mrachanis glanced around that they'd heard the words. Fortunately, by the time they got around to looking up, the Elder was gone. "But this is no place for such discussions," Thrr-mezaz improvised, gesturing again to the warriors and thankful for once that Elder voices couldn't be picked up by optronic microphones. "Your living area is across the landing field. Come with us."

The warriors fell in beside them, and together they all headed across the open space, the spotlights following their path the whole way. Klnn-vavgi and more warriors were waiting for them there, lined up beside the door to the storehouse that they'd hurriedly converted into living quarters for their visitors. "Here is where—" Thrr-mezaz broke off, glancing over his shoulder as the darklight beam connecting him with the interpreter belatedly caught up with him. "Here is where you will stay," he began again. "Two warriors will be on duty outside this door if you need anything. If you will tell me what you need from your spacecraft, I will have it brought to you."

"Thank you," the translator said in Thrr-mezaz's ear slits a few beats later. "Everything we need is in the five cases waiting inside our spacecraft at the top of the ramp. We do not need them quickly."

Or in other words, Lahettilas was fully expecting the Zhirrzh to search their luggage before turning it over to them. Not only expecting it, but rather magnanimously giving them his permission to do so.

Which was just as well. Thrr-mezaz had been planning to search the cases whether they liked it or not. "We will deliver them to you as quickly as possible," he promised the alien. "The warriors will show you inside. Someone will be here later to see you."

"And then there will be talk?" Lahettilas asked.

"Yes," Thrr-mezaz said. "Then there will be talk."

18

For a few brief hunbeats, just before sunset, the sky to the west had been reasonably clear. But that hadn't lasted long; and now, with the last reddish tinges fading from the edges of the clouds, the gap had mostly closed up. Standing at the door of his protector's dome, breathing deeply of the cool evening air, Thrr-tulkoj gazed out at the gathering clouds and wondered idly if they were heavy enough to spill some rain.

He hoped so. Nearly all of the Elders liked rainstorms, at least the quiet, civilized sort. The steady drumming of rain on the shrine; the gentle, almost tickling sensation of the drops that made it through the insect mesh to dribble onto their preserved *fsss* organs; the restless, capricious breezes whispering around the shrine's corners—it all made for a welcome change for them. A respite from the dreary routine and decreased sensory abilities that figured so strongly in an Elder's life.

He looked up at the sky again. On second thought, he amended, it would be better if the rain held off until next fullarc or at least much later this latearc. It would be a shame for the fleeting pleasures of a rainstorm to come when the Elders couldn't properly appreciate them. With virtually all of them clustered over in Cliffside Dales right now listening to the speakers at that Overclan-sponsored debate/discussion, the noise of a rainstorm would just be a distraction.

Across the path the other dome opened up, and a young Zhirrzh stepped outside. Thrr-aamr, freshly recruited to the position of protector of the Thrr family shrine. "Good latearc, Protector Thrr-tulkoj," he said, nodding politely at his superior. "You're here rather late."

"And going to be later still," Thrr-tulkoj told him. "I got a message a few hunbeats ago on the direct-link that Thrr-brov is ill, so I'll be taking his shift this latearc."

"I'm sorry to hear that," Thrr-aamr said. "Do you want me to call one of the Elders and have him track down a substitute?"

"Don't bother," Thrr-tulkoj said, flicking his tongue in a negative. "I'm not tired; and anyway, the Elders are all having a big argument over at Cliffside Dales. I wouldn't want to interrupt their fun."

Thrr-aamr grinned. "I understand. Anyway, I've finished the fullarc's statement and sent it across to your recorder for approval. I've also gone ahead and started the twenty-fullarc review of the current shrine population. Is there anything else I should be working on?"

"Nothing comes to mind," Thrr-tulkoj said, frowning at him. "Aren't we about two fullarcs early for a population review?"

Thrr-aamr shrugged. "I thought that, given how quiet it's likely to be this latearc, I might as well go ahead and get it started now."

Thrr-tulkoj smiled wryly. The kid might be young and fresh to the job, but already he'd caught on to the chief reason family shrines still bothered with protectors. Not to protect them, but to have someone on hand at all times for lonely Elders to talk to. "Point well taken," he said. "Sure, keep going with it."

"Yes, Protector."

Thrr-tulkoj glanced at the sky again. "On second thought, as long as you're already on your feet, why don't you go ahead and do a perimeter walk first. The initial section of a population review mostly runs itself, anyway."

"Yes, I know," Thrr-aamr said, reaching into the dome and picking up his laser rifle. "I'll be back soon," he added, slinging it over his shoulder and starting down the path toward the gate.

"No rush," Thrr-tulkoj said. "Might as well enjoy the air and make a really good check of the fence. As you said, it's going to be a quiet latearc."

"Sure thing," Thrr-aamr said.

Thrr-tulkoj stepped back into his dome and touched the door button. The curved wedge of material slid closed on its track and sealed; and as it did so, the dome abruptly seemed to vanish as the special ceramic turned one-way transparent. For a few beats he watched Thrr-aamr make his way toward the predator fence gate, now sealed for the latearc. Then, stretching once, he turned around and sat down on his couch, swiveled now to face the shrine. For a beat he gazed up at the brilliant white surface, growing dim as the sunlight faded out to the west. Then, dropping his attention to his desk, he activated his recorder and began reading Thrr-aamr's fullarc statement.

• • •

Across the darkened chambers came a quiet knock at the door. Frowning, the Prime looked up from his recorder. "Come in," he called.

The door opened. "Good latearc, Overclan Prime," Speaker Cvv-panav said as he stepped inside. "You're up late. I take it I'm not intruding?"

"Not particularly," the Prime said, not entirely truthfully. "Can I help you with something?"

"No," Cvv-panav said, closing the door behind him. "I just thought I'd stop by to tell you that it's started."

"What's started?"

"The retrieval of Thrr-pifix-a's *fsss* organ from her family shrine, of course," Cvv-panav said, settling himself down on the visitor's couch in front of the Prime's desk. "Surely you hadn't forgotten?"

"Hardly," the Prime said, looking at his armwatch. "I'm a bit surprised at the timing, that's all. It won't even be fully dark out in Kee'rr territory yet."

"It's dark enough," Cvv-panav assured him. "Certainly for a theft from a couple of simple and unsuspecting shrine protectors." He paused. "And, of course, the slightly early timing should help in getting the jump on all the rest of it, too."

The Prime eyed him. "All the rest of what?"

Cvv-panav smiled tightly. "Come now, Overclan Prime. You didn't really think I was foolish enough to take your story at face value, did you? Thrr-pifix-a being a threat to the stability of Zhirrzh culture, and all that?"

"That wasn't just a story," the Prime said quietly. In the darkness behind Cvv-panav, he could make out the image of the Eighteenth, hovering there listening. "Thrr-pifix-a's attitude is a genuine threat to the legal and traditional bases of Eldership. One that has cropped up more than once in the past five hundred cyclics."

"Oh, I have no doubt of that," Cvv-panav agreed. "And I have no doubt that you see it as a danger of sorts. But we both know what you see as the *real* threat to your power."

The Prime flicked his tongue. "You?"

"Very good," Cvv-panav said approvingly. "No feigned surprise; no false astonishment. And all by itself it proves that I'm right."

The Eighteenth was still there, still listening. An emergency communication link that Cvv-panav didn't know about, should this whole thing go badly wrong. "You're wrong," the Prime told Cvv-panav. "I guessed only because I understand how you think. That you see yourself as one of the High Warriors of old, who will lead the Dhaa'rr to glorious domination of the eighteen worlds. The breakwater that all other Zhirrzh must throw themselves against, to destroy or else be destroyed by."

"All politics is warfare, Overclan Prime," Cvv-panav said. "All of life is, for that matter. It's a battle of wills and of strength. Of course you're out to destroy me. That's the natural order of things."

"And where does cooperation come in?"

Cvv-panav sniffed contemptuously. "Cooperation was invented by people who didn't have enough strength to win what they really wanted. You and I are warriors, Overclan Prime. We're beyond such things."

The Prime flicked his tongue in disgust. "You've certainly recreated the attitude of the old High Warriors—I'll give you that much. Enough of this, and we won't need the Human-Conquerors to destroy our culture for us."

"I would say it's precisely that warrior attitude that we need right now," Cvv-panav countered. "You can bet the

Human-Conquerors didn't grow to dominate all within their reach by making compromises with inferior peoples. Tell me about CIRCE."

The Prime felt his tail twitch. "CIRCE?" he asked as casually as he could. "What's that?"

"Don't play coy with me, Overclan Prime," Cvv-panav warned. "You know perfectly well what CIRCE is. It's a Human-Conqueror weapon of great power. I want to know the details."

The Eighteenth was still there. "I don't know what you're talking about," the Prime said. "Where did you hear about this CIRCE?"

Cvv-panav snorted under his breath. "The High Warrior plays for time," he said, a note of disgust in his voice. "Fine; so be it. I have as much time as you do . . . and when your obvious little warrior net comes up empty, you'll tell me what I want to know. Or else I'll bring you down, and the entire Overclan along with you."

The Prime grimaced. So Cvv-panav knew all about the warrior net he'd set around the Thrr family shrine. "Perhaps," he said, his mouth and voice stiff. "We'll see. In the meantime, as you pointed out, it's rather late. If you'll excuse me, I have work to do."

"Certainly," Cvv-panav said, settling himself more comfortably on his couch. "Go right ahead. We have all latearc."

There was a flicker of light, just visible out of the corner of his eye, and with a frown Thrr-tulkoj looked up from his reader. Odd; the weather forecast hadn't made any mention of lightning. Letting his lowlight pupils widen, he scanned the sky beyond the shrine.

It was certainly cloudy enough in that direction, but they weren't the sort of clouds that generally spawned thunderstorms. Even as he studied them, though, there was another flicker of light, this one off to his right. He turned quickly, just in time to catch a third flash from over the hills that dotted the eastern horizon. And it had definitely not looked like lightning.

It had looked like laser fire.

Eyes still on the hills, he fumbled for the key that activated his direct-link to the other dome. "Thrr-aamr?" he called. "Take a look at the horizon due east."

There was no answer. "Thrr-aamr? Come on, look alive."

Again, no answer. Of course: Thrr-aamr was probably still walking the perimeter. Peering out at the predator fence half a thoustride away, Thrr-tulkoj keyed off the direct-link and reached instead for the control to the loud-speaker he used to summon Elders. The noise would cut into their debate over in Cliffside Dales, of course, but that couldn't be helped. Anyway, it wouldn't be any worse for them than if he stepped outside the dome and shouted.

He paused, his fingers resting on the switch. Thrr-aamr wasn't walking along the predator fence, at least not any part of it Thrr-tulkoj could see. In fact, the younger pro-tector was nowhere to be seen.

Thrr-tulkoj looked around the fence again, an unpleas-ant tingle running through him. No; no mistake. Thrr-aamr had vanished.

Unless he was back in his dome and the direct-link had simply malfunctioned. Sure; that was probably what had happened. All Thrr-tulkoj had to do was step outside, tap on Thrr-aamr's dome, and the two of them together could then have a nice calm discussion about what kind of phe-nomenon could produce lightning that looked like laser fire.

Thrr-tulkoj's hand was still resting on the loudspeaker switch. He let it go, inactivated, moving his hand instead to the laser rifle propped against the dome beside the door. Sliding off his couch, he punched the door release and slipped outside.

The sun was long gone beneath the horizon, and the shifting breezes had turned chilly. For a few beats Thrr-tulkoj crouched beside the dome, laser rifle held ready, ear slits straining for any unusual sounds. Nothing. His low-light pupils were already fully open, and now that he was outside the darklight-blocking effect of the dome, he let his darklight pupils widen as well. The landscape around him took on tinges of heat-radiant glow; carefully, methodically, he began a slow sweep of the parts of the shrine enclosure he could see.

Nothing.

Swearing under his breath, he moved a quarter of the way around the side of his dome and started the search again. This was stupid. It really was. Chances were good Thrr-aamr was sitting inside his dome right now, either completely oblivious to Thrr-tulkoj's antics out here or else watching in bemusement as his superior made a fool of himself. He ought to just go over and pound on the door—

He froze. There, across by the bluff overview, something was lying on the ground beside the predator fence. About the size of an adult Zhirrzh.

Not moving.

"Of course it was obvious to me from the start what you really had in mind when you suggested this operation," Cvv-panav commented. "People close to me, I believe you specified when we talked; people I could implicitly trust. People whose very identity would indict me along with them when your net of warriors caught them with a stolen *fsss* organ in hand."

"I had nothing of the sort in mind," the Prime said. "The Overclan warriors are surrounding the Thrr shrine solely to provide your people with cover. To make sure no one wanders into the area at an awkward time."

"Ah," Cvv-panav said. "So you admit that there are warriors there?"

"It wouldn't do much good to deny it," the Prime pointed out. "You've obviously already had word from your own people that they're there. *My* question is, what are you doing to them?"

"The High Warrior worried about his warriors?"

The Prime locked eyes with him. "The Overclan Prime concerned about those under his authority," he bit out. "What are you doing to them?"

Cvv-panav's mouth twitched. "It depends on how peacefully they surrender," he said, some of the arrogance gone from his voice. "Assuming the idea of Eldership holds no great fascination for any of them, they should all be lying on the ground by now with laser rifles held against their *fsss* scars. Unhurt."

"And if they decided instead to fight?"

Cvv-panav shrugged. "I sincerely hope that's not the case. I have no particular desire to raise any of them to Eldership."

"I'm pleased to hear that," the Prime said bitterly. "I don't suppose any of that altruism might come from the fact that raising them to Eldership would put them in instant contact with the Elder community and flash the alarm all across Oaccanv."

Cvv-panav shrugged again. "My people know what they're doing. Tell me about CIRCE."

"I trust your people will also remember that the Overclan warriors standing by near Reeds Village are there to arrest Thrr-pifix-a after her *fss* has been delivered to her," the Prime said, ignoring the other's question. "If they're delayed too long, she'll have time to destroy it."

"Ending any chance of burying the incident without a public trial," Cvv-panav nodded. "Don't worry, Overclan Prime. I'm watching over the Dhaa'rr clan's interests here. All of our interests. Now, are you going to tell me about CIRCE? Or shall I instruct the Dhaa'rr Elders to begin spreading the word about this mysterious Human-Conqueror weapon that has the Mrachanis so frightened?"

The Prime grimaced. So that was how Cvv-panav had found out about CIRCE. Bad; but not as bad as it might have been. The Mrachanis who'd landed at the Dorcas beachhead had said little more than CIRCE's name before Warrior Command had been able to stifle that line of discussion. It was too bad that one of the Elders in attendance had leaked the name to Cvv-panav, but at least he didn't have the whole story.

But even with just a name he had enough of a lever to do some serious prying with. And if he chose to have this out in public in the Overclan Seating, nothing about CIRCE would stay a secret for long.

So it all hung on what happened in the next couple of tentharcs out in Kee'rr territory—on his people's skill, and on the accuracy of his own perception of how Cvv-panav saw the universe and his own place in it.

"I have nothing to say right now about CIRCE," he told Cvv-panav. "Except that it's something that must be kept secret."

Cvv-panav smiled. "In other words, you still have hopes that your warriors will prevail out there and bring me down. Very well; I can wait. When word comes that my people have completed their mission and successfully vanished into the darkness of latearc, perhaps you'll recognize that your choices are between a private briefing or a public battle."

"Perhaps," the Prime said. "Or perhaps an entirely different word will come to you. Shall we wait here together and see?"

Cvv-panav eyed him, the first hint of uncertainty flicking across his face. "Certainly," he said. "Why not."

It was Thrr-aamr, all right, lying there in a crumpled heap at the base of the predator fence. Unconscious, a swelling lump already forming at the base of his skull where he'd been hit. Beside him was a neat cut in the mesh of the fence, just big enough for a Zhirrzh to crawl through, directly over the steepest part of the bluff.

Someone had penetrated the enclosure.

Thrr-tulkoj swore again, this time meaning it, as he dropped flat on the ground beside Thrr-aamr and swung his laser rifle around to firing position. He couldn't see anything moving or radiating near the shrine, but that didn't prove much. He—or they—could be around on the far side of the shrine right now, out of Thrr-tulkoj's sight. Besides, intruders clever enough to breach the fence at the one spot no protector would ever expect trouble would certainly be clever enough to be wearing darklight-suppressing combat suits while they did it.

They would also be clever enough to crawl across the ground, lest someone watching from the protectors' domes spotted them. Which would take time. Which meant that unless Thrr-aamr had happened to have the misfortune of catching them on their way out, the intruders were most likely still here.

Pressed against the ground, his tail spinning rapidly, Thrr-tulkoj peered across the open ground and wondered what in the eighteen worlds he was going to do. The simplest, most straightforward thing would be to shout as loud as he could and hope that at least some of the Elders on this side of the shrine would hear him. If he could get a warning into the Elder community, the whole planet could be aroused in a matter of hunbeats.

But there was no guarantee that his voice would carry well enough against the latearc breezes for anyone to hear him. Except maybe the intruders. And if they were armed —and they almost certainly were—then at the first sign of trouble from him they would do their best to raise him to Eldership.

Thrr-tulkoj wasn't afraid of Eldership. The threat of premature raising was supposed to come with this job. But if he was raised now, it would leave the Elders and the shrine completely defenseless.

Steady, he told himself firmly, pressing closer against Thrr-aamr. *Think it through. You're a trained protector, and you're a long way from being helpless here. Think it through.*

He should have used the loudspeaker right at the beginning, of course. In backsight that was painfully clear. But the procedures stated explicitly that the Elders were not to be alerted in cases of suspected intrusion, probably because every such incident for the past hundred cyclics had turned out to be a false alarm. Thrr-tulkoj *had* hit the direct-link emergency signal mounted to the side of the dome before heading over here; the fact that there hadn't yet been a response from Cliffside Dales implied that the intruders must have cut the cable somewhere before breaking in. Either that, or the system had simply fallen apart from disuse.

The best thing would be if he could get back to the dome. The loudspeaker would let him sound the alarm, not to mention the laser protection the one-way ceramic would afford him if it came down to a battle.

Unfortunately, nearly half a thoustride of open ground lay between him and the domes right now. Worse, he hadn't been particularly surreptitious on his way over to the fence. If the intruders had spotted him, they were undoubtedly watching and waiting for his next move. Probably with lasers already pointed his direction.

Which left him really only one option. He would have to slip through the hole the intruders had made in the fence, make his way down the bluff and over to the rail stop near the gate, and use the direct-link installed there to sound the alert. It would be a tricky climb, and it would mean leaving the shrine undefended, but there was nothing he could do about that. Keeping a close eye on the area around the shrine, he started to ease his way around Thrr-aamr—

And froze, listening. A new sound was drifting in to him over the latearc breezes. A transport, somewhere in the near distance.

The reinforcements from Cliffside Dales had arrived.

Moving his head as little as possible, Thrr-tulkoj searched the sky for the craft, a fresh surge of excitement rippling through him. Protector laser rifles were infinitely adjustable, in both intensity and spread angle, and there was a specified procedure for tuning the power and muzzle-coning down far enough to make the weapon into a safe flash-code signaler. A signaler, moreover, whose beam would be easily visible to the transport pilot and yet wouldn't sizzle the atmospheric water enough to produce emissions visible in any other direction. He could start with a simple three-two-three distress signal. . . .

He frowned, his hands pausing midway through the necessary adjustments. The hum of the transport's engines had choked suddenly, dissolving into the sharp crackle characteristic of a misfiring transkilmer. Was the transport in trouble? He looked around the sky again, but he couldn't spot any running lights in the direction the sound was coming from. Odd. Had the transport's optronics failed, too? No; of course, the warriors would be trying to make an invisible approach. The hum returned, crackled again; returned, crackled again; returned, crackled again—

And then, in the middle of the last crackle, he abruptly understood. The noise wasn't coming from engine failure, at least not from unintentional engine failure. It had been deliberately created, designed for a very specific purpose.

To cover up the sound of a *fsss*-niche cover being opened.

For a beat Thrr-tulkoj's mind flashed back four fullarcs to that attempt by Thrr-gilag's mother to steal back her *fsss*. Thrr-pifix-a herself couldn't have climbed the bluff, certainly, but she might have found friends or relatives to do it for her.

He glanced down at Thrr-aamr's unconscious form. No. He knew Thrr-pifix-a and her family, and none of them would ever have condoned violence of this sort against one of her shrine's protectors.

But then who? And why?

The transport's engines had settled down again to their normal hum, and from the sound of it, the vehicle was veering off. Apparently its sole job had been to cover the noise of the intruders opening their target niche.

Thrr-tulkoj gripped his rifle harder, the brief flicker of hope giving way again to frustrated indecision. The intruders had one of the niches open now, with free access to the *fsss* organ inside. But surely the owner would have felt their touch by now and come back to investigate.

But no Elder had yet appeared. Were they dealing with the *fsss* of someone who was still a physical, then?

Again Thrr-tulkoj's thoughts flicked to Thrr-pifix-a. But again he rejected the idea that she could possibly be behind this. This was something vicious, like the bitter living-death feuds of nine hundred cyclics ago.

He winced at the thought. *Living death:* the deliberate destruction of an enemy physical's *fsss*. The exquisite torture of leaving him to live out his physical life with the knowledge that nothing but certain death awaited him at the end of it. Such feuds had once been widespread on Oaccanv, ultimately precipitating the Second Eldership War. If someone was trying to resurrect the abominations of that era . . .

He stiffened. Over at the shrine a figure had raised itself up from the ground. For a beat it stood there, silhouetted against the white ceramic. Then, crouching low, it headed across the enclosure.

Directly toward Thrr-tulkoj.

Thrr-tulkoj pressed his tongue hard against the inside of his mouth, quickly readjusting his laser rifle back to full power. The figure was still coming, blatantly arrogant in his presumption that no protector would dare fire on him with a shrine at his back. Lifting his laser rifle a fraction, Thrr-tulkoj peered through its sights. Right or wrong, it was time to make a move. Taking a deep breath and holding it, he settled his thumbs against the rifle's triggers.

His only warning was a whisper of sound from above him . . . and by then it was too late. Too late to react; too late to move; too late to do anything but realize to his shame and chagrin that the enemy had outmaneuvered him one final time. Against the sudden hum of the returning transport came the faint flopping sound of something semirigid flying through the air toward him—

And suddenly he was hammered flat against the ground as the black stickiness of a tar slab slammed into him.

He dropped his weapon, turning half-over and pushing upward against the sticky, semisolid blackness. It molded itself around his hands, the sides folding gradually but inexorably in toward his body. He tried pulling his hands sideways in opposite directions, hoping to tear a hole in it. But the slab was too thick, the material too resilient, and he succeeded only in lowering the roof of the slowly shrinking cave he and Thrr-aamr were in. Desperately, he let go with one hand and grabbed for his laser rifle, swiveling it awkwardly in the cramped space and managing to get it jammed up into the tar like a tent pole. Mentally pleading for good luck, he pressed the triggers.

The entire tar slab didn't burst into flame, as he'd feared it might. Instead, a small section around the muzzle flashed into vapor. The slab dropped inward around the new hole; holding it back with one hand, Thrr-tulkoj repositioned the rifle to another spot and fired again.

It seemed to take forever but was probably no more than fifteen hunbeats before he had enough of the tar slab vaporized to pull himself out from under it. Breathing heavily, his tail going double time with the body heat he hadn't been able to get rid of in there, he got shakily to his feet and looked around.

Not that there was any need to do so. The intruders and their transport were long gone, having accomplished whatever it was they'd come there to do.

Swearing dully, he reached down and pulled Thrr-aamr partway out of the tar, making sure his face and tail were clear. Then, retrieving his rifle, he headed across the enclosure toward the dome. It was far too late to give the alarm now—whatever the damage, it was already done. But it was still part of his job to do so.

Very likely the last part of this job he would ever do.

"Yes, I'm coming," Thrr-pifix-a called as the insistent knock came a second time on her door. She'd spent much of the postmidarc in her garden, and her legs had now stiffened up as she sat fussing with her decorative edgework. "I'll be there in just a hunbeat."

Whoever was out there apparently heard her, because the knocking stopped. She made her way across the conversation room to the foyer, her legs thankfully loosening up somewhat in the process. Reaching the door, she opened it.

There was no one there.

Frowning, she took a half step outside, letting her low-light and darklight pupils widen as she looked around in the darkness. No one. Some child, perhaps, up late pulling pranks? She took another half step outside, shivering in the chilly latearc air—

Her foot kicked something solid. Frowning some more, she looked down.

It was a small pouch, of the sort she liked to practice her edgework on, just lying there in the dirt. Bending over with some difficulty—her back had stiffened up, too—she retrieved it and stepped back into the foyer. Pulling the fastening strip open, she looked inside.

And froze, her hands going suddenly rigid.

It was a *fsss* organ.

She hurried outside again, this time going all the way to the roadway. But Korthe and Dornt were nowhere to be seen. They must have just set the pouch and *fsss* down and run.

Something in the back of Thrr-pifix-a's mind found

that disturbing. But for right now it didn't seem to matter. What mattered was that they'd kept their pledge to her.

She had her *fsss*.

Slowly, she retraced her steps back into the house, closing and locking the door behind her. She had her *fsss*. Here, in her hands. Her own *fsss*. To destroy, if she so chose.

The question was, *did* she now so choose?

She groped her way to the kitchen table and sat down, staring into the open pouch as she did so, her mind a swirl of conflicting thoughts and emotions and questions. This was what she had wanted, wasn't it? Of course it was. She had her future—her life—here in her hands. All she had to do—

And suddenly, without challenge or warning of any sort, her door slammed open.

She spun around in her chair, the pouch somehow getting away from startled fingers. Three Zhirrzh were already in her house—big Zhirrzh, wearing the sort of warrior fighting suits she'd seen in pictures and dramas—with more of them piling in through the door behind them. All were carrying short, vicious-looking weapons; all were wearing grim expressions.

Weapons and expressions that were pointed directly at her.

"What's going on?" she demanded. Or rather, tried to demand. Even in her own ear slits, her voice sounded as weak and thin as that of a sickly child. "What do you want?"

The lead warrior didn't bother to answer. Stepping into the kitchen, he reached a long arm down to the floor and retrieved the pouch she'd dropped. "Is this yours?" he asked, his voice as cold as the latearc air as he held it up.

For the first time Thrr-pifix-a focused on the pouch itself. To find, to her utter amazement, that it *was* indeed hers. There was her edgework, plain as a sunny fullarc, edgework she'd completed not five fullarcs ago.

But how in the eighteen worlds had it wound up at her door?

The warrior was still waiting for an answer. "Yes," she murmured, still staring at the pouch. Korthe or Dornt must have stolen it. That was the only explanation. They must have stolen it while they were here last fullarc. Without her even noticing.

"And this," the warrior said, holding it open for her inspection. "You want to tell us what you're doing with this?"

Thrr-pifix-a stared up at his face, a horrible twisting sensation knifing through her. Suddenly, suddenly, it was clear. She'd been set up. For whatever reason, she'd been set up. "I didn't take it," she whispered. "It was two young male Zhirrzh. Korthe and Dornt, they called themselves. They said they were members of an organization called Freedom of Decision for All."

"Uh-huh," the first warrior grunted, handing the pouch to another warrior. "Korthe and Dornt, from Freedom of Decision for All. Right."

"It's true," Thrr-pifix-a insisted. "Really. They said they'd get my *fsss* for me. And they did."

"And did they happen to mention to you that *fsss* theft is a grand-first felony?" another warrior put in harshly.

"That's enough," the first warrior said before Thrr-pifix-a could stammer an answer. "We'll check it out. In the meantime—" He fixed Thrr-pifix-a with cold eyes. "Thrr-pifix-a; Kee'rr, you're hereby charged with grand-first theft and placed under detention. By authority of the Overclan."

Thrr-pifix-a squeezed her eyes shut. She made no comment, offered no resistance, as they helped her up and took her out into the cold latearc air.

The messenger turned and left the chambers, closing the door behind her. "Well?" the Prime asked as Cvv-panav opened the message. Though he was pretty sure he already knew what was in it.

He was right. "As expected," Cvv-panav said, tossing the message casually onto the desk in front of the Prime. "My people have completed their mission." He eyed the Prime, his expression just short of gloating. "Without any successful interference from either the Thrr protectors or your warriors."

"As I've already told you, my warriors weren't there to interfere," the Prime reminded him.

"Of course they weren't," Cvv-panav said. "Well. According to this, my people observed your warriors enter Thrr-pifix-a's house and take her away in a transport. You should be getting a report on that yourself before long."

"No doubt," the Prime agreed. In actual fact the report had already come in, transmitted via the direct-link to his reader nearly ten hunbeats ago. But Cvv-panav didn't have to know that. "I presume that finishes the latearc's excitement. You'll be going home now, I expect."

Cvv-panav eyed him. "Unless you're ready to tell me about the weapon called CIRCE."

The Prime flicked his tongue in a negative. "CIRCE is a warrior secret, Speaker. As I've already told you."

"And as I've already told *you,* you'll tell me or you'll tell the entire Overclan Seating," Cvv-panav countered. "And all the Elders who'll be listening. I'm not bluffing."

"You'd threaten to bring down the entire Overclan system in the middle of a war?" the Prime asked.

"Why not?" Cvv-panav shot back. "You were prepared this latearc to destroy me and alienate the entire Dhaa'rr clan from the Overclan."

"The warriors were not there—"

"Spare me," Cvv-panav cut him off, standing up. "You've got until the Overclan Seating session next postmidarc to tell me about CIRCE. After that what happens will be on your own shoulders, Overclan Prime."

Without waiting for a reply he turned and stalked out of the chambers, slamming the door behind him.

"Well," the Eighteenth commented in the sudden silence. "That seemed to go well."

"Or at least as expected," the Prime said, unclenching his hands.

The Eighteenth peered at him. "You're not worried, are you?" he asked. "Everything's worked out exactly as planned."

"Except for how he's going to react," the Prime said, gesturing in the direction Cvv-panav had gone. "He's got enough pride and stubbornness for any six Zhirrzh. What if he doesn't fold?"

"He will," the Eighteenth assured him. "He'll fold because he's also ambitious. Ambitious Zhirrzh do not bring the target of their ambitions down in flames around them. Not if there are any other options still remaining."

"He won't forget this, though," the Prime said. "There'll be more trouble with him down the line."

"We have the Human-Conquerors arrayed against us," the Eighteenth reminded him grimly. "Under the circumstances I think one vindictive Clan Speaker will be the least of our worries."

The Prime nodded. "I hope so. Still . . . you never know."

19 The doors of both domes opened simultaneously, and two protectors stepped out to flank the flagstone path, their laser rifles at the ready. "This is it," Klnn-dawan-a murmured. "You ready?"

"As ready as I'm going to be," Thrr-gilag murmured from beside her. "I just hope this works. If it doesn't, we're going to be in a lot of trouble."

Klnn-dawan-a nodded silently. Actually, even if it did work, there was going to be a lot of trouble. It would merely fall in on them a little later.

But the option was to do nothing and let Prr't-zevisti die. If the Human-Conquerors hadn't killed him already.

"Halt and stand," the protector on the left said in the words of the ancient Dhaa'rr ritual. "Speak your names to the protectors of the Prr."

"We obey the protectors of the Prr," Klnn-dawan-a

said, stopping between the twin racks of *kavra* fruit that flanked the path. "I am Klnn-dawan-a; Dhaa'rr."

"I am Thrr-gilag," Thrr-gilag said. "Kee'rr."

It seemed to Klnn-dawan-a that the protectors lifted their rifles just a little higher at Thrr-gilag's non-Dhaa'rr clan name. "How do you prove your goodwill?" the first protector demanded.

"With the rite of the *kavra*," Klnn-dawan-a said, selecting one of the fruit from the rack and slicing it. Out of the corner of her eye she saw Thrr-gilag doing likewise. "We stand now defenseless before the protectors of Prr," she continued, dropping the lacerated *kavra* into the disposal container.

The protectors had watched the whole operation closely. Particularly Thrr-gilag's part of it. "And who will offer you welcome?" the first protector asked.

"A friend and colleague," Klnn-dawan-a said. "Prr't-casst-a; Dhaa'rr."

The protector frowned. "Advance, Klnn-dawan-a," he said, lowering his rifle to not quite point at them. "What do you mean by calling her a colleague?"

"We're doing a small sensory experiment with *fss* organs," Klnn-dawan-a explained as she stepped away from Thrr-gilag and over to the protectors. "Prr't-casst-a has graciously volunteered to be one of our test subjects."

"What sort of experiment?" the second protector growled. "And do you have authorization?"

"Right here," Thrr-gilag said, holding out the forms they'd put together. "May I approach the protectors of Prr?"

The first protector didn't seem all that enthusiastic about it, but he nevertheless nodded. "Advance, Thrr-gilag."

Thrr-gilag rejoined Klnn-dawan-a and handed the protector the forms. Klnn-dawan-a watched as the other took them, striving hard to keep her tail motion steady. Right here was where this whole thing was most likely to come unraveled. The description/authorization forms were certainly official enough; the problem was that they were for experiments on non-Zhirrzh alien species like her cocooned Chig whelps back on Gree. If the protectors were suspicious enough or bored enough to read past the names and descriptions and get into the more detailed printing . . .

The first protector gestured to his partner as he glanced over the top page. "Give Prr't-casst-a call," he said. "Let's see what she has to say about this."

The other protector nodded and stepped back into his dome. A beat later his amplified voice echoed across the shrine enclosure, summoning Prr't-casst-a to the domes.

She was there almost before the echo of the loudspeaker had died away over the hills. "So you made it after all," she said, looking back and forth between Klnn-dawan-a and Thrr-gilag. "I didn't think you were going to have time."

"One of our other volunteers quit on us at the last hunbeat," Thrr-gilag said, pulling a small flat box from his waist pouch and lifting the lid. "We decided we had enough time to swing by here. If you'll clear us with your protectors, we can get started."

"Not so fast," the first protector growled, stepping forward and plucking the box from Thrr-gilag's hand. "I haven't been told anything about any experiments with Prr *fsss* organs."

"It's something new," Thrr-gilag told him. "A series of experiments to see if new sensory enhancements can be created for Elders. Don't worry, it's perfectly safe."

"We'll decide how safe it is, if you don't mind," the

protector said, frowning at block of reddish gel and the spoon with its thick, cylindrically shaped handle occupying the two parallel compartments in the box. "What is this stuff?"

"The complete composition report is in the authorization," Klnn-dawan-a said, pointing at the forms he still had in his other hand. "Basically, you could say it's similar to a very spicy Ghuu'rr basting sauce."

The protector blinked at her. "You're kidding. A *basting* sauce?"

"That's rather an oversimplification, of course," Thrr-gilag said curtly, throwing a look at Klnn-dawan-a that had just the right edge of professional annoyance to it. She winced slightly in response, the look of a subordinate nonverbally reprimanded by a superior. The more the protectors had the impression that Thrr-gilag was the one in charge—and therefore the one to watch most closely—the better. "What she means is that the glaze is similar to a basting sauce in that it's rich with selected spices and olfactory enhancements," Thrr-gilag continued. "We're hoping this will be a way to add an extra dimension to Elder life. Look, it's all in the authorization, and it's all perfectly safe. And we really are on a tight schedule."

The protector thrust the box back at Thrr-gilag. "Prove it's safe," he challenged. "Eat some."

Thrr-gilag shrugged. "Certainly." Picking up the spoon, he scooped up a small portion of the gel and licked it off. "Perfectly safe," he said, holding the spoon poised for another scoop. "Rather tasty, actually. Would you like to try some?"

The protector made a face. "No, thanks," he said. "Prr't-casst-a, you sure you want to go through with this?"

"Very much," the Elder said, her voice low and with a

quiet passion that required no acting at all on her part. "Please let them in."

The protector sighed. "All right, come on. Prr't-casst-a, go ahead and show us to your niche."

They headed off toward the shrine, Prr't-casst-a hovering in the lead, the second protector bringing up the rear. Klnn-dawan-a took a deep breath, not daring to look at Thrr-gilag and trying to exude a nonchalance she didn't feel. First stage: passed. Now all she had to do was hope this scheme she and Thrr-gilag had cooked up would work as well in practice as it did in theory. And that she could pull off her part of it.

Prr't-casst-a's niche was located about three strides up the northwestern wall of the shrine. Using a control set into one edge of the white ceramic, the first protector unfolded a mechanical top-tethered platform from the apex section at the peak. Just barely big enough for three, Klnn-dawan-a estimated as the motors brought it down to ground level. Which meant one of the protectors would probably insist on going along.

She was right. "I'll need to go up with you," the protector said, stepping through the gap in the guardrail onto the platform and moving to its right end.

"Other end, please," Thrr-gilag said, motioning him to the left side of the platform. "I need to be in the middle, with my assistant on my right."

The protector moved to the left end without comment. Klnn-dawan-a took up position at the right end, and Thrr-gilag squeezed in to stand between them. The protector gestured to his partner, and the platform began to rise. A few beats' worth of maneuvering later, they were there.

"Good," Thrr-gilag said briskly, handing the open box

to Klnn-dawan-a and pulling a pair of healer's gloves from his pouch. "If you'll open the niche for us, Protector?"

Klnn-dawan-a winced at the loud snap as the protector released the catch and swung Prr't-casst-a's mesh door open. Incredibly loud things, obviously designed that way so as to alert protectors and Elders alike to any unauthorized tampering. Standing there with a protector half a stride away, she knew there wasn't a chance in the universe that she would be able to open the door to Prr't-zevisti's niche without being noticed.

But then, she wasn't planning on opening his door. In fact, she was hoping very much not to.

"Good," Thrr-gilag said again, wiggling his fingers as he checked the feel of his gloves and peering in through the opening at Prr't-casst-a's *fsss*. "If you'll hold that door open for me, Protector? Excellent. You ready, Klnn-dawan-a?"

"I'm ready," Klnn-dawan-a told him. In her left hand she held the box for him, its open lid strategically positioned where it would block the protector's view of Prr't-zevisti's niche. In her right hand, also hidden from the protector beneath the box, she held the spoon where Thrr-gilag could reach it.

"Prr't-casst-a?"

"I'm ready," the Elder said, hovering half in and half out of the shrine in front of Klnn-dawan-a. Ostensibly watching Thrr-gilag and the experiment, she was positioned where her transparent form would do what little it could to help conceal what was about to happen.

"All right, then," Thrr-gilag said. "Here we go." Getting a good grip on the spoon, he pulled it away from Klnn-dawan-a.

And as he did so, the spoon's end cap came loose in her grasp. Leaving her holding the end of the needle-tipped tissue sampler that had been hidden inside the spoon's thick handle.

"Here we go," Thrr-gilag said again, adjusting his grip on the spoon so that his hand was covering the missing end cap as he scooped up some of the red gel. "Okay, Prr't-casst-a. Tell me how this feels."

He began smoothing the gel onto Prr't-casst-a's *fsss* organ, the two of them keeping up a running barrage of questions and comments as he worked. But Klnn-dawan-a didn't really notice. Carefully, keeping it beneath the box, she turned the sampler around in her hand and eased the slender needle through the mesh into Prr't-zevisti's niche. Working by touch, she located the *fsss* organ. Then, bracing herself, she pressed the needle firmly against the hardened outer layer and began to push.

For a beat it didn't work. Then, abruptly, the outer layer yielded and the needle slid into the softer part inside. Klnn-dawan-a winced in sympathetic pain—surely this would have been a stab of agony to an Elder anchored here. But in this case, of course, Prr't-zevisti wasn't in any position to feel anything. Touching the button on the end of the sampler, she got it started.

It seemed to take forever before the gentle vibration stopped. If she and Thrr-gilag had done their calculations correctly, the sampler tube should now contain the same volume of *fsss* cells as a standard *fsss* cutting. Whether it would work the same way, though, was something they wouldn't know until they got the sampler to Thrr-mezaz on Dorcas. If then.

Second stage: passed. Now came possibly the most delicate part of all. Easing the sampler back toward her until the *fsss* was pressed up against the ceramic mesh, Klnn-dawan-a braced a corner of the box against the door and began a steady pull. If the needle was so tightly embedded that its removal threw her back against the guardrail, the protectors couldn't help but notice. Worse, if the pressure snapped the catch and the door swung open with the *fsss* still impaled on the needle . . .

And then, so suddenly that she was almost caught unprepared, the needle was free. Catching her balance, she quickly slid the sampler back into position beneath the box. A handful of Elders had drifted in to watch the experiment on Prr't-casst-a's *fsss;* she could only hope that none of them had happened to notice her part of it. If they had—

Abruptly, an Elder appeared in front of Thrr-gilag. "Are you Thrr-gilag; Kee'rr?" she demanded.

Out of the corner of her eye Klnn-dawan-a saw Thrr-gilag's tail twitch violently. "Yes," he said.

"Message for you," the Elder said, her voice curt. "Wait here."

She vanished. Thrr-gilag looked at Klnn-dawan-a, his tail under control, his face a little pinched. "That's all right," she told him, nodding once. "You were about finished with this test anyway, weren't you?"

His expression relaxed a fraction. "Yes," he agreed. He offered her the spoon under the box again, turning it around as he did so. Deftly, Klnn-dawan-a inserted the tip of the sampler into the casing and pushed the device firmly back into its hiding place. Taking the reassembled spoon from Thrr-gilag, she returned it to its compartment in the box and closed the lid.

And then the Elder was back. "You're ordered to return at once to Unity City," she told Thrr-gilag. "By order of the Overclan Prime. End of message."

Klnn-dawan-a looked at Thrr-gilag, caught his slight frown. "Message understood," he told the Elder. "Thank you."

The Elder vanished. "By order of the Overclan Prime?" the protector echoed. "I thought you said this was a small experiment."

"It is," Thrr-gilag said. "But there are other projects I'm also involved in."

The protector frowned at him; and then, suddenly, he got it. "Thrr-gilag; Kee'rr," he said. "Sure. You were the speaker for that searcher group on Base World Twelve. The ones with the alien prisoner."

"That's right," Thrr-gilag said. "Now, if you'll set us back down, please, I have to get a flight for Oaccanv."

For a long beat the protector gazed hard at Thrr-gilag's face, and for that same long beat Klnn-dawan-a was sure the scheme had collapsed. A searcher who specialized in alien studies would hardly be going around Dharanv putting basting sauce on *fss* organs . . .

But to her relief the protector merely shrugged. "Sure," he said, swinging the mesh door down over Prr't-casst-a's niche and sealing it again. He looked over the guardrail and gestured to his partner, and the platform started down.

A hunbeat later they were walking down the flagstone path toward the predator-fence gate. "Well?" Prr't-casst-a muttered, hovering beside Klnn-dawan-a.

Klnn-dawan-a glanced around. There were no other Elders in sight. "We're all set," she said. "You can set up your secure pathway and tell Thrr-mezaz we've got it."

"I will." Prrt'-casst-a paused. "Thrr-glag, what is this summons by the Overclan Prime?"

"I wouldn't worry about that," Thrr-gilag assured her with a confidence Klnn-dawan-a could tell he wasn't feeling. "I'm sure it doesn't have anything to do with this. I'll get that straightened out, then we'll try to find a way to get our little prize out to Thrr-mezaz."

"In the meantime, you need to keep up your pressure on the Dhaa'rr and Prr leaders to postpone or cancel the ritual of fire," Klnn-dawan-a added. "There's no way we can guarantee that what we've got will work the same way as a proper cutting."

"I'll try," Prr't-casst-a said, her voice trembling. "Klnn-dawan-a; Thrr-gilag . . . I don't know what to say. How to thank you . . ."

"You can start by getting that message to my brother," Thrr-gilag said, gently cutting her off. "And after that perhaps you'll get hold of a travel communicator for me. I need to catch the next flight out to Oaccanv and Unity City from this part of Dharanv."

"Right," Prr't-casst-a said, pulling herself back from the edge of maudlin sentiment with obvious effort. "Right away."

She vanished. "So," Thrr-gilag said, looking at Klnn-dawan-a. "Did you have any problems?"

"Not really," Klnn-dawan-a said, flicking her tongue in a negative. "It went more smoothly than I expected."

Thrr-gilag grunted. "I just hope it works," he said darkly. "I can't help thinking that if it was really this easy, they ought to be taking cuttings this way all the time."

Klnn-dawan-a shrugged. "Never underestimate the power of tradition," she reminded him. "Especially with Elders. Cuttings taken with knives work. That's how it's done; that's how it's always been done. That's good enough for most of them."

"You're probably right. If it works, maybe we'll write up a procedure paper on it sometime."

"Sure," Klnn-dawan-a said dryly. "What do you suppose the Overclan Prime wants?"

"Probably something to do with our mission to the

Mrachanis," he said. "Maybe they're moving the departure up a few tentharcs or something."

They had passed the gate and were heading for the railcar stop when Prr't-casst-a reappeared. "I have the pathway to Thrr-mezaz," she said, her voice tight. "I sent the message, but he wants to speak to you."

"Sure," Thrr-gilag said, throwing a frown at Klnn-dawan-a. "Hello, my brother."

Prr't-casst-a vanished. "You think there's trouble?" Klnn-dawan-a asked hesitantly.

"Sounds like it," Thrr-gilag said. His expression was grim, his tail suddenly spinning faster. "I wonder if the Humans are up to something."

Prr't-casst-a returned. " 'Father's been trying to get hold of you for nearly two tentharcs, Thrr-gilag,' " she said without preamble. " 'You need to head back to Oac-canv immediately.' "

Thrr-gilag's hand groped for Klnn-dawan-a's, gripped it hard. "Is it about mother?" he asked.

The delay this time seemed to drag on forever. Klnn-dawan-a held tightly to Thrr-gilag's hand, her own tail spinning with tension. With the bulk of their attention focused first on the threat to their bond-engagement and then on this thing with Prr't-zevisti's *fsss*, she hadn't had a chance to get more than a rough idea of the problem with Thrr-gilag's mother. But she knew it involved Thrr-pifix-a's *fsss* and her reluctance to accept Eldership. . . .

Prr't-casst-a returned. " 'He wouldn't say,' " she quoted Thrr-mezaz. " 'In fact, he really didn't tell me anything at all except that he needed to see one of us as quickly as possible. He was worried, though. Really worried. I could tell that much.' "

"He probably didn't trust the pathway he was on," Thrr-gilag said. "All right, look, I've just been summoned back to Unity City anyway. I'll try to find a way to get over to him."

Prr't-casst-a vanished, returned a hunbeat later. " 'All right. You want me to call him and let him know?' "

"Yes, you'd better," Thrr-gilag nodded. "You can get a much more secure pathway than I can. No telling what kind of leakage we'd get if I tried calling him from here."

Klnn-dawan-a looked at Prr't-casst-a, wondering if she would take that as an implied insult to the reliability of Prr Elders. But if she was offended, she didn't show it before vanishing again. Maybe she was too preoccupied with her own troubles to notice. Or maybe she'd done her fair share of Elder gossiping and knew that Thrr-gilag was right.

Prr't-casst-a returned. " 'All right. Any idea how you're going to deliver your package to me?' "

"Not yet," Thrr-gilag said.

"Actually, I have an idea," Klnn-dawan-a spoke up. "We'll discuss it and get word back to you."

Prr't-casst-a looked a bit confused. "Do I repeat all of that?"

"Yes," Thrr-gilag told her. "Just make it clear along the pathway that Klnn-dawan-a said the second part."

"All right."

She vanished. "What idea is this?" Thrr-gilag asked Klnn-dawan-a.

"That I go out to Dorcas and deliver it to him," Klnn-dawan-a said. "With the leaders still making up their minds about our bond-engagement, I haven't got much else to do right now anyway."

"So naturally you want to spend this free time in a war zone?"

"Don't be sarcastic, dear," she chided. "And don't argue, either. You know as well as I do it's the only way. You have to get back to Oaccanv and get ready for your mission. And there's no one else we can trust with this."

Thrr-gilag made a face at her, but in his eyes she could see he knew she was right. That was one of the things she liked most about him: the fact that he judged other people's ideas against exactly the same standards and criteria as he did his own. "It *is* a war zone, though," he reminded her. "How would you get them to let you in?"

"There are a couple of ways," she said. "Best chance would be—"

She broke off as Prr't-casst-a reappeared. " 'The sooner the better. Things are beginning to happen here. I have to go now, my brother. Keep yourself safe, and I'll speak with you again soon.' "

"Right," Thrr-gilag murmured. "Farewell, my brother." He took a deep breath, nodded to Prr't-casst-a. "Deliver that message, then release the pathway. Then get me that travel communicator."

"I will," Prr't-casst-a said, and disappeared.

Klnn-dawan-a looked at Thrr-gilag. "What's the matter?" she asked him.

"I don't know," he said slowly, his face troubled. "Just the way he said that, about things beginning to happen there. It didn't sound good."

"You want to get the pathway back and ask him?"

Thrr-gilag's tongue flicked in a negative. "No. If he could talk about it, he would have." He waved a hand, as if trying to brush the thoughts and worries away. "Never mind that. He's a warrior; he knows what he's doing. You were telling me how you were going to get to Dorcas."

"I was saying the best way might be for me to collect some personal messages or items for Thrr-mezaz's second commander, Klnn-vavgi. He's a distant cousin of mine, remember."

"I didn't think you knew him very well."

"I don't," Klnn-dawan-a said. "But that doesn't matter. Close family or distant cousin are all the same to the Dhaa'rr. And personal messages are traditionally to be delivered by hand."

"Even in a war zone?"

"Even in a war zone. So. I can get regular passage from here to the Dhaa'rr routing center on Shamanv, and from there I should be able to get a ride on a supply ship headed out to Dorcas."

Thrr-gilag pondered that. "That should get you to orbit, anyway. But what if they won't let you land?"

"I'll just have to count on Thrr-mezaz to get me past that one."

They'd reached the railcar stop. "I don't like it," Thrr-gilag said, opening the door of the first car in line on the siding and ushering her inside. "But right now I can't see any better way to do it. All right. As soon as Prr't-casst-a finds us a travel communicator, we'll check on flights to Shamanv."

"Good," Klnn-dawan-a said as he sat down beside her and keyed in his value number and their destination. The car beeped, and they were off.

It was a good idea, she knew, her going off to Dorcas like this. The best delivery plan either of them had. Probably the best plan either of them were going to have.

But that didn't mean she had to like it. She'd faced the crossbows of a Chig war party and had had enough good luck to escape without being raised prematurely to Eldership. Whether that good luck would hold her against the far deadlier weapons of Human-Conqueror warriors wasn't a question she particularly wanted to test.

"You don't have to do this," Thrr-gilag said quietly from beside her. "We can find some other way."

"No," Klnn-dawan-a said, taking his hand again. "We all have responsibilities in life. Prr't-zevisti is a Dhaa'rr, and so am I. This is something I have to do."

Gently, he leaned over and touched her face with his tongue. "That's one of the things I really love about you, Klnn-dawan-a," he murmured. "That you're always willing to do what needs to be done."

She squeezed his hand hard. "Just keep telling me that."

20
"The *Imperative* picked it up about ten hunbeats ago," Klnn-vavgi said, pointing to the hazy image on the monitor. "It didn't show up on our own monitors until just a couple of hunbeats ago."

Thrr-mezaz frowned at the image. A small Human-Conqueror aircraft, framed against the mountains it was coming in from. "Must be going pretty slow."

"Slow and high both," Klnn-vavgi said. "Not exactly your optimum profile for sneaking in on someone."

"Rather implies they want us to see them."

"That would be my guess, too," Klnn-vavgi nodded. "Question is, are they serious or just a distraction?"

"That's the question, all right," Thrr-mezaz agreed, throwing a quick look around the room at the other monitors. A half-dozen Zhirrzh aircraft were in the air ready to intercept, all ground defenses were activated and standing ready, all warriors were on full alert.

And across the landing field in their converted storehouse, oblivious to all the activity going on around them, the two Mrachanis were resting quietly. . . .

"It's the Mrachanis," Thrr-mezaz said. "They saw the spacecraft land, and this is their response."

"Pretty fast reaction," Klnn-vavgi grunted. "You could be right, though. But it brings us right back to question one: what are they up to?"

Thrr-mezaz gazed at the image on the monitor, trying to put himself in the Human-Conquerors' commander's place. All right. He knew a Mrachani spacecraft had landed on Dorcas; one of his aircraft had observed the aliens' landing from a respectful distance. He'd had nearly five tentharcs now to mull over that fact, and to come up with this response. Whatever it was.

And the tone of the response might well indicate whether he considered the Mrachanis to be captive allies to be rescued or dangerous enemies to be destroyed.

Thrr-mezaz stepped over to the Stingbird monitor. "How many Stingbirds do we have in the air?" he asked.

"Four," the warrior at the monitor said. "The rest are standing ready and awaiting orders."

"Put them all up," Thrr-mezaz ordered. "Have them form a defense perimeter twenty thoustrides outside the village. They're to be alert for any Human-Conqueror activity."

"I obey, Commander," the warrior answered, setting to work.

"That goes for the Elders, too," Thrr-mezaz added, looking up at the Elders hovering overhead. "They're to keep close watch on all ground approaches."

"I obey," one of the Elders said, and vanished.

Thrr-mezaz stepped back to Klnn-vavgi. "Let's see how easily they can be scared off," he commented.

"You think it's a feint, then?" Klnn-vavgi asked.

"Actually, no, I don't," Thrr-mezaz told him. "I don't think they're going to be scared off, either. My guess is that that aircraft is on its way here to rescue our Mrachani guests. Or else to try to kill them."

"Really," Klnn-vavgi said, eying his commander. "A wide range of options, I must say. I trust you aren't going to allow them to do either."

"We're certainly going to try to stop them," Thrr-mezaz assured him. "On the other hand, whichever attempt they make should tell us something about their relationship with the Mrachanis."

Klnn-vavgi rubbed thoughtfully at the side of his face. "I don't know, Thrr-mezaz," he murmured. "Sounds to me like a pretty big risk. We're nowhere near knowing the full extent of Human-Conqueror weapons technology. And Warrior Command isn't going to be at all happy if you lose their Mrachani prisoners for them."

"True," Thrr-mezaz said. "On the other hand, the Overclan Seating is about to send an expedition out to the Mrachani homeworld anyway. Plenty of Mrachanis there for them to talk to." He gestured to the slowly approaching aircraft. "Besides, the Human-Conquerors don't have any idea where our guests are. They're going to have to land first and find some clever way to ask for directions."

"What if they just swoop overhead, drop some really high explosives, and obliterate the whole village?"

"If they had that capability, I think they'd probably have used it long before now," Thrr-mezaz said dryly. "No, we're taking some risk with this, but not as much as it looks."

"Well, you're the commander," Klnn-vavgi said. "In

the meantime, that Human-Conqueror aircraft is getting closer. About time we ran all this past Warrior Command?"

"Right." Thrr-mezaz looked up. "Communicator?"

Thrr-mezaz had expected the aircraft to do at least one surveillance circle over the village before putting down. To his mild surprise it came straight in to the western part of the landing field, putting to ground a respectful distance from both the Mrachani spacecraft and the hangar-size building where the Zhirrzh had set up their own aircraft service facilities. Apparently the Human-Conquerors aboard hadn't considered it necessary to look the place over first.

Or rather, the Human-Conqueror, singular. It was a lone enemy warrior who emerged from the small aircraft into the waiting semicircle of Zhirrzh warriors, his hands outstretched and empty of weapons.

"Just one?" Klnn-vavgi murmured at Thrr-mezaz's side as they stood in the long postmidarc shadows beside the headquarters building, fifty strides southeast of the aircraft. "At least the Mrachanis sent us two."

"Maybe there are more inside," Thrr-mezaz said. "I'll have someone take a look."

The Human-Conqueror was speaking now. A few beats later the translator-link in Thrr-mezaz's ear slits came to life. "I am Srgent-janovetz of the Commonwealth Peacekeepers. I have come to discuss (something) terms with the commander of the Zhirrzh."

One of the warriors stepped forward with a jumpsuit draped around his neck. "You will wear this," he instructed the alien, his words coming faintly across the distance.

An Elder appeared at Thrr-mezaz's left, hidden from

the Human-Conqueror's view by the headquarters building. "We have searched the enemy warrior, Commander," he reported. "He is carrying no obvious weapons."

"Understood," Thrr-mezaz said. Though that was of only limited comfort. As Klnn-vavgi had pointed out earlier, there was a lot they didn't know about Human-Conqueror weaponry. "What about other devices?"

"He carries several," the Elder said. "One of them is particularly troubling: a short, flat device that has been inserted into his body."

Thrr-mezaz frowned across the field at the Human-Conqueror, midway through the job of changing out of his clothing. "Where inside his body?"

"Just here," the Elder said, pointing a faint tongue at the left side of Thrr-mezaz's own face. "It seems to have been inserted beneath the skin, between the mouth area and the ear appendages."

"Odd sort of placement," Klnn-vavgi said. "Did you examine it?"

"We did," the Elder said, nodding. "None could decipher its purpose. But many of us suspect it to be a weapon."

"Let's not leap to conclusions quite yet," Thrr-mezaz cautioned. "It could be any number of other things. A timed chemical drip, perhaps, or something else healer-implanted."

The Elder snorted. "Do not allow yourself to be fooled, Commander," he said. "Aliens can be very clever. Let me tell you some of the things we found being used as weapons during the third assault on the Isintorxi homeland—"

"We'll be careful," Thrr-mezaz cut him off, not really in any mood to listen to a history lecture. "Come on, Second, let's go see what our new prisoner has to say for himself."

The Human-Conqueror was just sealing up his jump-suit as Thrr-mezaz and Klnn-vavgi reached the group of warriors surrounding him. "I'm Commander Thrr-mezaz; Kee'rr," Thrr-mezaz identified himself. "Why are you here?"

The optronic speaker on his shoulder gave out the Human-Conqueror translation. The Human-Conqueror spoke again— "I am Srgent-janovetz. I have come to discuss (something) terms."

"We don't understand all your words," Thrr-mezaz said. "Please rephrase."

The translation was made, and the Human-Conqueror seemed to consider. Then he spoke again. "I am here to ask what must be done for us to stop fighting for a while with each other."

Thrr-mezaz glanced at Klnn-vavgi. "Are you asking for terms of surrender?"

Srgent-janovetz's face changed as the translation came through. "No, not surrender," the translator-link said. "Just to stop fighting for a time."

Thrr-mezaz flicked his tongue in a negative. Srgent-janovetz seemed to flinch back at the gesture. "And what purpose would such a partial surrender serve?"

Again the Human-Conqueror seemed to consider. He spoke— "We saw that you have taken new prisoners. Since you are unfamiliar with our species, we would like to ask permission to treat any injuries they may have."

Thrr-mezaz smiled grimly. There it was; and he'd called it straight down the line. The Human-Conquerors wanted a crack at the Mrachanis. "Our new guests are not Human-Conquerors," he said. "Nor are they prisoners."

Srgent-janovetz's face changed again as he spoke. "We are called Humans," the translation came. "What was the word you used for us?"

"I called you Human-Conquerors," Thrr-mezaz said. "It means—"

And without warning a brilliant flash of light came from across the landing field to the northeast.

"Cover!" Thrr-mezaz snapped as the sharp *crack* of the explosion slapped across them. He leaped into the partial cover of the Human-Conqueror aircraft, Klnn-vavgi right beside him. Crouching down, he peered out past the aircraft's beak, just in time to get his midlight pupils dazzled by the flash of a second explosion. He twisted his head away with a curse; but he'd gotten enough of a look to locate the focal point of the attack.

The Mrachanis' storehouse.

"Communicators: full attack alert," he shouted as a third explosion flashed reflected light from the nearby buildings, the sound hammering into his ear slits. "Tell the warriors guarding the Mrachanis to get them out of there and to cover."

He got a faint shout of acknowledgment and threw a quick look around him. Two of the Zhirrzh warriors had the Human-Conqueror facedown on the ground; the others had unslung their laser rifles and were kneeling around the base of the aircraft, weapons swinging around uncertainly as they searched for something to use them on. Thrr-mezaz looked back toward the storehouse, wondering how in the eighteen worlds the Human-Conquerors had slipped this much attack power past his aircraft and Elders. From another edge of the landing field one of the ground defenses opened fire, sizzling rapid-fire laser pulses into the air in half a dozen directions. Somewhere in the distance he could hear the faint sound of laser rifles joining in—

"Commander!" An Elder appeared in front of Thrr-mezaz. "The warriors at the Mrachani storehouse are down!"

Thrr-mezaz swore under his breath. "Second, stay here and watch the prisoner," he ordered Klnn-vavgi. "Keep one warrior. The rest of you, come with me. Elders, find out where this cursed attack is coming from."

A fourth explosion lit up the landscape as he ducked under the beak of the aircraft and headed at a stopped-over run toward the Mrachanis' storehouse, the warriors fanning out around him on both sides. A pretty stupid tactic, running straight-out toward an obvious target zone this way, but there was no time for subtlety or finesse. Locked in their storehouse, the Mrachanis were as helpless as sleeping nornins before the Human-Conqueror assault. They wouldn't stand a chance if someone didn't get them out of there immediately.

No more explosions came before they made it to the storehouse. Bracing himself, trying to watch the sky in all directions, Thrr-mezaz led the way around the corner to the east wall where the building's doors were located.

Or rather, where the building's doors had once been located. One of the twin panels was hanging loosely by its top hinge, its lower section bent and blackened. The other door was on the ground, shattered into a hundred metal shards.

And sprawled amid the wreckage were the bodies of the two warriors who'd been on guard duty.

Raised to Eldership.

Thrr-mezaz grimaced. Two more early newcomers for the family shrines. Something else for Speaker Cvv-panav and the Dhaa'rr to blame him for. "Come on," he told his warriors. Picking his way through the splinters, preparing himself for the worst, he went inside.

It was bad, but not nearly as bad as he'd feared. There

were three good-sized holes in the north wall, and the storehouse itself was filled with smoke and dust. But aside from that there seemed to be little damage. More important, the two Mrachanis were huddled together beneath a table, obviously shaken but apparently unharmed.

They caught sight of the Zhirrzh and called something, their voices trembling oddly. Thrr-mezaz stepped toward them, waiting for the translation—

"Relay's gone," one of the warriors spoke up, pointing toward the spot on the wall where the darklight relay had been hanging.

"Probably knocked down by the vibrations," Thrr-mezaz said. "Go see if you can find it. The rest of you, get the Mrachanis out of here."

The warriors moved off toward their tasks. Thrr-mezaz took a last look around and then stepped outside the broken doors again. "Communicator?" he called.

An Elder appeared. "Report," Thrr-mezaz said.

"We've found no sign of any Human-Conqueror warriors," the Elder said, his voice tight. "But—"

"What do you mean, no sign?" Thrr-mezaz demanded. "None at all?"

"None at all," the Elder said. "No Human-Conquerors, no weapons emplacements, no vehicles."

Thrr-mezaz looked around. "What were the warriors shooting at, then?"

"I don't know, Commander," the Elder said tartly. "Possibly their own shadows. Wherever the Human-Conquerors were, though, they seem to have gone."

Thrr-mezaz frowned, listening. The Elder was right; there hadn't been anything since that fourth explosion. "We must have scared them off."

"Or else they just didn't want to give us enough time to

locate their attack site," the Elder said darkly. "Conveniently allowing them to use it again."

Thrr-mezaz eyed the Elder. He was angry, all right. Angry down to his core, and impatient and frustrated besides. One of those Zhirrzh warrior veterans who selectively remembered his own service to be exemplary and perfect, and fully expected the warriors who'd followed him to be likewise. "Perhaps," Thrr-mezaz said. "On the other hand, maybe the explanation is much simpler. Alert all aircraft and perimeter warriors to continue to keep watch."

"I obey," the Elder growled.

Thrr-mezaz glanced back across the landing field. "And tell the technics to get the interpreter going again."

The Elder vanished. A beat later the warriors and Mrachanis emerged from the damaged storehouse, the latter still gabbling in that same trembling tone of voice as they came toward Thrr-mezaz.

"We've got their luggage together, too, Commander," one of the warriors spoke up. "Where do you want us to take them?"

"There's a small subroom in the northwest corner of the aircraft service building," Thrr-mezaz said. "Take them there and put them under full guard. And I mean *full* guard."

"I obey, Commander."

From the corner of his eye he saw a darklight beam flick on from across the landing field: the interpreter was back in operation. "Hold it a beat," he told the warriors, turning to the chief Mrachani. "Lahettilas, the warriors are taking you to a new building. You should be safe there."

The chief Mrachani didn't even wait for the translation to come. He clutched at Thrr-mezaz's arm, babbling in that same trembling voice. "Did you see what the Humans did?" the translation demanded in Thrr-mezaz's ear slits. "They tried to destroy us."

"Yes, I saw," Thrr-mezaz agreed. "But they're no longer here, and we're—"

"We are not safe here, Commander of the Zhirrzh," Lahettilas cut him off. "Not anywhere on Dorcas. The Humans must know of our mission to the Zhirrzh. They will try again to kill us. Unless we are taken out of their reach. Commander of the Zhirrzh, I insist we be taken to a Zhirrzh world immediately."

"I understand your concerns, Lahettilas," Thrr-mezaz said, striving for patience. "But for right now, that's impossible. I'll speak to the Overclan Prime, though, and see what can be done."

"That will do no good," the Mrachani insisted. "I insist you send word to your homeworld."

Thrr-mezaz stared hard into the soft, alien face. "Let's get one thing straight right now, Lahettilas," he said coldly. "You and your companion are not in any position to insist on anything."

The alien face changed. More strikingly, so did his voice. Instead of the trembling tone, it was suddenly quiet and soothing. "I am sorry, Commander of the Zhirrzh," the translation came. "We understand that we are at your complete (something). I am (something) because I am afraid that we will die."

"I understand that," Thrr-mezaz said. Somehow this new voice of his was more irritating than the previous one had been. It reminded him of the condescending tone one of his teachers had used back in school whenever someone got the answer wrong. "We'll do whatever we can to protect you."

Lahettilas bowed half-over. "I understand, Commander of the Zhirrzh. We will trust you."

"Someone will be in to talk to you later," Thrr-mezaz said, catching the eye of one of the warriors and gesturing toward the aircraft service building. The warrior nodded and gestured to the others, and together they steered the Mrachanis across the landing field. Keeping the bulk of his attention on the sky, Thrr-mezaz headed off at an angle from their path back toward the Human-Conqueror aircraft.

Srgent-janovetz was sitting on the ground when he arrived, watching the Mrachanis out of the corner of his eye. "Is the attack over?" Klnn-vavgi asked.

"It seems to be," Thrr-mezaz said, reaching a hand up to block the darklight interpreter-link. "For now, anyway. Prisoner give you any trouble?"

"None," Klnn-vavgi said. "He stayed right where he was told to the whole time. Didn't even sit up, in fact, until I prodded him to do so."

Srgent-janovetz was looking up at him now. "Was he doing anything that maybe didn't really qualify as trouble?" Thrr-mezaz asked. "Any hand or leg movements, for example?"

"Nothing that I noticed," Klnn-vavgi said.

"Um." Thrr-mezaz withdrew his hand from the interpreter-link. "As you can see," he said to Srgent-janovetz, pointing across at the Mrachanis, "your warriors missed their target. They're still alive."

The Human-Conqueror's face changed as the translation came through. He spoke— "I know nothing about that attack. I came here to speak about (something) terms."

"So you said," Klnn-vavgi said. "Events seem to be indicating otherwise. Why do you want to kill the Mrachanis?"

"We don't," Srgent-janovetz protested. "The Mrachanis aren't our enemies."

Thrr-mezaz reached a hand to the interpreter-link again. "What do you think?" he asked Klnn-vavgi.

"What's there to think?" Klnn-vavgi countered, blocking his own link. "Those sure weren't *our* explosives raining down on us."

Thrr-mezaz glanced back at the damaged storehouse. "Yes, but how did they do it? Neither the Elders nor anyone else was able to find any trace of an attack site. Nor did they see anything coming in across the village perimeter."

Klnn-vavgi shrugged. "Maybe you were right about the Human-Conquerors having a network of underground tunnels, and the Elders just haven't found them yet." He looked pointedly up at the aircraft beside them. "Or maybe they had everything they needed already inside the perimeter."

"Yes, I was thinking the same thing a hunbeat ago," Thrr-mezaz told him, eying the aircraft. "Problem is, we're southwest of the building right here, but all four explosions were on the east and north walls. How could they have gotten their projectiles to go around corners that way? Especially projectiles small enough that we couldn't spot them?"

"I don't know." Klnn-vavgi looked down at the Human-Conqueror still sitting on the ground. "I do know, though, that we shouldn't be discussing this in front of the prisoner. They may have picked up more of our language than we know."

"Good point." Thrr-mezaz gestured a pair of warriors over. "Any suggestions on where to put him?"

"The storehouse springs to mind," Klnn-vavgi said

dryly. "Let's see how he likes it there when his friends start firing again."

"Tempting, but impractical," Thrr-mezaz said. "The place has no doors left. Not to mention three brand-new exits."

"How about the optronics supply room, then?" Klnn-vavgi suggested. "After we've pulled all the optronics out of it, of course."

Thrr-mezaz considered. It was a little risky—the room was in the same building as the interpreter and was near other sensitive equipment. But the prisoner should be safe enough there until they could come up with something a little more permanent. "Fine," he told Klnn-vavgi. "Go ahead and get that set up for him. And detail some warriors to start converting some of the private homes in the village into guest quarters. Seal over the windows and secondary exits—you know what I mean."

Klnn-vavgi nodded. "I'll get right to it. If we're going to keep getting company, I suppose we might as well have a real place to put them."

"Right." Thrr-mezaz looked up at the aircraft. "And while they're doing that, have the technics start on this thing. I want to know about everything that's in there. Especially anything that could possibly be a weapon."

The sun had set in the west, and the long shadows were fading into a general dimness along the ground. Thrr-mezaz stepped carefully across the broken storehouse door, wincing as the shards crackled beneath his feet. Two Zhirrzh warriors had been raised to Eldership at this spot. Two warriors under his command . . .

He stepped into the storehouse, lowlight pupils widening to adjust to the gloom. A half-dozen warriors were at work inside, cleaning up the wreckage. The one he was looking for was over by one of the holes in the north wall: Vstii-suuv, one of his two climbing companions on that abortive attempt to penetrate Human-Conqueror territory two fullarcs ago.

Thrr-mezaz walked over to him. "Rather a mess, isn't it?" he commented.

Vstii-suuv straightened up from where he'd been crouching. "It certainly is," he agreed.

Thrr-mezaz gestured to take in the room. "So what's the consensus? Any ideas how the Human-Conquerors did it?"

"Not really." Vstii-suuv flicked his tongue in an annoyed negative. "I suppose it's possible they could have used missiles or projectiles that were small enough to sneak in without any of us seeing them. But I really don't like that theory."

"I know what you mean," Thrr-mezaz agreed, looking at the debris around the blast hole. "If they had an explosive this powerful, why haven't we seen them use it before?"

"Right," Vstii-suuv nodded. "And it's not nuclear, either. It would have left radiation behind."

"Still, just because they haven't used it before doesn't mean they don't have it," Thrr-mezaz said, gingerly touching the splintered wood at the edge of the hole. Fairly thin wood, actually, but the damage was still impressive. "We'll have to check and see if any of the other beachheads has come under this kind of attack. Should there be that many wood splinters out there?"

"I have no idea," Vstii-suuv said, stepping closer to the hole and peering at the ground outside. "But you can see there are a lot of splinters inside, too."

"True," Thrr-mezaz agreed, stepping back away from the hole. "One of the few halfway positive side effects of warfare: everyone learns so much along the way. We're certainly going to learn a lot about explosions and explosives by the time this is over."

"How about talking to the guards who were raised to Eldership when the door was destroyed?" Vstii-suuv suggested. "They might be able to tell you more about what happened."

"I've already tried getting a pathway to them," Thrr-mezaz said. "Unfortunately, they're both still twisted in anchoring shock. No telling when they'll come out of it, either—we're a long way from the eighteen worlds." He lowered his voice a bit. "The main reason I stopped by was to let you know that we're going to be doing another climb soon. Probably sometime in the next four or five fullarcs."

Vstii-suuv's midlight pupils narrowed. "You have something to take up there?"

"We will soon," Thrr-mezaz said, mindful of the other Zhirrzh in the room and the Elders floating around nearby. However Thrr-gilag had managed to pull off his illegal cutting of Prr't-zevisti's *fsss*, the theft seemed to be undetected as yet. He wanted to keep it that way as long as possible. "Anyway, pass the word on to Qlaa-nuur."

"I obey, Commander," Vstii-suuv said firmly. "We'll be ready whenever you want us."

"Good."

Thrr-mezaz took a few steps away from the wall, crunching wood shards underfoot, feeling a frown settling across his face as he looked around the open area. Something about this whole thing didn't feel right, somehow. "Communicator?"

An Elder appeared. "Yes, Commander?"

"Who was watching the Mrachanis when the Human-Conqueror attack began?" Thrr-mezaz asked.

"As it happens, I was," the Elder said.

"Who was with you?"

"Actually, I was alone," the Elder said. "The other two had been pulled off for perimeter sentry duty."

"I see," Thrr-mezaz said, making a mental note to discuss proper priorities later with the Elders' speaker. "Can you tell me what exactly the Mrachanis were doing when the first explosion occurred?"

"I've already been through this with the speaker—" The Elder broke off at the look on Thrr-mezaz's face. "They weren't doing anything in particular, Commander," he said. "Just sitting there at the table."

"The same table we found them hiding beneath?"

"Yes," the Elder said. "They were just talking together when the door blew up."

Thrr-mezaz looked across at the table. It was fairly close to where the darklight relay had been hanging. "Go to the interpreter room and find out for me what they were talking about."

"I can tell you right now, Commander: we don't know," the Elder said. "They'd accidentally covered over the darklight relay a few hunbeats earlier."

"What do you mean, accidentally covered it over?"

"The Mrachanis had hung out decorative cloths at various points along the walls," the Elder explained. "One of them happened to be over the relay."

Which meant the technics had no recording of the aliens' conversation. How very convenient for someone. "And you didn't think it worth telling one of the warriors about?"

The Elder was starting to look a little uncomfortable. "The alert had been sounded, Commander," he said. "Everyone's attention was out at the perimeter or on the approaching Human-Conqueror aircraft. I didn't think it was vital that it be fixed immediately. And anyway, I was watching them. They couldn't have done anything."

"Except that they could have—"

Thrr-mezaz broke off, his lungs tightening into an almost-gasp. Abruptly, for the briefest flicker of a shattered beat, a strange and dizzying tingle had splashed across his mind—

And in front of him the Elder screamed, his face contorted with agony and fear.

And suddenly Thrr-mezaz knew what had happened.

"Commander!" one of the warriors shouted from across the room. "What—?"

"Elderdeath weapon!" Thrr-mezaz shouted back, fighting off the residual disorientation. "Full alert: all warriors."

Another Elder appeared. "Commander, Second Commander Klnn-vavgi requests your presence immediately in the command/monitor room," he reported, his voice tightly controlled. "He asks permission to lift the Stingbirds into defensive positions."

Thrr-mezaz looked at the holes in the storehouse walls. "Give him permission," he told the Elder. "Then tell him to collect some warriors and meet me at the optronics supply room."

The Human-Conqueror was standing against the back wall of his temporary cell when the Zhirrzh warriors arrived. Still alert, still fully dressed. Almost as if he'd been expecting them. "Tell me where it is," Thrr-mezaz said without preamble. "Now."

The Human-Conqueror's face changed as the translation came through, the ridges of short hairs over his eyes pressing closer together. "Where what is?" his reply came in Thrr-mezaz's ear slits.

Thrr-mezaz flicked his tongue in contempt. With the

deceit unmasked he could have hoped the Human-Conqueror would at least be reasonable about it. "The Elderdeath weapon," he bit out. "The one you or your warriors just used against us. Is it aboard your aircraft, or are there other warriors nearby?"

The prisoner's face remained the same. "I heard the shouts, but whatever happened wasn't our doing. And I don't know anything about this—what did you call it? The Elderdeath weapon?"

"Don't act stupid," Klnn-vavgi snarled. "You know what the commander's talking about."

"And we know you know," Thrr-mezaz added. "Furthermore, we're prepared to do whatever is necessary to—"

And suddenly there it was again: an abrupt flicker of disorientation tingling through his head, sharper this time, with an edge of pain to it. He darted a hand to the door frame for support against the flash of dizziness, dimly aware of the Human-Conqueror still standing against his wall. Beside him Klnn-vavgi shouted something; a half-dozen laser rifles swung up toward the prisoner—

"Hold!" Thrr-mezaz snapped. "Don't fire."

The rifle muzzles paused uncertainly. "Commander?" Klnn-vavgi demanded.

"I said don't fire." The last of the dizziness faded away, and Thrr-mezaz straightened to face the prisoner again.

The Human-Conqueror was still standing there, making no move to take any advantage of his enemies' sudden weakness. Observing their reaction, perhaps? "By all rights I should kill you for that," Thrr-mezaz told him. "I should have let them shoot you down right there. I trust you realize that."

"Whatever happened to you wasn't my fault," the prisoner said, his voice quiet. Almost earnest. Almost believable.

Almost. "Fine," Thrr-mezaz said. "If that's the way you want to play it." He turned to Klnn-vavgi. "Second, I want you to collect some technics and go take another look at that aircraft. And give the healers a call—I want that device hidden under the skin on his face to be removed."

He turned back at the Human-Conqueror. "You can cooperate or not. It's your choice."

For a long beat the alien gazed back at him. Then his face seemed to twitch. "All right," he said. "But there's no need for healers."

He reached both hands up to his face, to the side where the Elders had discovered the hidden device. The laser rifles lifted again in warning as, slowly and carefully, he began to peel away a section of his skin.

Klnn-vavgi muttered an awed-sounding curse under his breath as the flap of loose skin grew larger. Thrr-mezaz nodded his agreement; Thrr-gilag had never mentioned anything about Human-Conquerors being able to do *that*.

The edge of the device was visible now: small and flat, very much the same color as the Human-Conqueror's skin but easily distinguishable by the differences in its darklight radiance. He finished with the flap of skin and dropped it onto the bed in front of him; then, just as carefully, he peeled the device itself from its place.

"Drop it on the bed," Thrr-mezaz ordered him. "And then stand away from it."

The prisoner did as instructed. Thrr-mezaz gestured, and one of the warriors gingerly retrieved both the device and the skin flap and handed them over.

"Ycch," Klnn-vavgi growled deep in his throat. "Did

you see that, Commander? He just ripped it right off his—"

"It's not skin," Thrr-mezaz said.

"What?"

"It's not skin," Thrr-mezaz repeated, turning it over. "At least not his own skin. See? No blood anywhere."

"Well, I'll be cursed," Klnn-vavgi said, peering closer. "That's an incredibly good imitation."

"I'm sure that was the intent." Thrr-mezaz looked up at the prisoner. "This must have been pretty important for your technics to have gone to so much work to hide it," he commented, hefting the skin-colored device in his other hand. "What is it?"

The Human-Conqueror shook his head back and forth to the side. "It's not a weapon."

"What is it?"

The other remained silent. "Fine," Thrr-mezaz said. "We'll figure it out for ourselves."

He gestured, and together the warriors left the room, locking it securely behind them. "Guard posts as previously," he ordered the warriors when they were out in the cool latearc air again. "Well, Second. Comments?"

"Ten to one it's our Elderdeath weapon," Klnn-vavgi said sourly.

"Yes," Thrr-mezaz murmured, gazing down at the device in his hand. "Perhaps."

"You don't sound convinced."

Thrr-mezaz shrugged. "Oh, you're probably right. It's just that the whole exercise seems to have been pretty futile. Yes, they got us stirred up a little, but that's about it. There was no attack on us, no further attack on the Mrachanis, not even an attempt by the prisoner to break out. So what did it gain them?"

"Information, maybe," Klnn-vavgi suggested. "They know now what levels it takes to affect us."

"They knew that after the first battle," Thrr-mezaz countered. "No, there's something here we're not getting. I just wish we had some idea what it was."

For a beat they stood there in silence. Then, with a sigh, Thrr-mezaz dropped the device and fake skin flap into Klnn-vavgi's hand. "Anyway. See what the technics can make of these."

"Right," Klnn-vavgi said. "You still want them to look at the aircraft, too?"

"Oh, yes," Thrr-mezaz confirmed grimly. "I want them to get in there and tear it apart. Down to individual molecules, if that's what it takes."

"And the prisoner?"

Thrr-mezaz looked back at the warriors standing guard. "The same goes for him," he said. "Something's going on here, Klnn-vavgi. It's time we found out what that something is."

21

There was an Elder waiting as Thrr-gilag came in through the side entrance of the Overclan complex. An Elder whose face was set in transparent stone. "You are Thrr-gilag; Kee'rr?" he demanded.

"Yes," Thrr-gilag said, holding up his pass for inspection. "I was told to come here—"

"I know," the Elder cut him off. "The Overclan Prime awaits you in his private chambers. Follow me."

Without waiting for a reply he set off down the corridor. Thrr-gilag followed, his tail spinning nervously behind him. There was trouble in the air. Big trouble. He'd seen it in the hardened faces of the perimeter protectors who had directed him to this particular door instead of to any of the main entrances. He could see it in the eyes of the Overclan warriors whom he passed and could hear it in the low tones as they conversed among themselves as he went by.

Big trouble. And all of it focused on him.

And to Thrr-gilag it was obvious what had happened. Somehow they'd found out about that little stunt he and Klnn-dawan-a had pulled with Prr't-zevisti's *fsss* back on Dharanv. They'd found out, and he was being led off to summary trial and judgment. All was lost: his career, his honor, his bond-engagement to Klnn-dawan-a. And Prr't-zevisti's last chance for survival.

It was over. And yet, even as Thrr-gilag's emotions swung violently between panic and resignation at the looming disaster, a small part of his mind refused to let go of the nagging sense that something here wasn't right. Why would the Overclan Prime get personally involved with such a sordid matter? For that matter, why had they trusted him to obey the summons to Oaccanv? Shouldn't they at least have brought him back here under warrior guard?

The fears and doubts and apprehensions were still chasing through his mind when he and the Elder arrived at their destination. It was a different room from the private offices he'd been brought to—could it really have been only eight fullarcs ago?—just after the ignominious return of the alien study group from Base World 12. "Enter," the Elder said, and vanished. Trying vainly to slow his tail's dizzying spin, Thrr-gilag gripped the wooden ring and pulled the door open.

It was a smaller room than the Prime's private office had been, and even more simply furnished. But it was imbued with the same sense of age and history. Two Zhirrzh were waiting for him: the Overclan Prime and Speaker Cvv-panav of the Dhaa'rr. "Come in, Searcher

Thrr-gilag," the Prime said gravely. "You know the Speaker for Dhaa'rr."

"I do," Thrr-gilag said, nodding respectfully to each of them in turn and noting the odd lack of a *kavra*-fruit rack. Here in the Prime's private chambers, apparently, such formalities were dispensed with.

"I'm afraid I have bad news for you, Searcher," the Prime said, "concerning a matter of grave importance. For reasons that will become apparent, I've decided to personally intervene. Please; sit down."

Thrr-gilag lowered himself onto the indicated couch, fighting to keep from blurting out the words boiling up within him. Whatever they knew—whatever they thought they knew—he must above all else not help them by volunteering information. He and Thrr-mezaz had fallen into that trap with their parents innumerable times as children. "What is it?" he asked as calmly as he could.

"It concerns your mother, Thrr-pifix-a," the Prime said quietly, his gaze steady on Thrr-gilag's face. "She's been detained on charges of grand-first theft." He paused. "She —or rather, persons unknown employed by her—broke into the Thrr family shrine last latearc. And stole her *fsss* organ."

Thrr-gilag stared at him, shock freezing his muscles into immobility. "What?" he whispered.

"You heard him," Cvv-panav said, the harshness of his voice slashing across the brittle stillness like a ragged ax against kindling reeds. "She hired some thugs and stole her *fsss*."

Thrr-gilag looked at him, the face not really registering against the swirling paralysis in his mind. She'd done it. She'd actually done it. His mother had stolen her *fsss*. Had had it there, in her hands.

There in her hands . . . "What happened then?" he asked, afraid to hear the answer. "I mean afterward?"

"Don't worry, her *fsss* was recovered intact," the Prime assured him. "Which is about the only good part of all this. At least she won't have to stand trial for *fsss* destruction."

Trial. The word sent a fresh shiver through Thrr-gilag. "Will she have to stand trial at all?" he asked. "I mean, if there was no harm done—"

"There was most certainly harm done," Cvv-panav cut him off. "Her thugs broke into the shrine, damaging Thrr property and injuring one of the protectors in the process. That's worth two trials right there." He sniffed contemptuously. "What makes it all the worse is that she refuses even to admit her complicity in the crime. Claims that two unnamed Zhirrzh from a nonexistent organization came to her out of nowhere and offered to help her."

Thrr-gilag looked at the Prime. "Maybe she's telling the truth."

"The organization she named doesn't exist, Searcher," the Prime said, flicking his tongue in a negative. "We've had plenty of time to check. It simply doesn't exist."

"I see." Thrr-gilag took a careful breath. This couldn't be happening. It couldn't be. "So she will have to go to trial."

"Under normal circumstance, undoubtedly," the Prime said. "In this case, however"—his eyes flicked to Cvv-panav—"Speaker Cvv-panav has asked me to intervene on behalf of you and your mother."

Thrr-gilag looked at Cvv-panav, a sudden surge of hope flickering into flame within him. Cvv-panav, Speaker of the most powerful Zhirrzh clan . . .

"It's obvious such a trial would be highly damaging to the Kee'rr," the Prime went on. "Because of your bond-engagement to Klnn-dawan-a, however, the prestige of the Dhaa'rr would also be affected. Naturally, Speaker Cvv-panav would like to avoid that at all costs."

"I see," Thrr-gilag said, the flicker of hope vanishing. He could see where this was going now, all right. And why Cvv-panav had decided to get involved with it. "And how would the Speaker propose that be done?"

"There will be no trial," Cvv-panav said. "Your mother will spend a few fullarcs under guard and then be allowed to return to her home. The Thrr and Kee'rr recorders will unobtrusively add the record of her crime to their archives, and the matter will be over."

"I see," Thrr-gilag said. "And what will the price be for all this official forgiveness?"

"There is no price per se," Cvv-panav said, his tone steady and unreadable. "I'm doing this for the Dhaa'rr, not you. However." He paused. "It is, of course, impossible to completely bury what has happened. The protectors of the Thrr shrine know; so do the warriors who detained Thrr-pifix-a; so do the recorders of the Thrr and Kee'rr and the Overclan. Your family is shamed, Searcher Thrr-gilag. My overriding concern is that the Dhaa'rr not be shamed along with you."

"What will the price be?" Thrr-gilag repeated.

The Speaker locked gazes with him. "Your bond-engagement to Klnn-dawan-a will end. Right here. Right now."

Thrr-gilag nodded bitterly. He'd been right. Cvv-panav had taken this tragedy and was going to twist it to his own purposes. "Suppose I refuse?"

"The bond-engagement is over, Searcher," the Prime said, his voice quiet but firm. "Accept it in private now, or accept it in public, with public humiliation, when your mother goes on trial."

Thrr-gilag looked at him, a sense of finality settling over him. Finality, and an odd sort of peace. The feeling of freedom that came of having nothing left to lose. "Are you threatening me, Overclan Prime?" he asked. "Because if you are—"

"That's enough," Cvv-panav snapped. "How dare you talk that way to—?"

"The Speaker for Dhaa'rr will be silent," the Prime said. His voice was still quiet, but suddenly there was an overpowering strength of authority to his tone. Cvv-panav flashed him a startled look and subsided, glowering.

For a beat the Prime continued to look at him. Then, slowly, he turned back to Thrr-gilag. "That was not a threat, Searcher Thrr-gilag," he said. "It was a statement of fact. Without Speaker Cvv-panav's support and assistance, there's no possibility for this to end without bringing Thrr-pifix-a to trial."

"I see," Thrr-gilag said. So it was over. The two most powerful Zhirrzh in the eighteen worlds had discussed the matter and had made their decision. "I don't seem to have any choices left. Do I."

The Prime's tongue flicked in a negative. "No. You don't."

For a few beats the room was silent. "Then I suppose it's settled," Thrr-gilag said, standing up. "Thank you for your time, Overclan Prime. And for your efforts on behalf of my mother."

"Merely repayment for your service to the Zhirrzh." Something in the Prime's face seemed to twitch— "Service which must, unfortunately, now come to an end. Under the circumstances I'm sure you understand that it would be best if you didn't represent the Kee'rr on the Zhirrzh mission to the Mrachani homeworld."

Thrr-gilag nodded, noting peripherally that Cvv-panav

seemed surprised. Perhaps he hadn't expected this one. A final parting shot from the Prime himself, then. "I understand."

"I'm sorry it has to be this way," the Prime said. "On the other side, this war isn't going to be over for a long time. There will surely be other ways for you to serve the Zhirrzh people in the future."

Thrr-gilag gazed at him, filled suddenly with the almost overwhelming desire to throw the lie back into that impassive face. This war could be a very short one indeed, ended by the Human-Conquerors' devastating CIRCE weapon. He wondered if the Prime had gotten around to telling the Overclan Seating about CIRCE yet. Or what Speaker Cvv-panav's reaction would be if he learned the truth. Right here and right now . . .

Thrr-gilag sighed, the rage and hatred draining out of him. No. CIRCE was not his secret to tell. And the reasons for keeping that secret had not changed. "I'm sure there will be," he said instead. "When that time comes, I will of course serve to the fullest of my abilities."

"I'm sure you will," the Prime said. "Good fullarc to you, Searcher Thrr-gilag."

It was a dismissal. Thrr-gilag nodded to both of them and turned to go—

"One other thing," the Prime said from behind him. "Thrr-pifix-a is currently in the detention center at Unity City. As she'll be there for several more fullarcs, you might wish to go to her home and select a few personal items for her use there. The server at the main Overclan desk has the key to her house, as well as a list of the sorts of things she can be allowed to have."

"I appreciate the courtesy, Overclan Prime," Thrr-gilag said. "I'll have to see if I can find a way to get out there."

"Speak with the server when you pick up the key," the

Prime offered. "If there are any Overclan flights heading that direction within the next couple of tentarcs, I'll see to it you're authorized to ride along."

"Thank you," Thrr-gilag said. After that last shot, a token coating of salve. Just to show there hadn't been anything personal or vindictive about this. Appearances were everything. "Again, I appreciate your courtesy."

"You'd best go, then," the Prime said.

Another dismissal. This time, clearly, he meant it. Nodding once again to the two Zhirrzh, Thrr-gilag turned and left the room.

For a few hunbeats he wandered randomly down the corridors, not really seeing or hearing the Zhirrzh he passed, his mind and emotions too frozen to think or feel anything at all. But the numbness couldn't last for long. Certainly not long enough. Slowly, inexorably, like a deep wound from which the anesthetic was receding, the bitterness and pain began to flow back in.

So it had happened. All the fears he'd taken into the room had now been realized. He'd feared the worst; and the worst had happened. In that single stroke the Dhaa'rr and the Overclan Prime had taken everything he truly valued away from him. His career, his honor, and especially Klnn-dawan-a. Everything.

Halfway down the corridor, a group of Zhirrzh looked around as an Elder appeared beside them. There was a brief, inaudible conversation, and the Elder vanished.

And Thrr-gilag realized he'd been wrong. He'd feared the worst, all right. But the worst had not, in fact, happened. In all their zeal the Overclan Prime and Speaker Cvv-panav had missed something.

Prr't-zevisti.

Thrr-gilag took a deep breath, a sudden surge of resolve slicing through the despair. No, it wasn't hopeless yet.

Not yet. If Klnn-dawan-a could get that tissue sampler to Thrr-mezaz, they might still have a chance of bringing Prr't-zevisti back from the almost certain death the Dhaa'rr were trying to force on him. And if they did, maybe they could use it as a lever right back at Speaker Cvv-panav again.

The odds were vanishingly small. Thrr-gilag knew that. But it didn't matter. He had fresh hope, and new purpose, and that was what he needed most right now.

Straightening up, Thrr-gilag got his bearings and headed at a brisk walk down the corridor toward the main Overclan desk. He would take the Prime up on his offer and go get some things to take to his mother. And when he saw her, he would be cheerful and comforting and helpful.

Because the Prime and Cvv-panav hadn't taken his family away from him, either. And maybe, ultimately, that was what really mattered.

"Well," Cvv-panav said, resettling himself on his couch. "All things considered, I'd say that went quite well."

"I'm pleased you were satisfied," the Prime said, trying to ignore the twinges of guilt prodding at him. It had all been necessary, but that didn't mean he had to like it. Decisions of state, he was rapidly coming to realize, were much easier when one didn't have to face those who were affected. "Now, if you'll excuse me, I have some film to review before the Overclan Seating session this postmidarc."

"Come now, Overclan Prime," Cvv-panav chided, making no move to stand up. "Surely you haven't forgotten our agreement. You were going to tell me about the CIRCE weapon, remember?"

"Of course I remember," the Prime said, tapping a key on his reader. "But first I'd like to view this film. Perhaps you'd be so kind as to watch it with me." The wall behind him lit up, and the Prime turned to look.

And from the direction of Cvv-panav's couch he heard a stifled gasp. "You recognize the setting, I see," the Prime commented. "You'll note the excellent quality of the pictures, despite the somewhat inadequate lighting. See there, too—how clearly the faces of both Korthe and Dornt can be seen as they lay the pouch containing her *fsss* at Thrr-pifix-a's door? And the detail on the pouch itself, of course. An ideal record for, shall we say, identification purposes?"

"I'm sure we could say that, yes," Cvv-panav ground out. "Who took this film? Thrr-pifix-a?" He cursed under his breath. "So I was right, after all. She was one of your agents, and the whole thing was nothing more than a gigantic setup. Designed to destroy me."

The Prime flicked his tongue in weary negative. "You flatter yourself, Speaker, and in the same breath underestimate the strength of my position along with it. Neither you nor the Dhaa'rr are the threat to my authority you seem to believe."

"And yet you seek to destroy me," Cvv-panav accused, jabbing his tongue toward the film.

"Not true," the Prime disagreed. "You continue to insist on seeing this in terms of the ancient battle standards. With yourself as the great and glorious leader of the Dhaa'rr, who must be destroyed or else surrendered to."

"What else is there?"

"Cooperation," the Prime said. "Working together toward a common goal. Subordinating personal or clan preferences when necessary for the good of the whole."

Cvv-panav gestured contemptuously. "You dream in

impossible ideals, Overclan Prime. You see five hundred cyclics of nonwar, and you think the Zhirrzh have changed. But we haven't. Conflict, competition, rivalry— it's all still there. Life in the eighteen worlds is still a contest to see who will dominate and who will submit. No different, really, from this war against the Human-Conquerors."

"You're wrong," the Prime said quietly. "Peaceful clan rivalry is nothing at all like the devastation of open warfare. And this war with the Human-Conquerors is not a contest of supremacy, at least not on our side. It's a battle for our survival."

Cvv-panav sniffed. "Strong words—"

"You wanted to hear about CIRCE," the Prime cut him off harshly. "Fine. Let me tell you about CIRCE."

He gave Cvv-panav all of it. Everything the Human-Conqueror prisoner Pheylan-Cavanagh had said; everything the technics had been able to draw from the alien recorder; everything Warrior Command had deduced or pieced together or speculated on.

It took ten hunbeats . . . and at the end Cvv-panav was as shaken as the Prime had ever seen him. "It's incredible," the Speaker breathed, his tail twitching uncontrollably. "Utterly incredible. How could such a thing exist?"

"I don't know," the Prime said. "If we knew, perhaps we'd be able to find a way to protect ourselves against it. But we don't. And we can't."

"That's why Warrior Command is driving so many different offensives," Cvv-panav murmured, gazing unseeingly into the air. "Trying to take as many Human-Conqueror worlds as possible to try to isolate the CIRCE components."

"Yes," the Prime nodded. "The price being that we've spread our forces dangerously thin. Ripe for a Human-

Conqueror counteroffensive. But we have no other choice."

Abruptly, Cvv-panav's attention came back to him. "What if it's too late? Are you sure it's not already too late?"

"We're not sure at all," the Prime said grimly. "For all we know, they could be assembling CIRCE right now."

"And what happens if they do?"

The Prime looked him straight in the eye. "Then the Zhirrzh race will most probably die."

For a long beat they sat in silence. "What do you want from me?" Cvv-panav asked at last.

The Zhirrzh race will die. With an effort the Prime pushed aside the words that still echoed through his mind. It was the first time that he'd put his fear into actual, explicit words. Somehow that very act had made it all the more real. And all the more terrifying. "I want what I've always wanted," he told Cvv-panav. "The full cooperation of you and the Dhaa'rr."

"And you thought you needed *that*"— Cvv-panav gestured distastefully at the film still playing—"to insure my cooperation?"

"I want your cooperation," the Prime said. "Not your leadership. I trust you see the difference."

"And what if I don't agree with some aspect of how you're handling the war?"

"You're welcome to question me," the Prime said. "To discuss your point of view, either privately or in the Seating. But when my final decision is made, you will accept it. Without further argument."

"And if I don't?"

The Prime locked gazes with him. "Then I'll release the film. And you'll be destroyed."

There was another long beat of silence. "You play dangerous games, Overclan Prime," Cvv-panav said at last.

"I'm not playing games," the Prime countered. "This is real. And very serious."

"Oh, I know it's serious," Cvv-panav agreed. "You seem to be having far too much fun with it, that's all."

The Prime flicked a negative. "I'm not having fun, Speaker. I'm simply doing what has to be done."

"I wish I could believe that." Cvv-panav stood up. "Regardless, you've made your point. And you've won this round. But there will be others."

"When the war is over," the Prime warned.

Cvv-panav smiled tightly. "Of course, Overclan Prime. When the war is over."

22 The previous fullarc had been devoted to an operation involving a Human warrior named Srgent-janovetz and the application of some sort of device to the side of his face, an operation Prr't-zevisti had found fascinating if thoroughly incomprehensible. He'd rather hoped that Doctor-Cavan-a would be doing a repeat of it this fullarc so that he could have another look; but for right now, at least, it was back to prodding and poking yet another sample from his *fsss* cutting.

He was getting tired of it. Not that it was painful, really, though the low-level Elderdeath emissions that usually accompanied her studies were growing more and more annoying. But it was boring. More importantly, it didn't give him any new information on the Humans or their technology. And there was so much more he needed to learn.

There was the sound of a muffled clank, transmitted by his *fss* cutting: the door being opened. Cautiously, Prr't-zevisti came up to the edge of the lightworld for a look.

It was the Human commander. "Hello Doctor-Cavan-a," he said, pulling the door closed. "Any progress?"

"A little," she answered. "I think I may have isolated the (something) source for the (something) activity."

"That's good," the commander said, stepping over to her and looking down at the latest *fss* sample. "Seen any more of the (something) from the (something) end?"

"I don't know," she said, looking up at his face. "I sometimes think I see something at the (something) of my eye. But when I look, there's nothing there."

"Try to (something) it down," he told her, throwing a quick look of his own around the room. Prr't-zevisti ducked down a little deeper into the grayworld, just to be on the safe side. "Try real hard. Bad enough they can (something) (something) across light (something). If they can (something) right through the walls of this room, too, it'll be just that much worse."

"Something's wrong, isn't it?" Doctor-Cavan-a asked, her voice suddenly quiet. "What?"

Prr't-zevisti heard the faint hissing sound of the commander's breath. "It's Srgent-janovetz. He and his (something) went silent last (something)."

"I hadn't heard," Doctor-Cavan-a said. "Do you think they've kill (something) him?"

"I don't know," the commander said. "We got one (something) (something) from him and sent one back. And that was all." He paused. "But what's really trouble (something) is what that (something) show (something). (Something), there was an attack on the Zhirrzh base."

Prr't-zevisti came up to the edge of the lightworld in time to see Doctor-Cavan-a's face change, her overeye hair tufts pressing toward each other. "You didn't tell me we were go (something) to attack."

"We didn't," the commander said. "That's what's so trouble (something). We didn't attack; and it doesn't make much sense for the Zhirrzh to have attack (something) themselves. Which leaves only one (something)."

"The (something)? But that's (something). They're prisoners."

"That's what we've been assume (something)," the commander said. "But we really don't know that for sure. The (something) we got show (something) them be (something) take (something) across the land (something) field. They didn't seem to be wear (something) anything like that (something) suit described in the report from your brother."

There was a beat of silence. "What was this attack like?" Doctor-Cavan-a asked.

"Our (something) angle wasn't very good," the commander said. "Near as we could tell, it seem (something) to be a series of explosions."

"Damage?"

"Again, we couldn't tell. But they all seem (something) to be locate (something) in the same general area. Why? You have an idea?"

"Not really," Doctor-Cavan-a said. "But you're right: by process of (something), it has to have been the (something) behind it. But what they're play (something) at, I can't begin to understand."

"Something (something), though," the commander said, his voice lowering in pitch. "I'd bet my (something) on that."

"Well, maybe—"

Doctor-Cavan-a stopped speaking as the door opened. "Commander?" a warrior called. "Observation Post Five report (something) enemy air activity."

"Probably just their (something) (something)," the commander said, pulling a metal cylinder from his waist as he moved to the door. "Hold that thought, Doctor. I'll be right back."

He stepped outside, leaving the door open behind him. Stealthily, Prr't-zevisti slipped out behind him. It was the first chance he'd had in nearly three fullarcs to get out of the metal room, and no matter what the risks, he was determined to make the most of it.

Not much had changed out there since his last trip. A few more of the equipment piles had disappeared, and it occurred to him that it might be possible to deduce from that whether or not the Humans were running low on supplies. But on the other side, it might just mean they were moving things around to other parts of the stronghold.

"(Something) here," the commander's voice said. Prr't-zevisti looked around, spotted the other standing a couple of strides off to the side next to one of the equipment piles. He had a flat rectangular device propped up on top of the pile, with the metal cylinder he'd taken from his waist held up near his mouth. Some sort of recorder, obviously—

"Post Five, Commander," a faint voice came from the cylinder.

Prr't-zevisti frowned, moving as close to the commander as the walls of the metal room allowed. So it wasn't a recorder, but a communication device. Probably would have recognized that sooner if he'd had the same darklight sensitivity now that he'd had before he was raised to Eldership. He looked around as the voice continued talking, wondering if he could spot the darklight relay. Or, for that matter, would even know what a Human darklight relay looked like.

"Interest (something)," the commander said, turning back toward the metal room. Prr't-zevisti's attention snapped back with the movement; he didn't want to risk either being seen or getting caught by a closing door. "Hang on; let me check something." The commander rounded the corner of the room and stepped into the doorway—

And abruptly, the faint background of Elderdeath annoyance exploded into a knife edge of pain.

Prr't-zevisti gasped, the sheer unexpectedness of it freezing him writhing to the spot. He barely heard the commander and Doctor-Cavan-a speaking, his full attention on the torment driving through him like a million twisting needles. The universe seemed to swirl around him as waves of dizziness joined with the pain and nausea—

And then, as suddenly as if a switch had been thrown, it was gone. He gasped again, fighting to bring the world back into focus. The commander was still standing in the doorway talking to Doctor-Cavan-a, pointing to his right away from the metal room with the hand that held the cylinder. He finished the gesture, brought the hand back in front of him again—

And Prr't-zevisti jerked in agony as the Elderdeath pain again lanced through him.

But only for a beat. He had barely enough time to gasp when the pain again shut off.

It seemed harder this time to regain his balance and equilibrium; the Human commander seemed to be walking up a slanted wall as he stepped away from the doorway and back to his equipment pile. With an effort Prr't-zevisti fought his way through the dizziness, almost too drained to be angry. So it had finally happened. His captors had finally tried a full-fledged Elderdeath attack on him. But he'd survived it, and he hadn't given himself away.

Maybe they hadn't expected him to. Doctor-Cavan-a had stepped to the door of the metal room now, looking at the commander and paying no attention to either his *fsss* cutting or Prr't-zevisti himself. The commander, for his part, was still talking into his cylinder as if nothing at all had just happened.

The cylinder.

Prr't-zevisti stared at the device, an icy chill creeping across the last residue of Elderdeath ache. The cylinder. Moved into the doorway, into direct line with his *fsss* cutting, as the Elderdeath attack began. Taken away as it ended. And moved briefly out of line with the commander's gesture during the equally brief lull in the attack.

And suddenly Prr't-zevisti had it. The truth. The horrifying, devastating truth.

The Humans' Elderdeath weapons weren't weapons at all. They were communication devices.

Prr't-zevisti hovered there, staring at the commander and Doctor-Cavan-a, his mind spinning with shock. The report from the study group on Base World 12 had included a claim by the Human prisoner that it was the Zhirrzh survey ships that had started the space battle. Warrior Command and the Overclan had dismissed it as a lie.

But it hadn't been a lie. Not from the prisoner's point of view. As far as he knew, the Humans had done nothing more aggressive than attempting to communicate.

And had promptly been fired on. In what the Zhirrzh commanders had naturally considered to be pure self-defense.

Which meant that this entire war was nothing but a gigantic mistake.

Numbly, Prr't-zevisti made his way back into the metal room, settling into his corner and down into the grayworld. A mistake. A horrible blunder of misunderstandings.

And if this war, then why not all the others? All of Zhirrzh history—all the wars of defensive conquest against aliens who'd attacked them on sight. Had all of those wars been sparked by similar mistakes?

There was a sound, and Prr't-zevisti moved back to the edge of the lightworld. Doctor-Cavan-a had come back inside the room, followed by the Human commander. They held a brief conversation, something with a lot of words Prr't-zevisti didn't understand, and then the commander went out again, closing the door behind him.

For a few beats Doctor-Cavan-a sat quietly, staring at the door. Then, exhaling audibly, she turned back to her work on the *fsss* sample. Trying, if her conversations could be believed, to understand its importance to the Zhirrzh.

And Prr't-zevisti came to a decision.

He came up to the closest edge of the lightworld, a small dark voice in the back of his mind reminding him as he did so that this whole thing could be nothing more than an elaborate stratagem, a trick to draw him finally out into the open. But it was a risk he had to take. If there was even a small chance that he'd stumbled on the truth here . . .

His movement caught Doctor-Cavan-a's attention. She turned her head and froze, her mouth dropping soundlessly open as she saw him—

"Hello, Doctor-Cavan-a," he said, speaking the alien words as clearly as he could. "I am Prr't-zevisti; Dhaa'rr."

23 The suborbital transport put Thrr-gi-lag down at a small private landing field fifteen thoustrides south of Reeds Village. The Overclan pilot loaned him a one-person runabout, promised to be back in two tentharcs, and lifted off again.

It was a long, lonely drive down the dusty roadway that led north toward his mother's house. Thrr-gilag saw only a few buildings along the way, farmhouses and related outbuildings, most of them fairly distant from the roadway. The only other vehicles he passed were lumbering planters out working the fields. Little to see, little to do except for the largely automatic process of driving down a deserted roadway.

It left him a lot of time for thought.

They weren't pleasant thoughts. He tried to concentrate on the attempt to save the possibly alive Prr't-zevisti from probable death, and to speculate on how such a success might be bartered into reinstatement of his bond-engagement to Klnn-dawan-a. But there were too many ifs in the whole equation; too many ifs and possibles and maybes and doubtfuls. And even if it all worked out perfectly, there would always be the weight of his mother's crime working against it.

His mother. Thrr-gilag sighed, feeling a twinge of guilt. With all the rest of the flurry that had accompanied it, the truly basic consideration hadn't even occurred to him until midway through the flight from Unity City. Thrr-pifix-a had tried to steal her *fsss* because she didn't want to become an Elder.

She'd failed. Which meant that choice had now been taken away from her. And Thrr-gilag still couldn't decide whether he was relieved or saddened by that.

There were a half-dozen Elders hovering around his mother's house as he pulled up in front of it. "Hello," one of them said as he stepped out of the runabout. "Who are you?"

Thrr-gilag eyed him. "Why?"

The other seemed taken aback. "I was just wondering. I'd heard something happened here last latearc, something involving Overclan warriors and some kind of criminal activity. Just wondered if you knew anything about it."

Thrr-gilag grimaced. So the rumors had already started. Inevitable, really. With so little to occupy their time, Elders were to rumors as liquid fuel was to fires. "Sorry," he said shortly, striding past the Elder toward the door.

"Wait a beat," a second Elder said, moving into Thrr-gilag's path. "What are you going to do?"

"I'm going inside," Thrr-gilag said. "Is that any business of yours?"

"Do you have permission from the occupant to enter?"

"I have the key," Thrr-gilag said, holding it up.

"But do you have permission?" the Elder repeated.

Thrr-gilag stopped. "I have all the permission I need," he ground out. "I'll ask again: what business is this of yours?"

"This is our land," a third Elder said, his voice and manner huffy. "It's both our privilege and our duty to protect it."

And suddenly Thrr-gilag was sick and tired of Elders. "That's dead bisfis effluvia," he said flatly. "And you know it. You never paid the slightest bit of attention to Thrr-pifix-a until you smelled a chance at some gossip. That's all you want, and you can forget it."

"How dare you speak that way to your Elders?" the third Elder demanded. "We are—"

"What you are is invited to get lost," Thrr-gilag cut him off. Pushing past and through the whole group of them, he unlocked the door and went in.

He half expected the Elders to join him, at least long enough to drop a few scathing comments about his manners and the importance of respect. But if they had in fact followed him in, they were keeping quiet about it.

More likely they'd simply returned to their family shrines, to tell in great detail about the rude young male who had shown up at the mystery-shrouded home of Thrr-pifix-a; Kee'rr.

His mother hadn't lived there for very long, but even so the house was rich with memories. For a few hunbeats Thrr-gilag just wandered through the various rooms, looking at the furniture and pictures he remembered from his childhood, fingering the various pieces of edgework she'd loved to do and been so proud of. Here and there was a pouch or scarflin she'd been working on, as yet unfinished. Beside the kitchen sink were her gardening tools, painstakingly cleaned from the previous fullarc's work and laid neatly out to dry. The trowel still held a drop of water in its curved surface; picking it up, he turned it over, watching the drop dribble off.

From the edge of his eye he caught a flicker of movement. So not all the Elders had gone away. Thrr-gilag spun toward the figure, drawing a breath to tell these nosy gossips once and for all what he thought of them—

"Hello, my son," Thrr't-rokik said, his voice grave. "I'm glad you've come."

Thrr-gilag's breath went out of him in a startled gasp. "Father," he murmured when he finally got his voice back.

Thrr't-rokik's serious expression cracked, just a little. "I take it you weren't expecting me," he suggested with a wry smile. "At least not if you were about to say what you looked like you were about to say."

"No, not at all," Thrr-gilag hastened to assure him, waving an arm in the general direction of the front door. "I was expecting it to be one of the local—"

He froze, his arm still raised toward the door, the words dying on his tongue as the second shock suddenly hit him. This wasn't the Thrr family shrine. He was *here,* just south of Reeds Village, 115 thoustrides away.

Fifteen thoustrides outside his father's anchorline range.

"No, it's not a hallucination," Thrr't-rokik said quietly. "I'm really here."

"But how?" Thrr-gilag asked, tongue flicking in confusion.

"Highly illegally, I'm afraid," Thrr't-rokik confessed. "Of course, we'd never intended that anyone would ever find out about it." He shrugged uncomfortably. "Under normal circumstances I'm sure no one ever would have. But the circumstances are hardly normal anymore."

"Wait a beat," Thrr-gilag said. "Wait just a beat, all right? How can you be here? What did you do, have a cutting taken or something?"

"No 'or something' about it," Thrr't-rokik said. "I talked a friend into taking a cutting for me. So that I could keep an eye on your mother."

Thrr-gilag nodded slowly. Of course. Obvious, now that he thought about it. It was exactly the sort of thing his father would do. "Without her knowing about it, I suppose."

Thrr't-rokik turned away. "I couldn't tell her, Thrr-gilag. She didn't want any part of me. Never wanted to see me again. But I couldn't accept that. Couldn't just let go."

Thrr-gilag sighed. It certainly wasn't proper, spying on her that way. But on the other side, he could hardly blame his father for doing so. "You took a big chance," he told Thrr't-rokik. "I trust you realize that. If she'd ever gotten around to checking with the local cutting pyramids, you'd have been caught for sure."

"Oh, I took a chance, all right," Thrr't-rokik said grimly. "But not the one you imagine. You see, my cutting isn't in any of the local pyramids. Or in the local shrines, or anywhere else it's supposed to be. It's . . . well, it's been rather informally placed, let's say."

Thrr-gilag frowned; and then it hit him, like a tongue edge in the neck. "You mean you just tossed it into a—a box or something?"

"Exactly correct, I'm afraid," Thrr't-rokik admitted. "It's in a sealed container buried out back beneath the Kyranda bushes." He eyed Thrr-gilag, his face pinched in anxious anticipation. "You're shocked, of course. I can't say I blame you."

Thrr-gilag sighed, acutely aware of the irony of it all. He and Thrr-mezaz were conspiring to put their illegal cutting of Prr't-zevisti's *fsss* in a predator-proof box on Dorcas; and here their father had already done the same thing. It must run in the family. "Actually, I'm not nearly as shocked as you probably think," he told Thrr't-rokik. "Who did you talk into doing this for you?"

"I suppose there's no real harm in telling you," Thrr't-rokik said. "After what's happened, it's all bound to come out soon anyway. They'll undoubtedly do a complete check of all the *fsss* organs at the family shrine to see if any of them were tampered with."

Thrr-gilag nodded. Once again, it was obvious. "It was Thrr-tulkoj, wasn't it?" he asked. "Only a shrine protector would have that kind of access."

"Yes." Thrr't-rokik nodded heavily. "And he's going to be in serious trouble when it's discovered. But for now there's nothing we can do about that." He looked at Thrr-gilag, a sudden fire in his eyes. "What we *can* do something about—maybe—is the trouble your mother's in. You see, I didn't attend that big Elder meeting last latearc. I was here."

Thrr-gilag's tail twitched. "You were *here?*" he echoed. "I mean, right here at this house?"

"Right here," Thrr't-rokik agreed soberly. "And I saw everything. There were two of them, two young males, dressed in the sort of outfits you sometimes see in warrior entertainment dramas. They came up to the door and laid the pouch on the ground, then knocked twice and ran."

"Why didn't you alert the rest of the Elders?"

"I wish I had," Thrr't-rokik sighed. "But I didn't recognize the significance of what I'd seen. Not until the warriors came up out of cover and charged toward the house—"

"Wait a beat." Thrr-gilag frowned. "The warriors came out of cover? Where out of cover?"

"Oh, pretty much everywhere," Thrr't-rokik said, waving vaguely around him. "From the various farmers' outbuildings, out of ditches, behind scrub-plant clusters—all around the area. I didn't even notice them until they started moving."

Thrr-gilag pressed the tip of his tongue hard against the top of his mouth. "But then that means it wasn't just some sudden news or anonymous warning that got them here in time to stop mother from destroying her *fsss,*" he said slowly. "They were waiting for it to show up. And yet you say they deliberately let those two males leave?"

"I don't know how deliberate it was," Thrr't-rokik said. "They could simply have been caught off guard. As I said, it happened very quickly."

"Maybe," Thrr-gilag growled. "But a few properly positioned Elders ought to have been able to give the warriors enough warning to catch them." He glared at his father. "Assuming, of course, that they *wanted* to catch them."

"Be very careful, my son," Thrr't-rokik warned. "What you're hinting at could get you into serious trouble."

Thrr-gilag flicked a tongue contemptuously. "I'm already in serious trouble. Or I will be soon, anyway."

"That's no reason to make things worse by announcing unproved accusations," Thrr't-rokik countered. "It doesn't help you or your mother."

With an effort Thrr-gilag forced down his growing anger. "Then we'll get some proof," he said. "You say you saw these two Zhirrzh. Would you recognize them if you saw them again?"

"I'm sure I would," Thrr't-rokik said.

"All right, then," Thrr-gilag said, fingering his mother's gardening trowel. "What we'll do is put their description out into the Elder network and see if we can track them down."

"Risky," his father said, flicking his tongue in a negative. "They certainly aren't going to want to be found; and if they catch even a hint that someone saw them, they're likely to bury themselves where we'll never find them."

Thrr-gilag grimaced. "I know. But it's all we've got."

"Actually, maybe not," Thrr't-rokik said. "I told you they left on foot. What I haven't yet told you is they didn't travel that way for long. They had a small transport waiting about a hundred strides to the west."

"Probably how they got here from the shrine," Thrr-gilag said, hearing an edge of bitterness in his voice. "A whole transport. I wonder how the Overclan warriors missed *that*."

"It's not impossible, Thrr-gilag," Thrr't-rokik cautioned. "Please don't stumble to false conclusions here. The vehicle had no lights or markings and looked to be darklight-shielded as well."

"Which all by itself proves *someone* important was involved," Thrr-gilag countered. "Transport modifications like that don't come cheap. They're only used when someone has something to hide."

"Perhaps," Thrr't-rokik said. "But they may have missed a bet. My cutting's a bit subsized, and I didn't have much time to look over the transport before they flew out of range. But I did get a chance to look at the floater engines, which turned out to be quite warm. Best guess is that they floated in at ground level for the last thoustride or so."

"Which you're probably going to say is why the Over-clan warriors didn't spot them," Thrr-gilag sighed. "They're sure not making this easy to prove, are they?"

"I'm sure that's their goal," Thrr't-rokik agreed. "Whoever 'they' are, and whatever 'they' were doing. But you miss my point. As I said, the floater engines were warm. Warm enough to give off a fair amount of dark-light." He smiled grimly. "Enough darklight, as it happens, for me to read the manufactural identification numbers."

Thrr-gilag felt his midlight pupils narrow. "You got the numbers?" he breathed. "Well, then—well, then, we're in. We've got them. We've got them by their tongues."

"Easy, son, easy," Thrr't-rokik said, holding up a hand. "It's not going to be that easy. We can't just announce the numbers and call for a public explanation. As you said, *someone* important is likely involved in this, and political power almost always comes with importance. We can't risk a countermove that crushes our entire family beneath it."

"So what do we do?" Thrr-gilag demanded. "Keep quiet and let them get away with it?"

"Of course not," Thrr't-rokik said. "All I'm saying is that the obvious, public way isn't going to work here. For right now Thrr-pifix-a is all right: she's shamed, but for whatever reasons, whoever's behind all this doesn't seem to want it made public. That means we have time. So what I'll do is—"

He broke off. Across the house there was a quiet knock at the door.

For a beat Thrr-gilag just looked at Thrr't-rokik, wondering if he'd imagined the sound. The knock came again; and Thrr't-rokik flickered and was gone.

He was back two beats later. "I don't know," he hissed

to Thrr-gilag. "One Zhirrzh, male, middle-aged. He looks very familiar, somehow, but I can't place him."

There was a third knock, a more insistent one this time. "Keep watch," Thrr-gilag told his father, crossing the kitchen to the door. Bracing himself, trying to prepare himself mentally for anything, he pulled it open.

"Hello, Searcher," the Overclan Prime said. "I'm glad you were able to find your way out here. May I come in?"

Thrr-gilag swallowed. This was not anywhere on his impromptu mental list of possibilities. "Certainly, Overclan Prime," he said, moving back out of the way.

"Thank you." The Prime stepped inside; and as he passed, Thrr-gilag noticed the irritating pulsating tone that followed along with him. A hummer, already activated. Whatever was about to happen, the Prime was obviously determined that it be confidential.

But even if Thrr't-rokik couldn't hear, he would certainly be watching. It was a comforting thought.

"I'm sorry I had to twist you around the way I did in order to get you here," the Prime said, turning back around to face Thrr-gilag as the latter closed the door. "But I needed to talk to you in private."

"Is it about my mother?" Thrr-gilag asked.

"It concerns the war," the Prime said. "And your theory that there may be a biochemical basis for Human-Conqueror aggression."

Thrr-gilag suppressed a grimace. All the way out here; and for this? "That theory is hardly a deep secret, Overclan Prime," he pointed out impatiently. "I've already filed a note about it. We could have discussed this back at the Overclan complex."

"Perhaps," the Prime said calmly. "But we could hardly have discussed the unauthorized cutting you and Klnn-dawan-a took of Prr't-zevisti's *fsss* organ. Could we."

Thrr-gilag stared at him, his mind freezing in shock. So they knew. They'd known all along. Klnn-dawan-a was probably at this very beat being hauled into a detention cell on Shamanv, her family shamed as his now was. . . . "No," he heard his voice say through a suddenly stiff mouth. "I suppose we couldn't have."

The Prime smiled faintly. "Relax, Searcher, it's not as bad as you're obviously thinking. Though you may change your mind about that in a hunbeat or two. For right now, at least, no one outside your little conspiracy knows anything about this."

With an effort Thrr-gilag forced his mind to start working again. The Prime could be lying, of course. But Thrr-gilag couldn't see what that would gain him. Either way, at this point he had little choice but to play this out and see where it led. "May I ask how you found out?" he asked.

"Through one of the Elders in Prr't-casst-a's supposedly secure pathway, of course," the Prime said. "As it happens, I already had an order in place that all of your communications were to be routed through an Overclan Elder. Prr't-casst-a's selection of Elders made it difficult, but not impossible. But that's not really the point. The point is that you probably want to go to Dorcas with Searcher Klnn-dawan-a. Fine; because I want you to go there, too."

Thrr-gilag frowned. Was he serious? "I don't understand."

"It's very simple," the Prime said. "The Dorcas beach-head has just taken three prisoners. Or possibly ambassadors; we're not really sure. One of them is a Human-Conqueror warrior." He gazed hard at Thrr-gilag. "The other two are Mrachanis."

Thrr-gilag felt his midlight pupils narrow. Mrachanis.

"I should tell you, Overclan Prime, that I don't really trust the Mrachanis."

"Yes, I know," the Prime said. "Which is precisely why I want you to be the one to go talk to them. Especially since there's a Human-Conqueror prisoner there for you to do your biochemical tests on."

"I see," Thrr-gilag said, eying the Prime closely. "Do I take it that all of this is . . . somewhat unauthorized?"

The Prime locked gazes with him. "*I'm* authorizing it, Searcher. That's all the authorization you need."

"Yes, I understand that. What I meant—"

"I know what you meant," the Prime cut him off. "And I have neither the time nor the inclination to detail for you the full range of political realities involved. Your qualifications are simple: you're good at what you do, and you're not overly intimidated by authority or tradition when you see something that has to be done. The question is equally simple: will you go, or won't you?"

"Of course I'll go," Thrr-gilag said. "When?"

"Immediately," the Prime said, a flicker of something that might have been relief touching his face. "There's a spacecraft waiting for you at the private field the transport dropped you off at. You can leave the runabout there to be picked up later."

"All right," Thrr-gilag said. "I don't have any luggage or equipment, though."

"There are changes of clothing for you already aboard the spacecraft," the Prime said. "You'll be making a stop at Base World Nine along the way; chances are most of the equipment you'll need can be picked up there. Have the spacecraft commander send me a list of whatever you want, and it'll be assigned to you. Anything Base World Nine doesn't have on hand will be sent to Dorcas from here. Acceptable?"

"Very much so," Thrr-gilag said, nodding. "Thank you."

"You'd best be on your way, then," the Prime said. "One other thing before you go. Commander Thrr-mezaz has reported the fact that the Human-Conquerors on Dorcas have made possibly two separate attempts to enter the region north of the Zhirrzh beachhead."

"Yes," Thrr-gilag said, shivering. "He told me."

"The commander was of course at a loss to explain their motivations." The Prime's expression hardened. "You and I, however, don't have to wonder."

"No," Thrr-gilag murmured. No, they didn't have to wonder at all. "CIRCE."

"Yes," the Prime agreed soberly. "And if one of its components is in fact hidden out there, there's no chance the Human-Conquerors will let it just sit there. If it becomes necessary, you're authorized to tell your brother everything you know about the device. And to do whatever it takes to make sure the Human-Conquerors don't retrieve it. Understood?"

Thrr-gilag nodded. "Understood."

"Good," the Prime said. "Then you'd better get going. Not a word or hint of any of this, of course. To anyone."

"Not to anyone," Thrr-gilag confirmed, moving toward the door.

"And," the Prime added softly, "good luck to you."

He managed a few words to his father before the runabout moved beyond Thrr't-rokik's range. Nothing beyond the fact that he was leaving Oaccanv, and that there was nothing to worry about.

Not that Thrr-gilag was entirely convinced of that himself. This whole thing could easily be a trap, for one thing. A trap to catch him and Klnn-dawan-a with the stolen *fss* cutting, perhaps, with the purpose of bringing disastrous shame onto both of their families and clans. For arcane political reasons he could only guess at.

Or the target could be Thrr-mezaz. This could be a plot to catch him in collusion with dubious and technically unauthorized civilian experiments on an enemy prisoner, providing a quick and easy reason to relieve him of his command.

Or it could be something even simpler. A scheme to get Thrr-gilag out of the way while the two Zhirrzh who had framed Thrr-pifix-a quietly buried themselves away beyond all possibility of finding or identifying them.

But it could also be completely legitimate. And if it was —and if there was even a chance that going to Dorcas might help the Zhirrzh win this war—then it was a risk that Thrr-gilag had to be willing to take.

Foolishness, or bravery. Only time would tell which.

24

The air of Shamanv was crisp and tangy, smelling of exotic plants and the more familiar odors of the superconducting-materials processing the planet was famous for. Klnn-dawan-a inhaled deeply as she walked across the courtyard toward the Dhaa'rr routing-center annex, savoring both the aromas and the fresh feelings of optimism growing within her. True, she'd professed great hope for this plan when she'd spun it out for Thrr-gilag and Prr't-casst-a back on Dharanv. But privately she'd never been really convinced she could make it work.

But so far, and to her honest amazement, she'd had no problems at all. Collecting enough personal messages and items back on Dharanv to justify a personal visit to Dorcas had been amazingly easy; if anything, she'd had to turn down requests. Now, here on Shamanv, the Dhaa'rr servers were similarly speeding her along her way, taking the time to guide her through the necessary forms and brushing aside the unnecessary ones. The Dhaa'rr clan, all working together.

She grimaced. Or else the word had spread as to who she was and what had just happened to her, and the servers were merely feeling sorry for her. After all, the message had come through to her nearly two tentharcs ago. Plenty of time for a loudmouthed Elder to have spread it through the entire routing center. Short and final: her bond-engagement to Thrr-gilag was ended.

She glanced up at the cloudless sky, glaring in Dharanv's general direction. Short and final the message had been; but at the same time disturbingly empty of information. There had been no indication of how the clan and family leaders had come to their decision, for one thing. Nor had there been any details on the vote itself, which she seemed to recall was usually required. Nothing but the plain fact of the decision itself.

Klnn-dawan-a wouldn't accept that. She couldn't accept that. Nor, she was sure, would Thrr-gilag. Somehow they had to find some way to continue this fight.

But that would have to wait. Right now the most important thing was to get Prr't-zevisti's *fsss* sample out to Thrr-mezaz on Dorcas. Once that was done, she could return to Dharanv and try to find a way to get the bond-engagement reinstated . . .

She paused, frowning up at the sky again. Had she just seen . . . ?

She had. Three dark dots were visible in the sky near the horizon. Coming this way, if she wasn't mistaken.

Muttering under her breath, she broke into a jogging run. The servers had told her that the ships for the Dorcas trip wouldn't be there for at least another tentharc. If they were this far ahead of schedule, it was going to be a race to get the forms processed before they lifted off again. Maybe the servers and their pleasant, helpful smiles weren't feeling as sorry for her as she'd thought. Glancing at the sky, she picked up her pace—

And came abruptly to a halt. Lifting her hand, she shielded her eyes from the glare of the sunlight and peered at the approaching aircraft. They were much closer now; still coming toward the routing complex, traveling much faster than she'd realized. She watched them come, feeling her tail picking up speed of its own. . . .

And then suddenly they were there, shooting not quite directly overhead, with a roar and a blast of heat and a violent thunderclap that nearly slammed her to the ground. Three small aircraft, colored black and white, rapidly shrinking again to tiny dots as they made for the horizon.

Like nothing Klnn-dawan-a had ever seen before.

Too late now—far too late—the warning sirens were starting to blare around her. In the near distance she could hear the roar of Stingbirds and other warrior aircraft as they scrambled for pursuit, adding more useless noise to that already filling the complex. Klnn-dawan-a stared at the receding aircraft, feeling suddenly naked and helpless and terrified beneath the empty sky. The comforting sense of safety and seclusion was gone, never to return.

The Human-Conquerors had found them.